D0031737

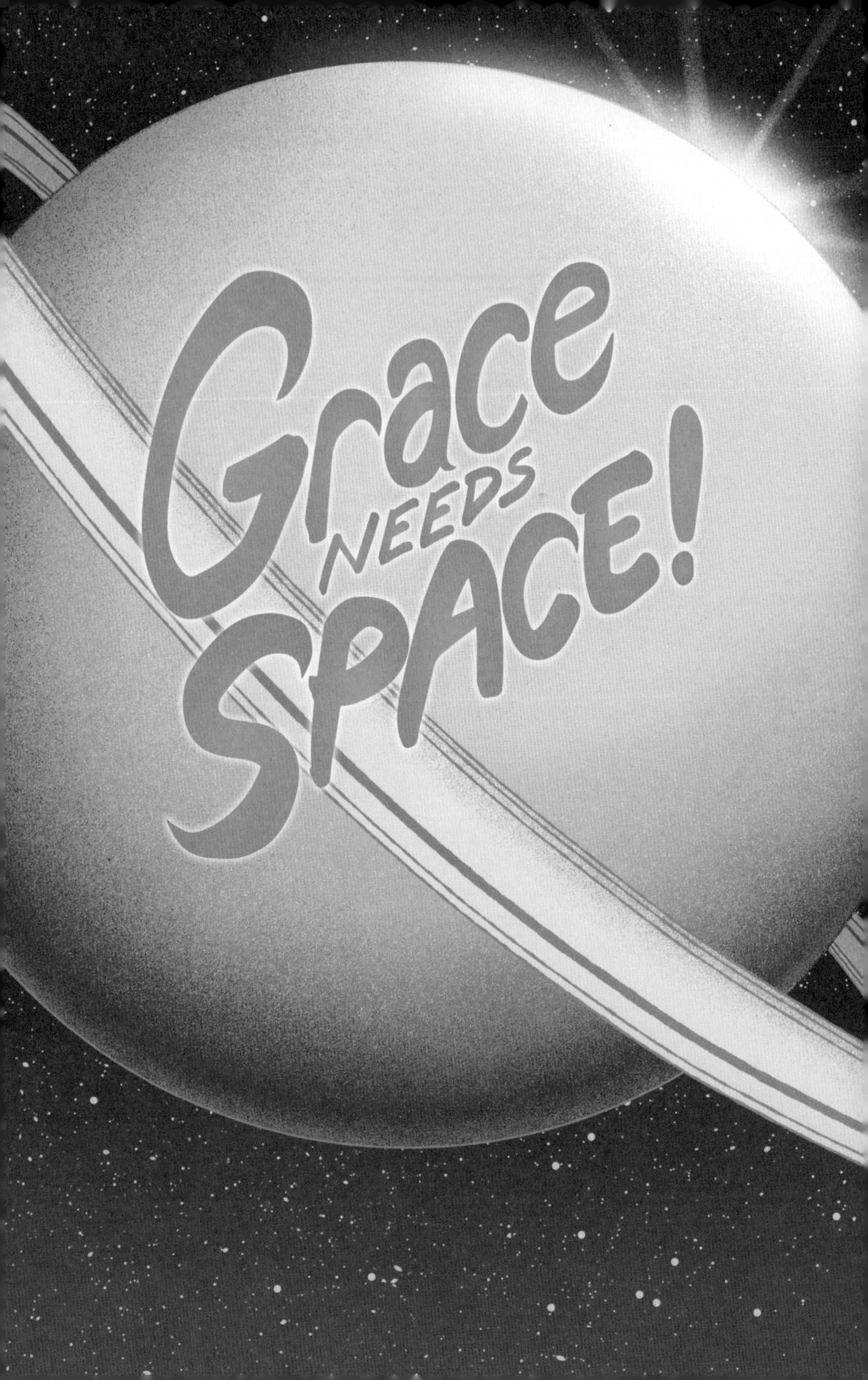
Grace
NEEDS
SPACE!

Also by Benjamin A. Wilgus

Chronin

The Mars Challenge with Wyeth Yates

Flying Machines: How the Wright Brothers Soared with Molly Brooks

Also by Rii Abrego

The Sprite and the Gardener with Joe Whitt

Grace NEEDS SPACE!

Benjamin A. Wilgus

Rii Abrego

RH
GRAPHIC

NEW YORK

Grace Needs Space! was illustrated and colored with Clip Studio Paint.

Text copyright © 2023 by Benjamin Alison Wilgus
Cover art and interior illustrations copyright © 2023 by Rii Abrego
Photographs on page 201 courtesy of NASA

All rights reserved. Published in the United States by RH Graphic, an imprint of Random House Children's Books, a division of Penguin Random House LLC, New York.

RH Graphic with the book design is a trademark of Penguin Random House LLC.

Visit us on the web! RHKidsGraphic.com • @RHKidsGraphic

Educators and librarians, for a variety of teaching tools, visit us at RHTeachersLibrarians.com

Library of Congress Cataloging-in-Publication Data is available upon request.
ISBN 978-0-593-18239-0 (hardcover) — ISBN 978-0-593-18238-3 (paperback)
ISBN 978-0-593-18240-6 (library binding) — ISBN 978-0-593-17944-4 (ebook)

Designed by Patrick Crotty

MANUFACTURED IN CHINA
10 9 8 7 6 5 4 3 2 1
First Edition

A comic on every bookshelf.

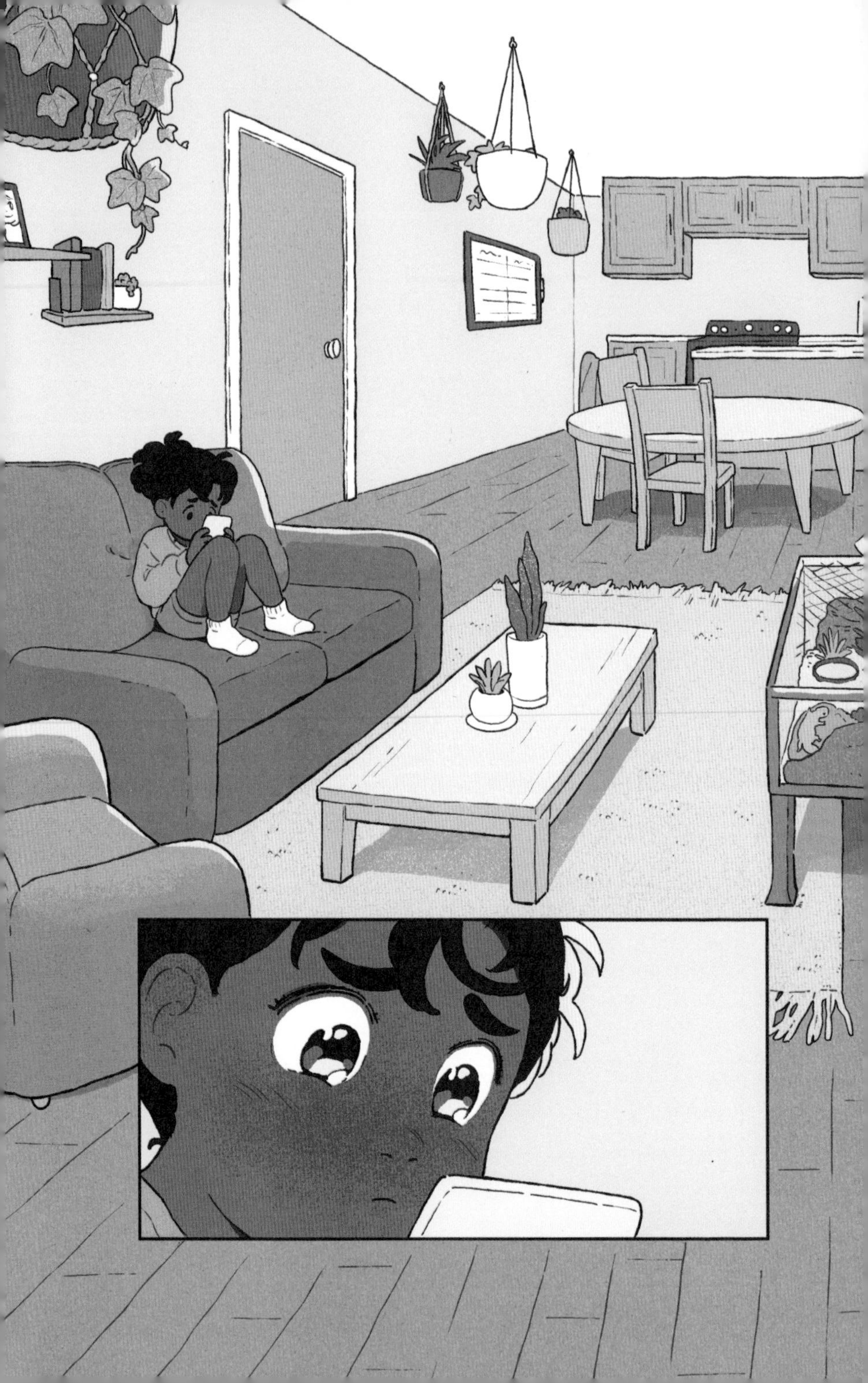

Grace?

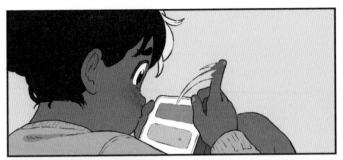

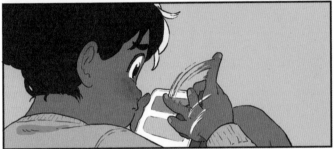

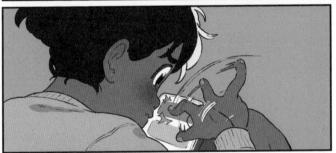

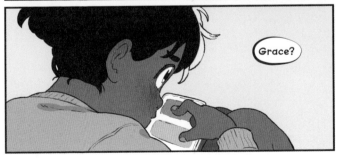

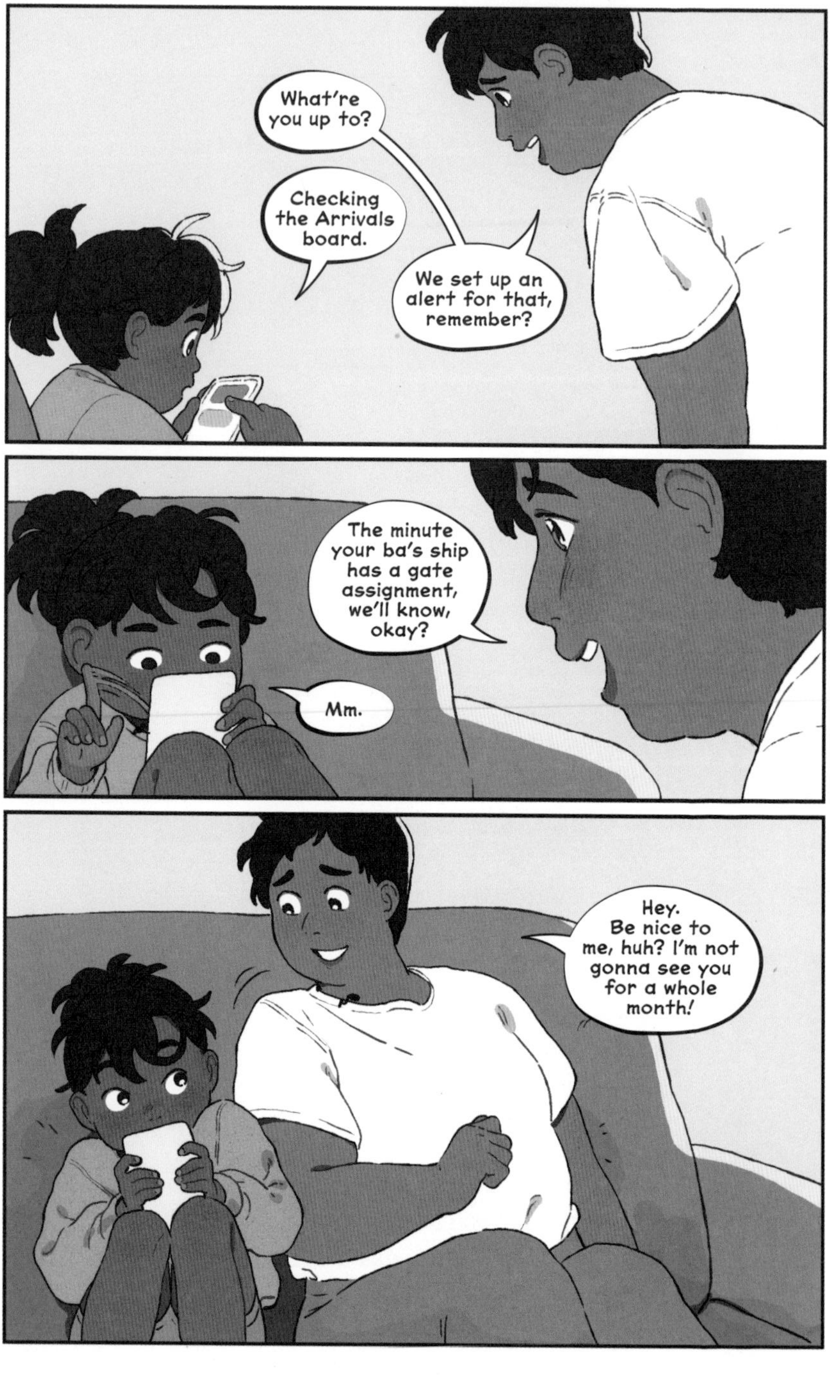
What're you up to?
Checking the Arrivals board.
We set up an alert for that, remember?
The minute your ba's ship has a gate assignment, we'll know, okay?
Mm.
Hey. Be nice to me, huh? I'm not gonna see you for a whole month!

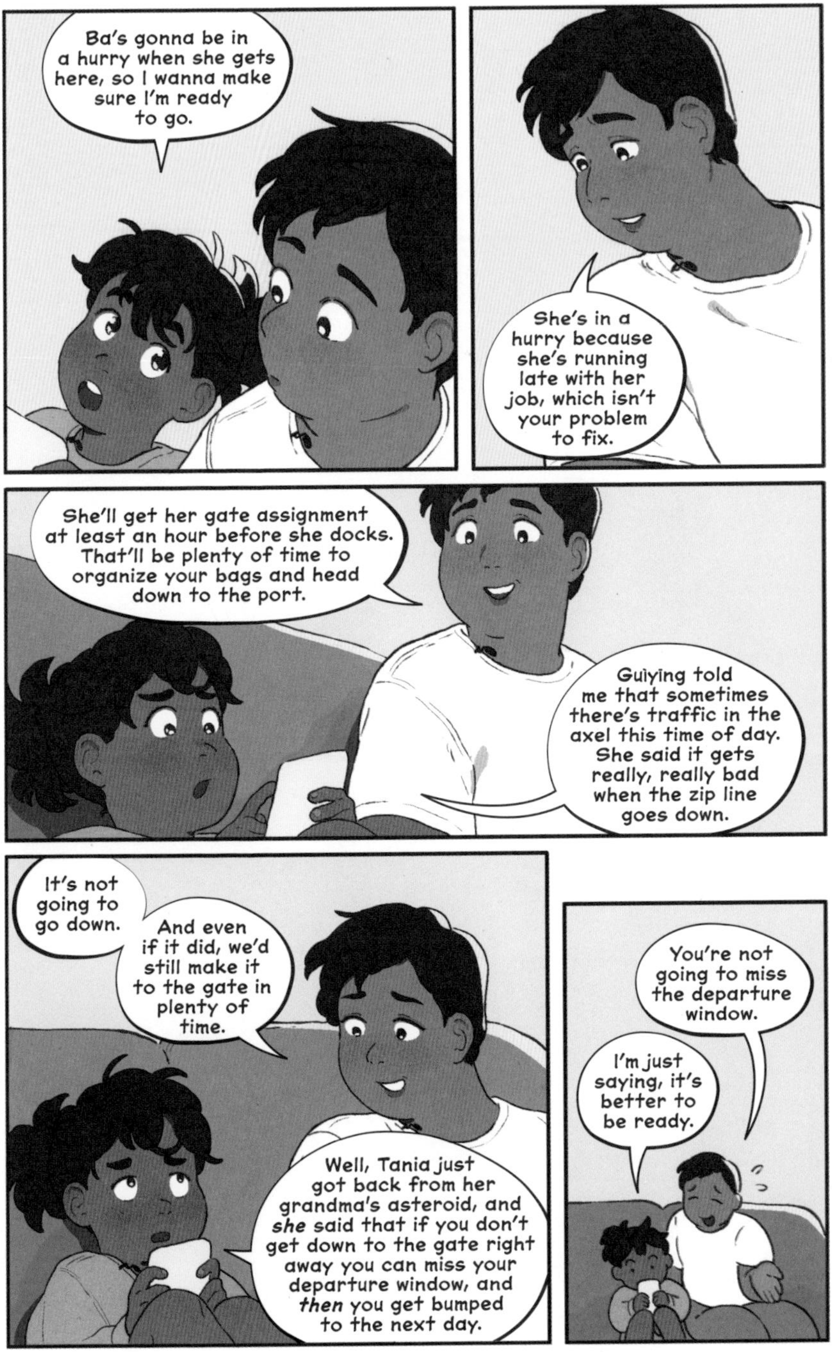
Ba's gonna be in a hurry when she gets here, so I wanna make sure I'm ready to go.
She's in a hurry because she's running late with her job, which isn't your problem to fix.
She'll get her gate assignment at least an hour before she docks. That'll be plenty of time to organize your bags and head down to the port.
Guiying told me that sometimes there's traffic in the axel this time of day. She said it gets really, really bad when the zip line goes down.
It's not going to go down.
And even if it did, we'd still make it to the gate in plenty of time.
Well, Tania just got back from her grandma's asteroid, and *she* said that if you don't get down to the gate right away you can miss your departure window, and *then* you get bumped to the next day.
You're not going to miss the departure window.
I'm just saying, it's better to be ready.

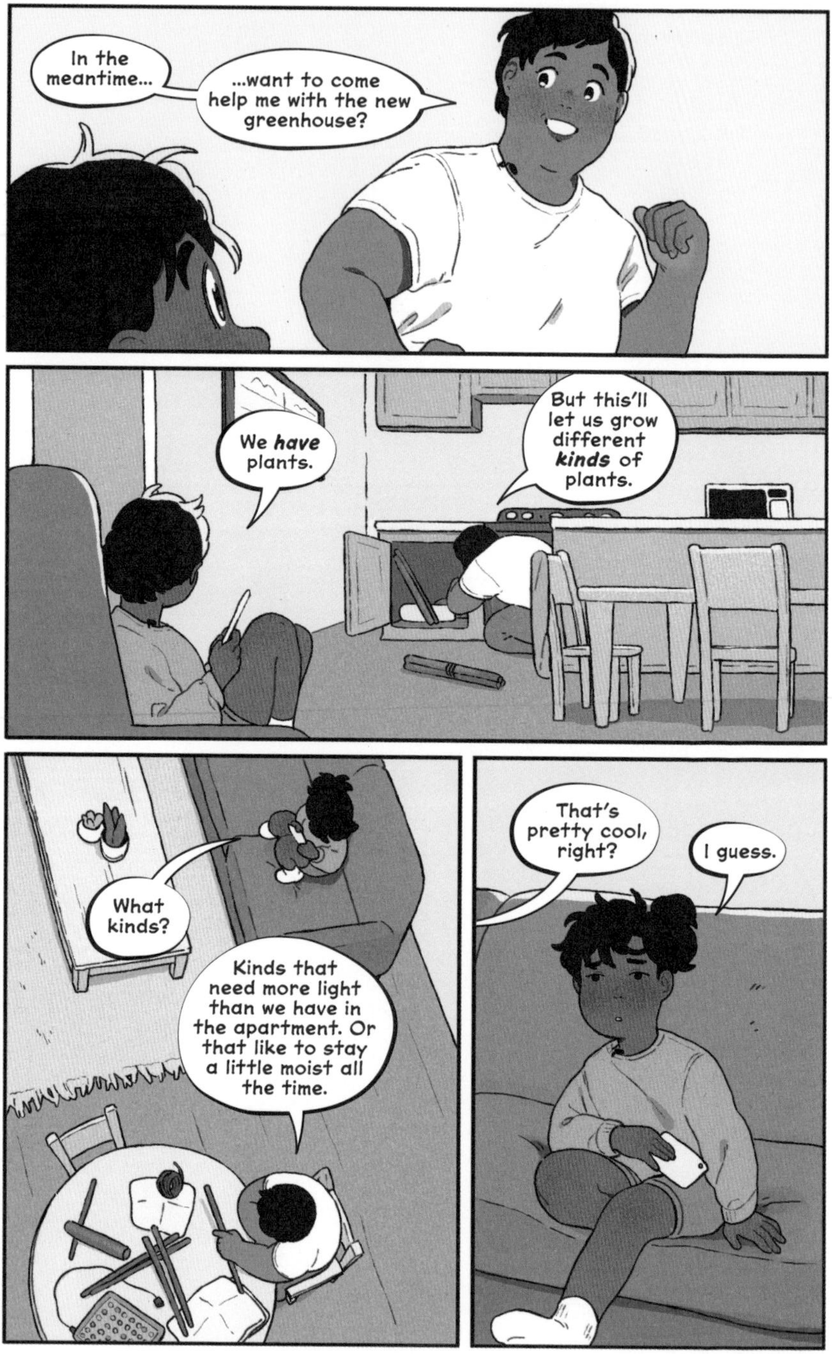
In the meantime...
...want to come help me with the new greenhouse?
We *have* plants.
But this'll let us grow different *kinds* of plants.
What kinds?
Kinds that need more light than we have in the apartment. Or that like to stay a little moist all the time.
That's pretty cool, right?
I guess.

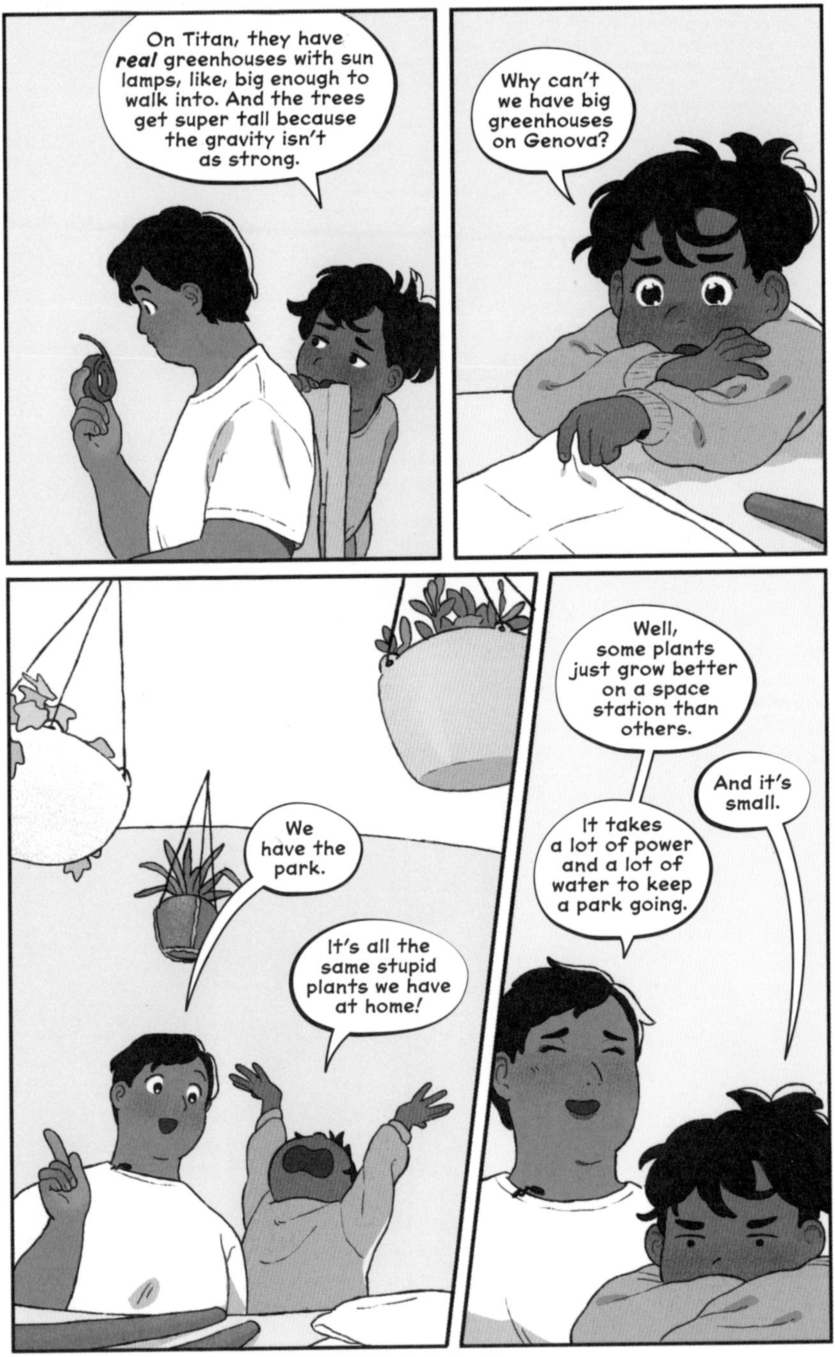
On Titan, they have *real* greenhouses with sun lamps, like, big enough to walk into. And the trees get super tall because the gravity isn't as strong.
Why can't we have big greenhouses on Genova?
We have the park.
It's all the same stupid plants we have at home!
Well, some plants just grow better on a space station than others.
It takes a lot of power and a lot of water to keep a park going.
And it's small.

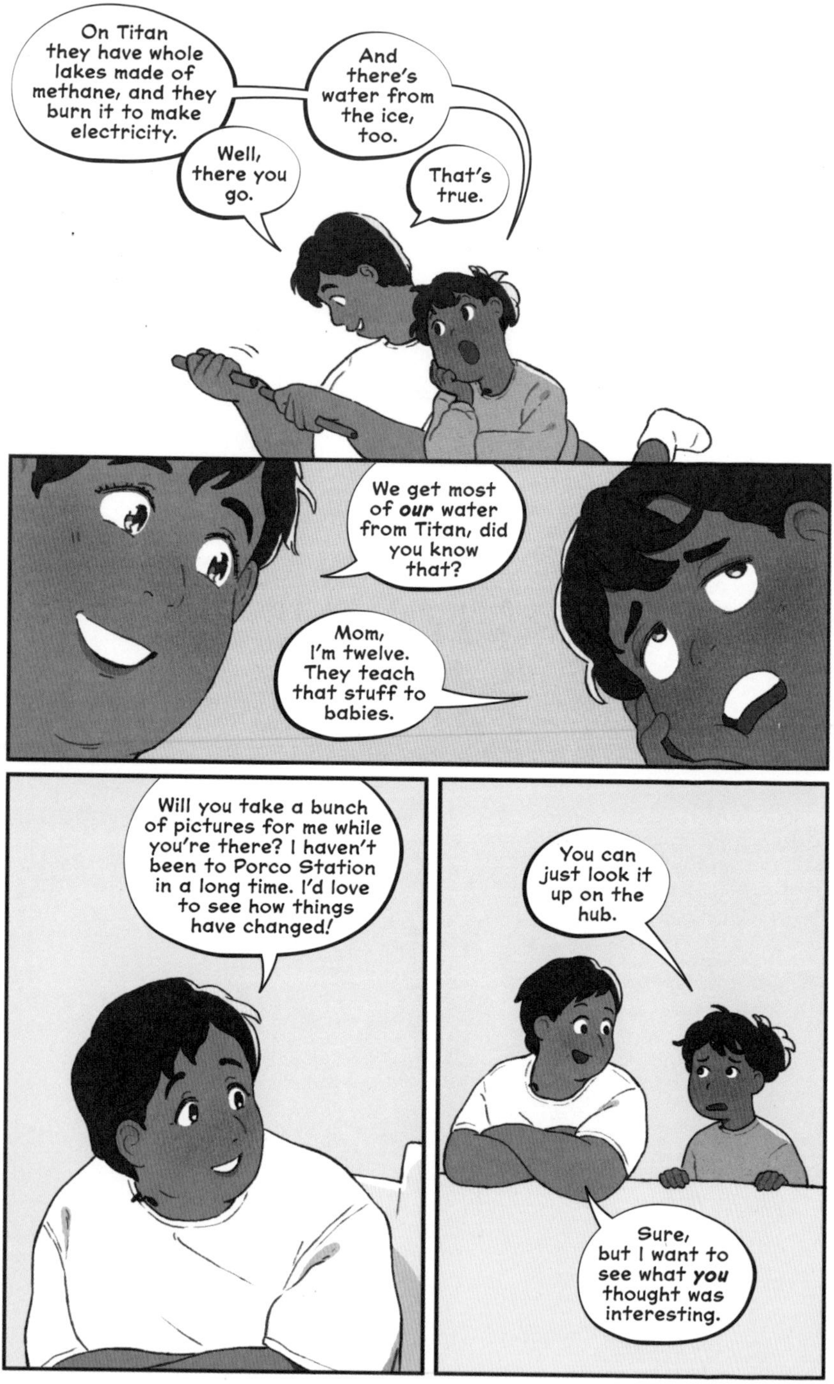
On Titan they have whole lakes made of methane, and they burn it to make electricity.
And there's water from the ice, too.
Well, there you go.
That's true.
We get most of ***our*** water from Titan, did you know that?
Mom, I'm twelve. They teach that stuff to babies.
Will you take a bunch of pictures for me while you're there? I haven't been to Porco Station in a long time. I'd love to see how things have changed!
You can just look it up on the hub.
Sure, but I want to see what ***you*** thought was interesting.

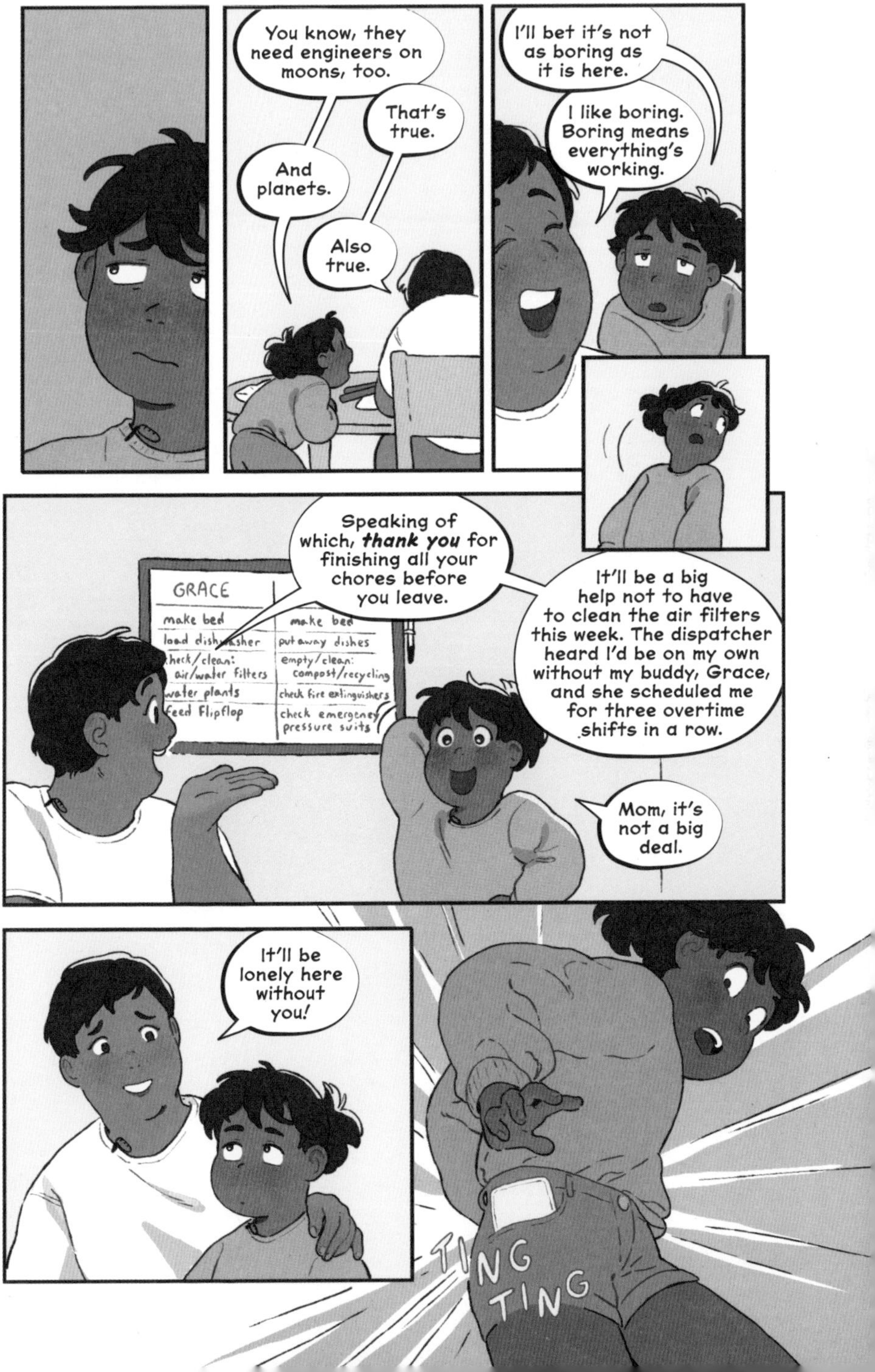

You know, they need engineers on moons, too.
That's true.
And planets.
Also true.
I'll bet it's not as boring as it is here.
I like boring. Boring means everything's working.
GRACE
make bed
load dishwasher
check/clean: air/water filters
water plants
feed Flipflop
make bed
put away dishes
empty/clean: compost/recycling
check fire extinguishers
check emergency pressure suits
Speaking of which, ***thank you*** for finishing all your chores before you leave.
It'll be a big help not to have to clean the air filters this week. The dispatcher heard I'd be on my own without my buddy, Grace, and she scheduled me for three overtime shifts in a row.
Mom, it's not a big deal.
It'll be lonely here without you!
TING TING

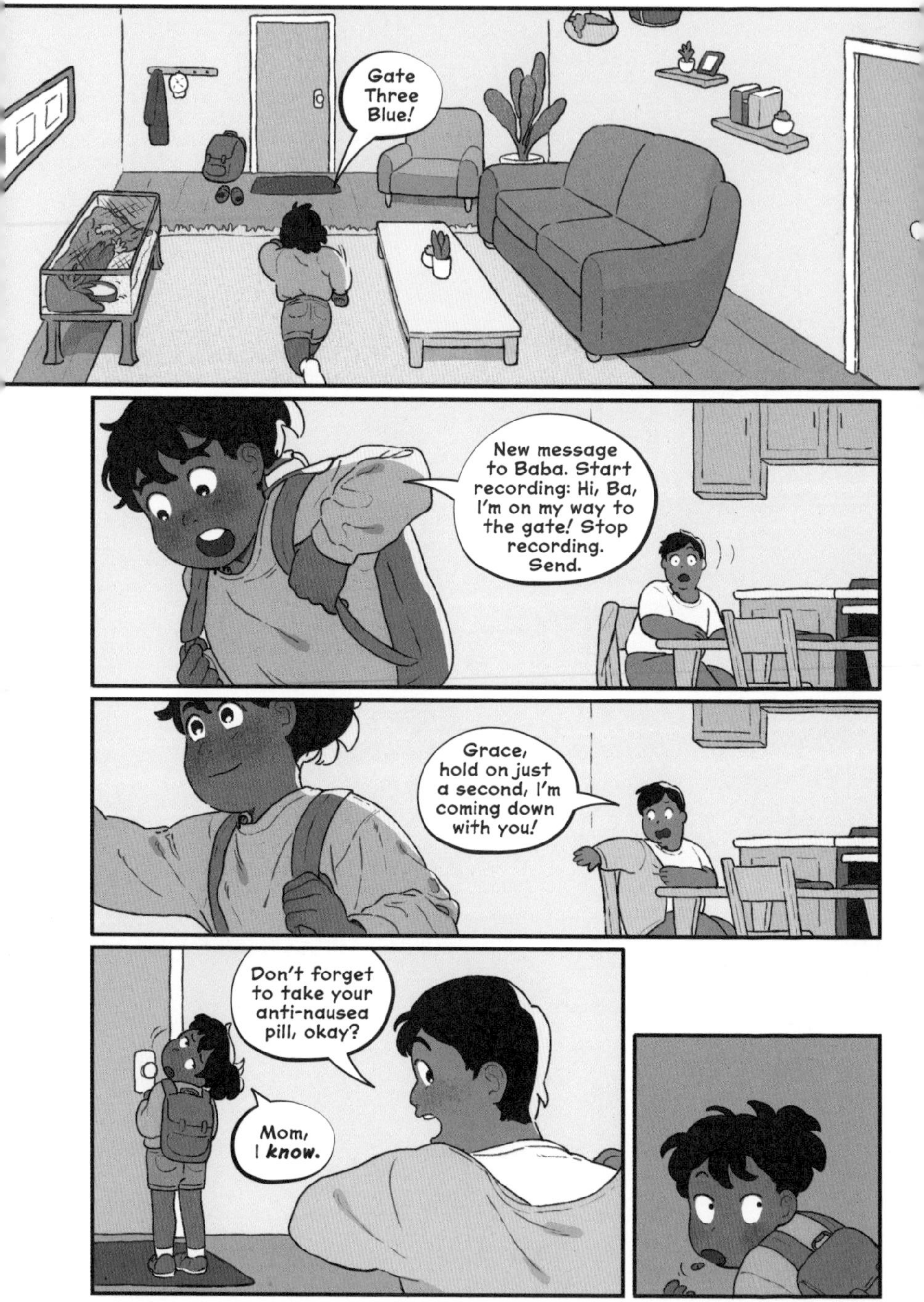
Gate Three Blue!
New message to Baba. Start recording: Hi, Ba, I'm on my way to the gate! Stop recording. Send.
Grace, hold on just a second, I'm coming down with you!
Don't forget to take your anti-nausea pill, okay?
Mom, I *know*.

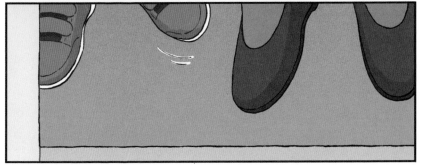

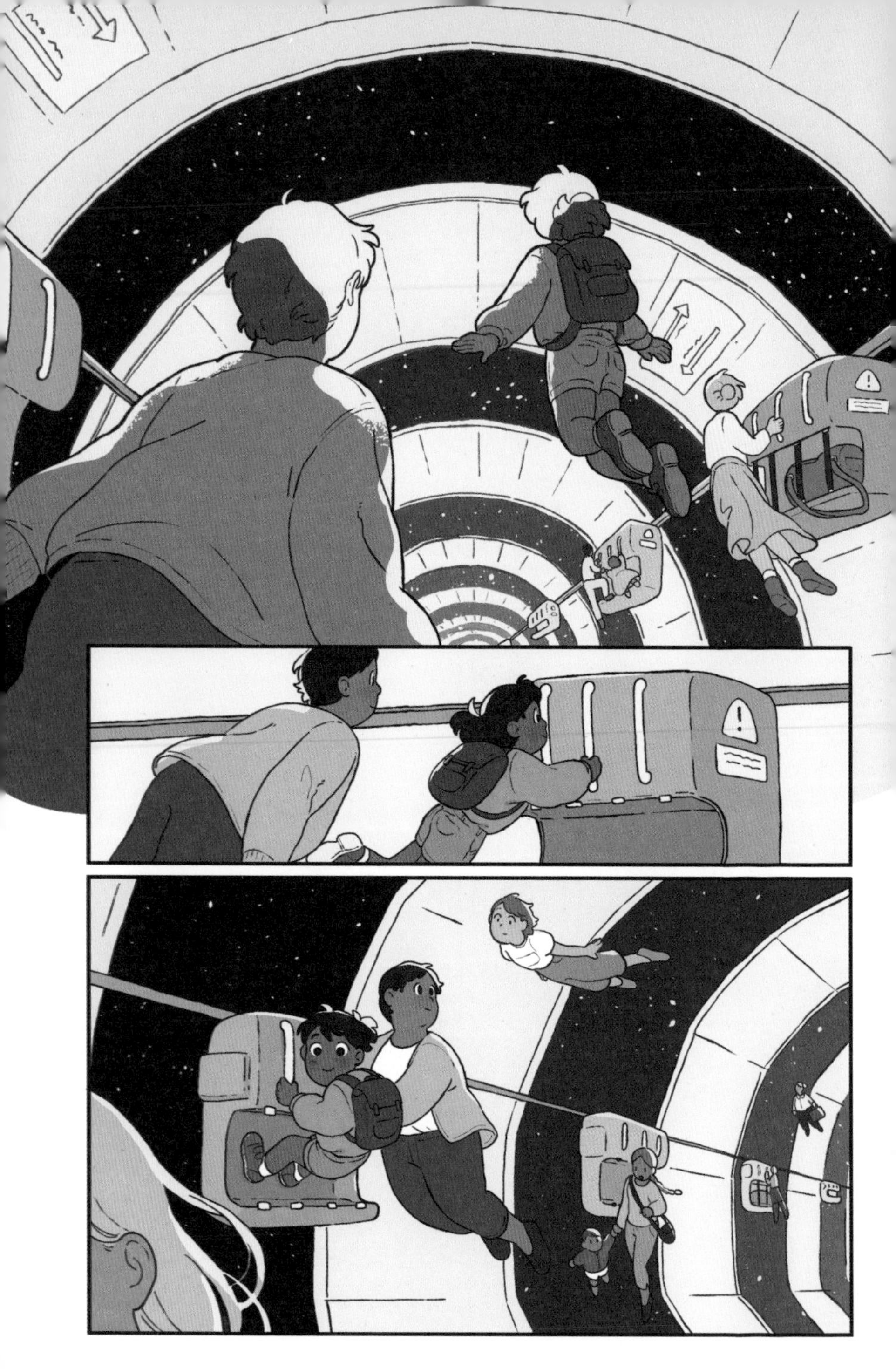

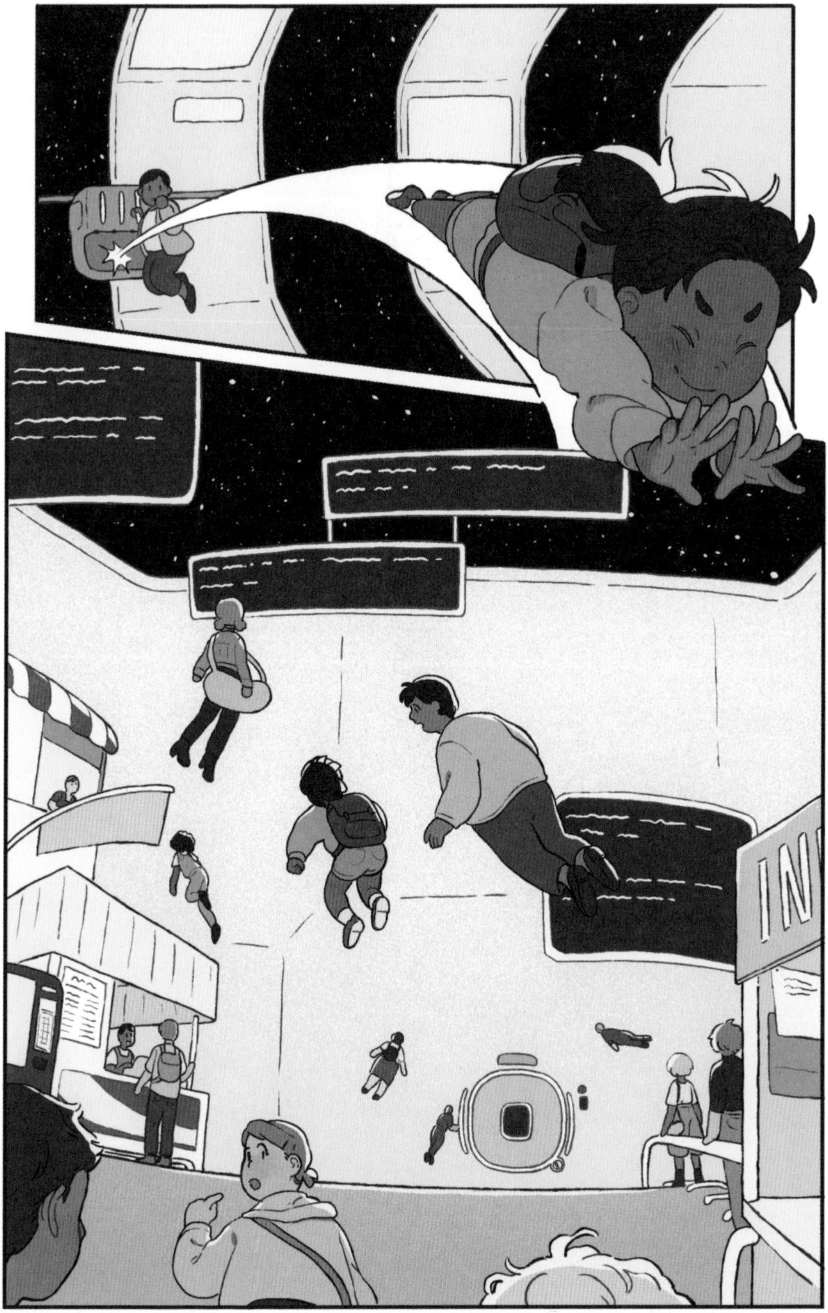

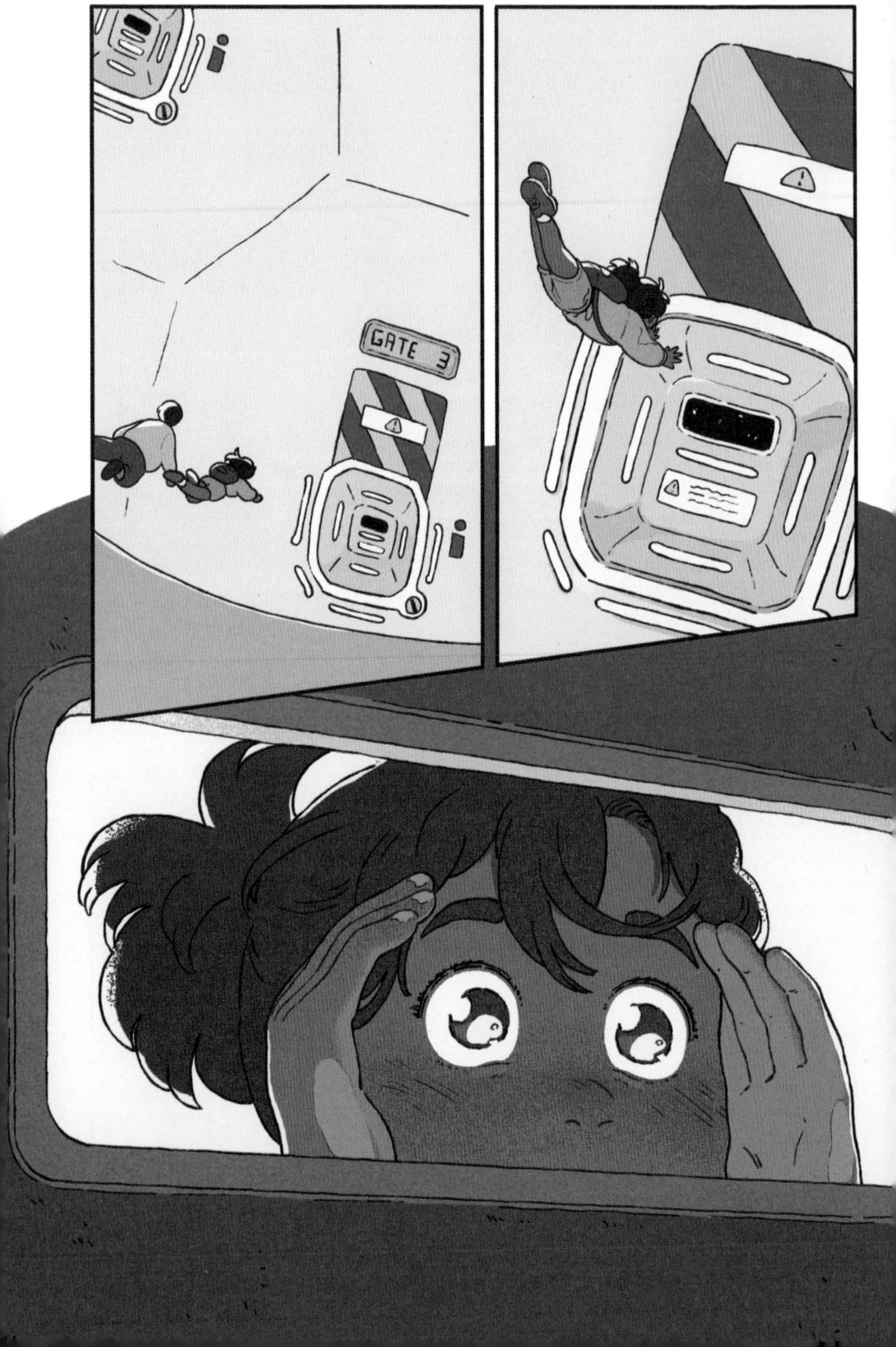
GATE 3

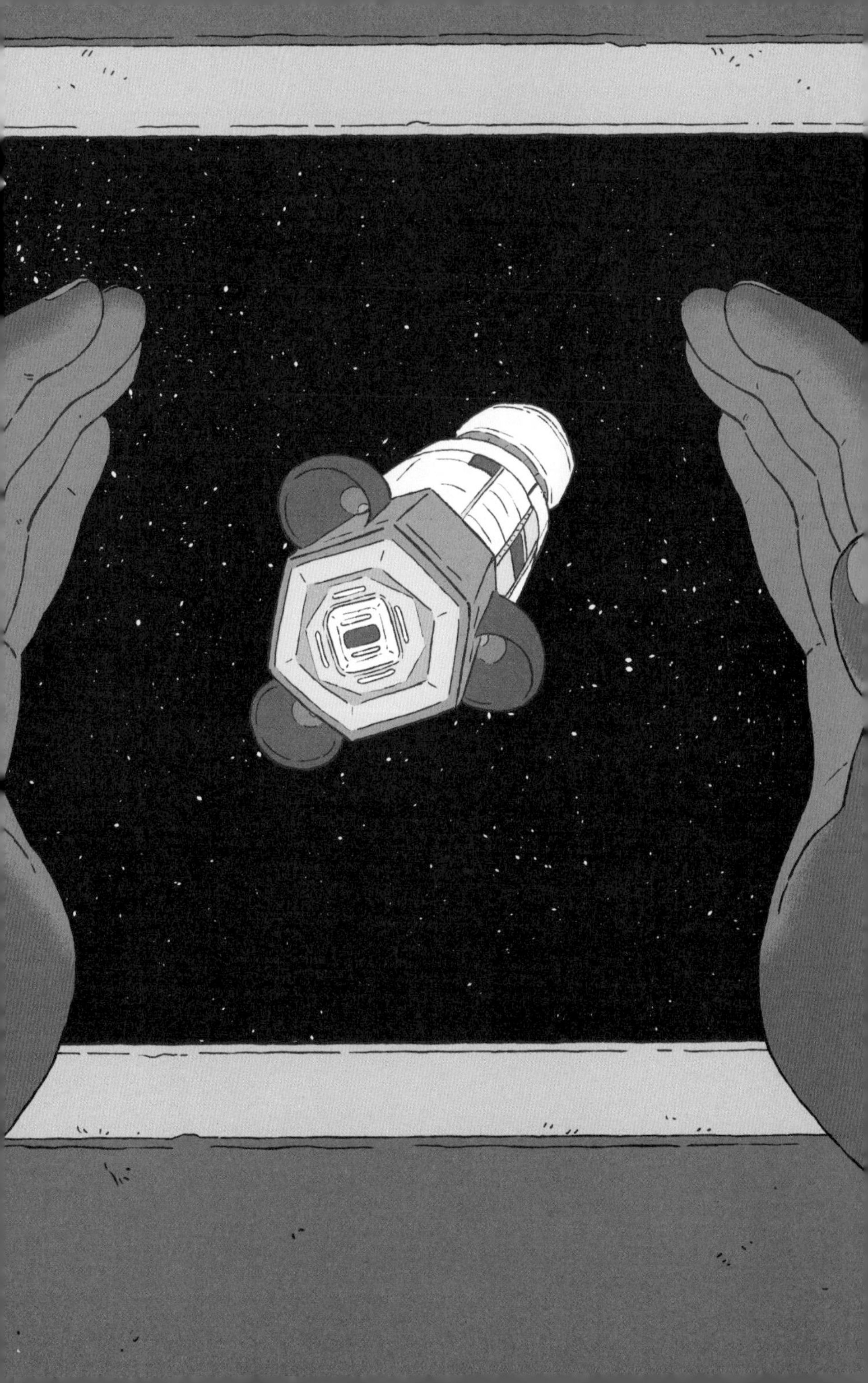

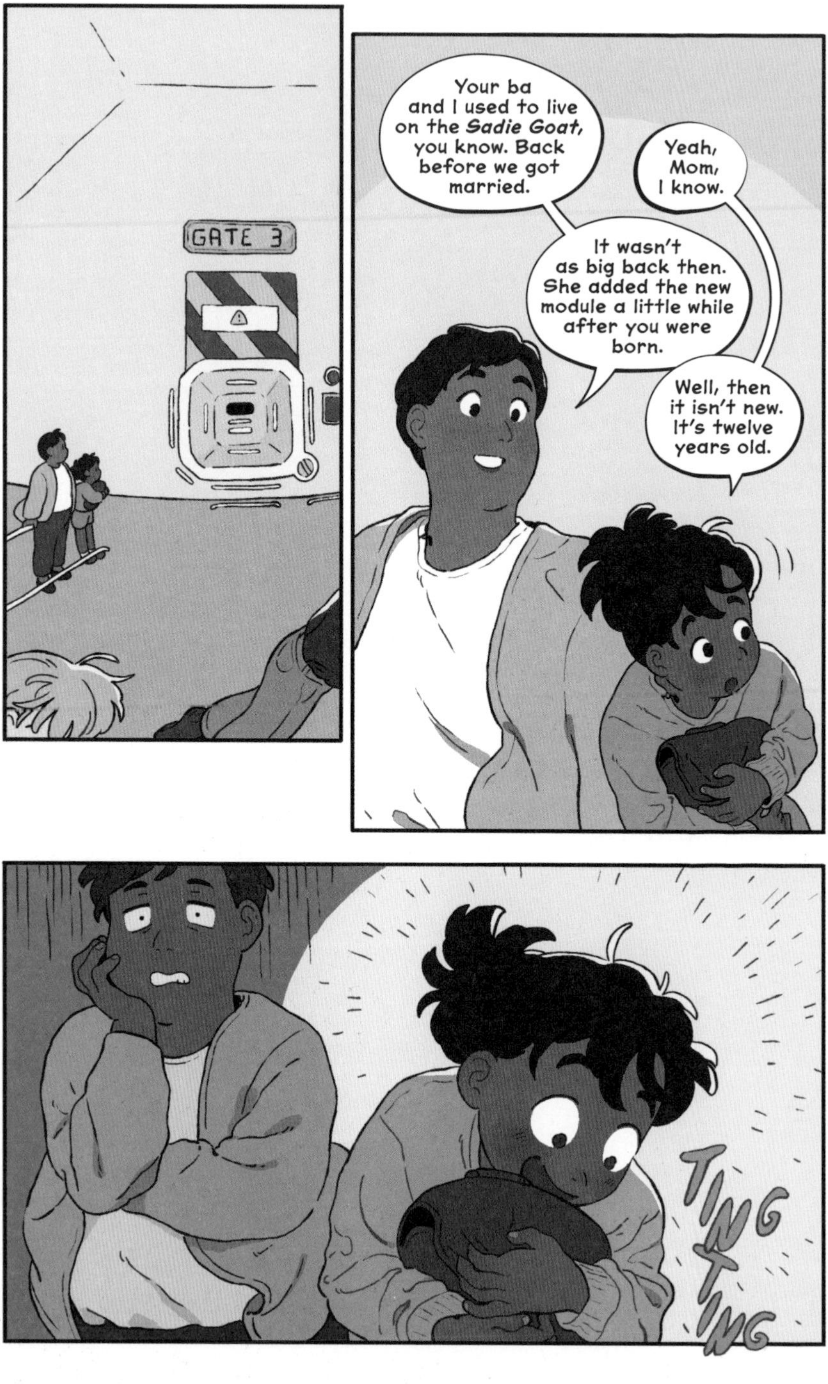
GATE 3
Your ba and I used to live on the *Sadie Goat,* you know. Back before we got married.
Yeah, Mom, I know.
It wasn't as big back then. She added the new module a little while after you were born.
Well, then it isn't new. It's twelve years old.
TING TING TING

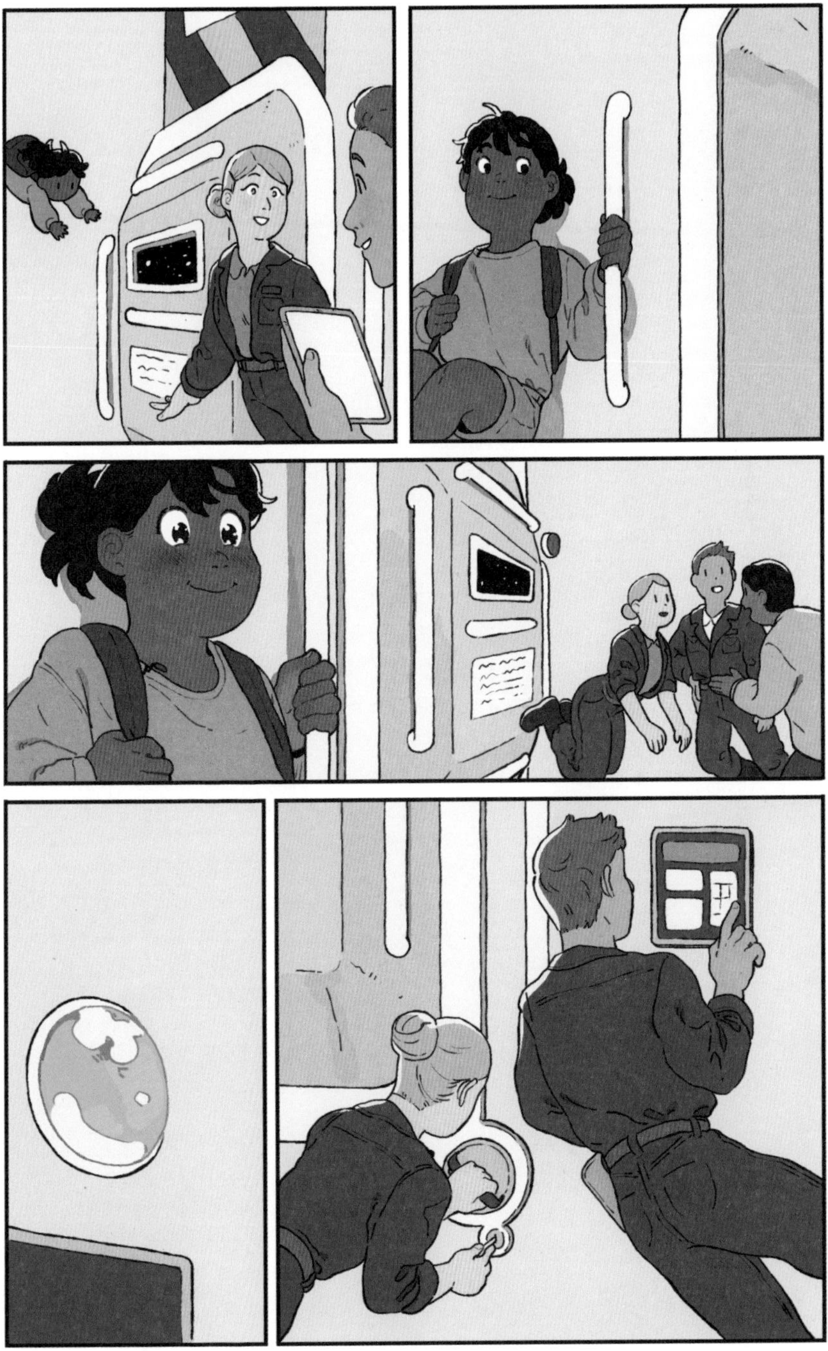

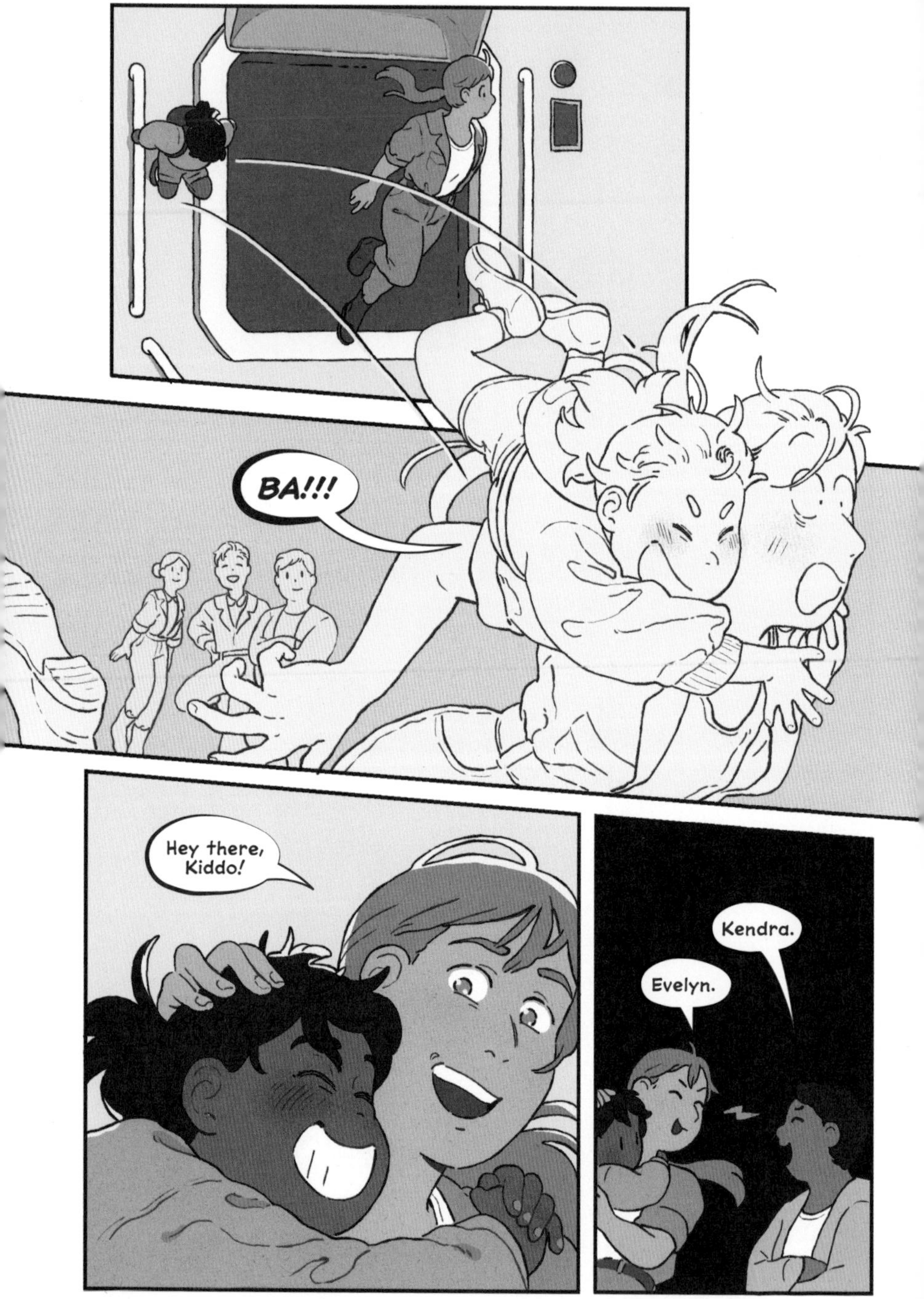
BA!!!
Hey there, Kiddo!
Kendra.
Evelyn.

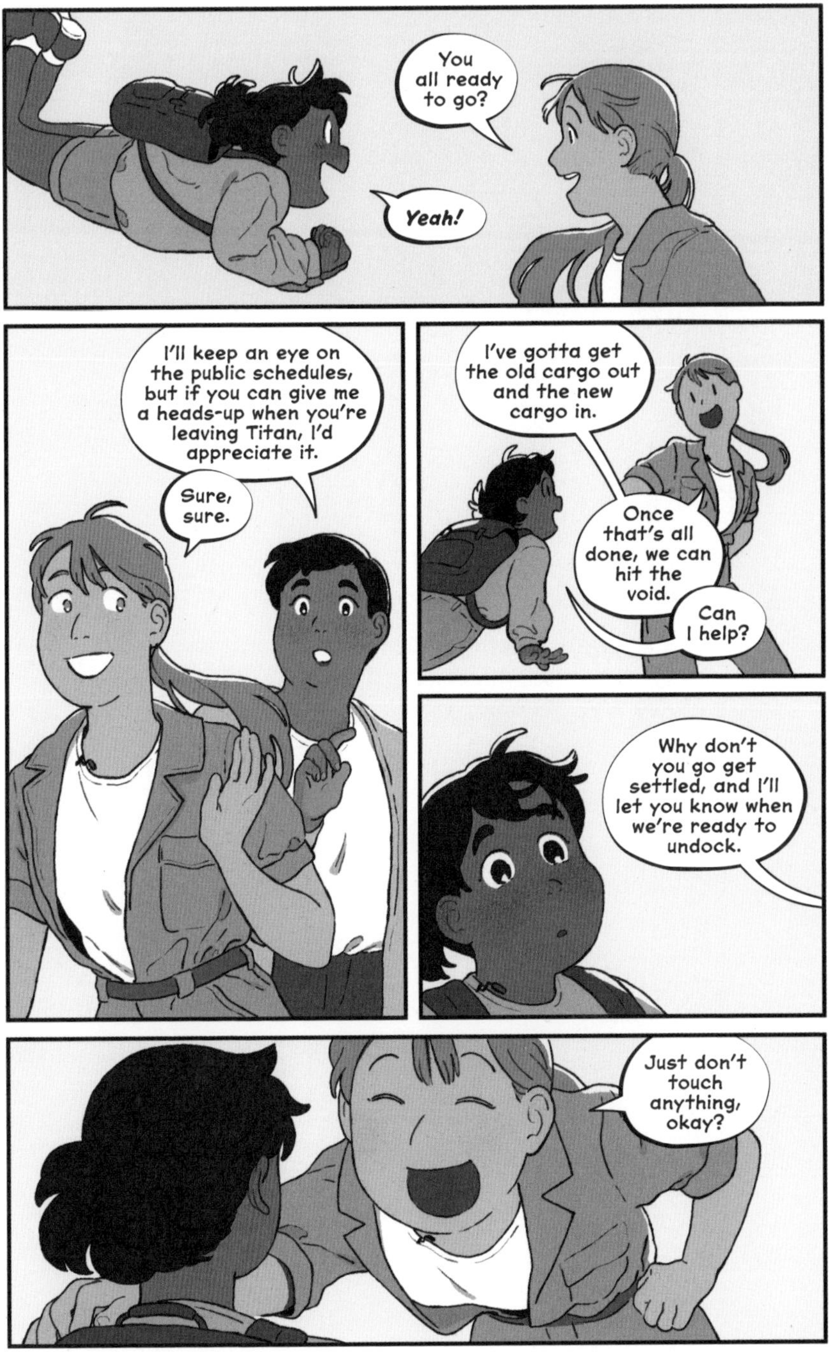
You all ready to go?
Yeah!
I'll keep an eye on the public schedules, but if you can give me a heads-up when you're leaving Titan, I'd appreciate it.
Sure, sure.
I've gotta get the old cargo out and the new cargo in.
Once that's all done, we can hit the void.
Can I help?
Why don't you go get settled, and I'll let you know when we're ready to undock.
Just don't touch anything, okay?

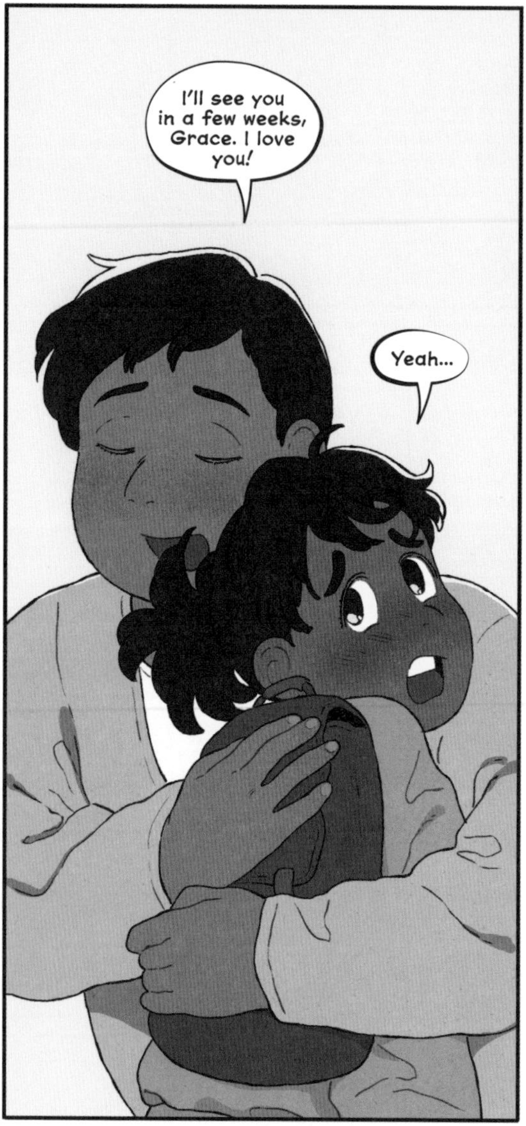
I'll see you in a few weeks, Grace. I love you!
Yeah...

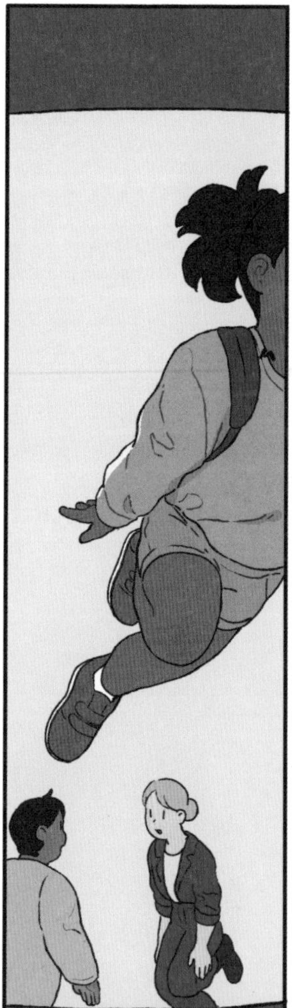

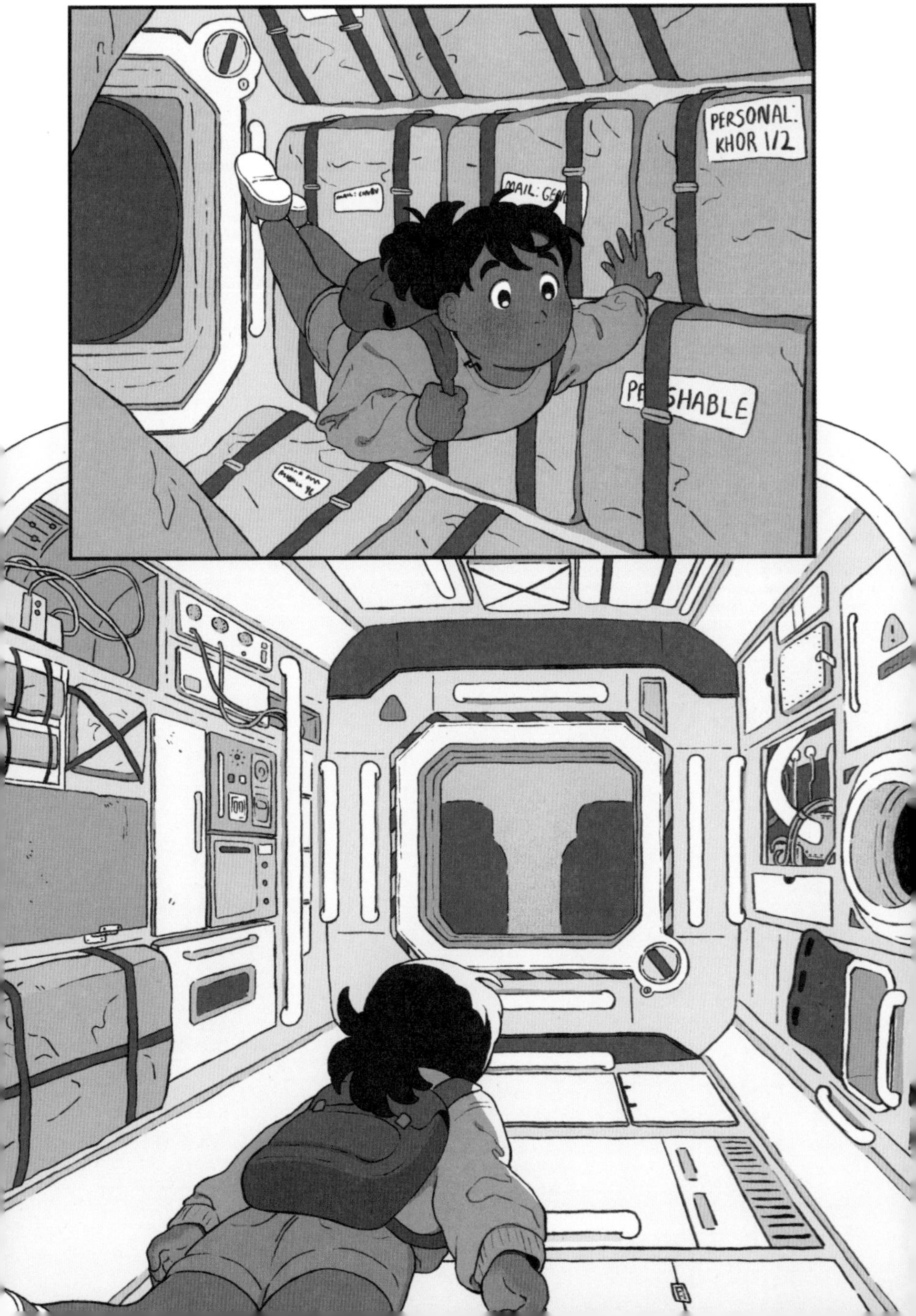
PERSONAL:
KHOR 1/2

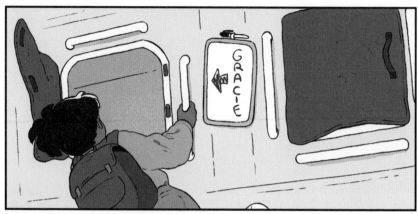

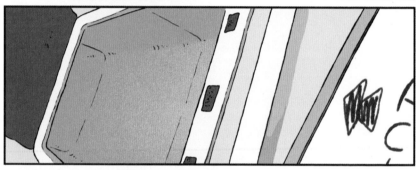

—second-most populous moon, with six thousand permanent residents calling it home.

Nestled safely within the magnetosphere of Saturn, Titan's dense atmosphere, plentiful water ice, and hydro-carbon lakes made it irresistible to early pioneers, and the first settlement was established in—

22

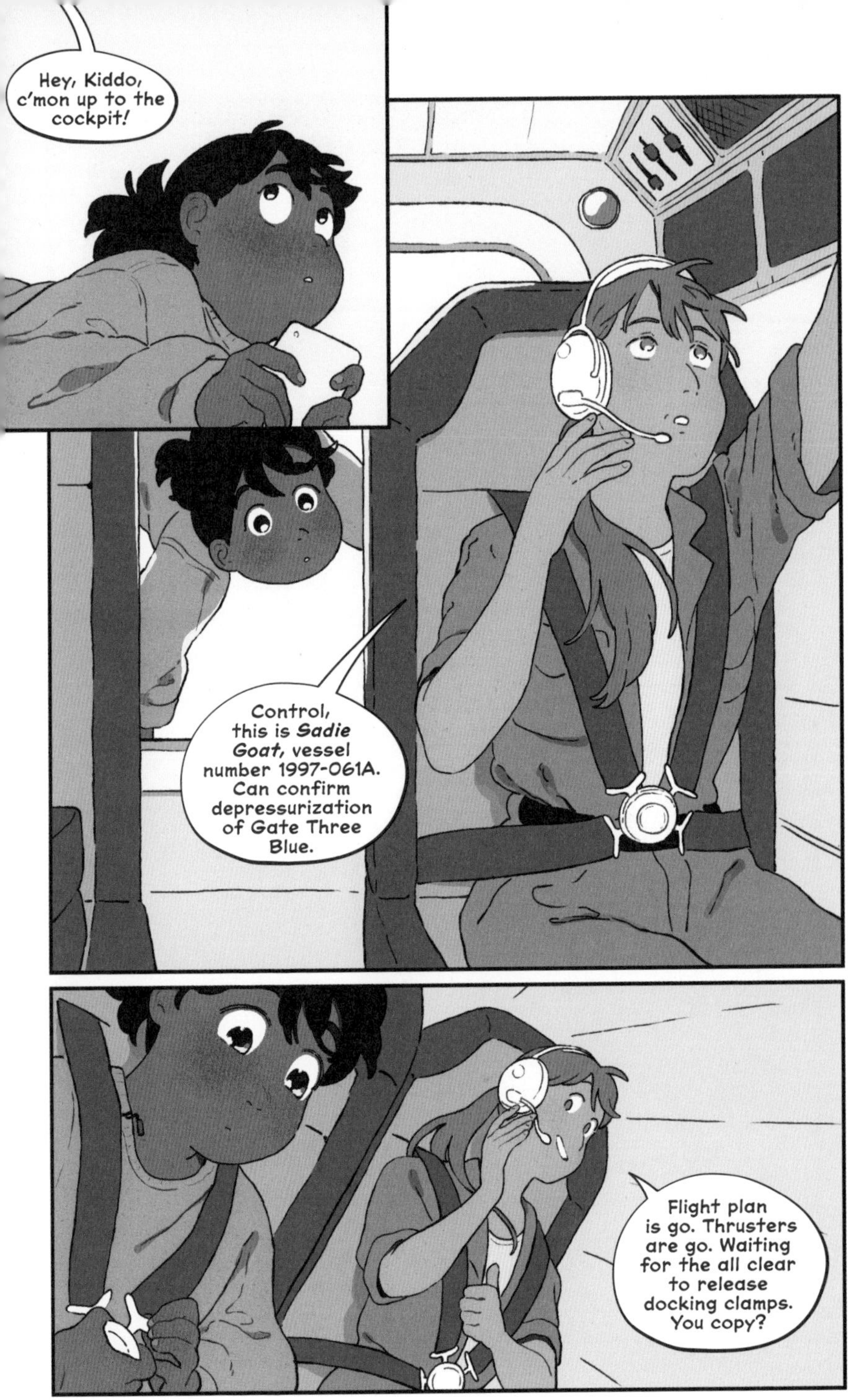
Hey, Kiddo, c'mon up to the cockpit!
Control, this is *Sadie Goat,* vessel number 1997-061A. Can confirm depressurization of Gate Three Blue.
Flight plan is go. Thrusters are go. Waiting for the all clear to release docking clamps. You copy?

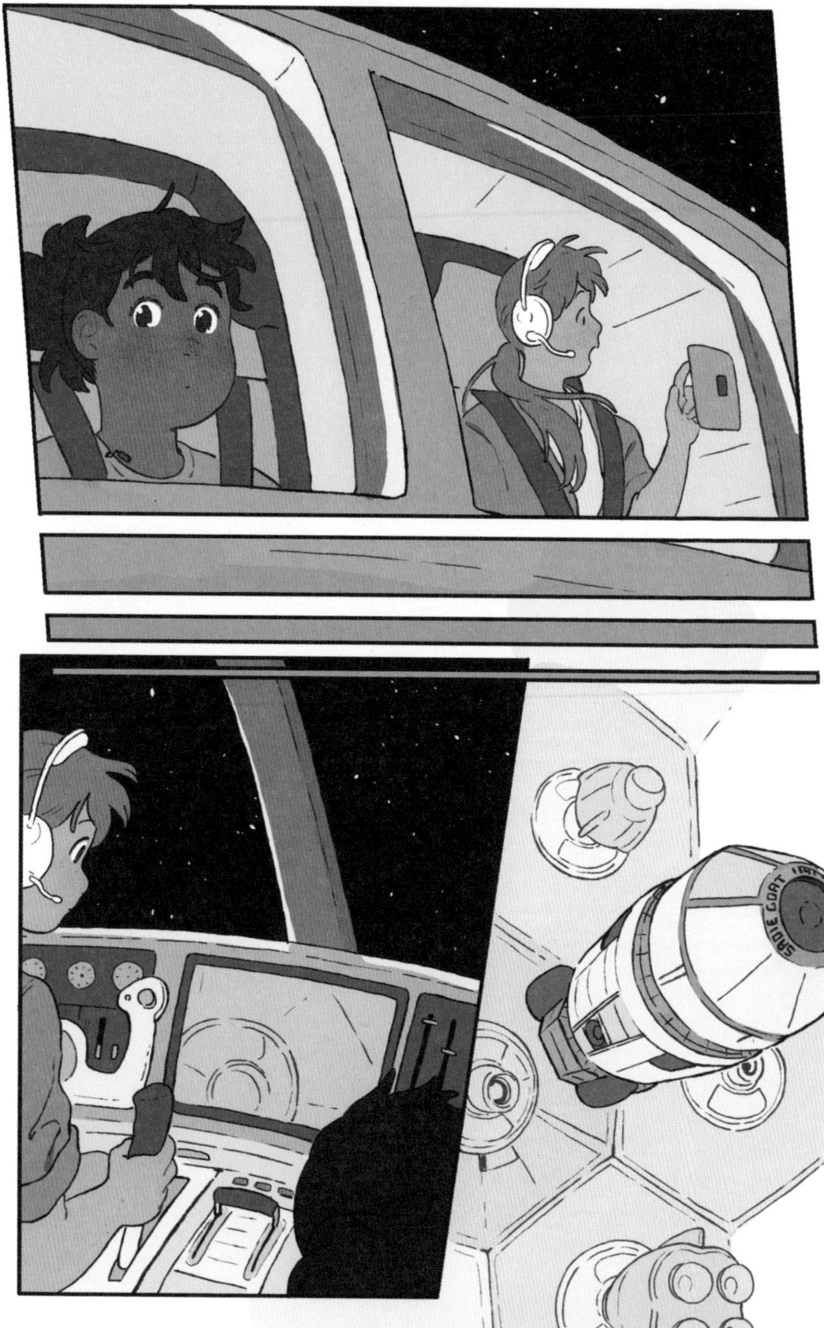
SADIE GOAT

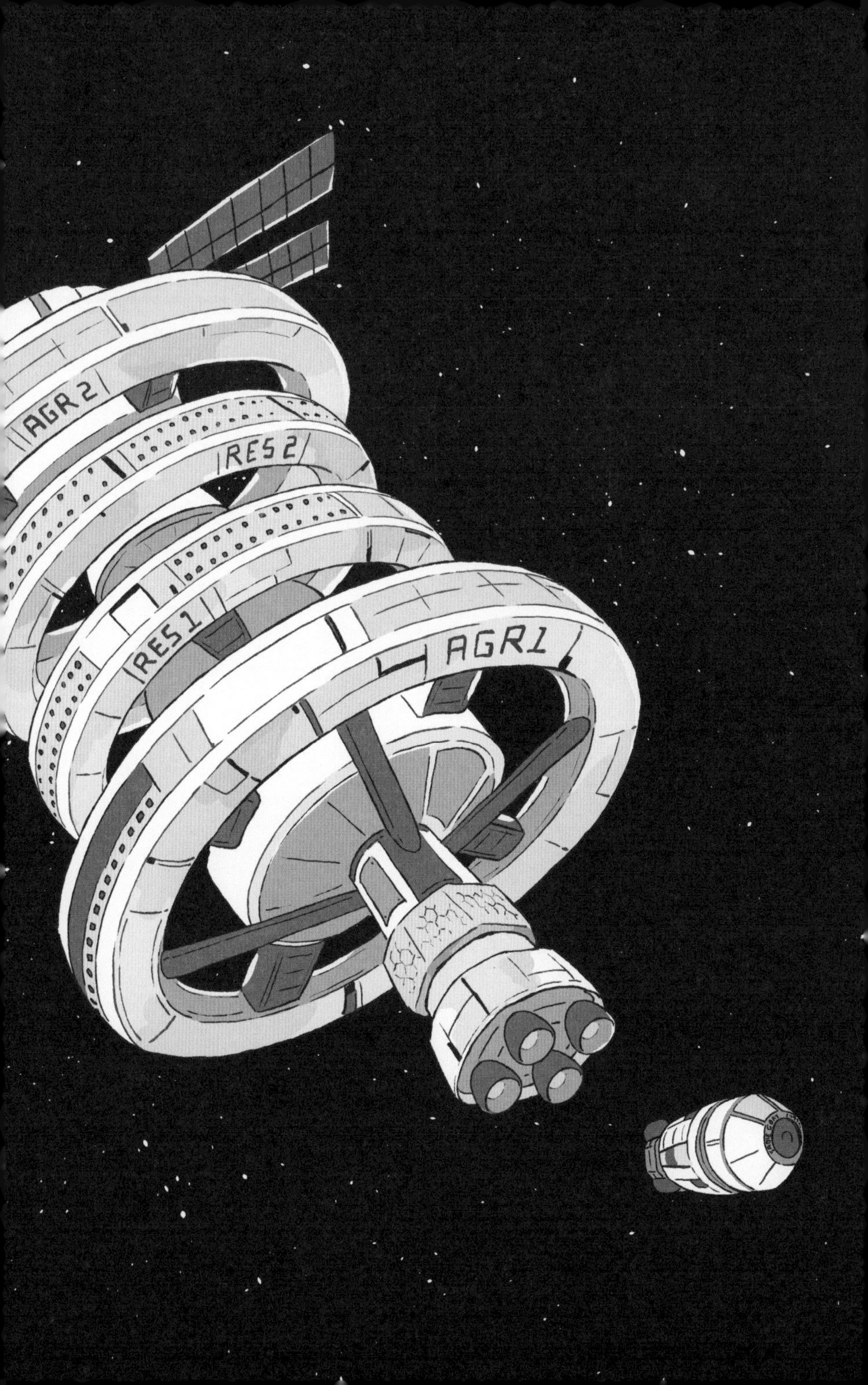
AGR 2
RES 2
RES 1
AGR1

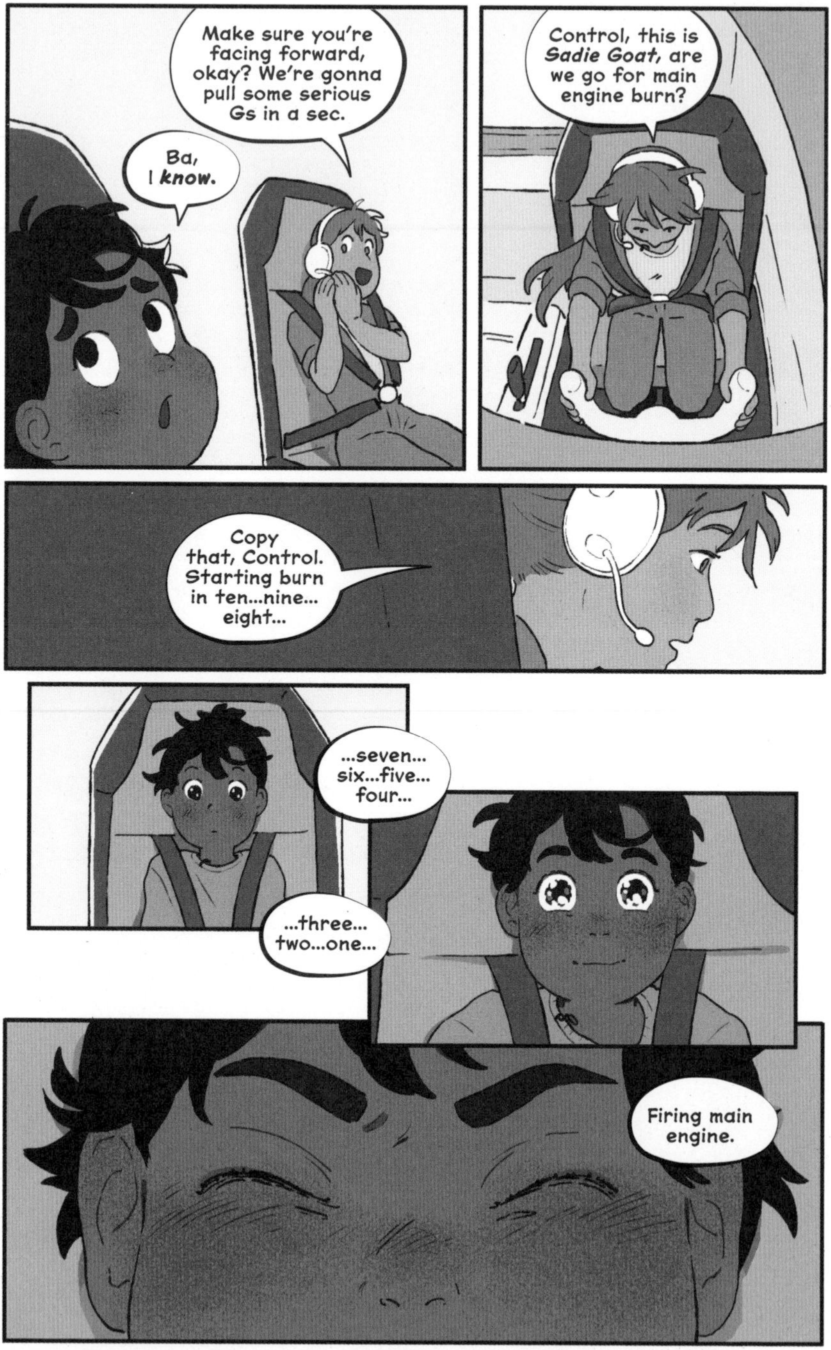
Make sure you're facing forward, okay? We're gonna pull some serious Gs in a sec.
Ba, I *know*.
Control, this is *Sadie Goat*, are we go for main engine burn?
Copy that, Control. Starting burn in ten...nine... eight...
...seven... six...five... four...
...three... two...one...
Firing main engine.

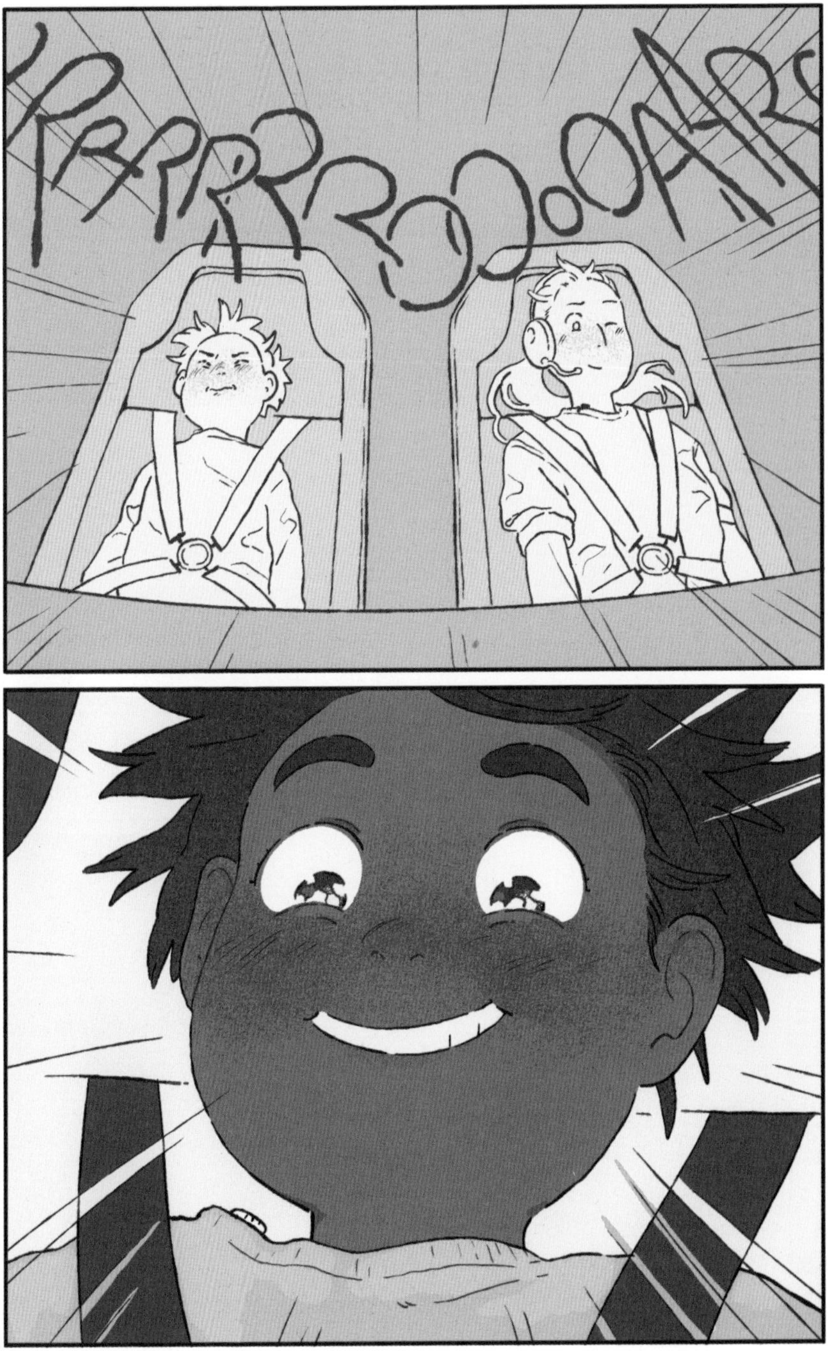
VRRRRRROOOOARR

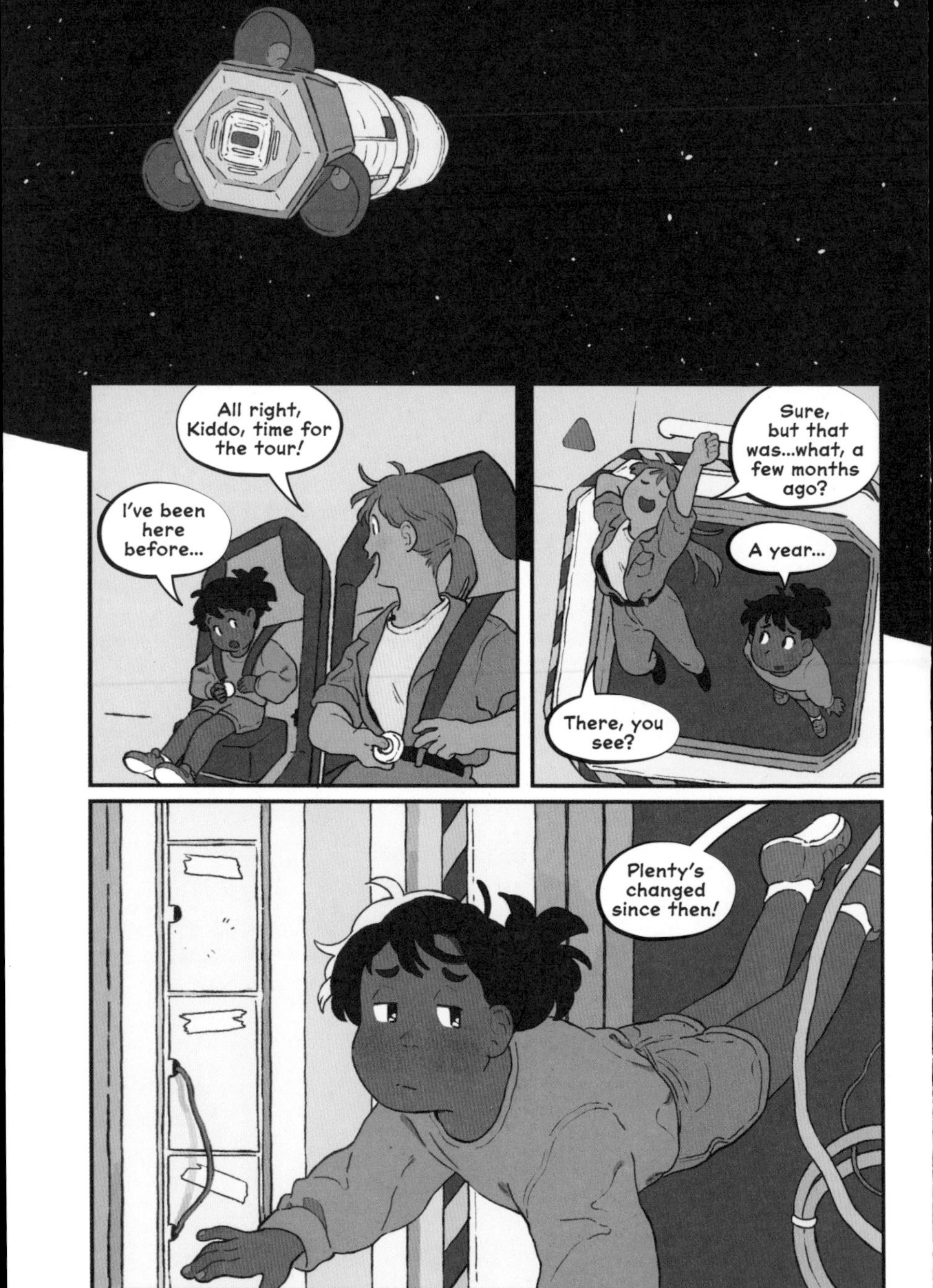
All right, Kiddo, time for the tour!
I've been here before...
Sure, but that was...what, a few months ago?
A year...
There, you see?
Plenty's changed since then!

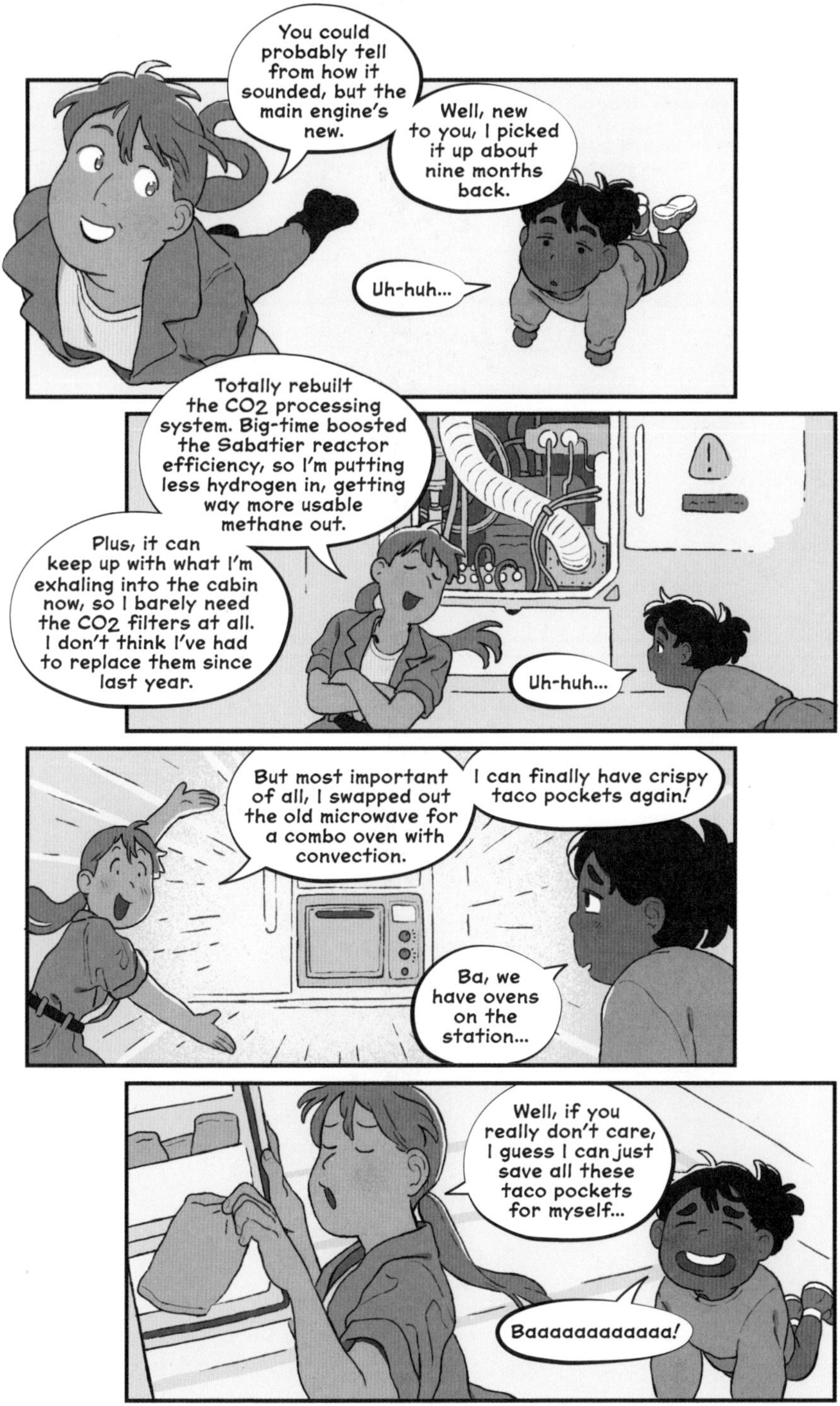
You could probably tell from how it sounded, but the main engine's new.
Well, new to you, I picked it up about nine months back.
Uh-huh...
Totally rebuilt the CO2 processing system. Big-time boosted the Sabatier reactor efficiency, so I'm putting less hydrogen in, getting way more usable methane out.
Plus, it can keep up with what I'm exhaling into the cabin now, so I barely need the CO2 filters at all. I don't think I've had to replace them since last year.
Uh-huh...
But most important of all, I swapped out the old microwave for a combo oven with convection.
I can finally have crispy taco pockets again!
Ba, we have ovens on the station...
Well, if you really don't care, I guess I can just save all these taco pockets for myself...
Baaaaaaaaaaa!

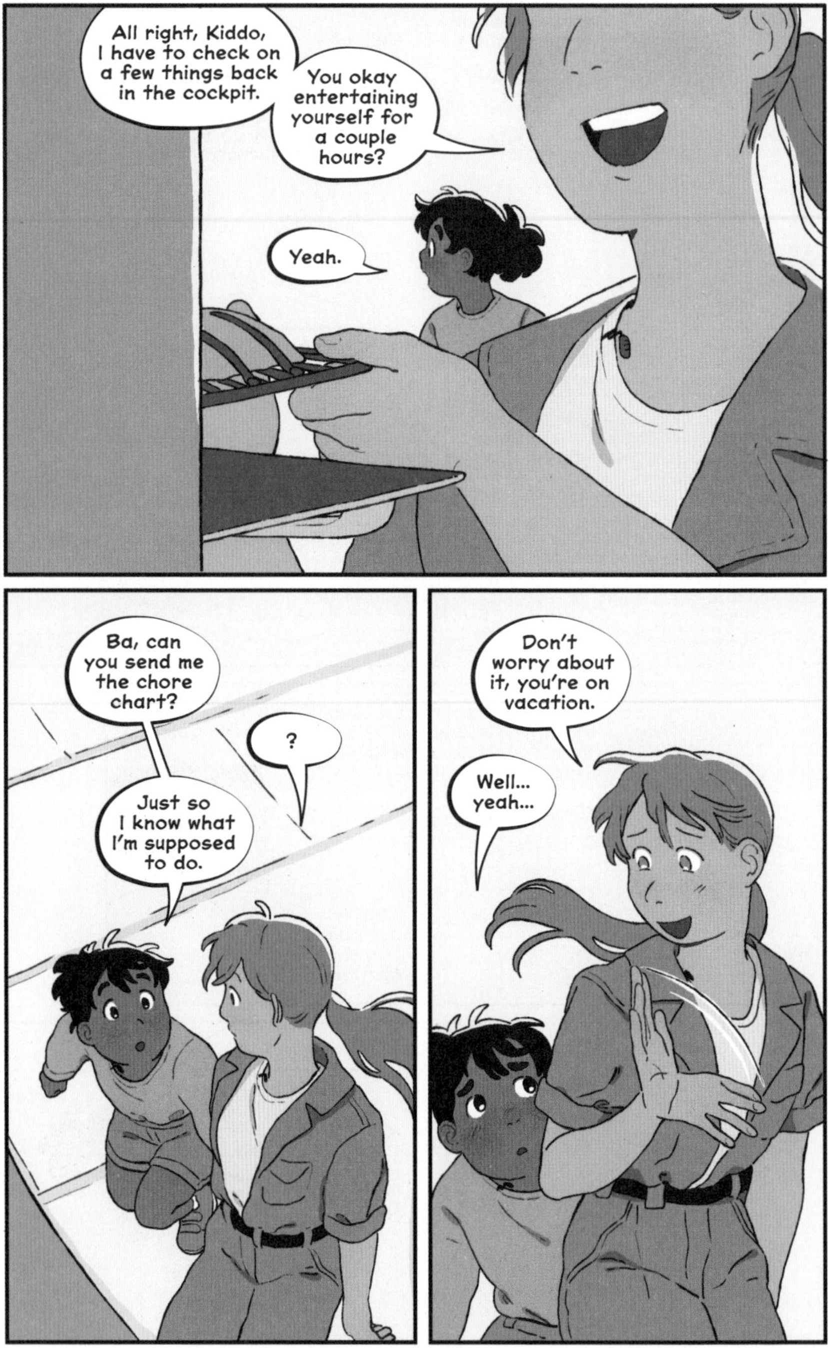
All right, Kiddo, I have to check on a few things back in the cockpit.
You okay entertaining yourself for a couple hours?
Yeah.
Ba, can you send me the chore chart?
Just so I know what I'm supposed to do.
?
Don't worry about it, you're on vacation.
Well... yeah...

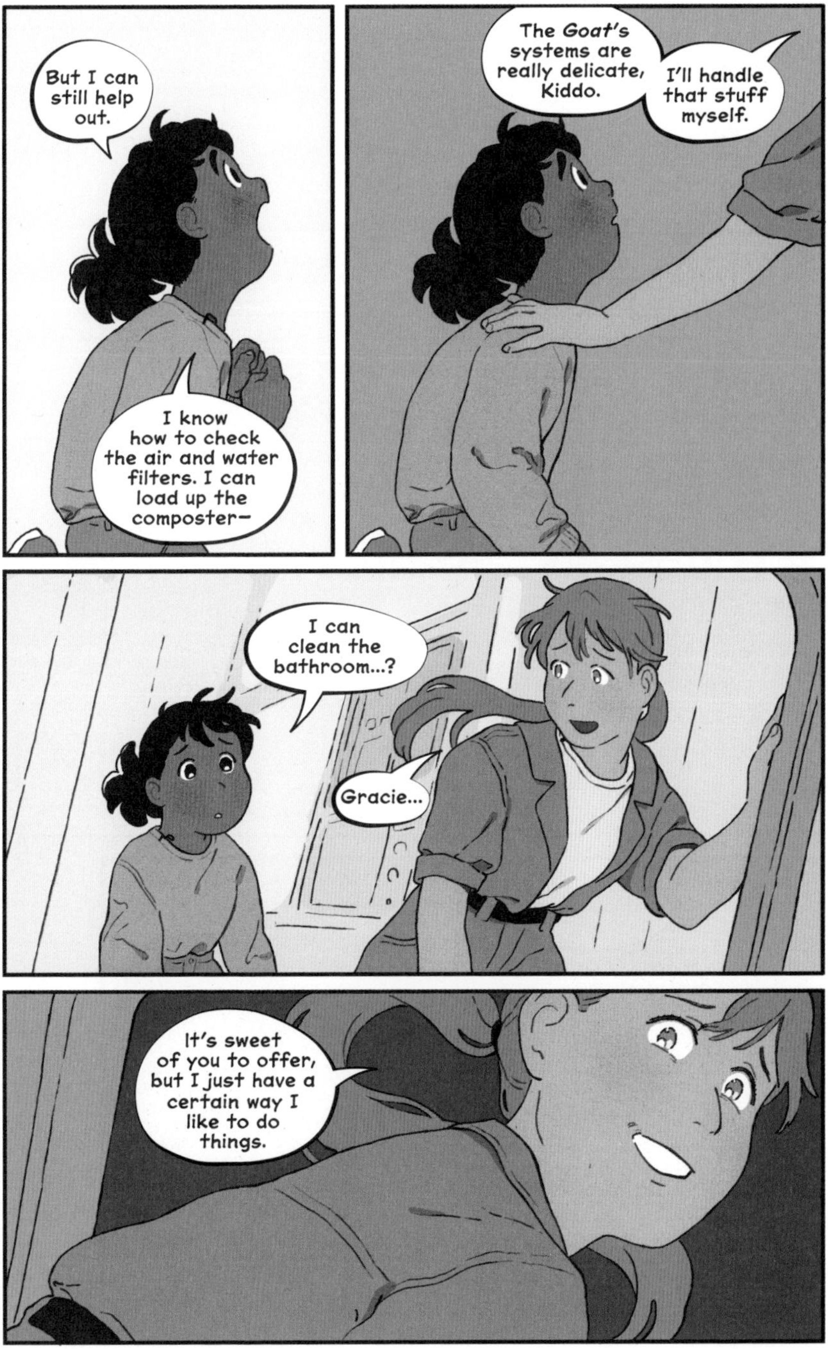
But I can still help out.
I know how to check the air and water filters. I can load up the composter—
The Goat's systems are really delicate, Kiddo.
I'll handle that stuff myself.
I can clean the bathroom...?
Gracie...
It's sweet of you to offer, but I just have a certain way I like to do things.

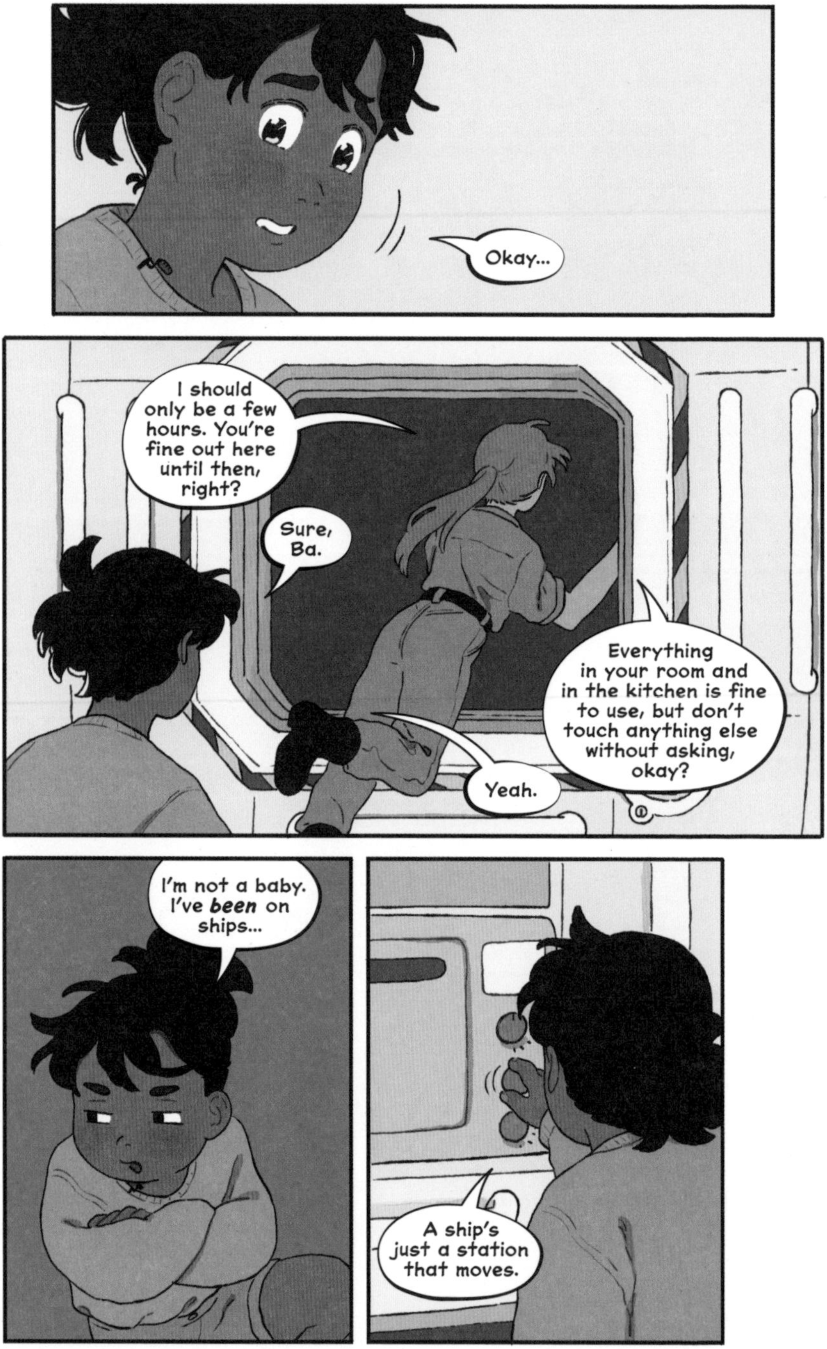
Okay...
I should only be a few hours. You're fine out here until then, right?
Sure, Ba.
Everything in your room and in the kitchen is fine to use, but don't touch anything else without asking, okay?
Yeah.
I'm not a baby. I've *been* on ships...
A ship's just a station that moves.

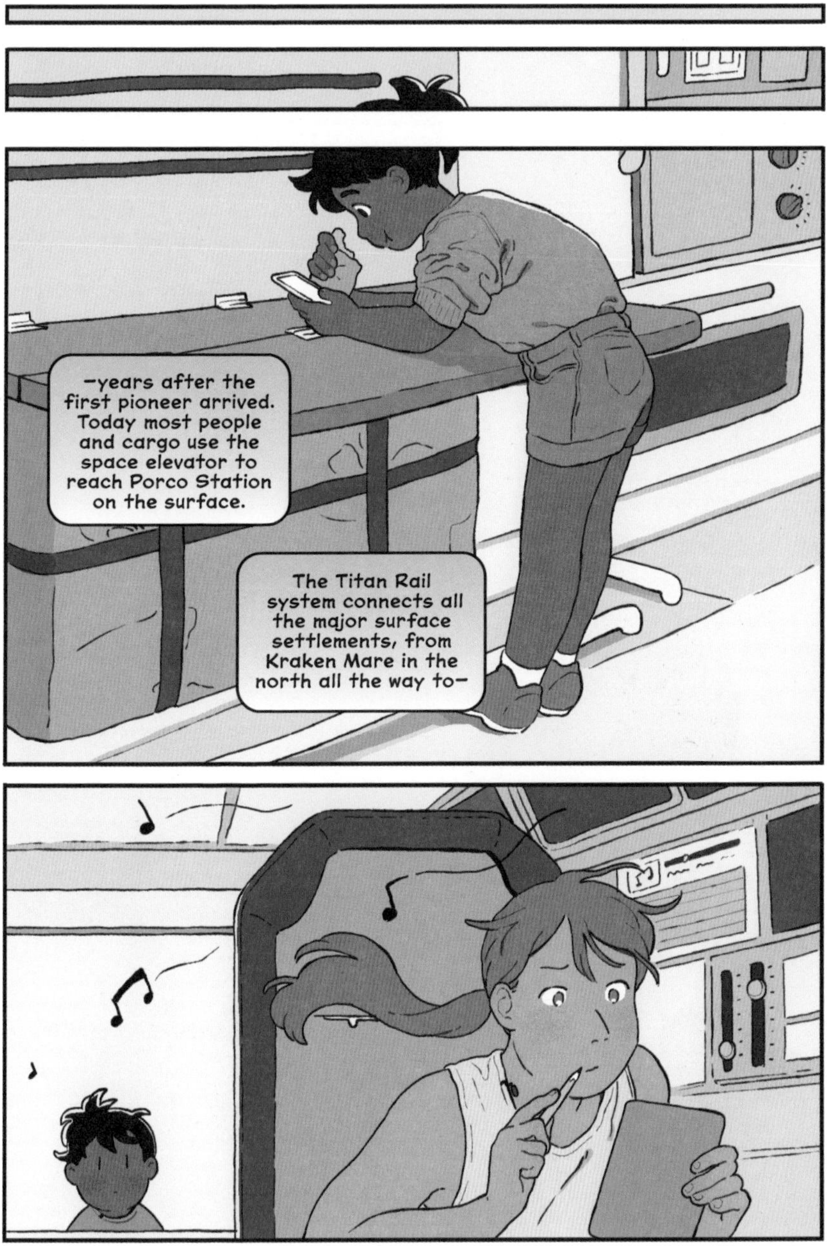
-years after the first pioneer arrived. Today most people and cargo use the space elevator to reach Porco Station on the surface.
The Titan Rail system connects all the major surface settlements, from Kraken Mare in the north all the way to-

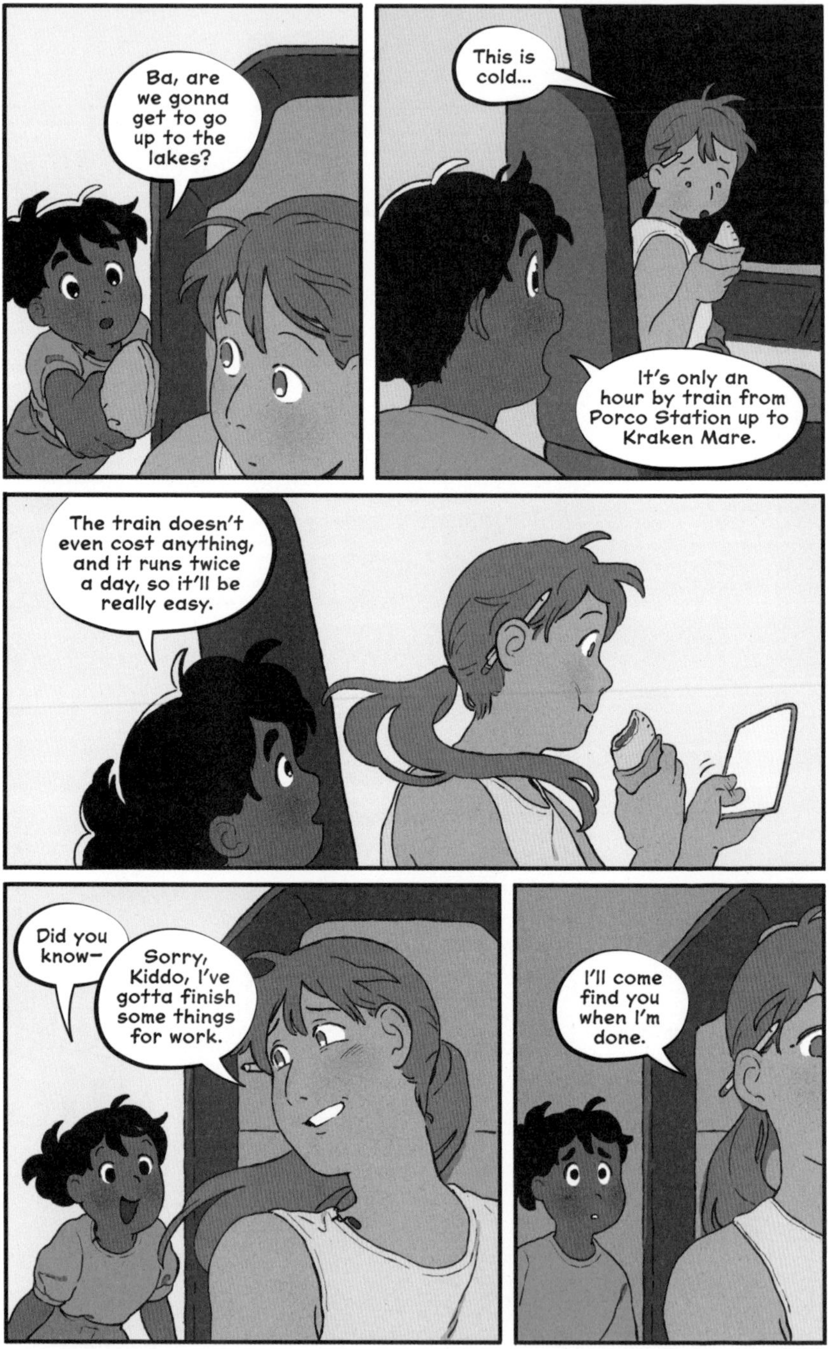

Ba, are we gonna get to go up to the lakes?
This is cold...
It's only an hour by train from Porco Station up to Kraken Mare.
The train doesn't even cost anything, and it runs twice a day, so it'll be really easy.
Did you know—
Sorry, Kiddo, I've gotta finish some things for work.
I'll come find you when I'm done.

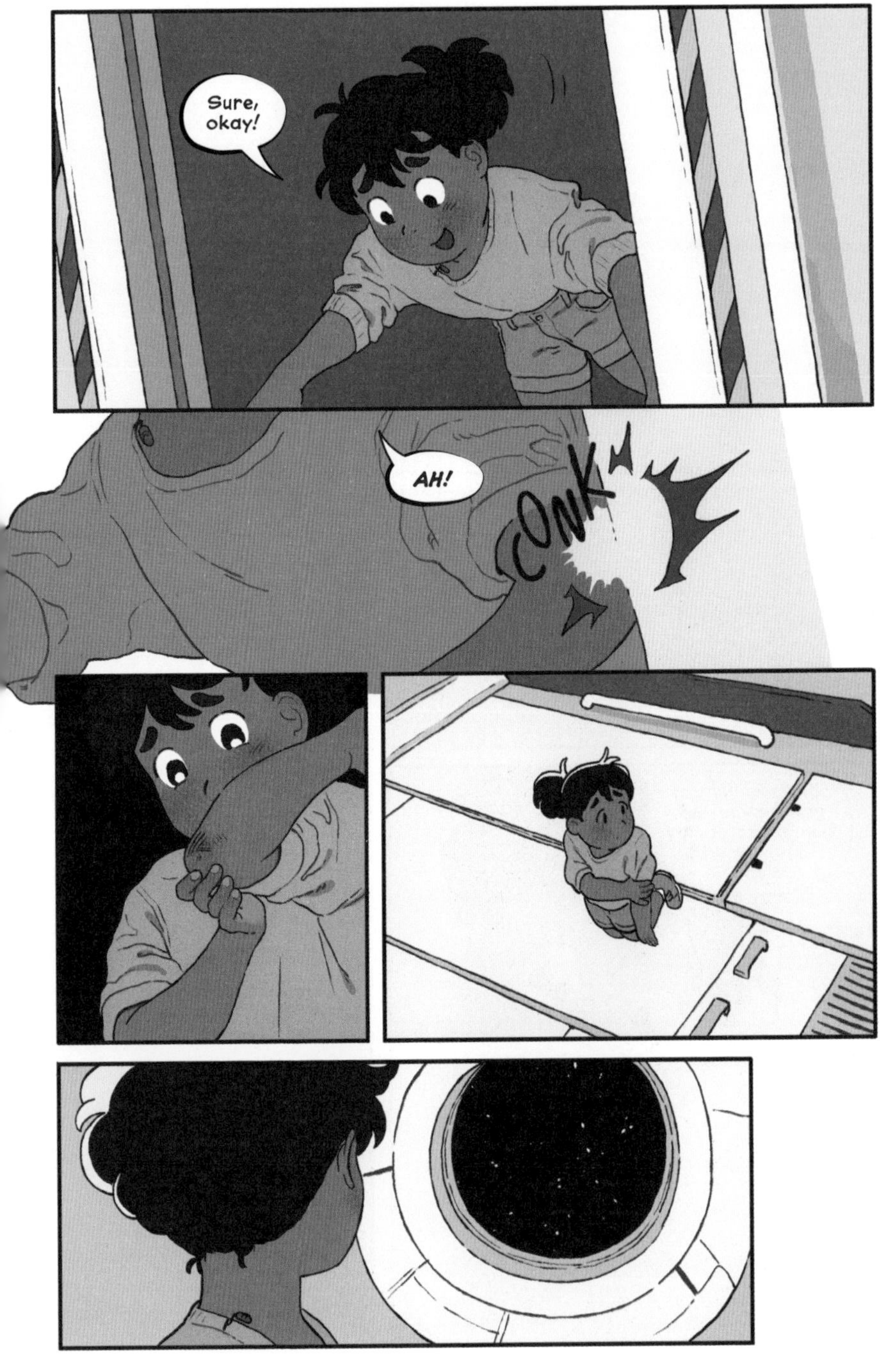
Sure, okay!
AH!
CONK

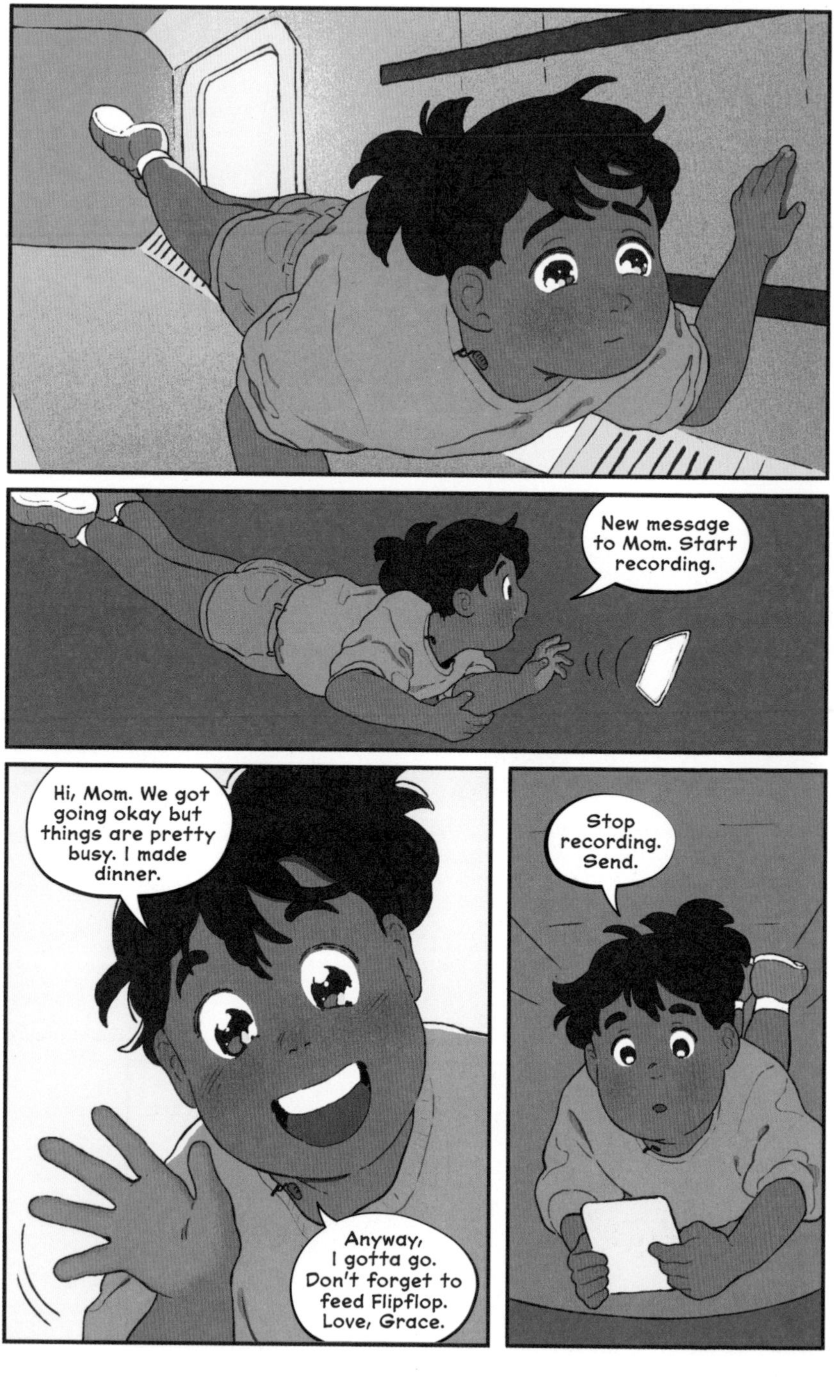
New message to Mom. Start recording.
Hi, Mom. We got going okay but things are pretty busy. I made dinner.
Anyway, I gotta go. Don't forget to feed Flipflop. Love, Grace.
Stop recording. Send.

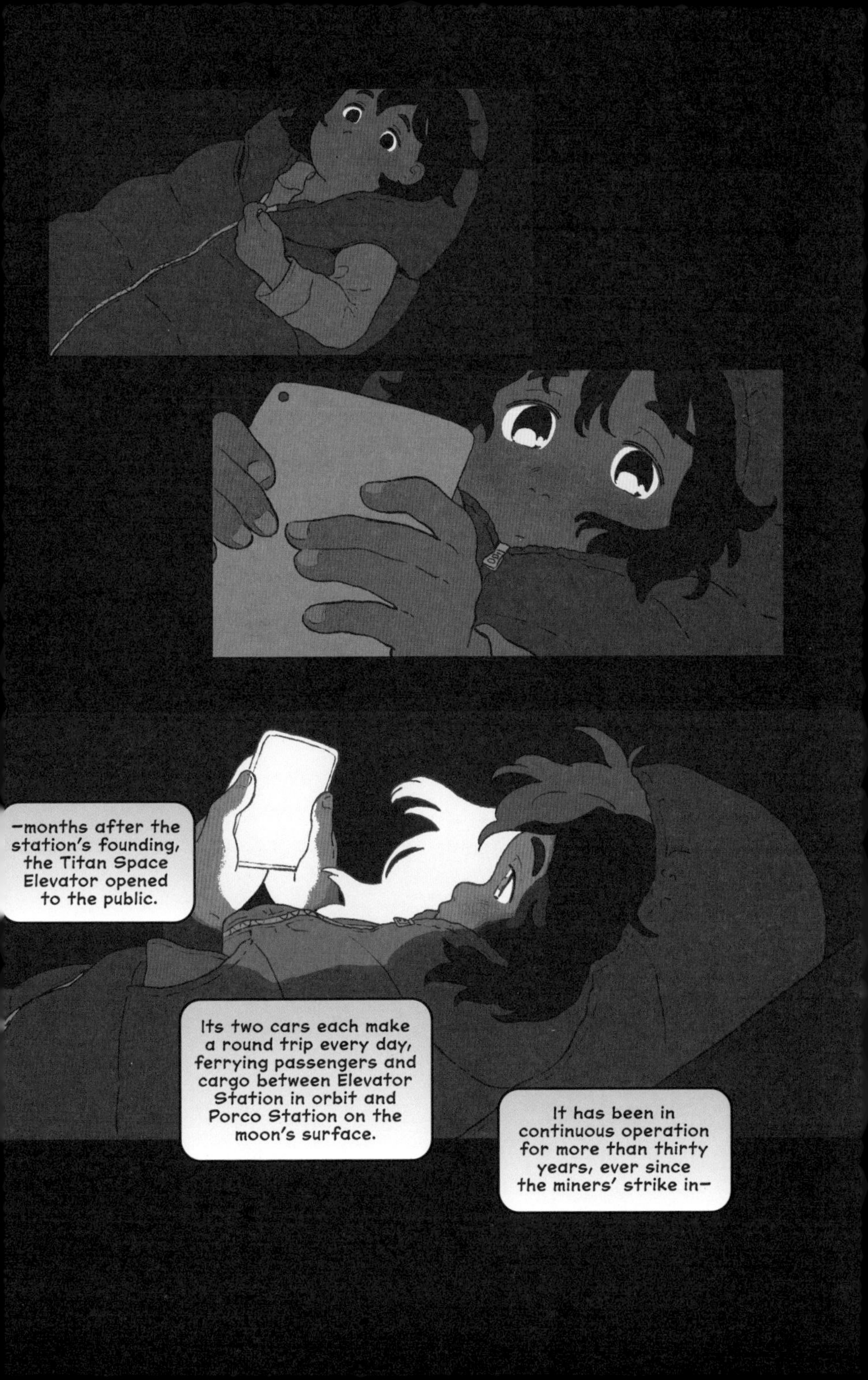
—months after the station's founding, the Titan Space Elevator opened to the public.
Its two cars each make a round trip every day, ferrying passengers and cargo between Elevator Station in orbit and Porco Station on the moon's surface.
It has been in continuous operation for more than thirty years, ever since the miners' strike in—

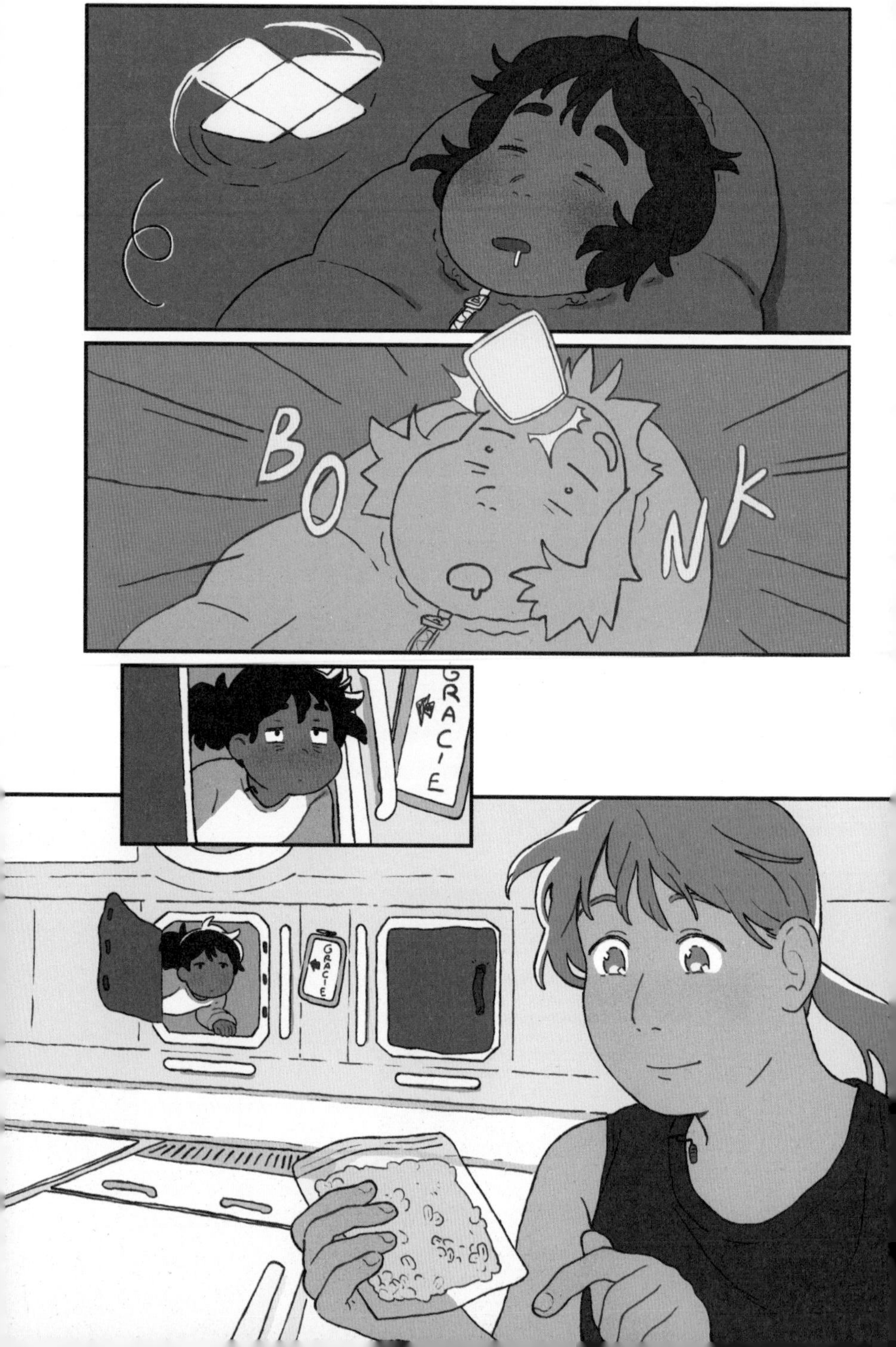
BONK
GRACIE
GRACIE

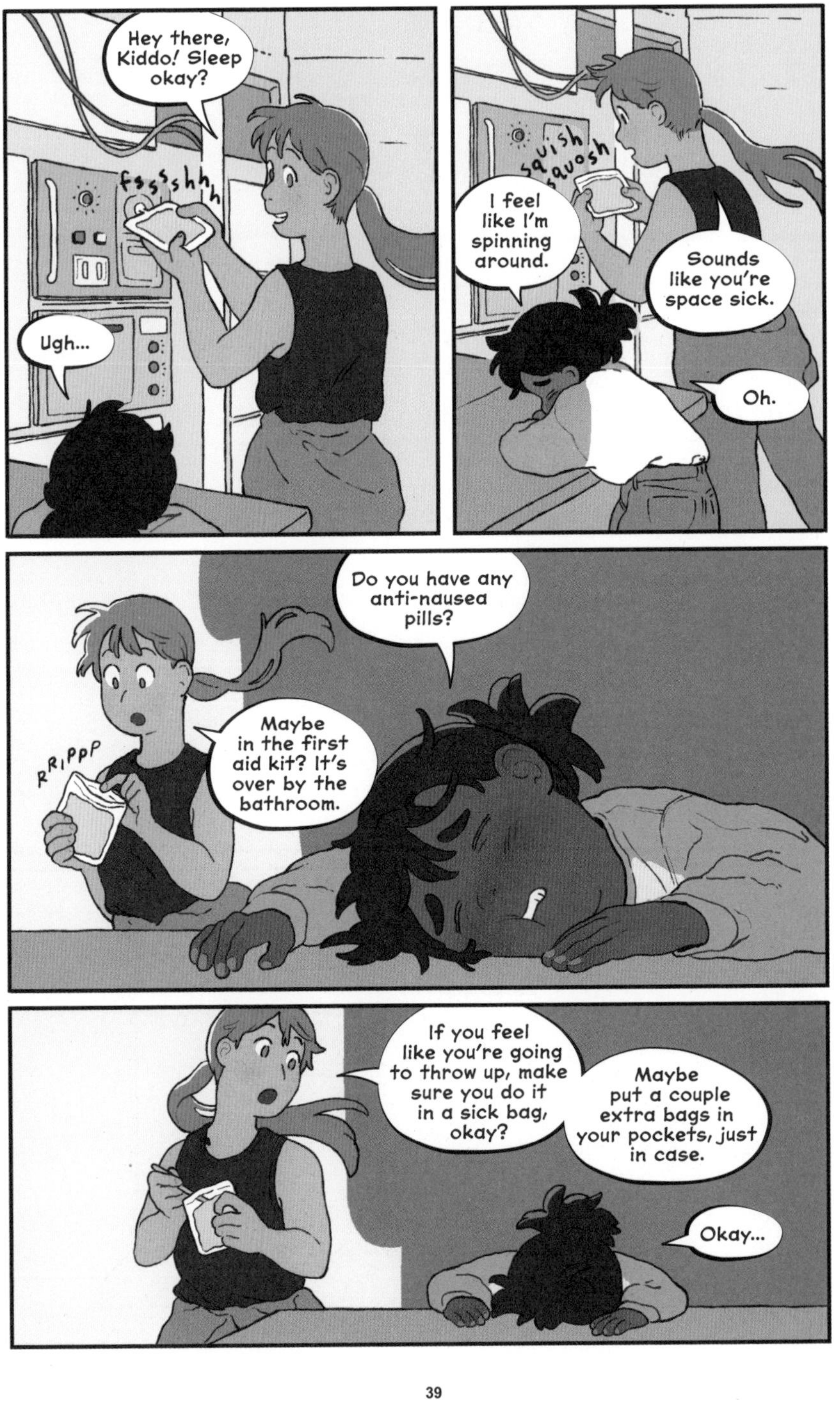
Hey there, Kiddo! Sleep okay?
fsssshhh
Ugh...
squish squosh
I feel like I'm spinning around.
Sounds like you're space sick.
Oh.
Do you have any anti-nausea pills?
Maybe in the first aid kit? It's over by the bathroom.
RRIPPP
If you feel like you're going to throw up, make sure you do it in a sick bag, okay?
Maybe put a couple extra bags in your pockets, just in case.
Okay...

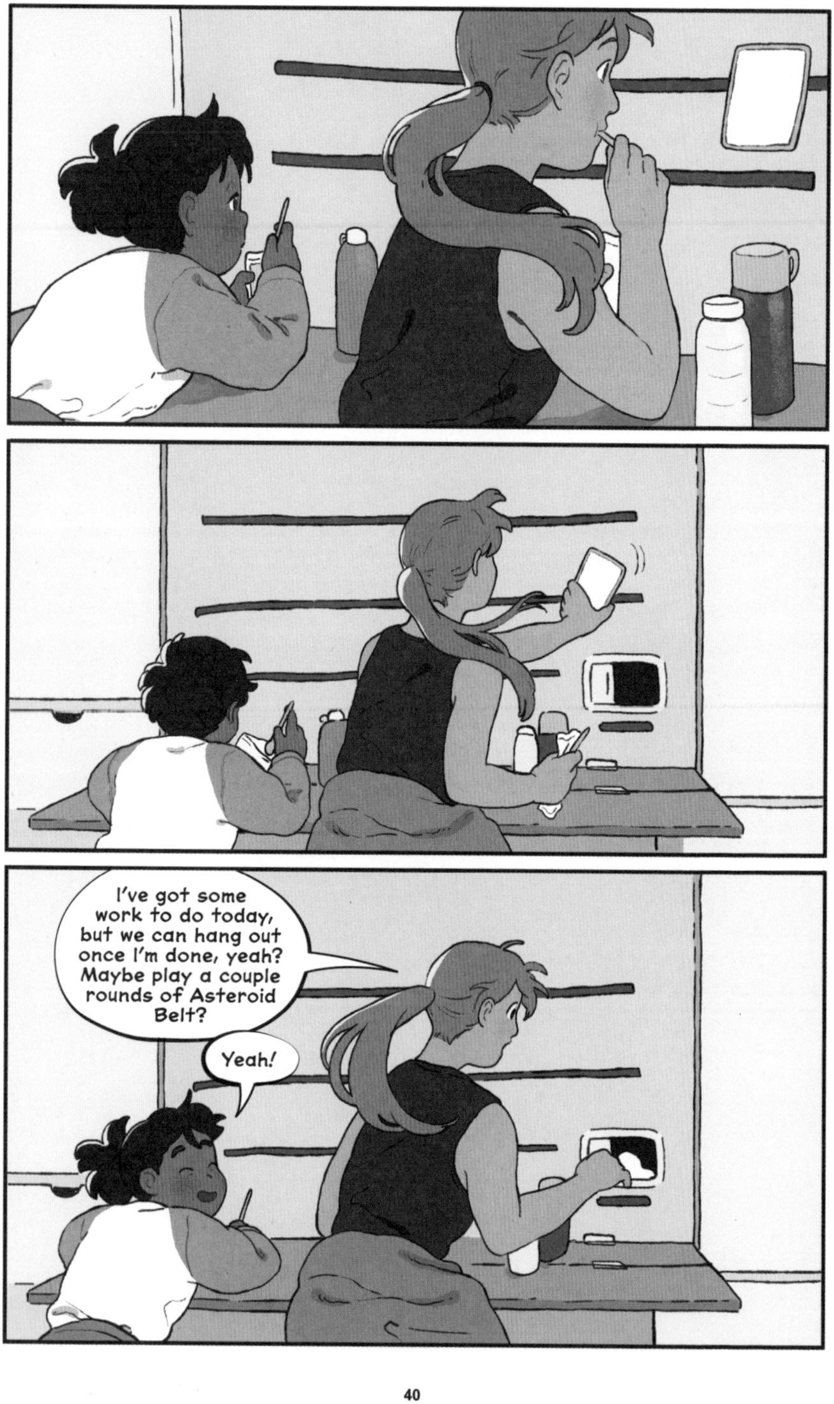
I've got some work to do today, but we can hang out once I'm done, yeah? Maybe play a couple rounds of Asteroid Belt?
Yeah!

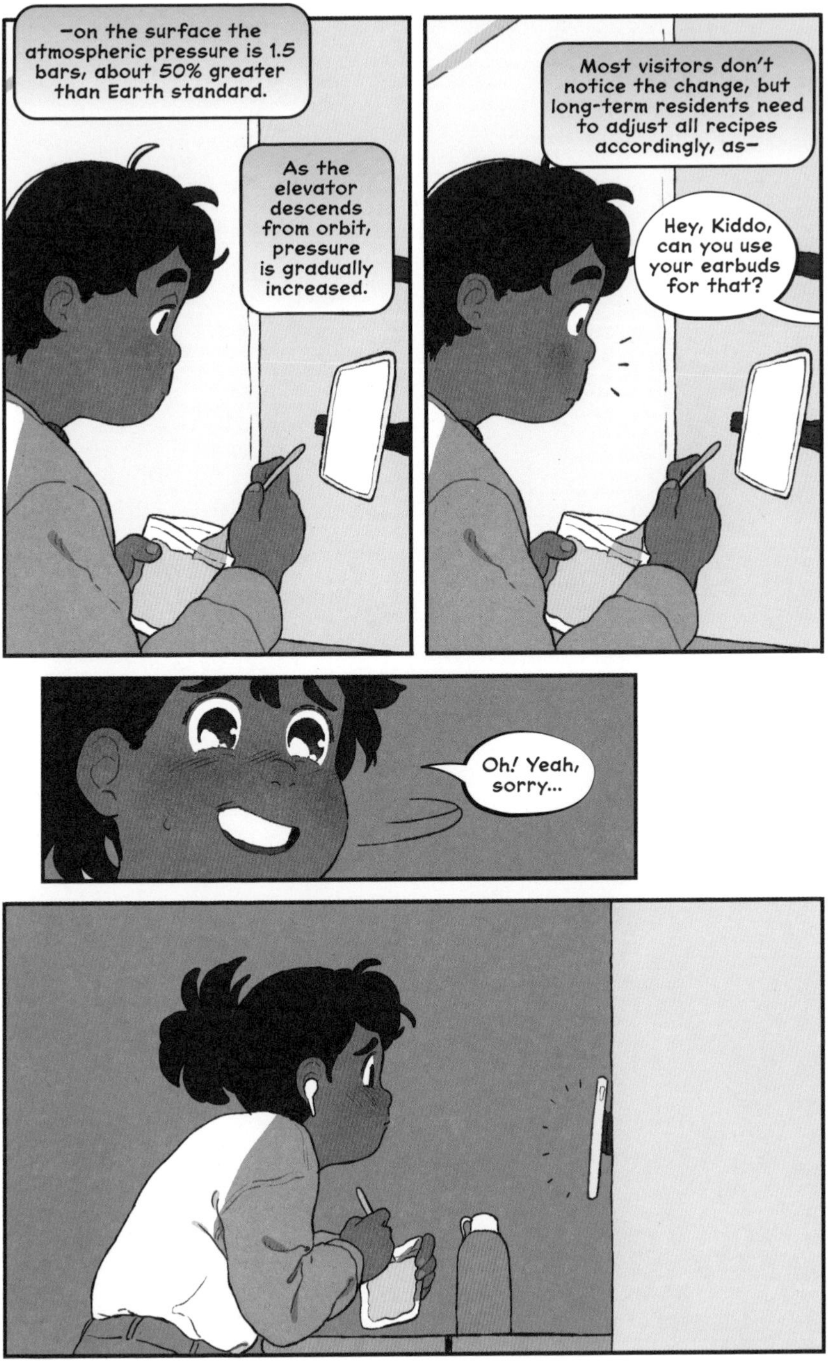
–on the surface the atmospheric pressure is 1.5 bars, about 50% greater than Earth standard.
As the elevator descends from orbit, pressure is gradually increased.
Most visitors don't notice the change, but long-term residents need to adjust all recipes accordingly, as–
Hey, Kiddo, can you use your earbuds for that?
Oh! Yeah, sorry...

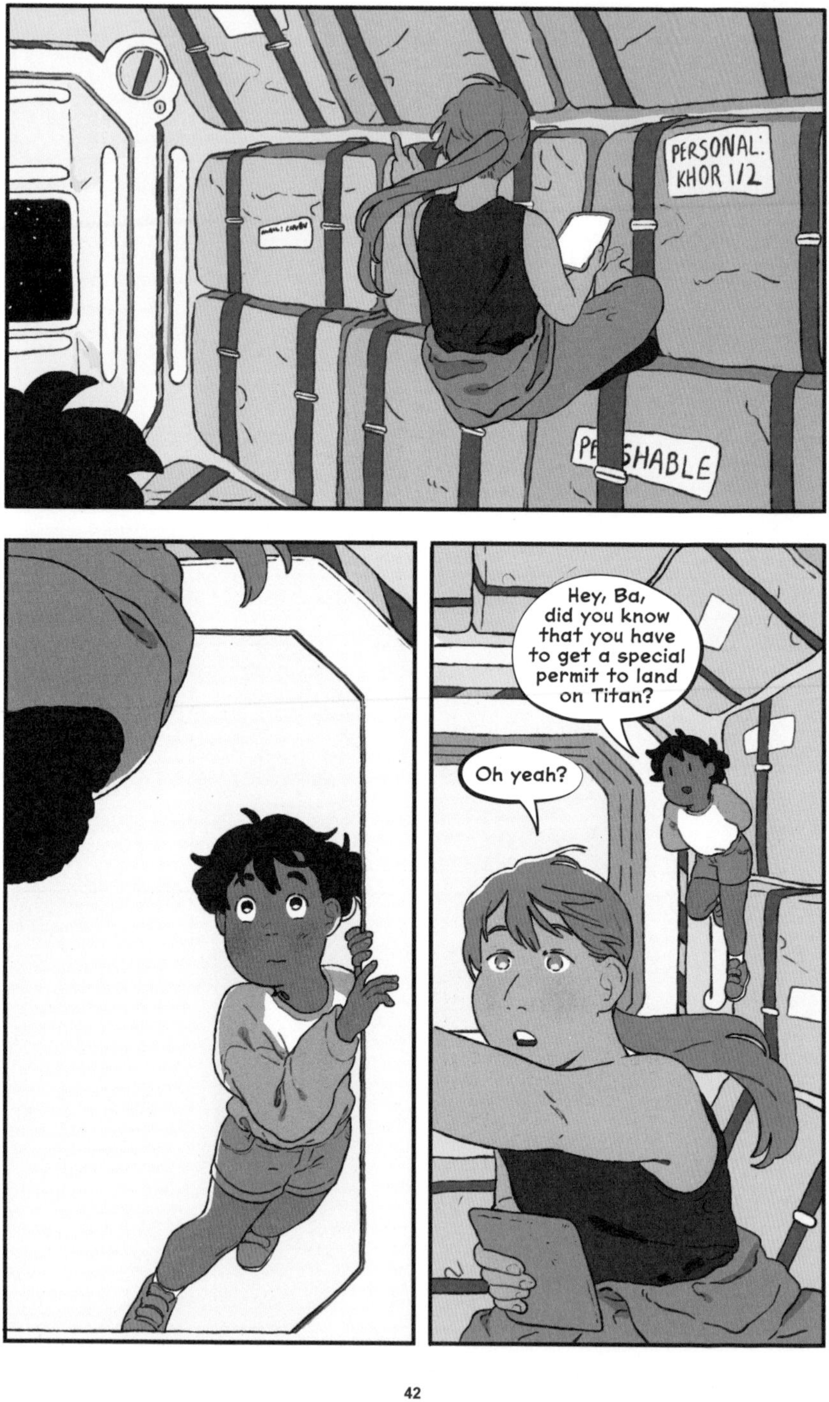
PERSONAL: KHOR 1/2
Hey, Ba, did you know that you have to get a special permit to land on Titan?
Oh yeah?

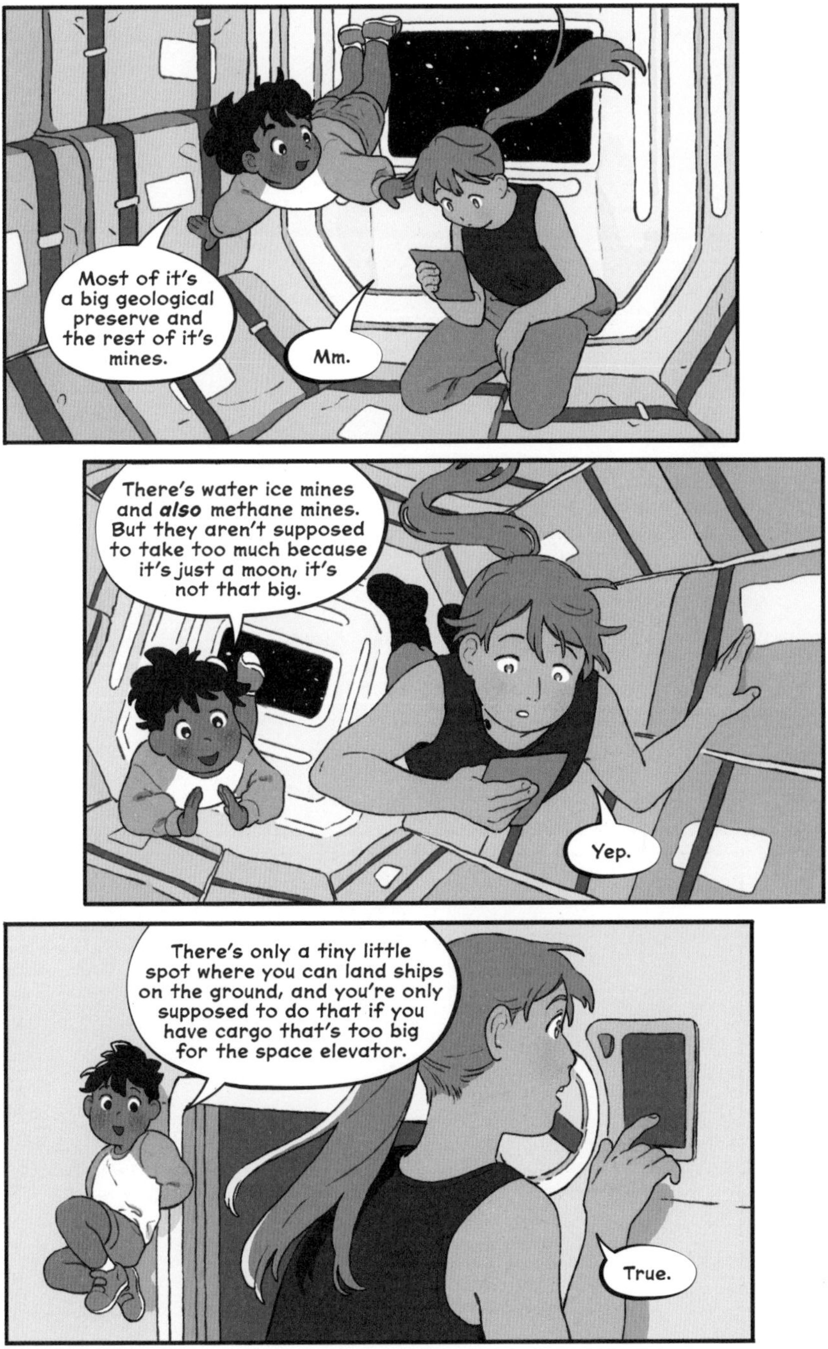
Most of it's a big geological preserve and the rest of it's mines.
Mm.
There's water ice mines and *also* methane mines. But they aren't supposed to take too much because it's just a moon, it's not that big.
Yep.
There's only a tiny little spot where you can land ships on the ground, and you're only supposed to do that if you have cargo that's too big for the space elevator.
True.

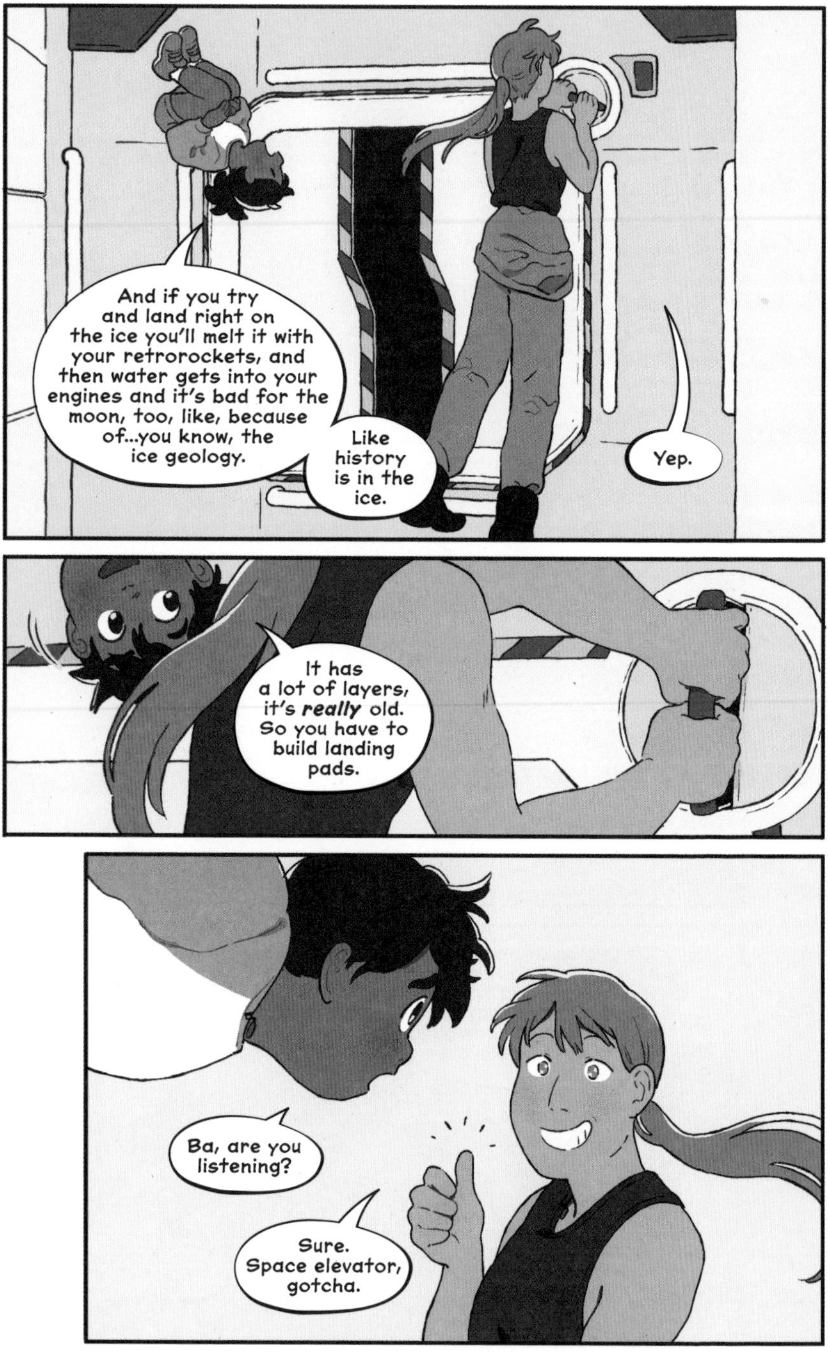
And if you try and land right on the ice you'll melt it with your retrorockets, and then water gets into your engines and it's bad for the moon, too, like, because of...you know, the ice geology.
Like history is in the ice.
Yep.
It has a lot of layers, it's *really* old. So you have to build landing pads.
Ba, are you listening?
Sure. Space elevator, gotcha.

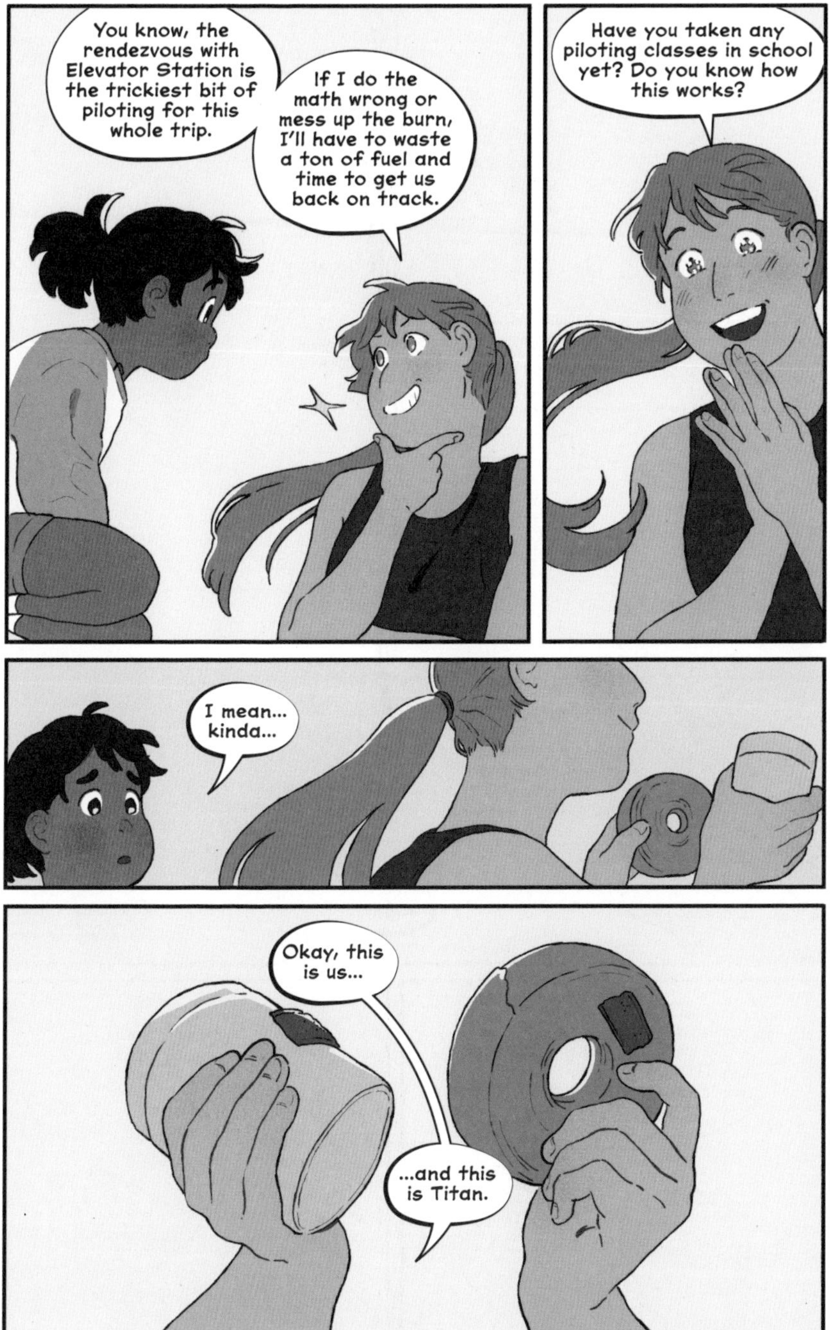
You know, the rendezvous with Elevator Station is the trickiest bit of piloting for this whole trip.
If I do the math wrong or mess up the burn, I'll have to waste a ton of fuel and time to get us back on track.
Have you taken any piloting classes in school yet? Do you know how this works?
I mean... kinda...
Okay, this is us...
...and this is Titan.

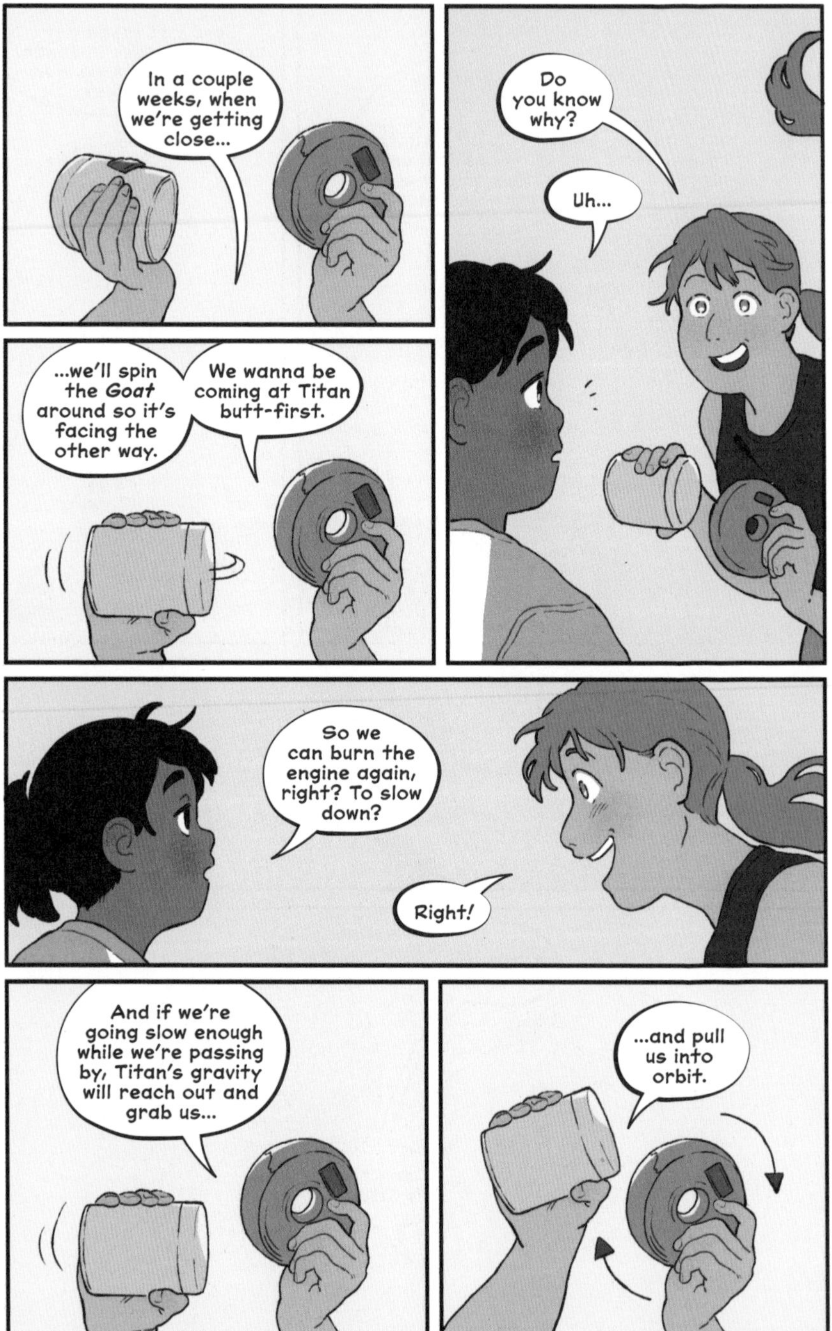
In a couple weeks, when we're getting close...
Do you know why?
Uh...
...we'll spin the *Goat* around so it's facing the other way.
We wanna be coming at Titan butt-first.
So we can burn the engine again, right? To slow down?
Right!
And if we're going slow enough while we're passing by, Titan's gravity will reach out and grab us...
...and pull us into orbit.

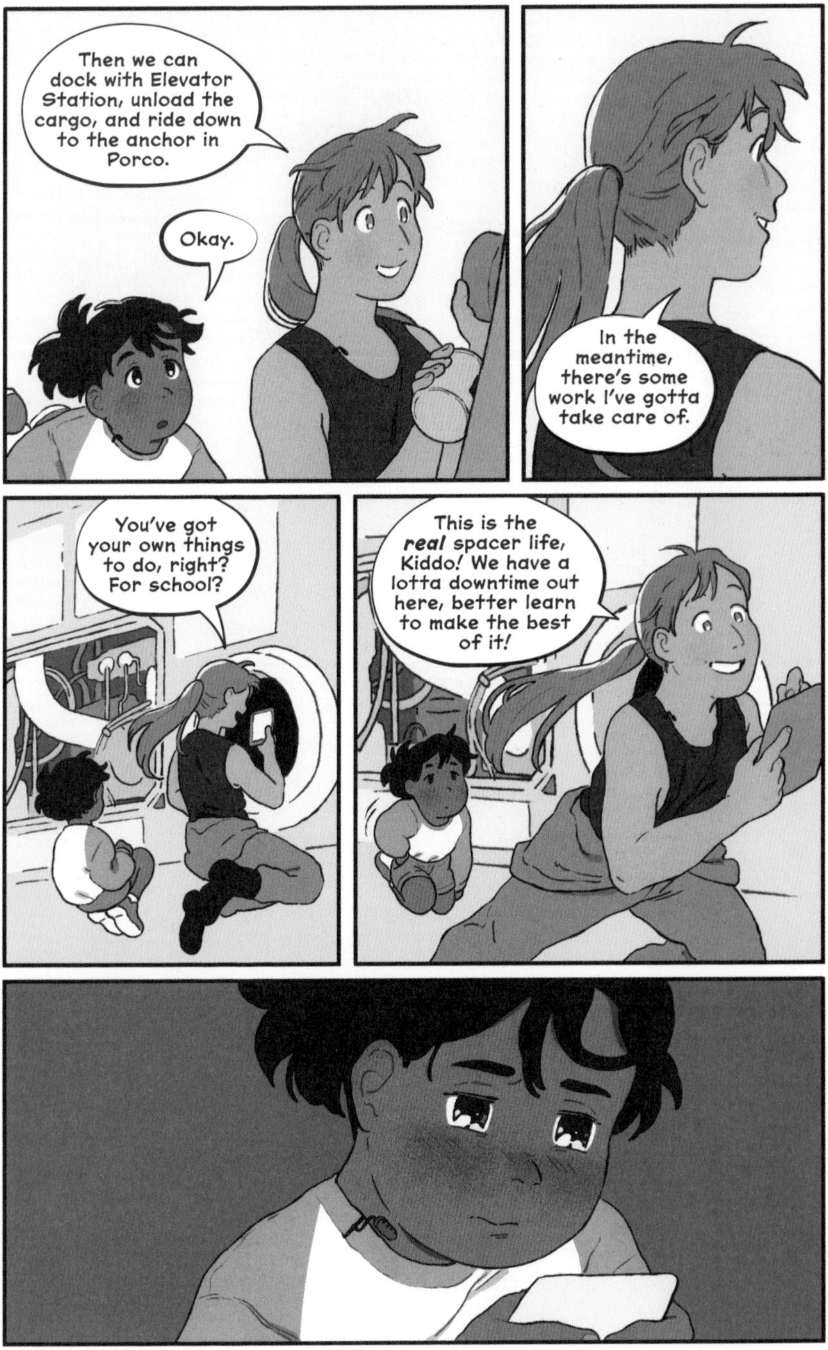
Then we can dock with Elevator Station, unload the cargo, and ride down to the anchor in Porco.
Okay.
In the meantime, there's some work I've gotta take care of.
You've got your own things to do, right? For school?
This is the *real* spacer life, Kiddo! We have a lotta downtime out here, better learn to make the best of it!

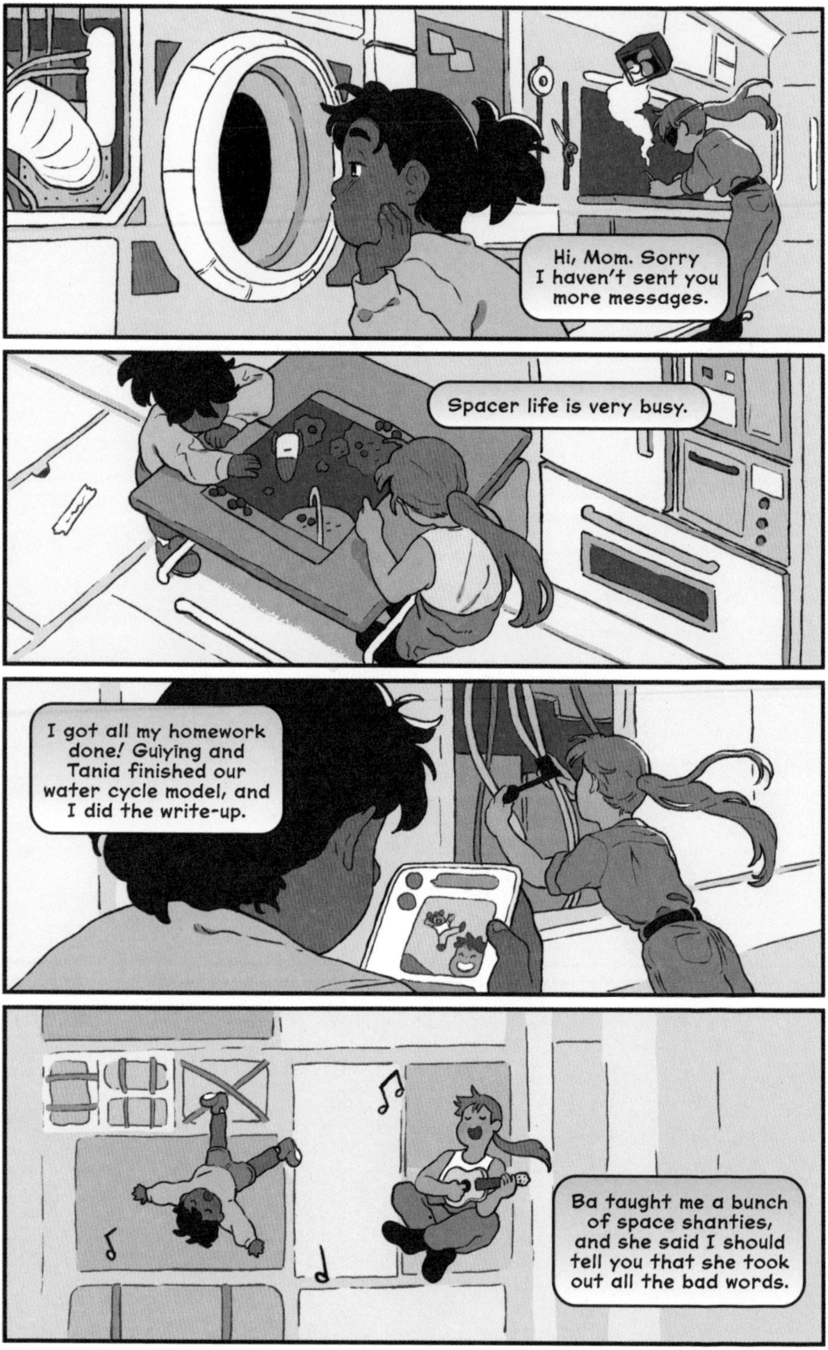
Hi, Mom. Sorry I haven't sent you more messages.
Spacer life is very busy.
I got all my homework done! Guiying and Tania finished our water cycle model, and I did the write-up.
Ba taught me a bunch of space shanties, and she said I should tell you that she took out all the bad words.

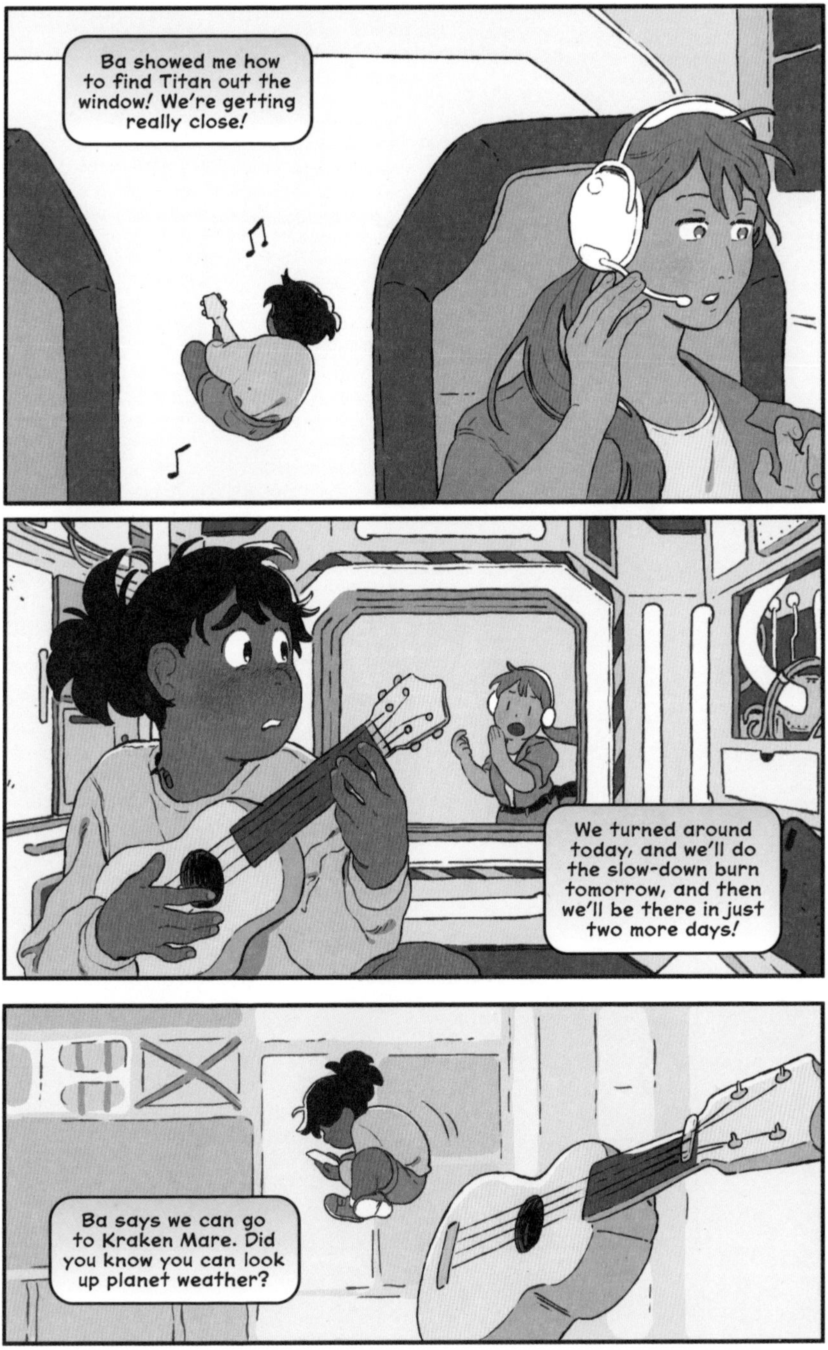
Ba showed me how to find Titan out the window! We're getting really close!
We turned around today, and we'll do the slow-down burn tomorrow, and then we'll be there in just two more days!
Ba says we can go to Kraken Mare. Did you know you can look up planet weather?

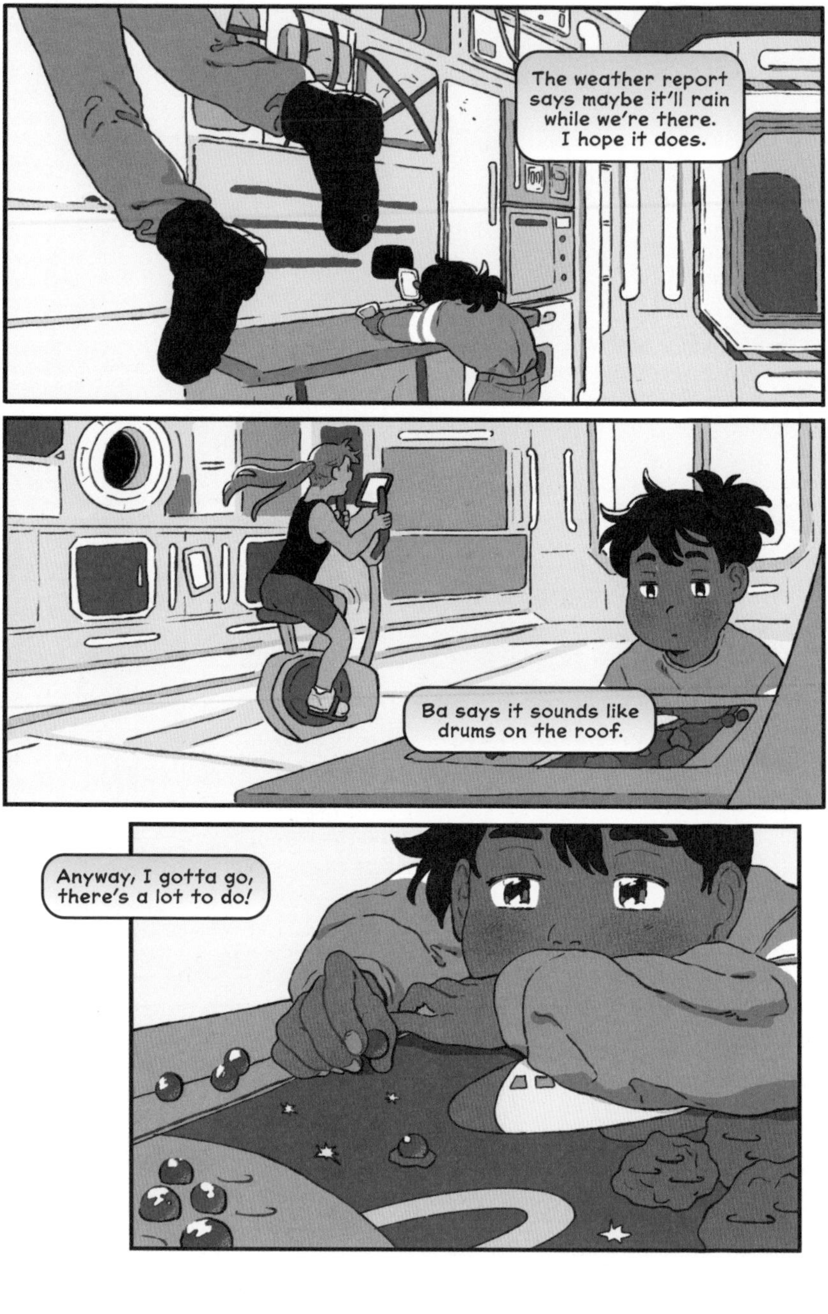
The weather report says maybe it'll rain while we're there. I hope it does.
Ba says it sounds like drums on the roof.
Anyway, I gotta go, there's a lot to do!

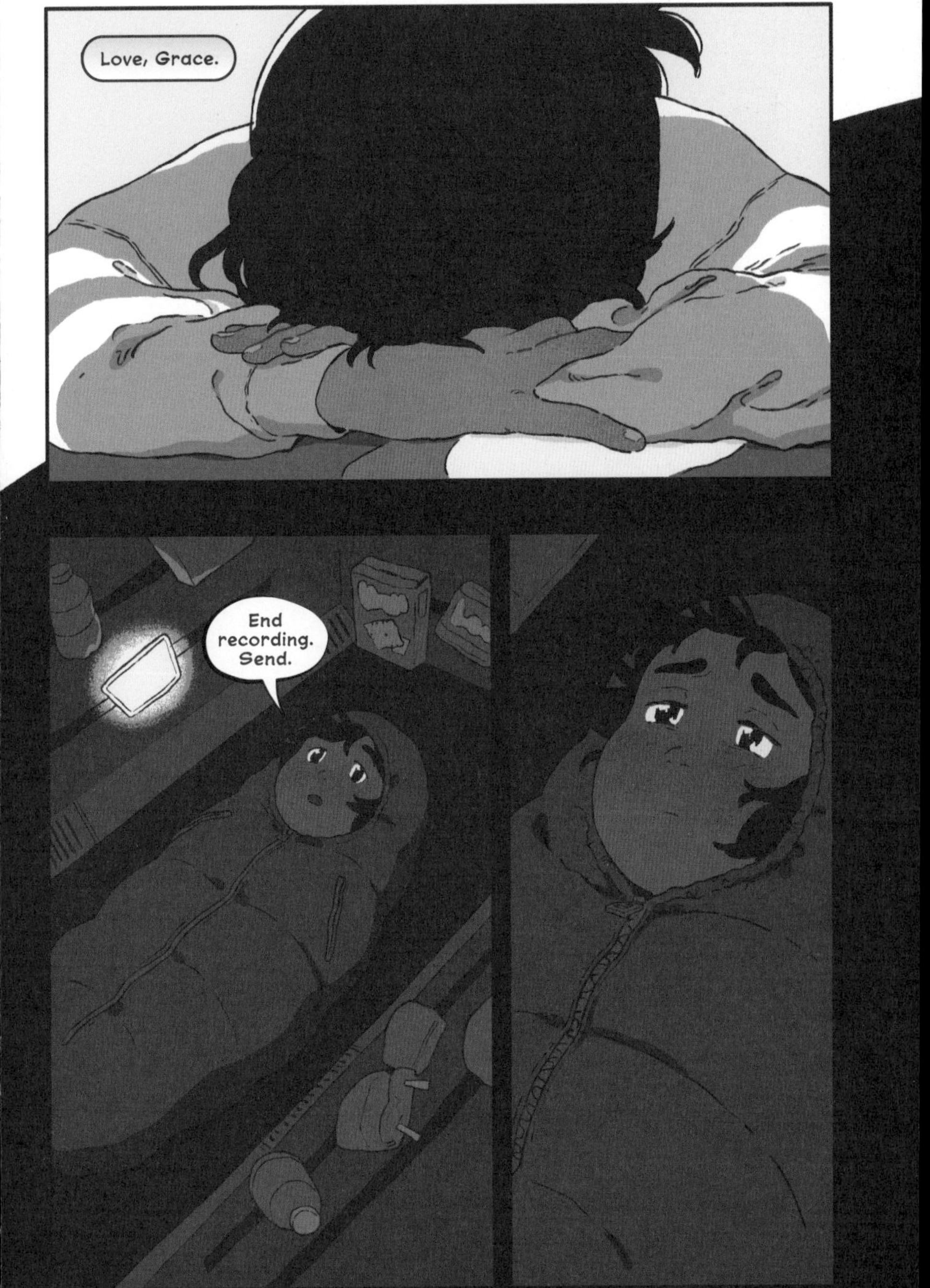
Love, Grace.
End recording. Send.

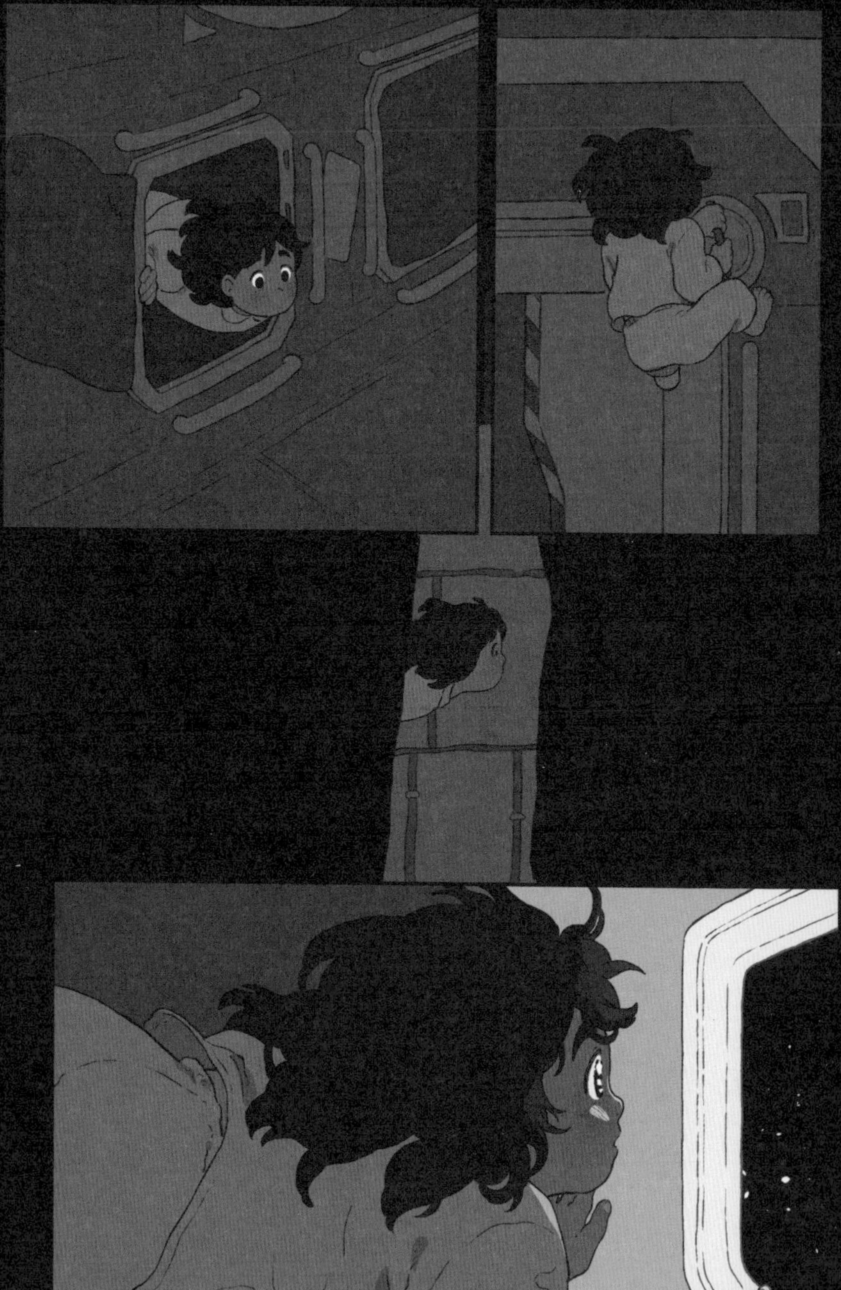

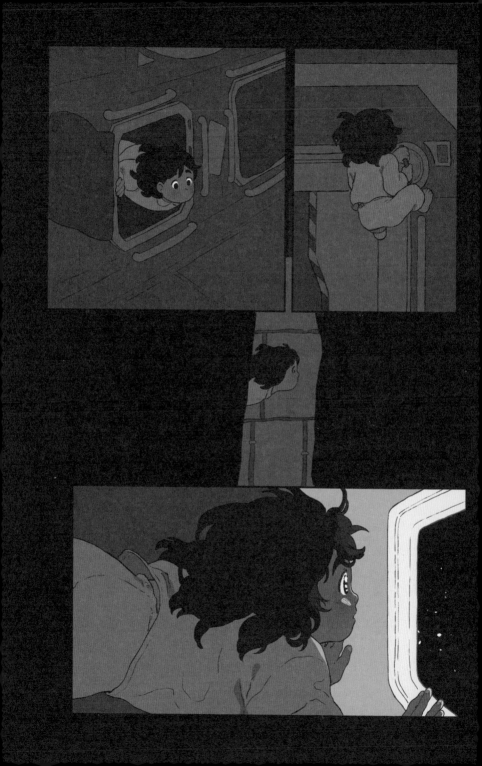

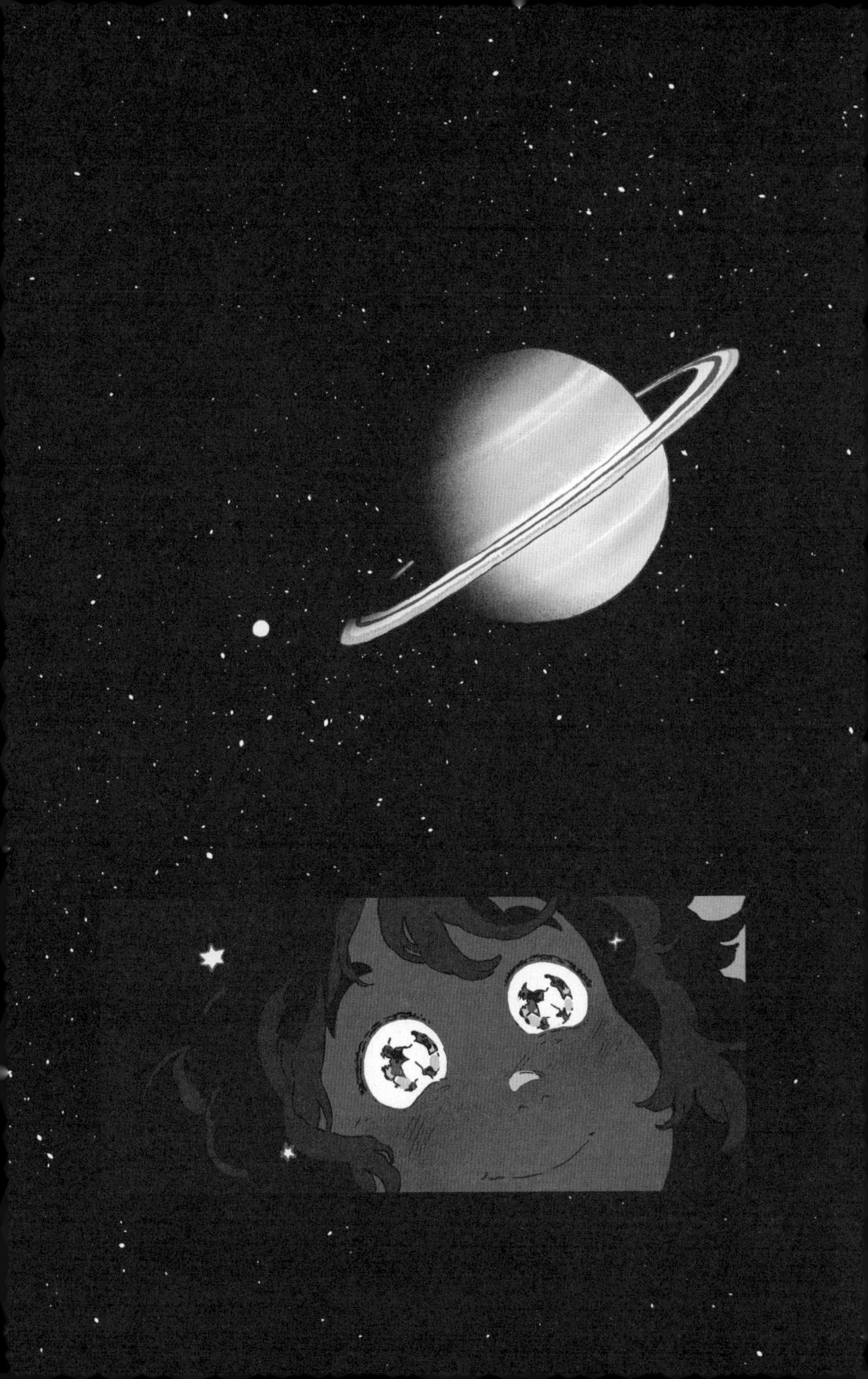

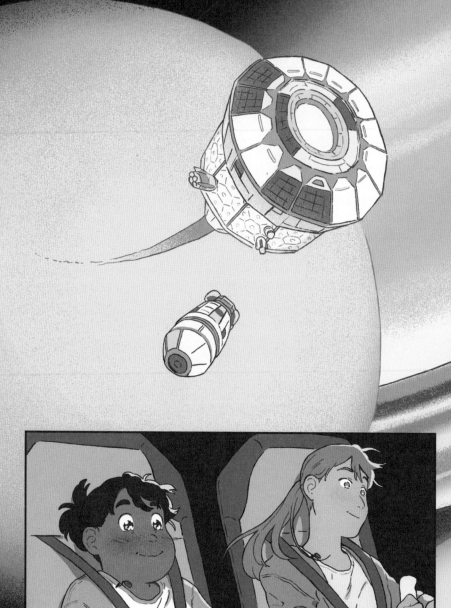

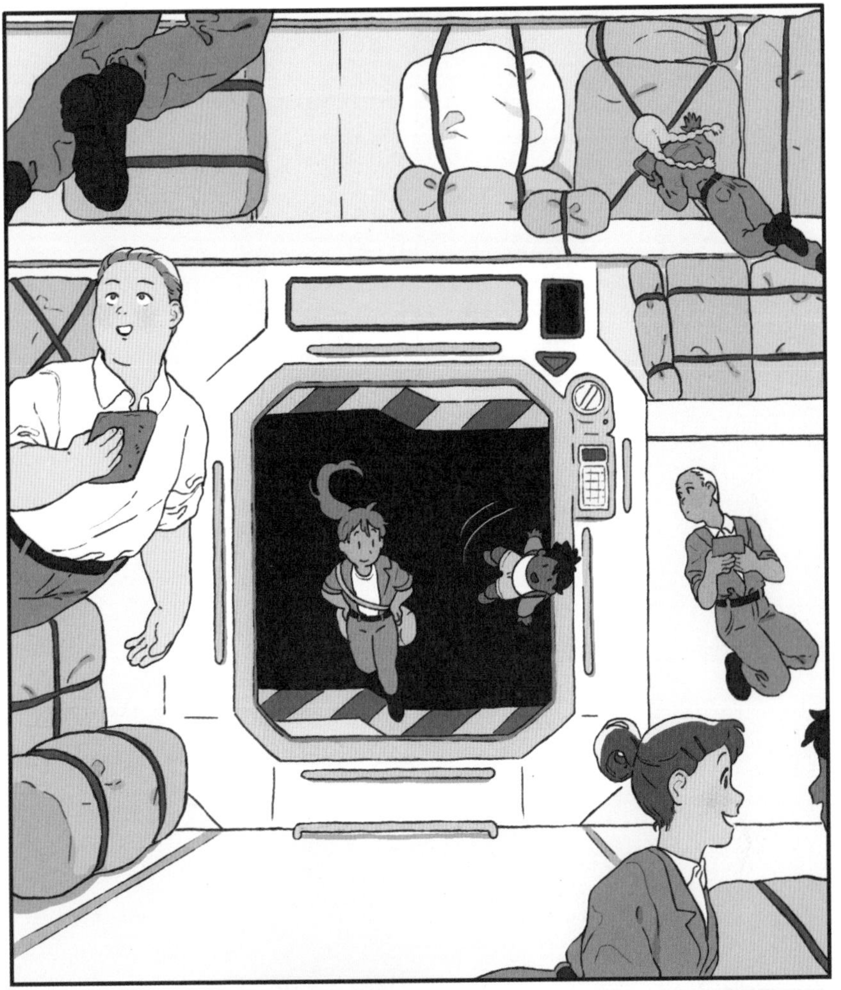

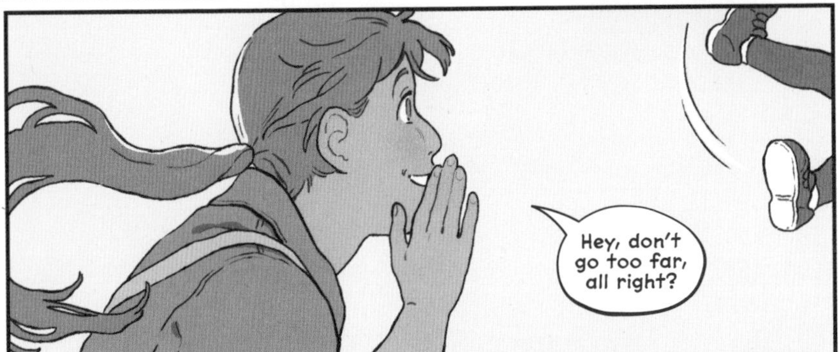
Hey, don't go too far, all right?

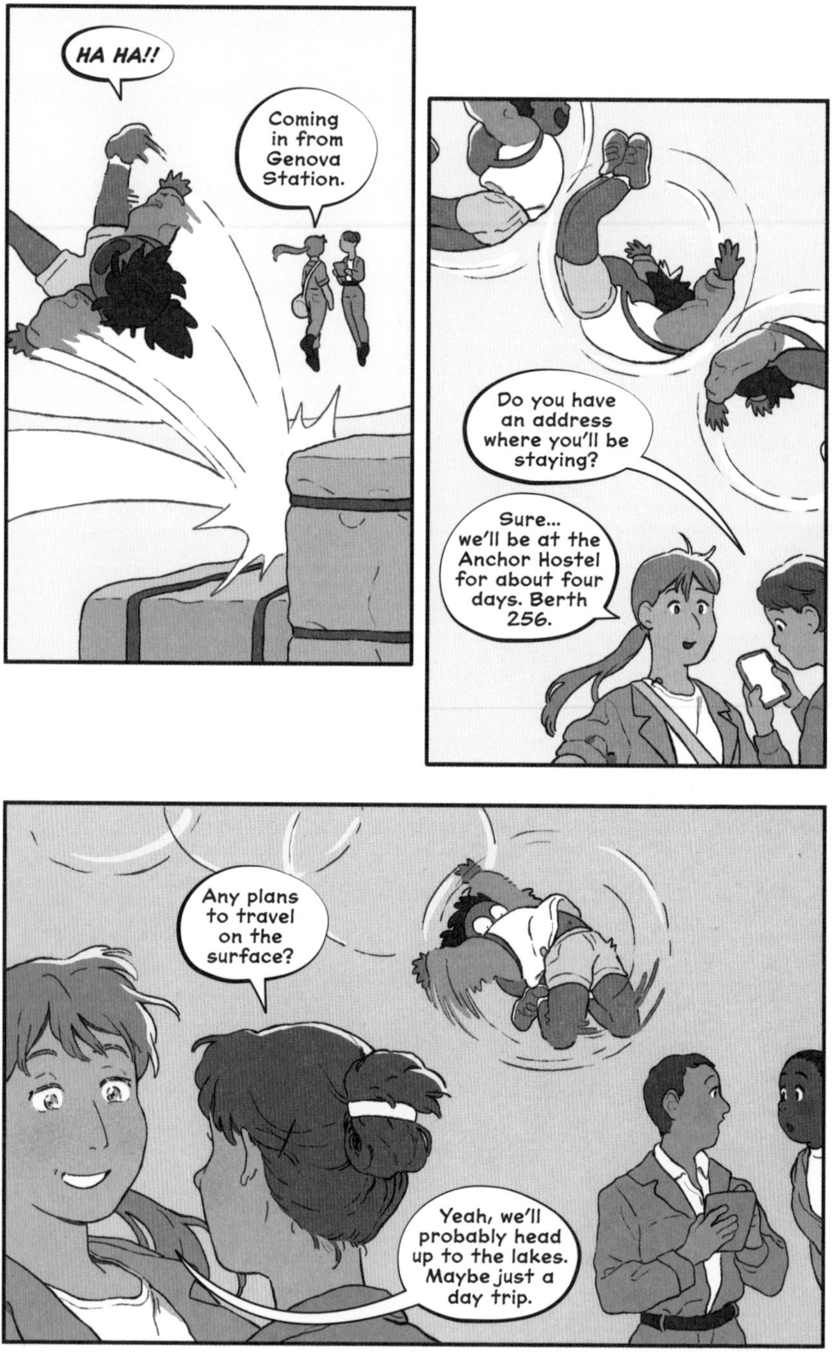
HA HA!!
Coming in from Genova Station.
Do you have an address where you'll be staying?
Sure... we'll be at the Anchor Hostel for about four days. Berth 256.
Any plans to travel on the surface?
Yeah, we'll probably head up to the lakes. Maybe just a day trip.

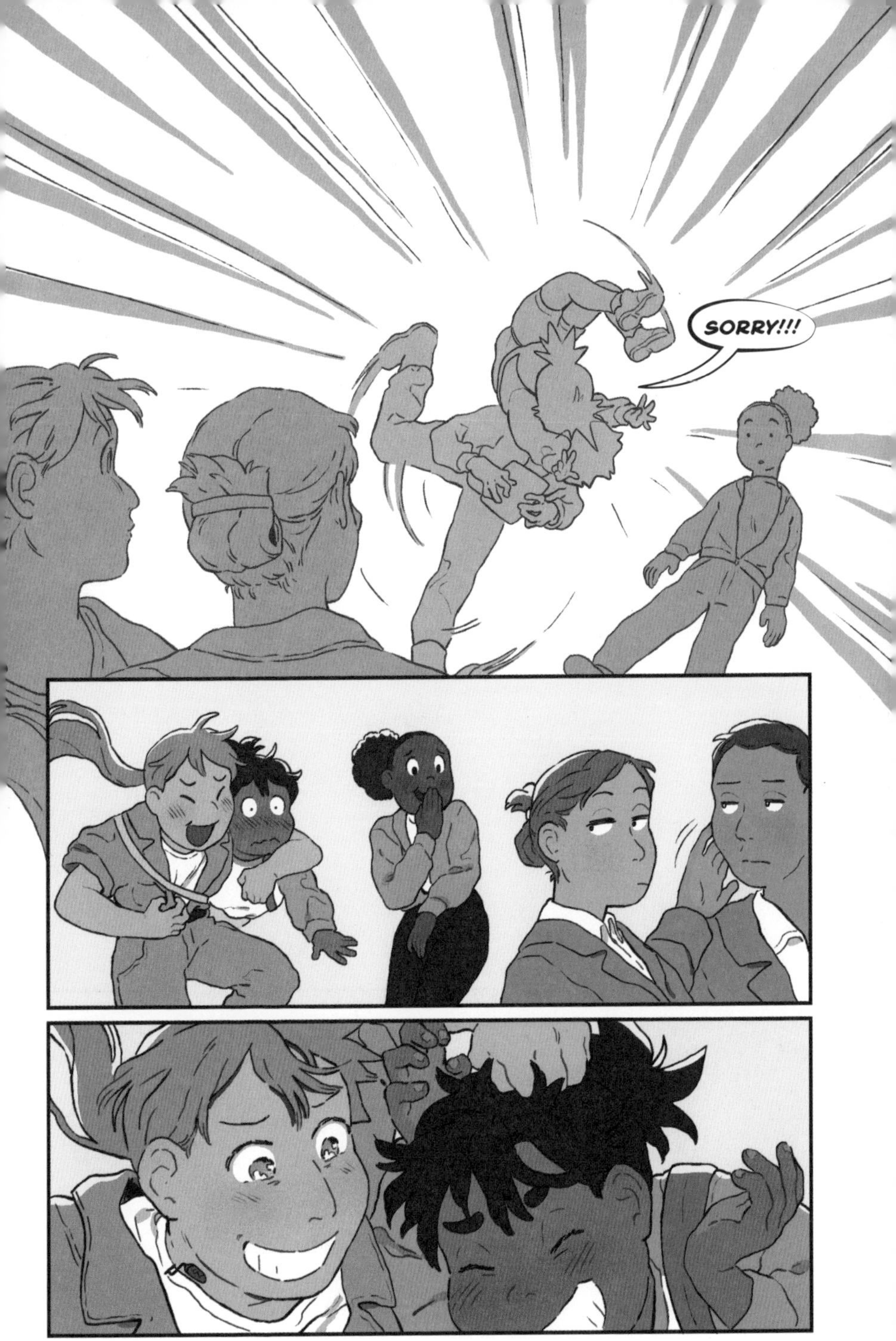
SORRY!!!

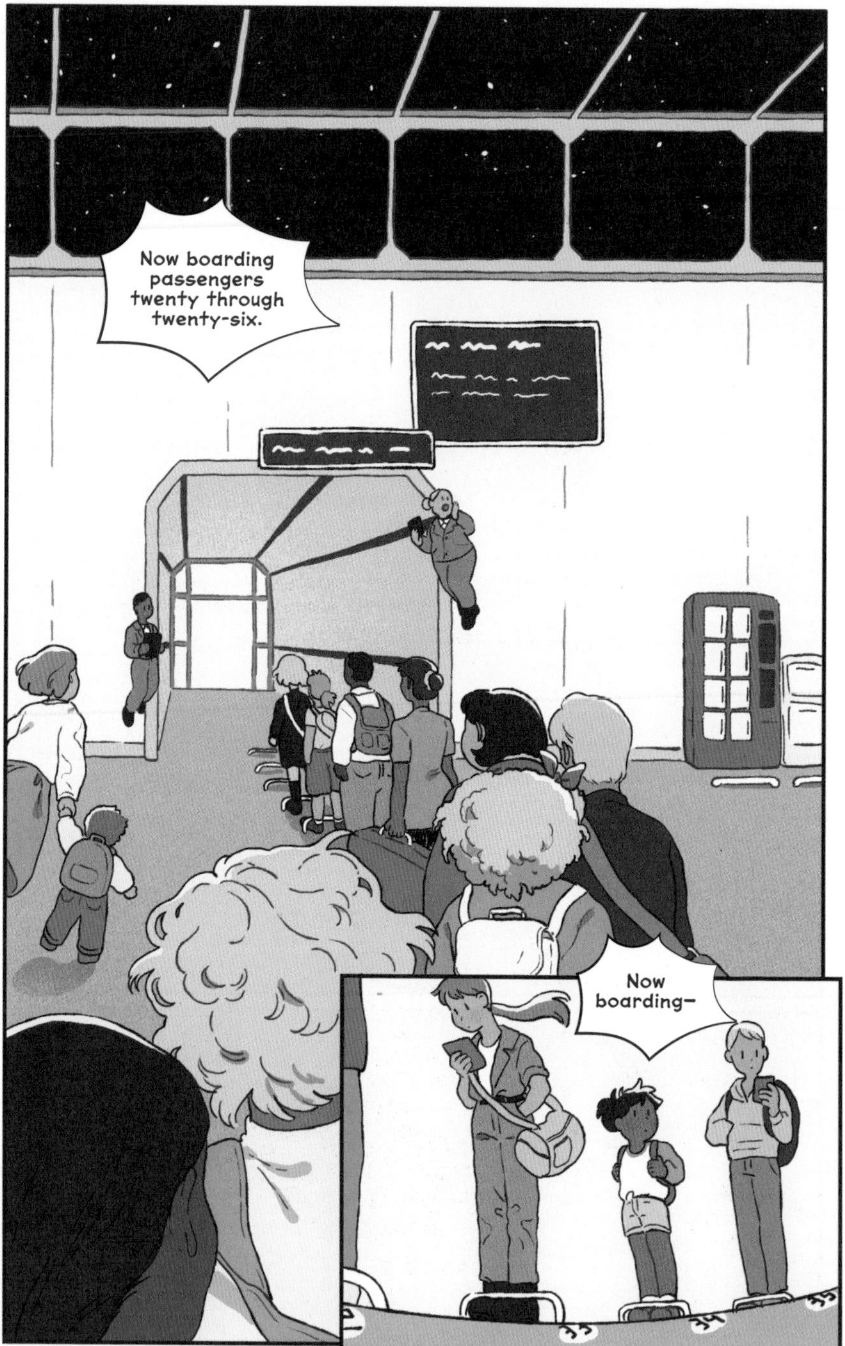
Now boarding passengers twenty through twenty-six.
Now boarding–

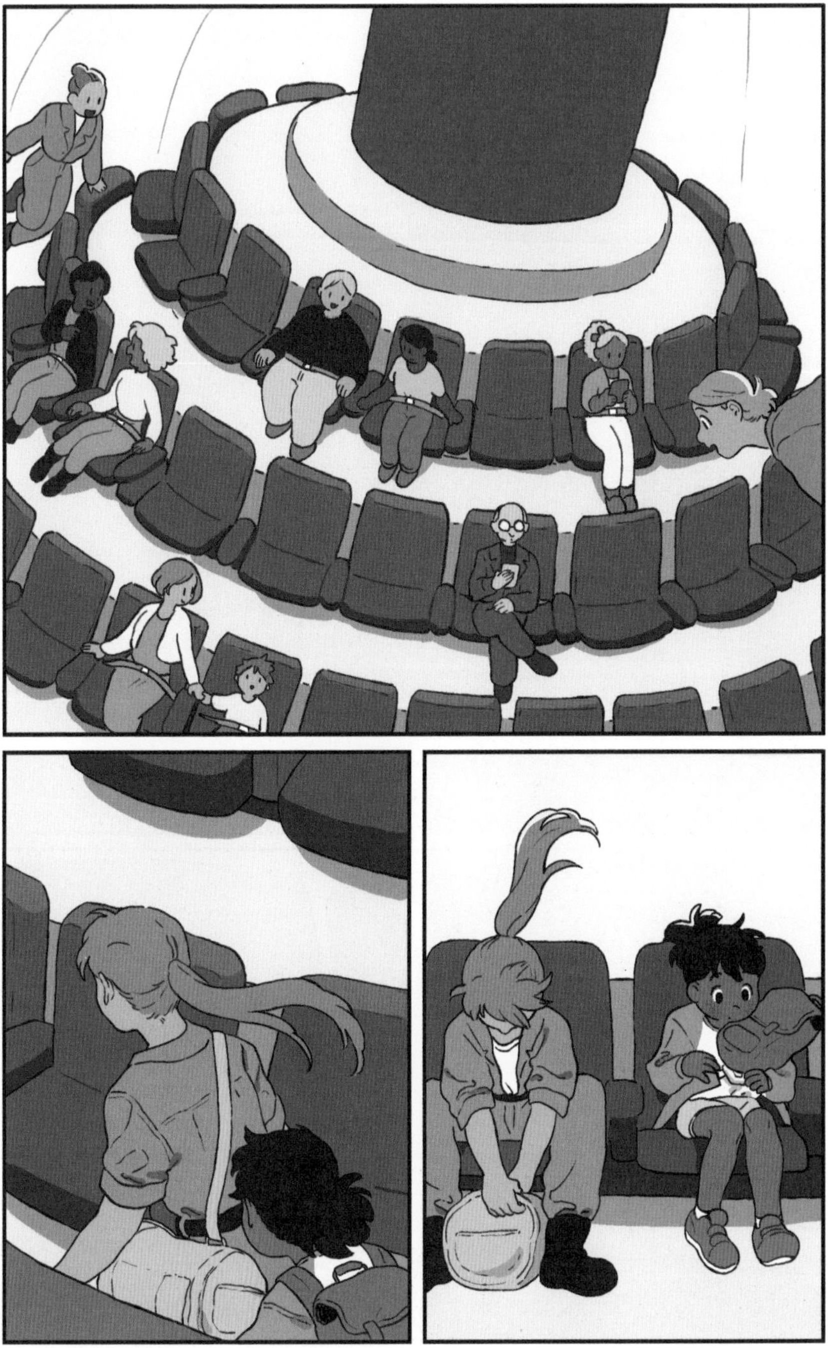

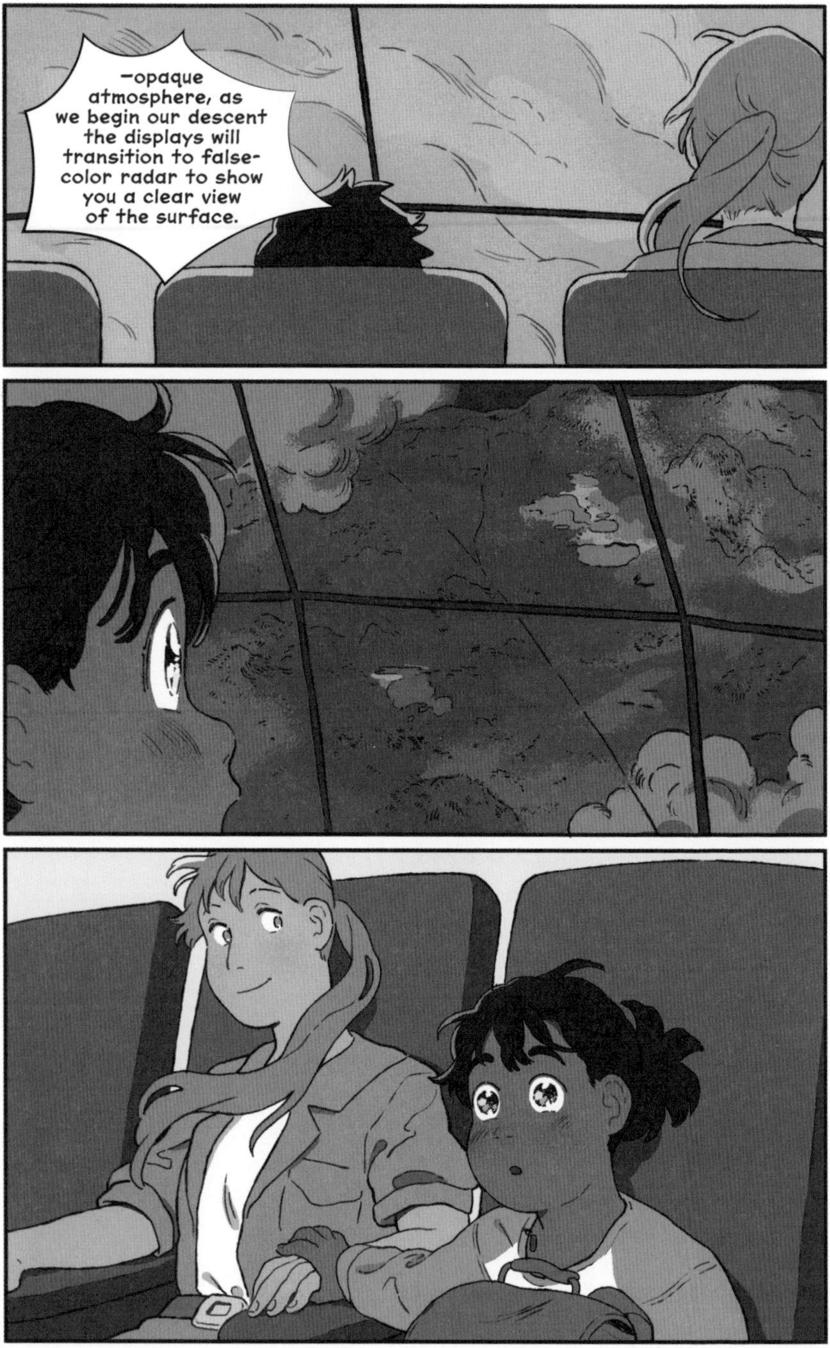
–opaque atmosphere, as we begin our descent the displays will transition to false-color radar to show you a clear view of the surface.

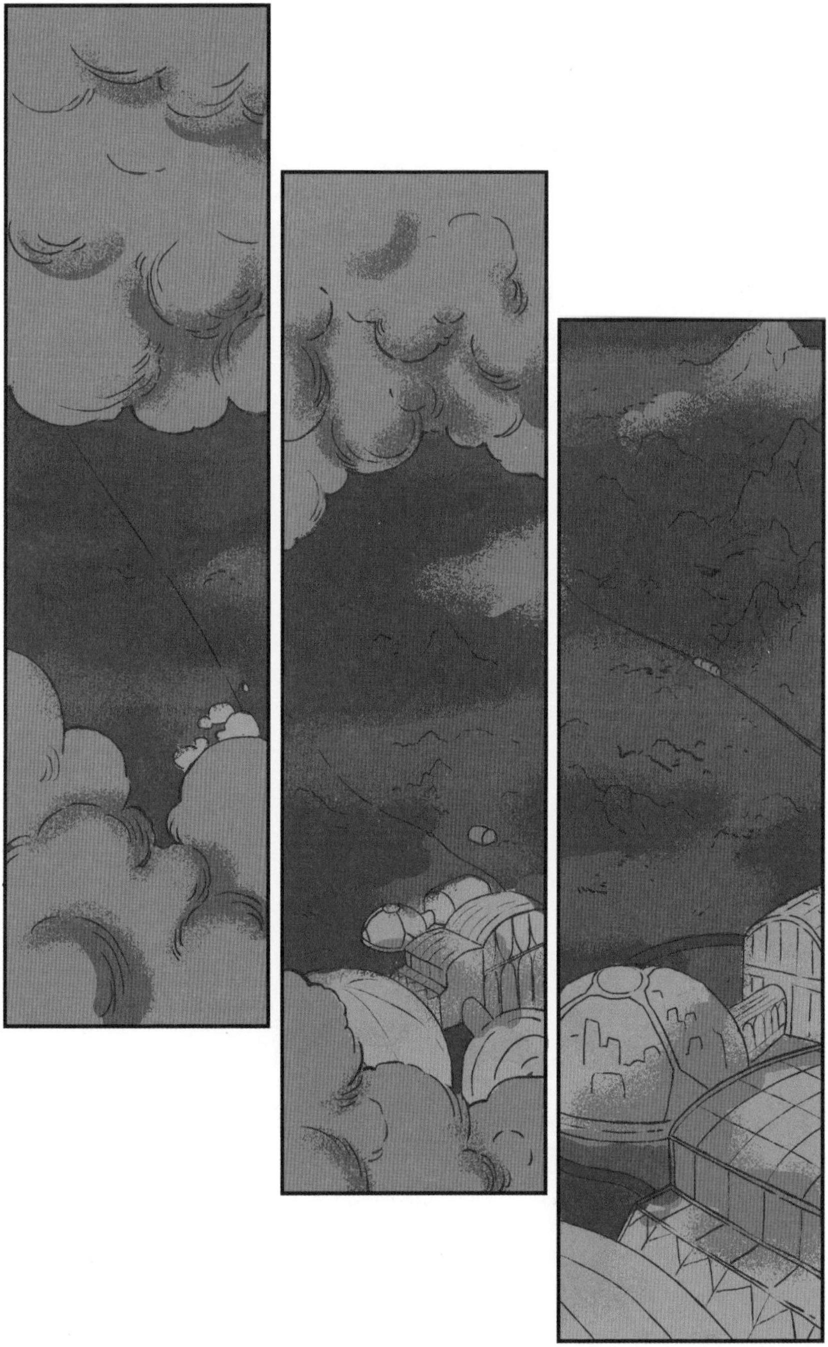

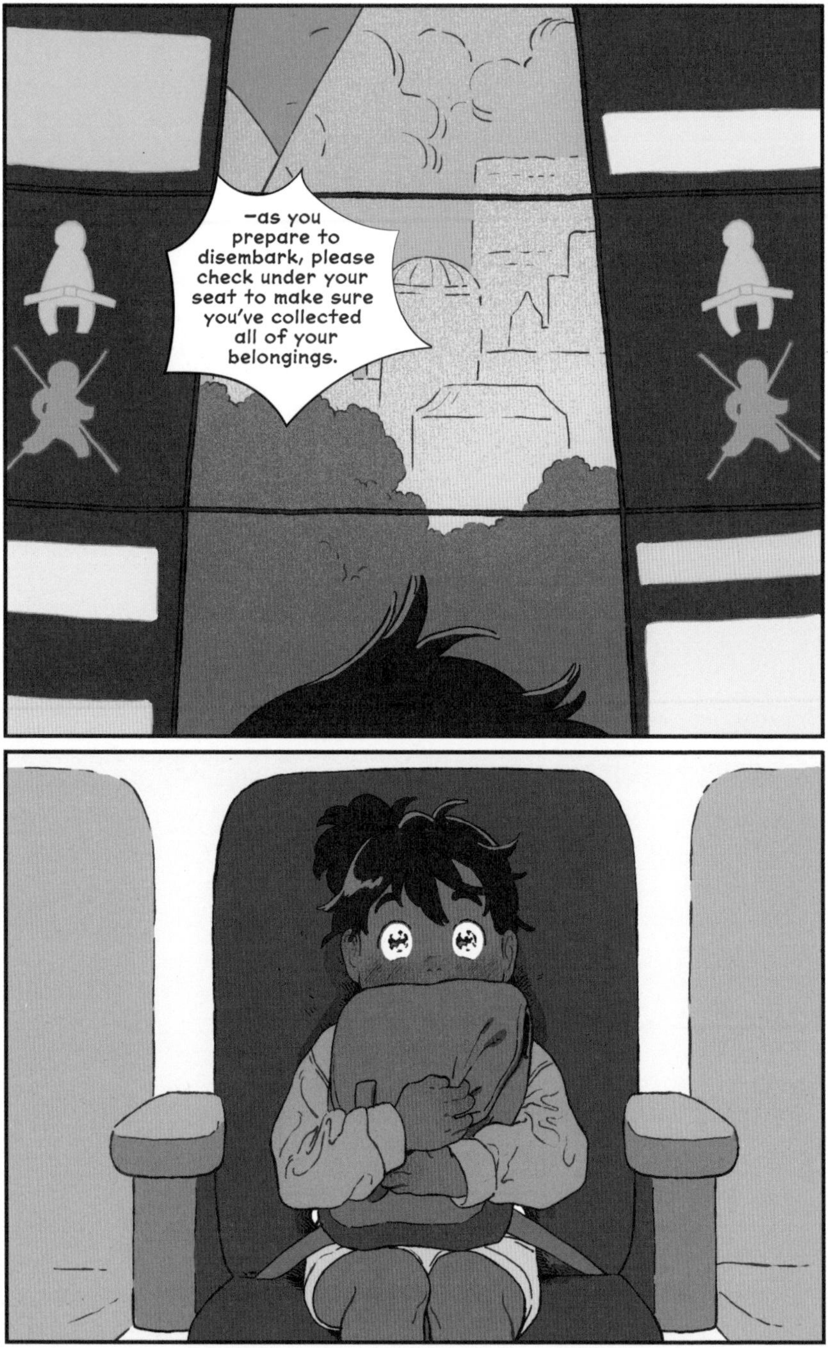
-as you prepare to disembark, please check under your seat to make sure you've collected all of your belongings.

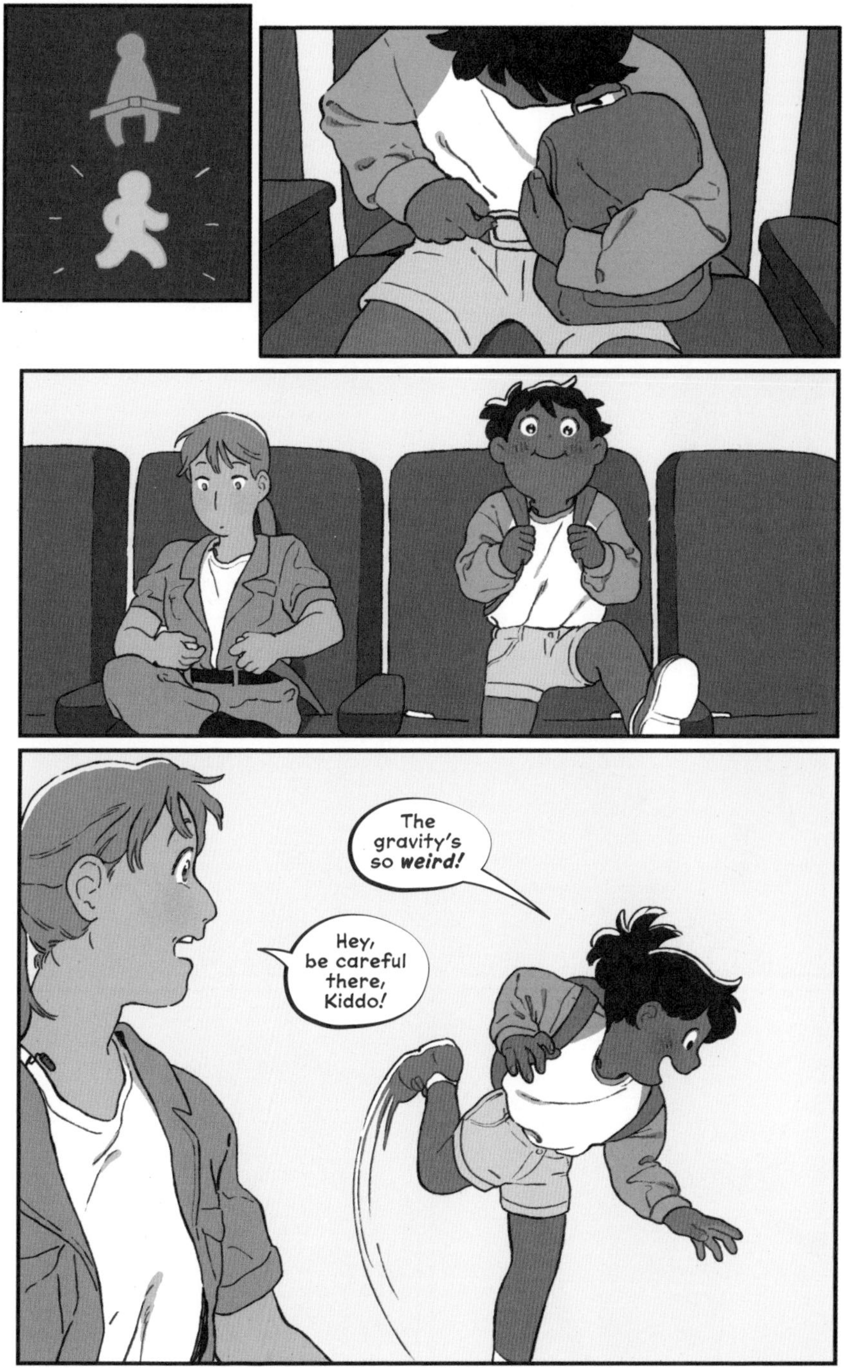
The gravity's so *weird!*
Hey, be careful there, Kiddo!

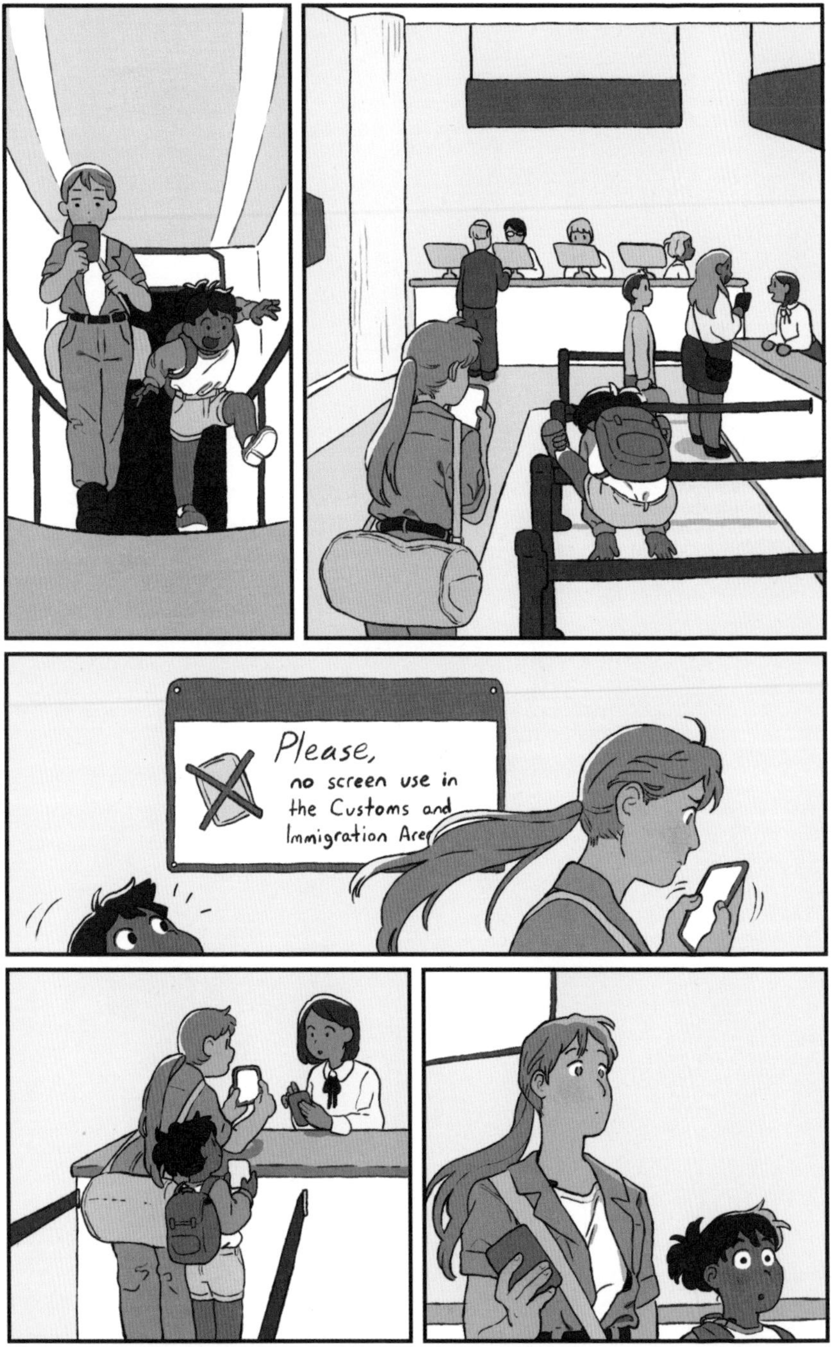
Please,
no screen use in
the Customs and
Immigration Are

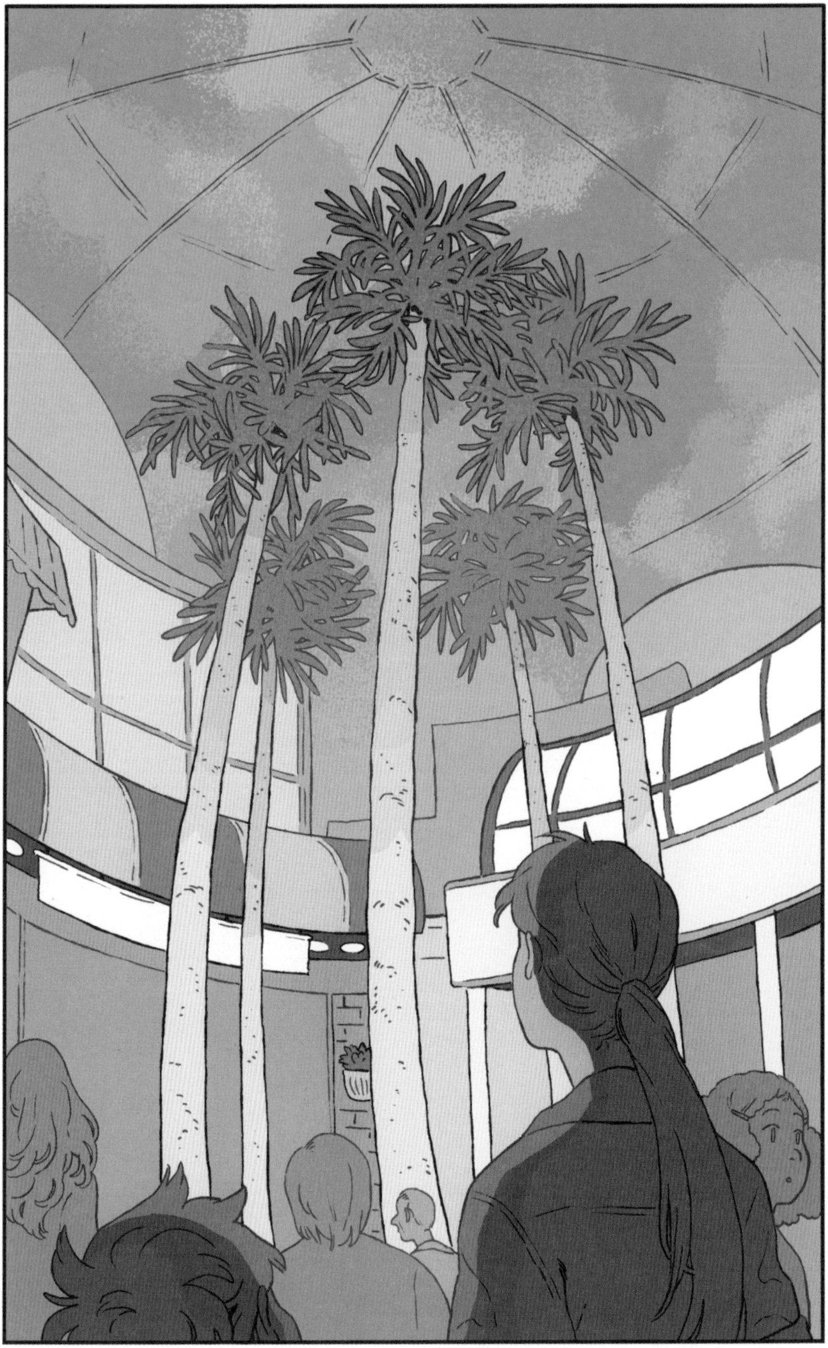

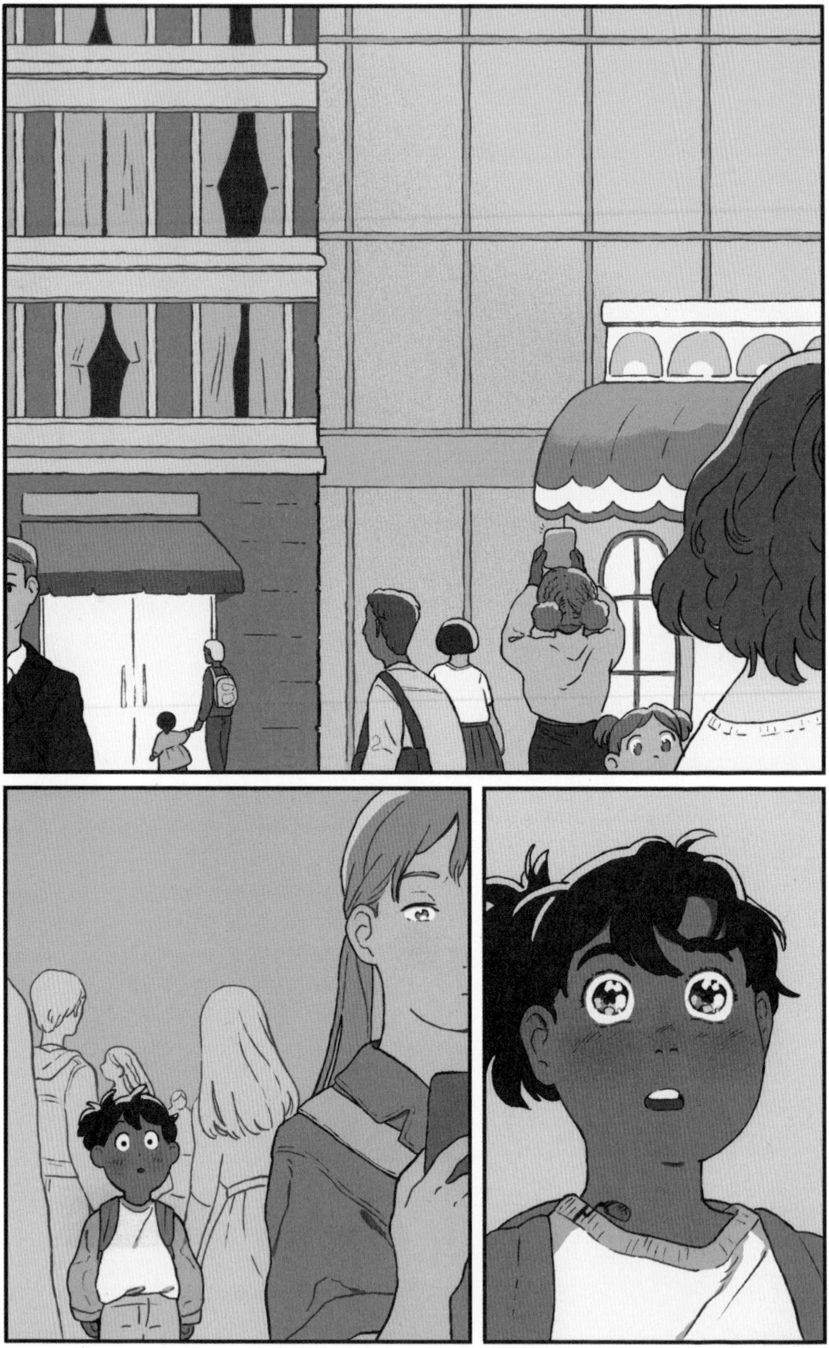

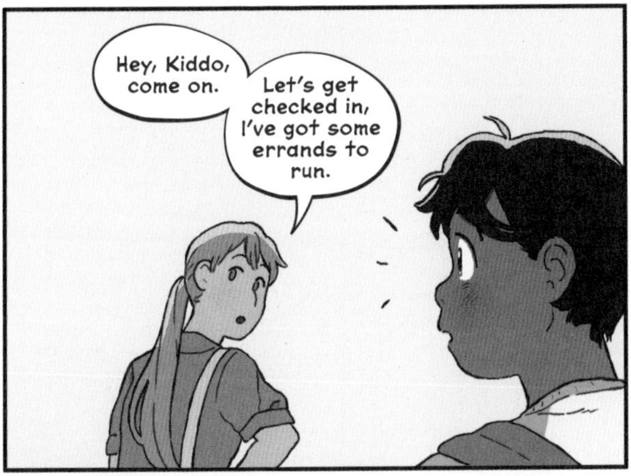
Hey, Kiddo, come on.
Let's get checked in, I've got some errands to run.

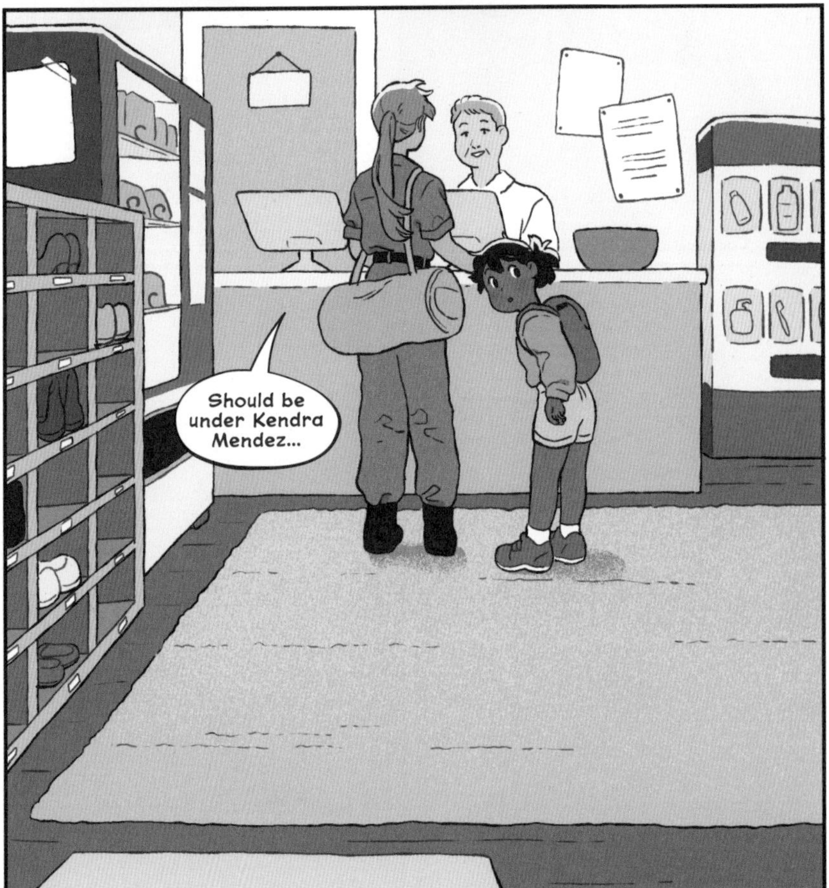
Should be under Kendra Mendez...

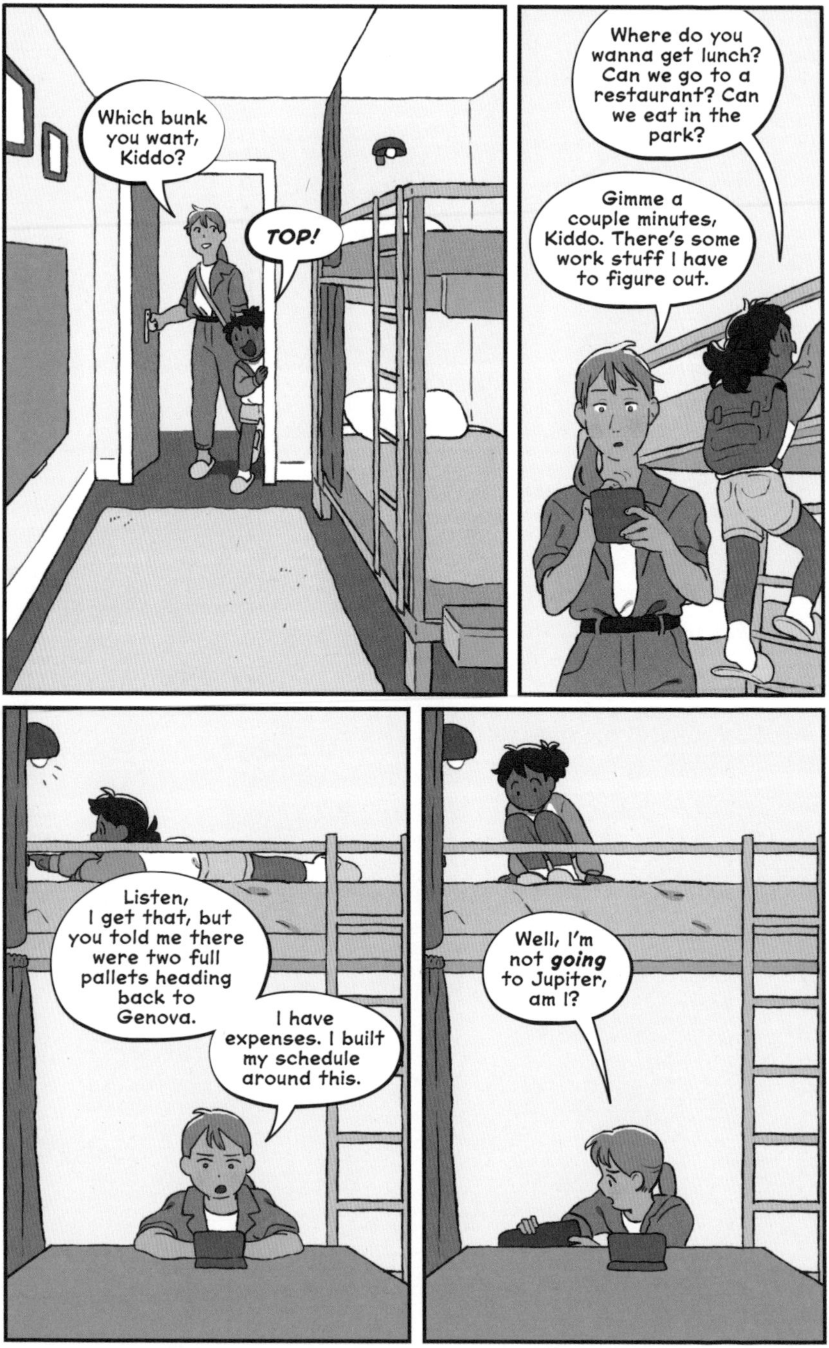
Which bunk you want, Kiddo?
TOP!
Where do you wanna get lunch? Can we go to a restaurant? Can we eat in the park?
Gimme a couple minutes, Kiddo. There's some work stuff I have to figure out.
Listen, I get that, but you told me there were two full pallets heading back to Genova.
I have expenses. I built my schedule around this.
Well, I'm not *going* to Jupiter, am I?

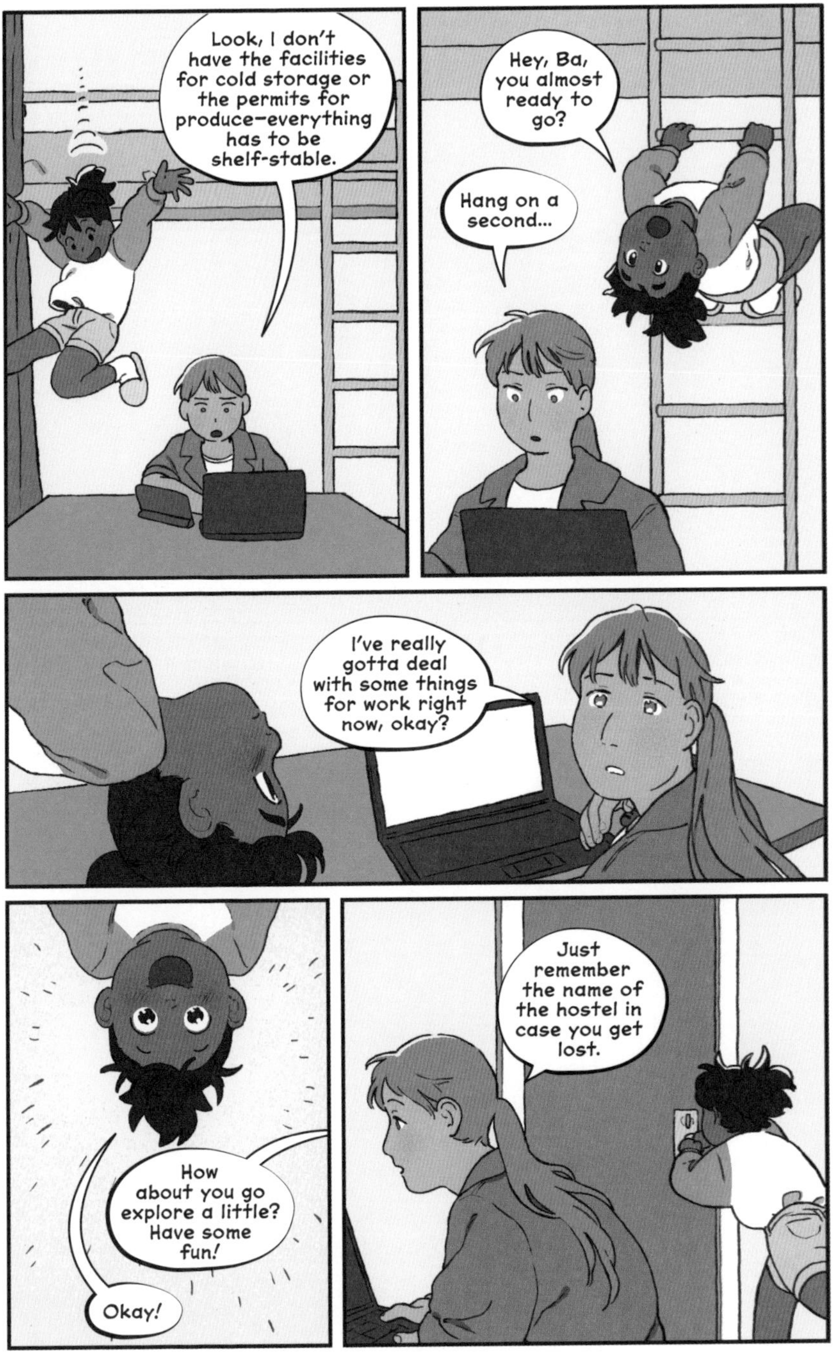
Look, I don't have the facilities for cold storage or the permits for produce—everything has to be shelf-stable.
Hey, Ba, you almost ready to go?
Hang on a second...
I've really gotta deal with some things for work right now, okay?
How about you go explore a little? Have some fun!
Okay!
Just remember the name of the hostel in case you get lost.

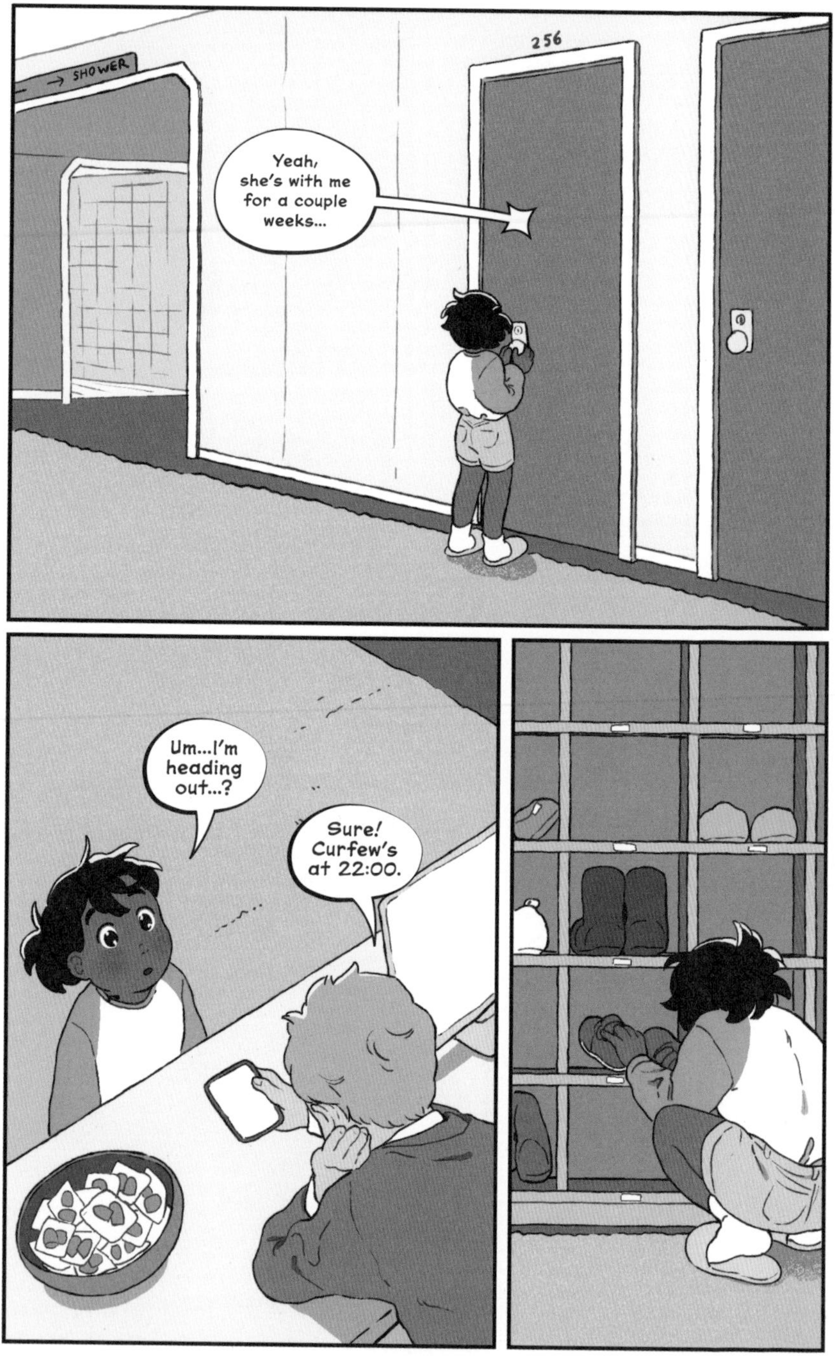
SHOWER
256
Yeah, she's with me for a couple weeks...
Um...I'm heading out...?
Sure! Curfew's at 22:00.

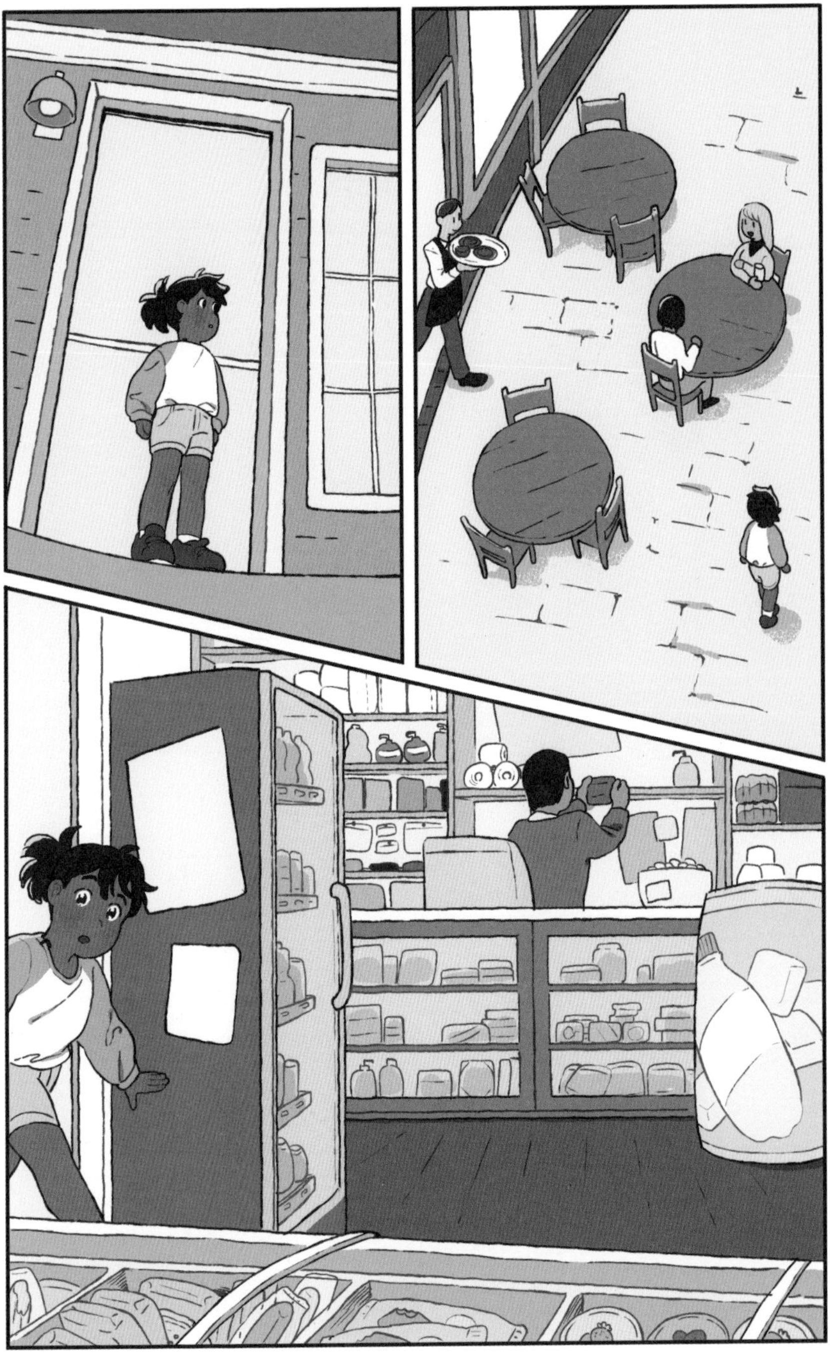

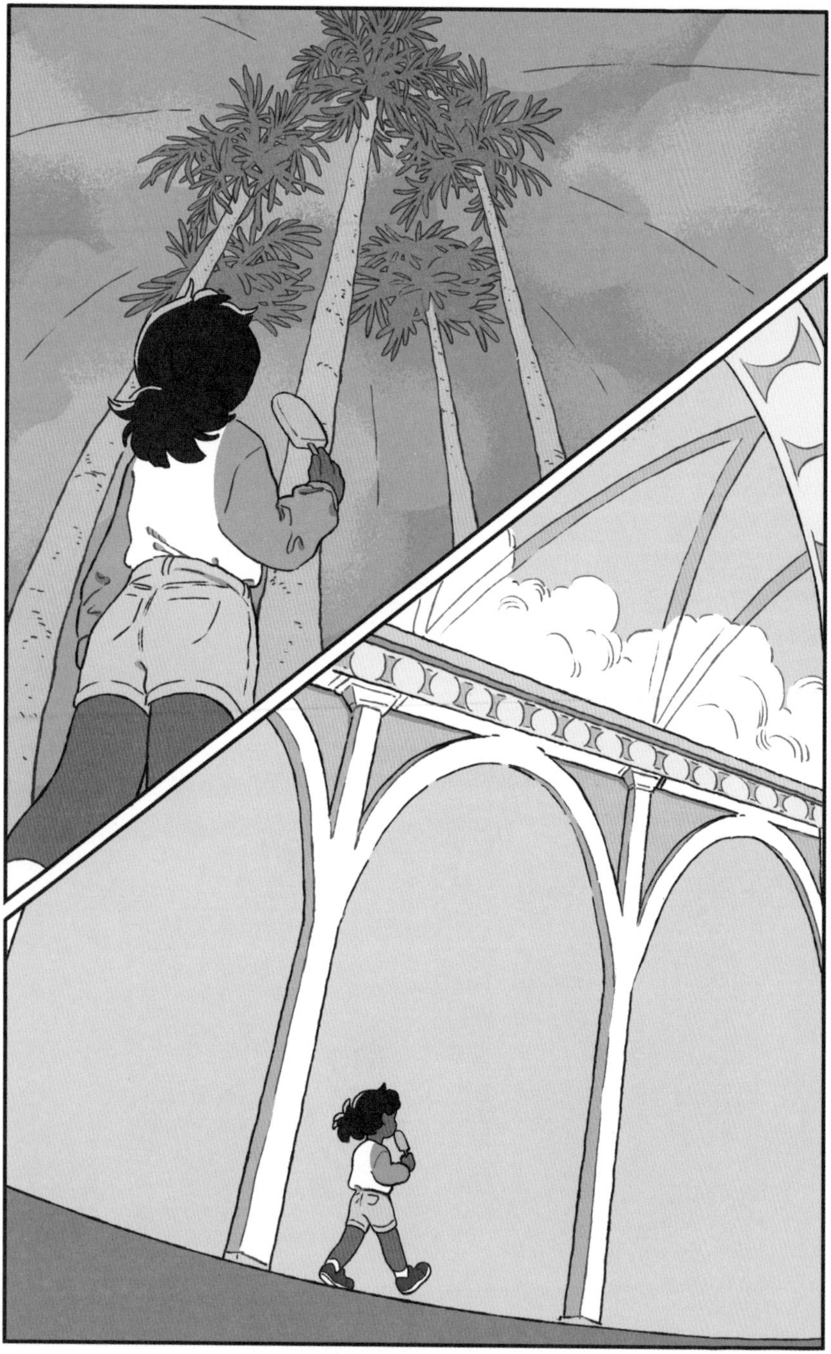

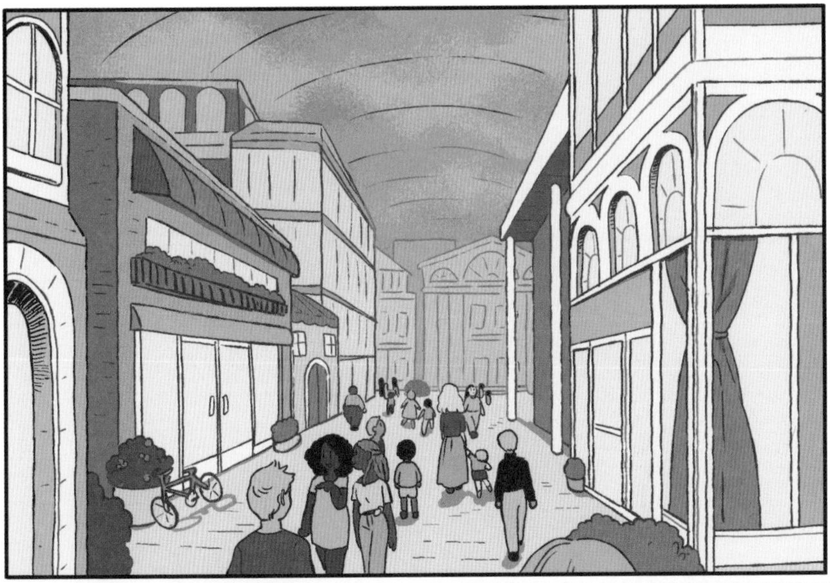

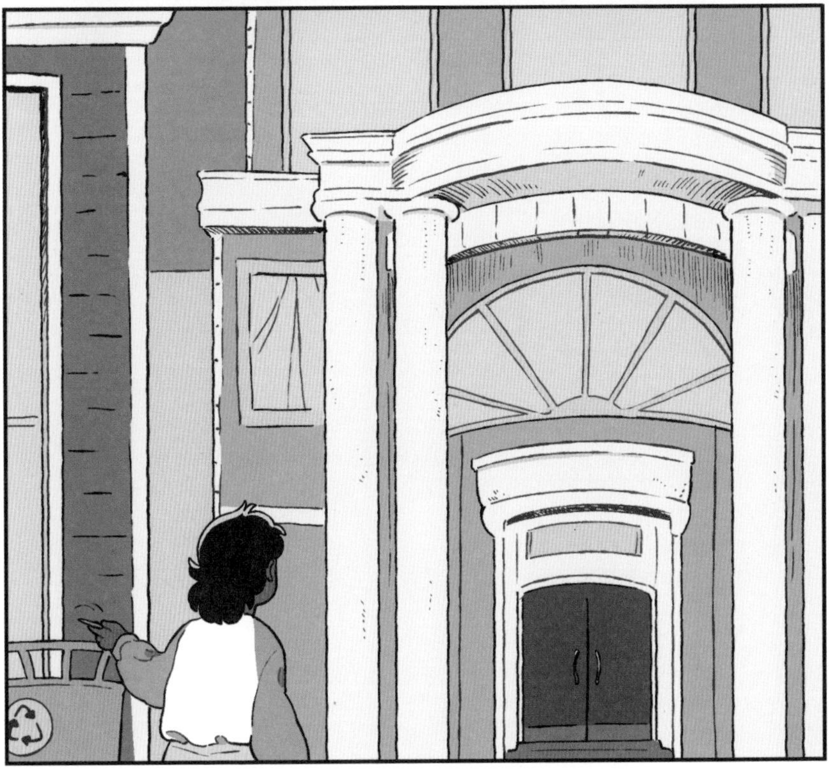

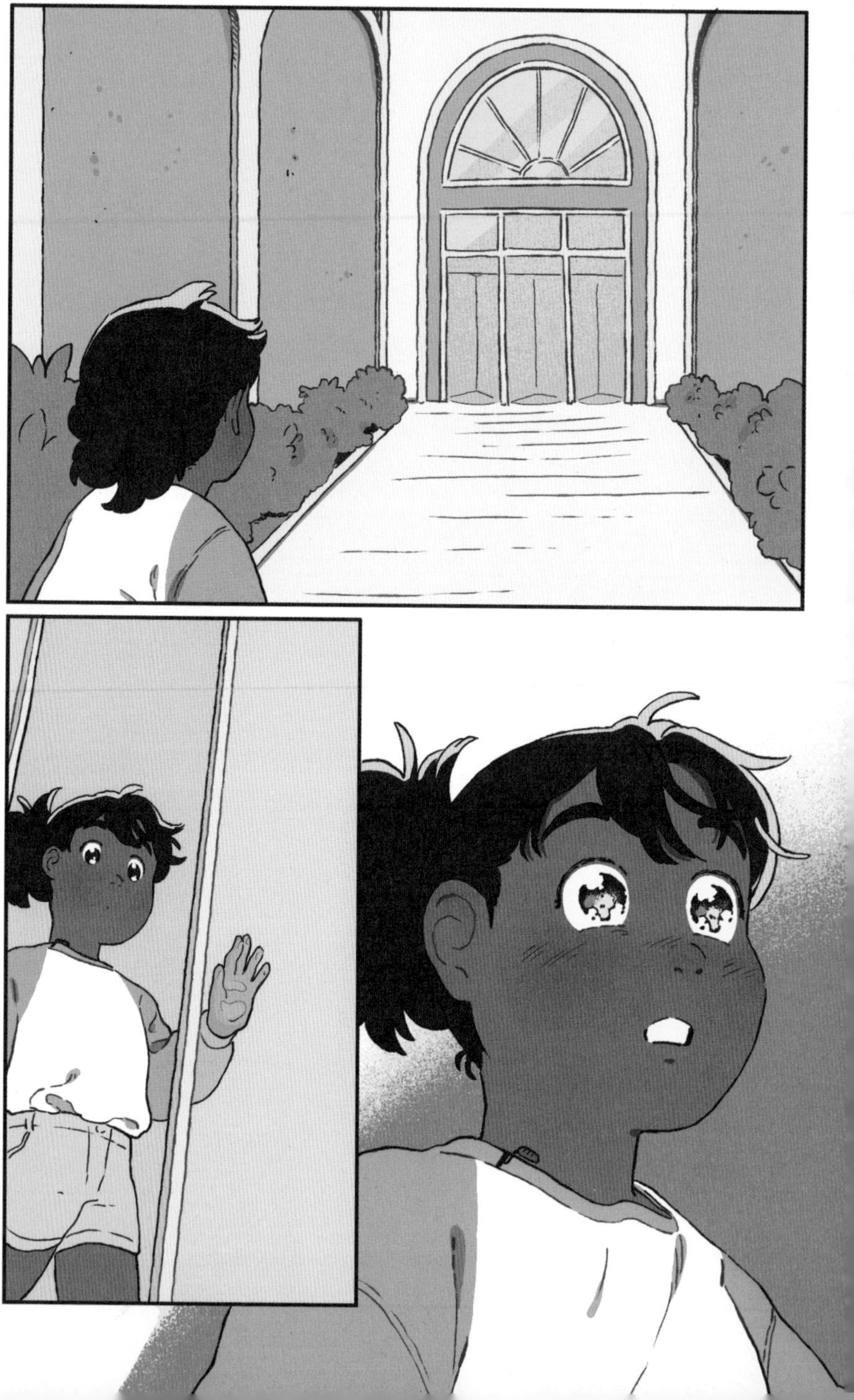

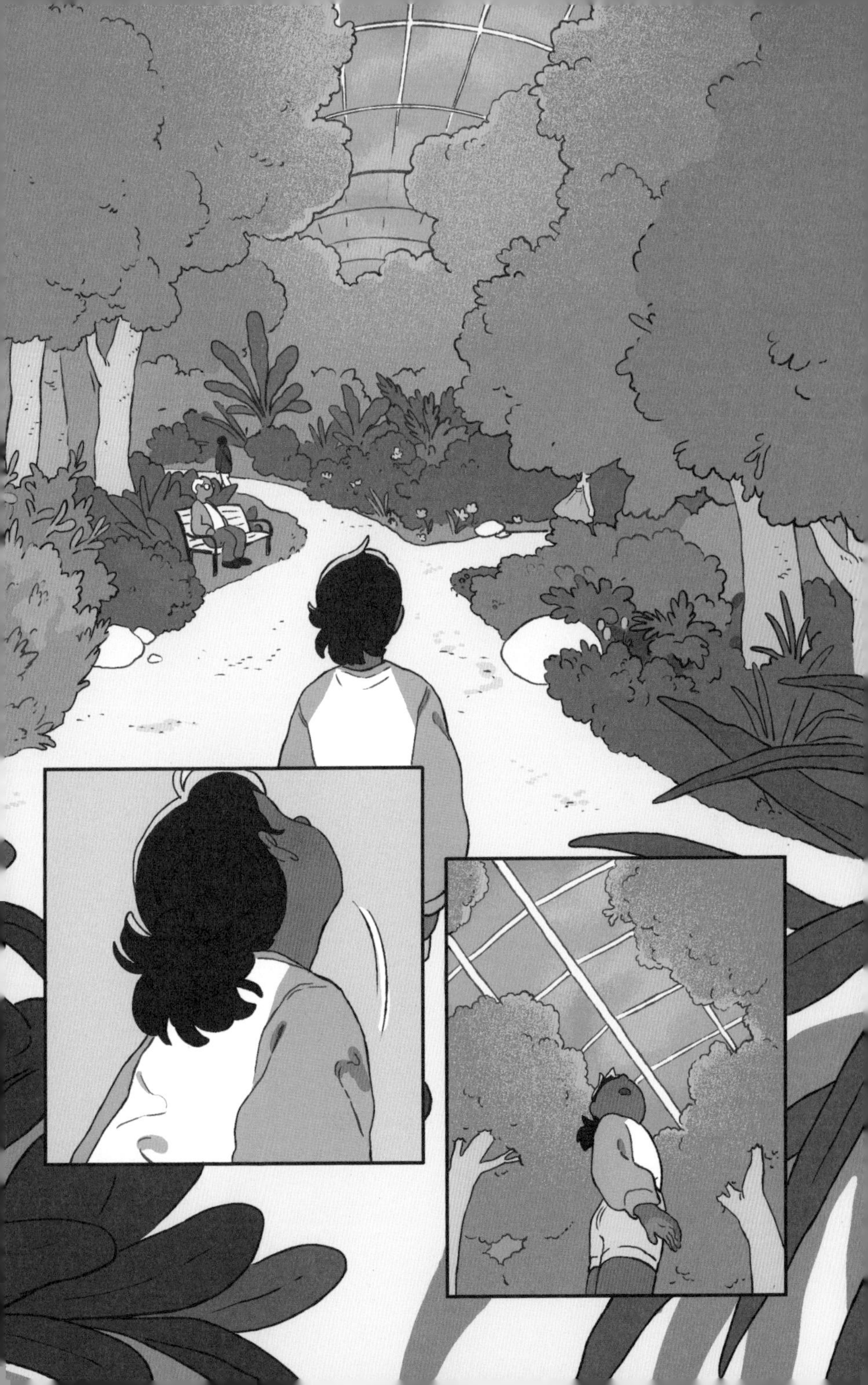

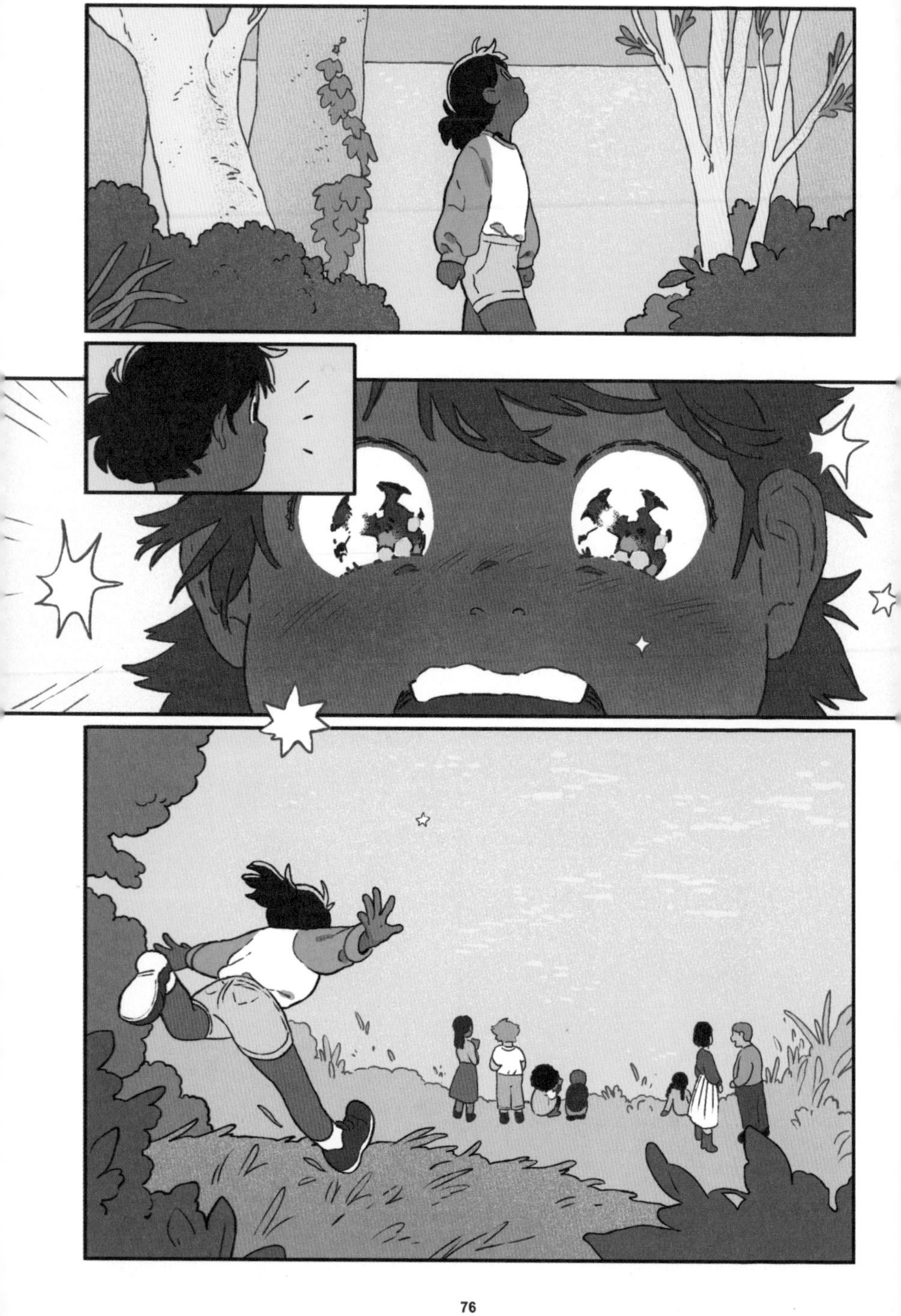

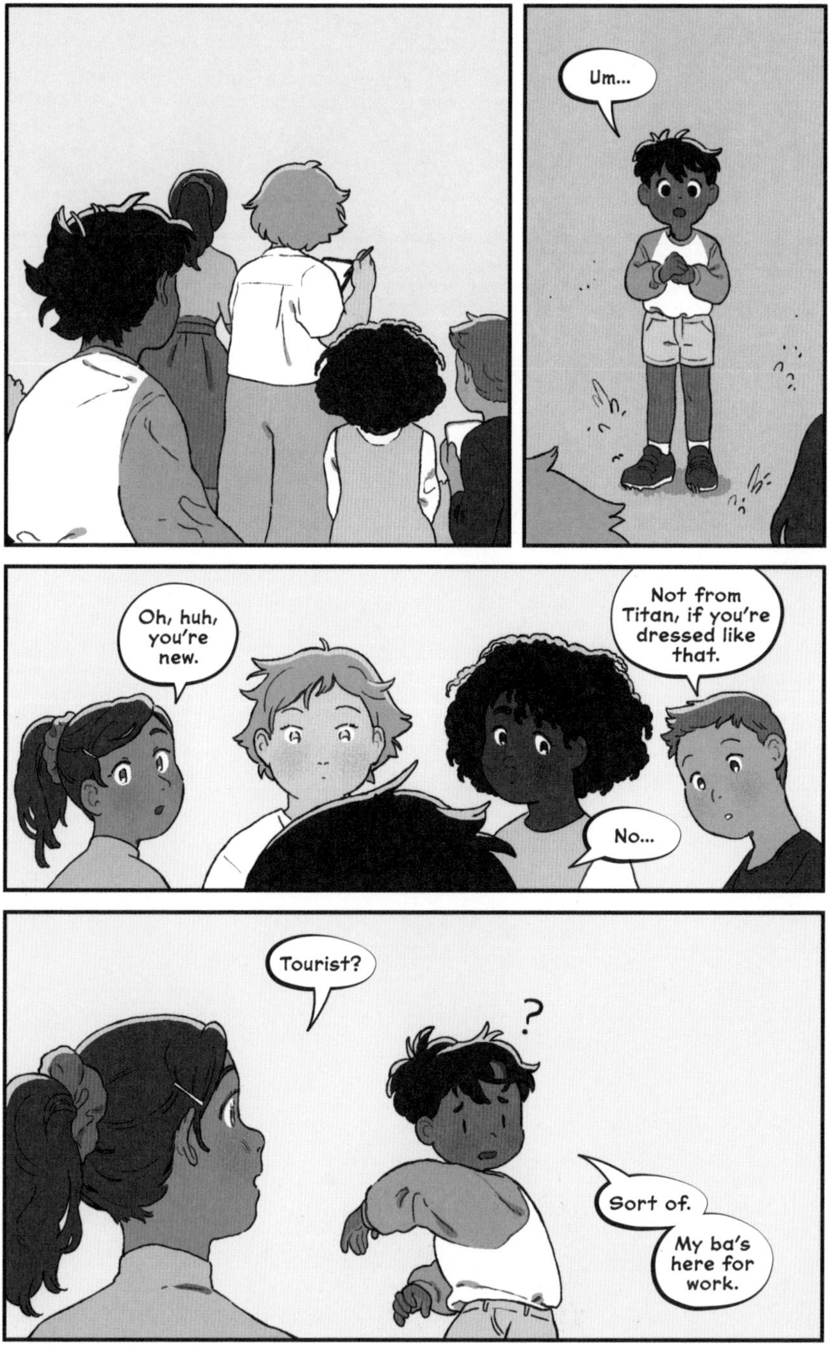
Um...
Oh, huh, you're new.
Not from Titan, if you're dressed like that.
No...
Tourist?
?
Sort of.
My ba's here for work.

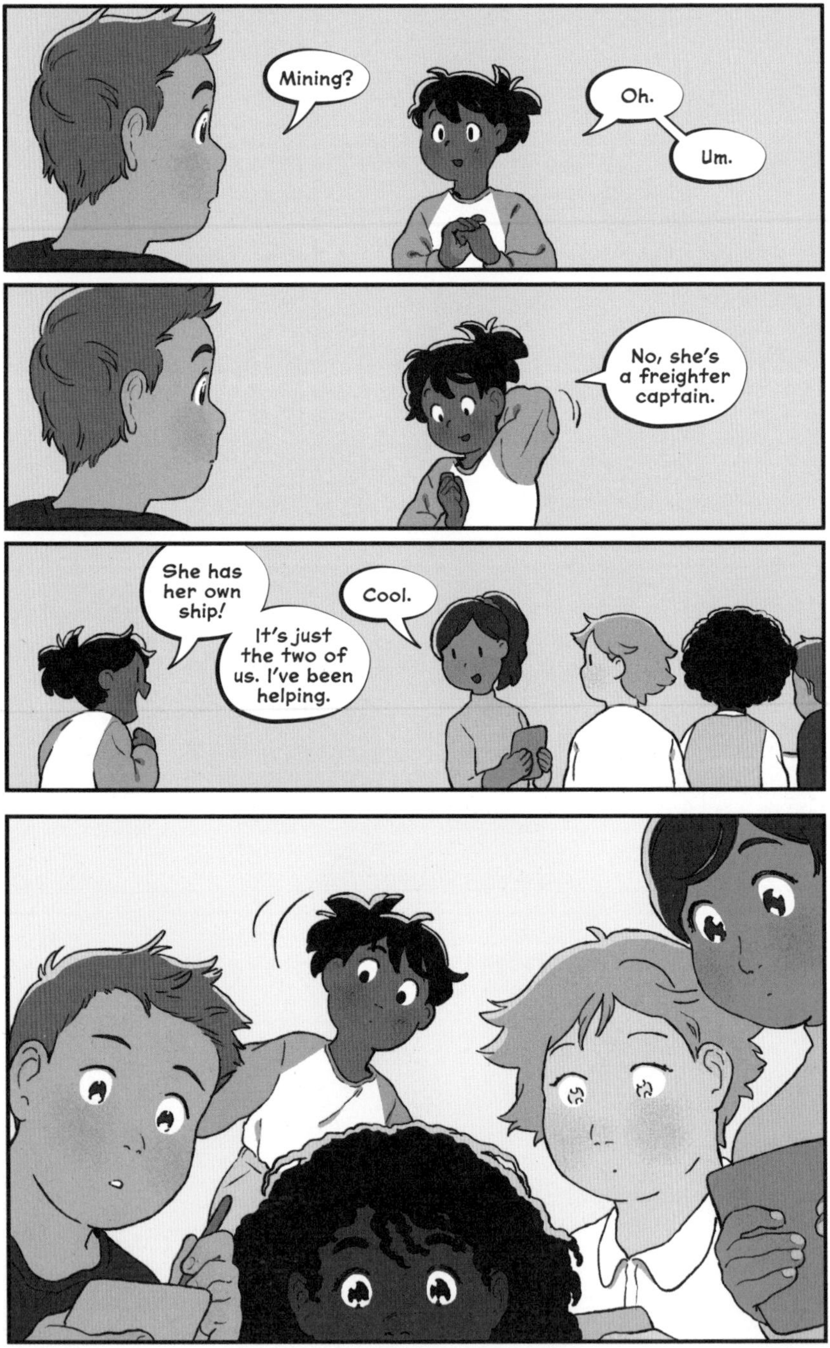
Mining?
Oh.
Um.
No, she's a freighter captain.
She has her own ship!
It's just the two of us. I've been helping.
Cool.

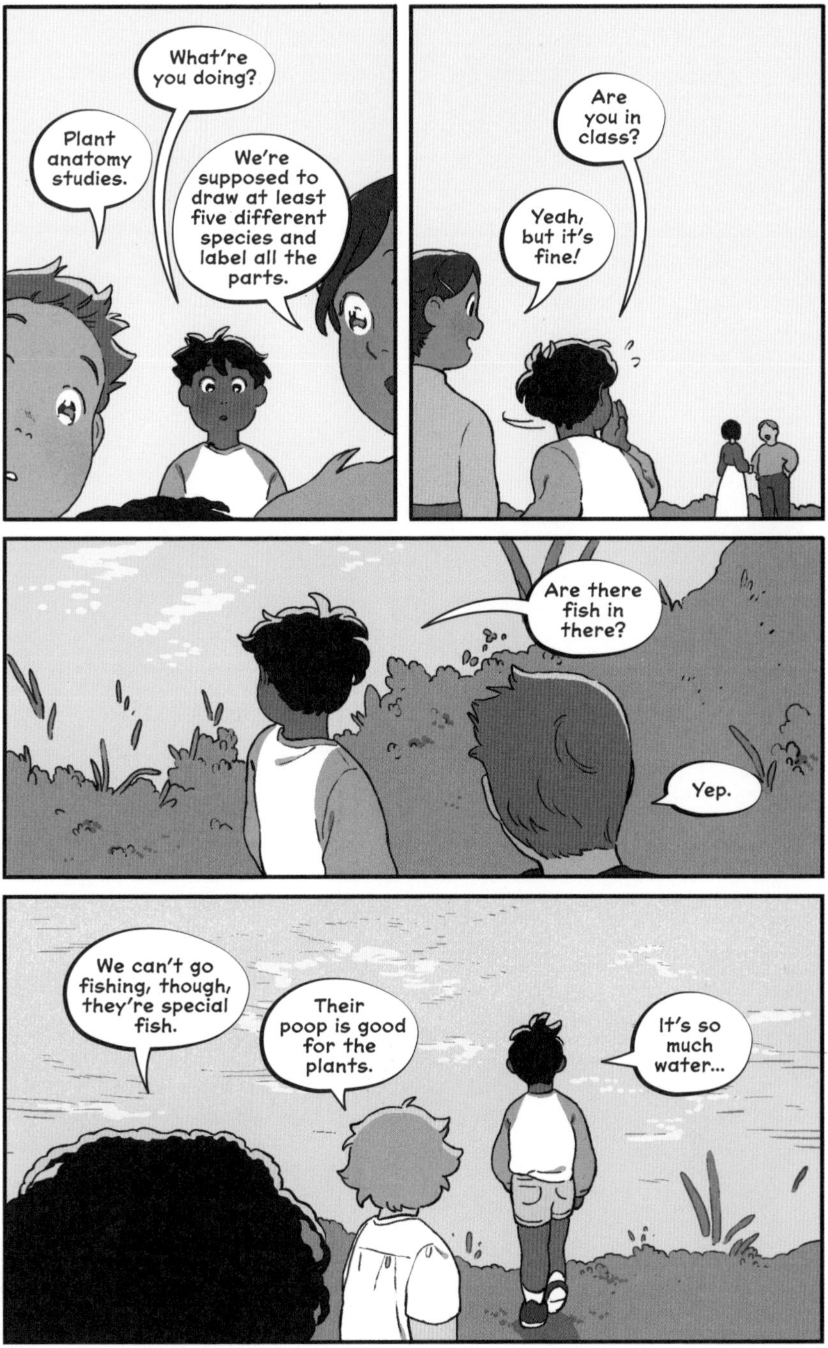
What're you doing?
Plant anatomy studies.
We're supposed to draw at least five different species and label all the parts.
Are you in class?
Yeah, but it's fine!
Are there fish in there?
Yep.
We can't go fishing, though, they're special fish.
Their poop is good for the plants.
It's so much water...

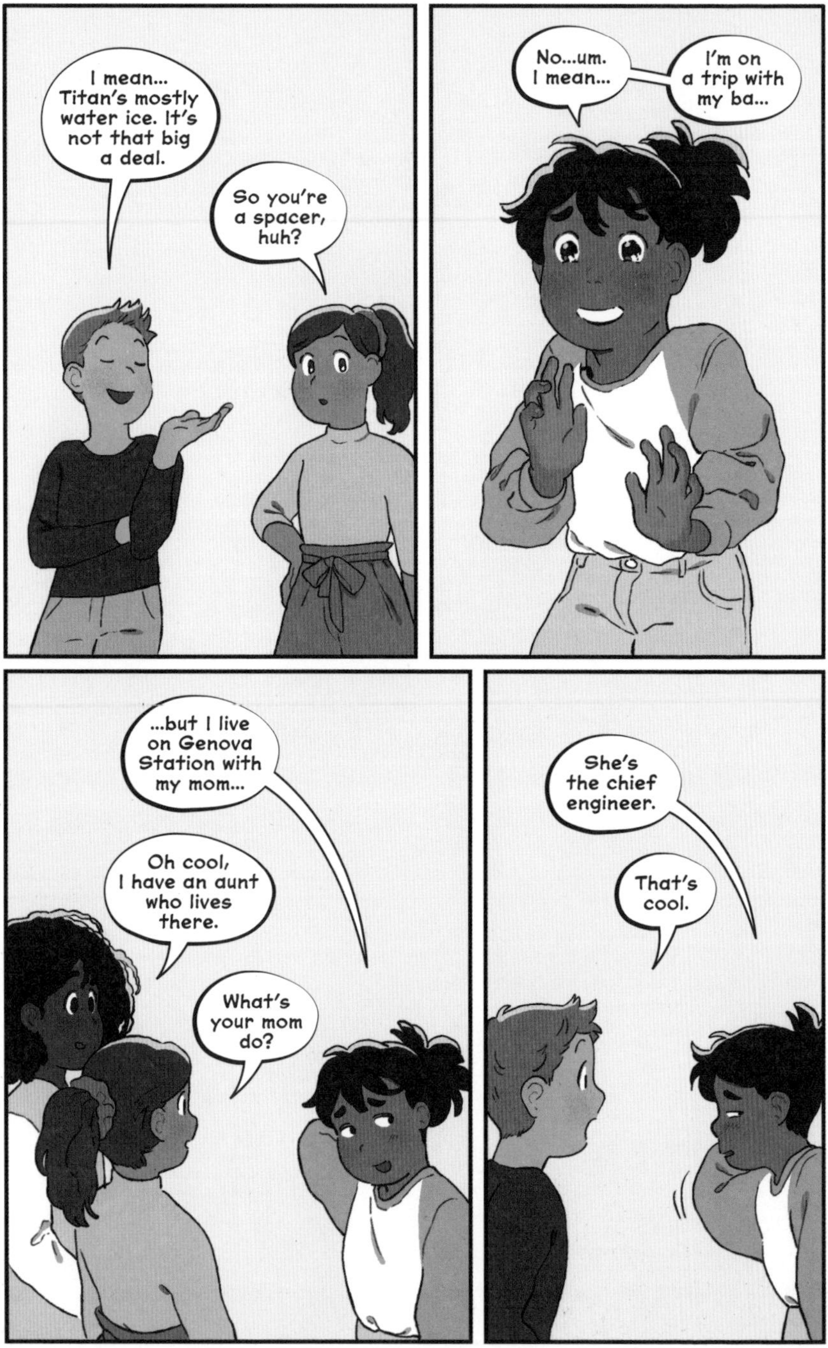
I mean... Titan's mostly water ice. It's not that big a deal.
So you're a spacer, huh?
No...um. I mean...
I'm on a trip with my ba...
...but I live on Genova Station with my mom...
Oh cool, I have an aunt who lives there.
What's your mom do?
She's the chief engineer.
That's cool.

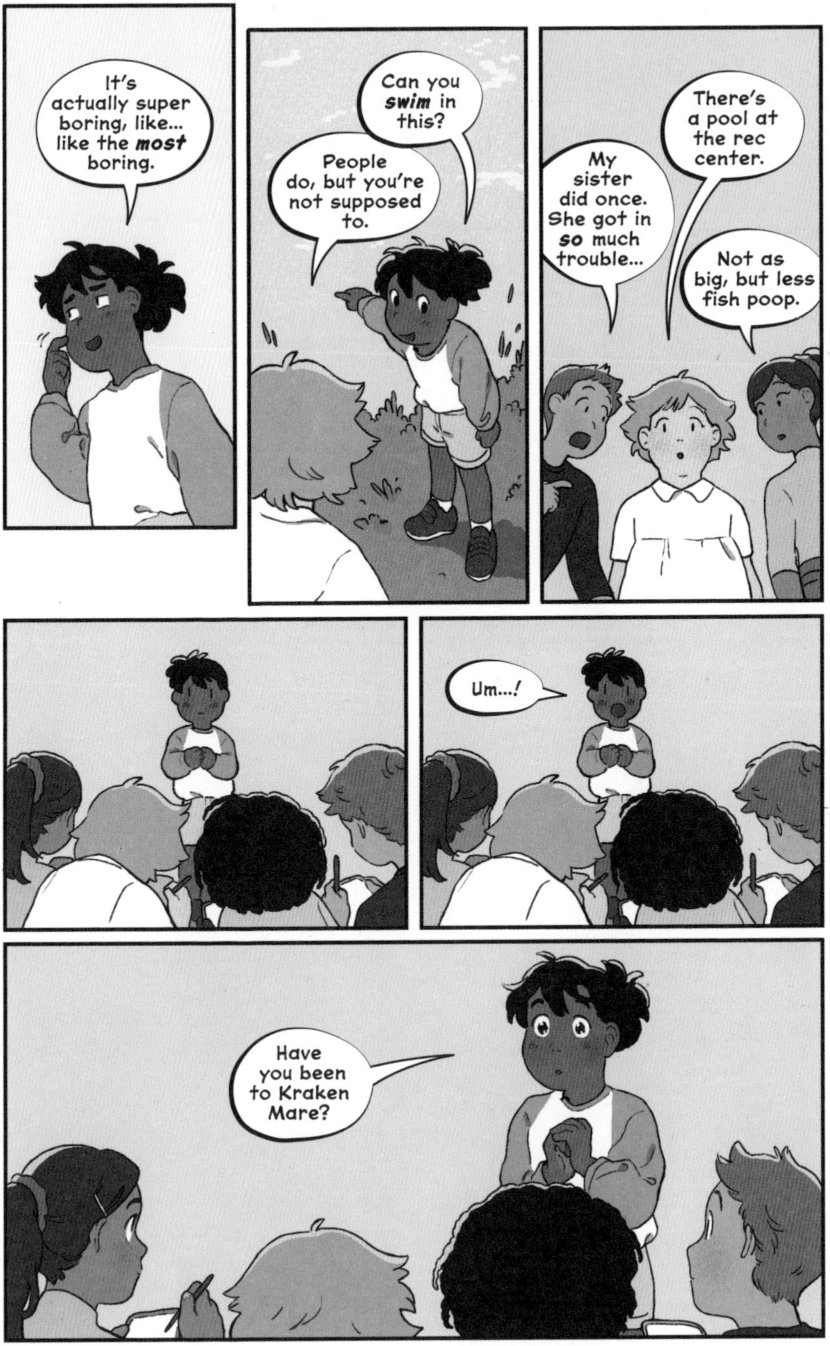
It's actually super boring, like... like the *most* boring.
Can you *swim* in this?
People do, but you're not supposed to.
There's a pool at the rec center.
My sister did once. She got in *so* much trouble...
Not as big, but less fish poop.
Um...!
Have you been to Kraken Mare?

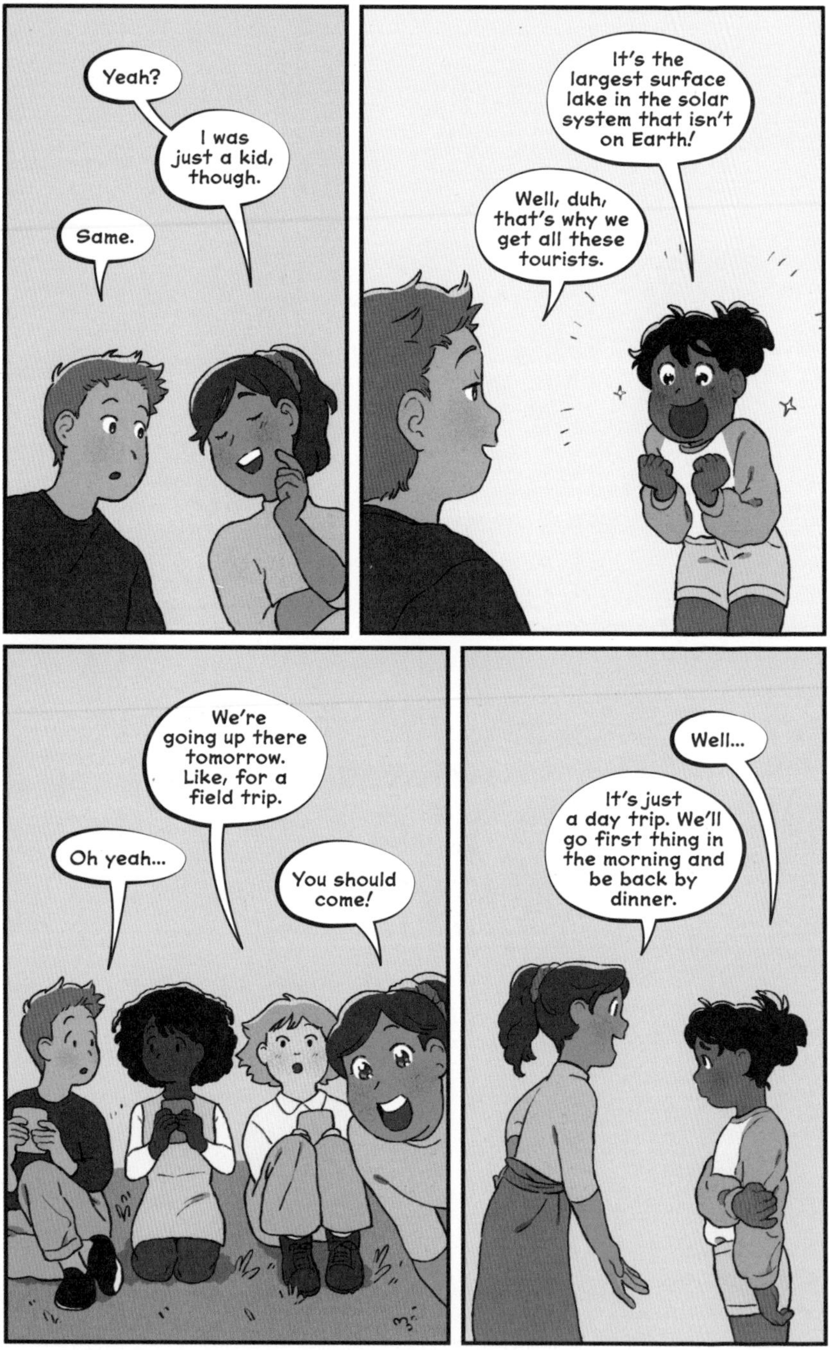
Yeah?
I was just a kid, though.
Same.
It's the largest surface lake in the solar system that isn't on Earth!
Well, duh, that's why we get all these tourists.
We're going up there tomorrow. Like, for a field trip.
Oh yeah...
You should come!
Well...
It's just a day trip. We'll go first thing in the morning and be back by dinner.

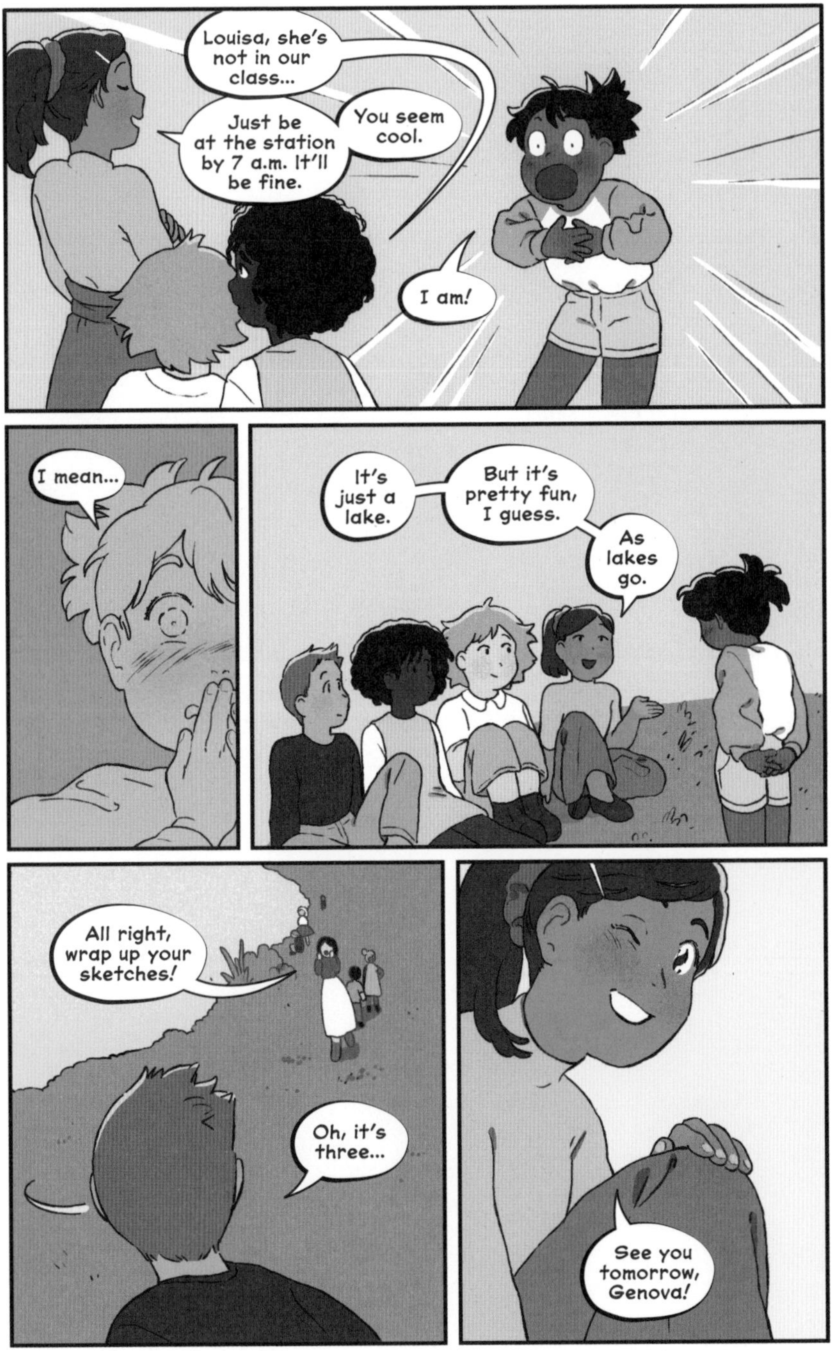
Louisa, she's not in our class...
Just be at the station by 7 a.m. It'll be fine.
You seem cool.
I am!
I mean...
It's just a lake.
But it's pretty fun, I guess.
As lakes go.
All right, wrap up your sketches!
Oh, it's three...
See you tomorrow, Genova!

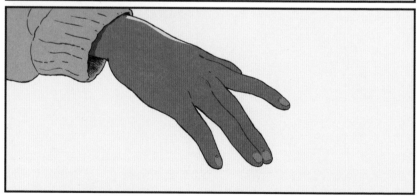

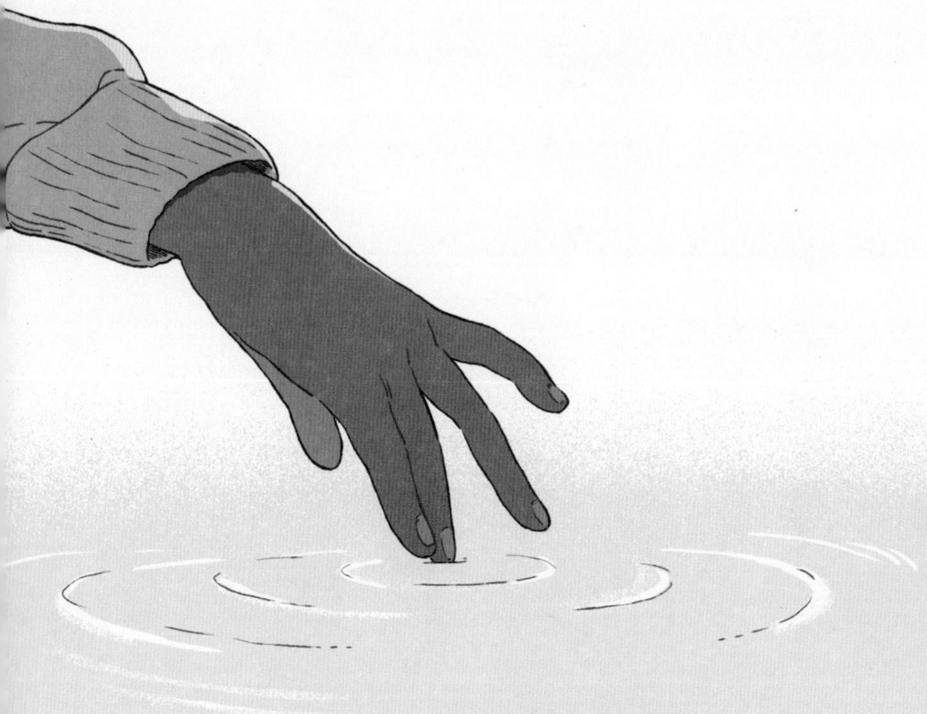

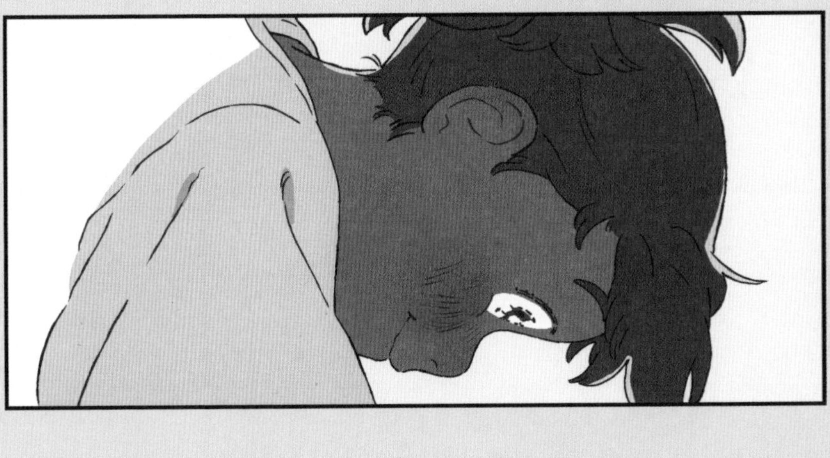

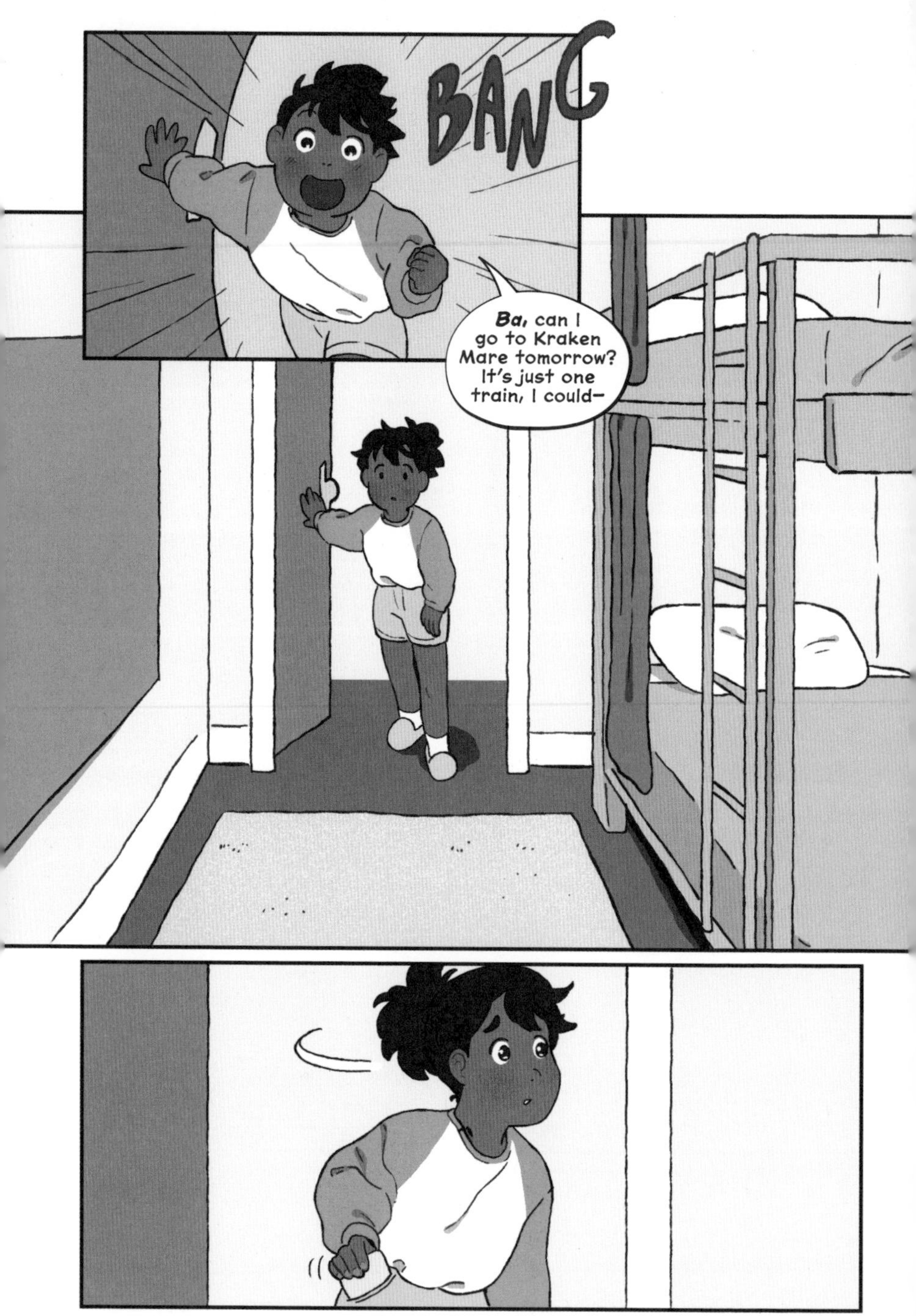
BANG
Ba, can I go to Kraken Mare tomorrow? It's just one train, I could–

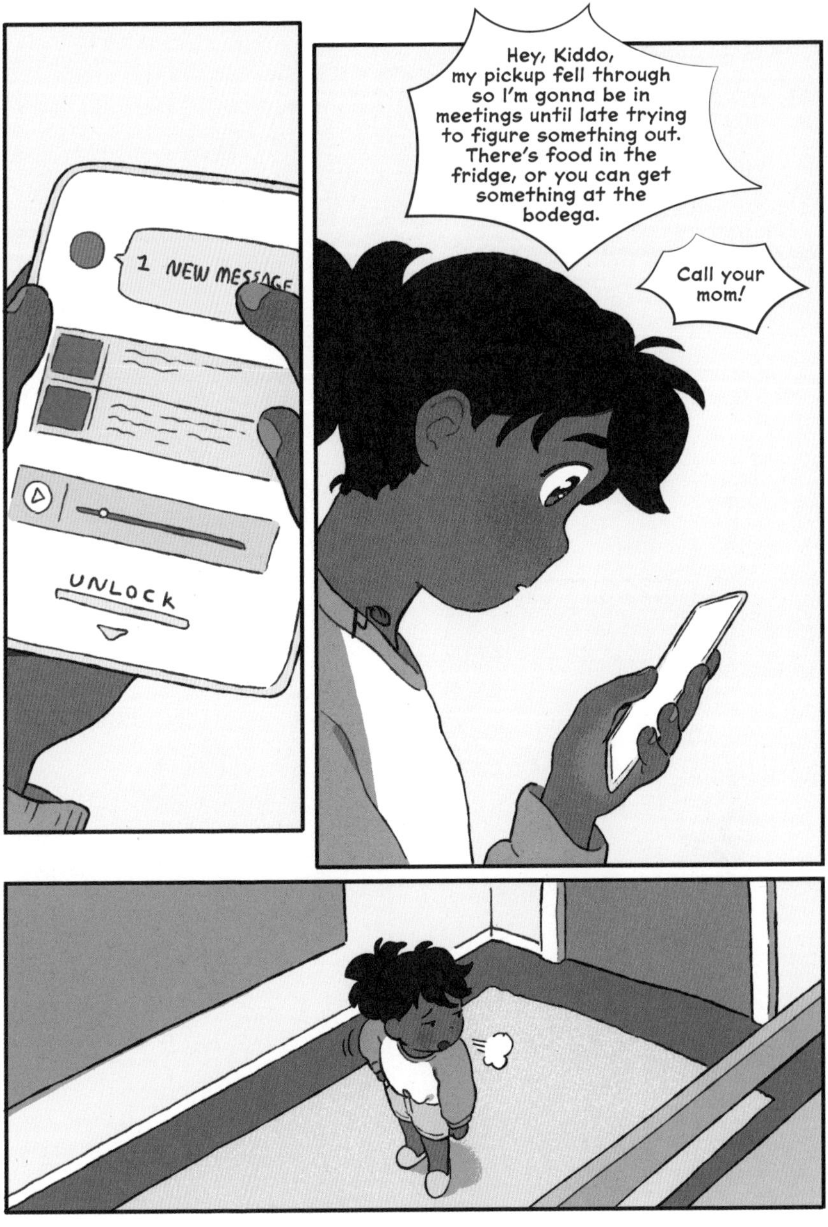
1 NEW MESSAGE
UNLOCK
Hey, Kiddo, my pickup fell through so I'm gonna be in meetings until late trying to figure something out. There's food in the fridge, or you can get something at the bodega.
Call your mom!

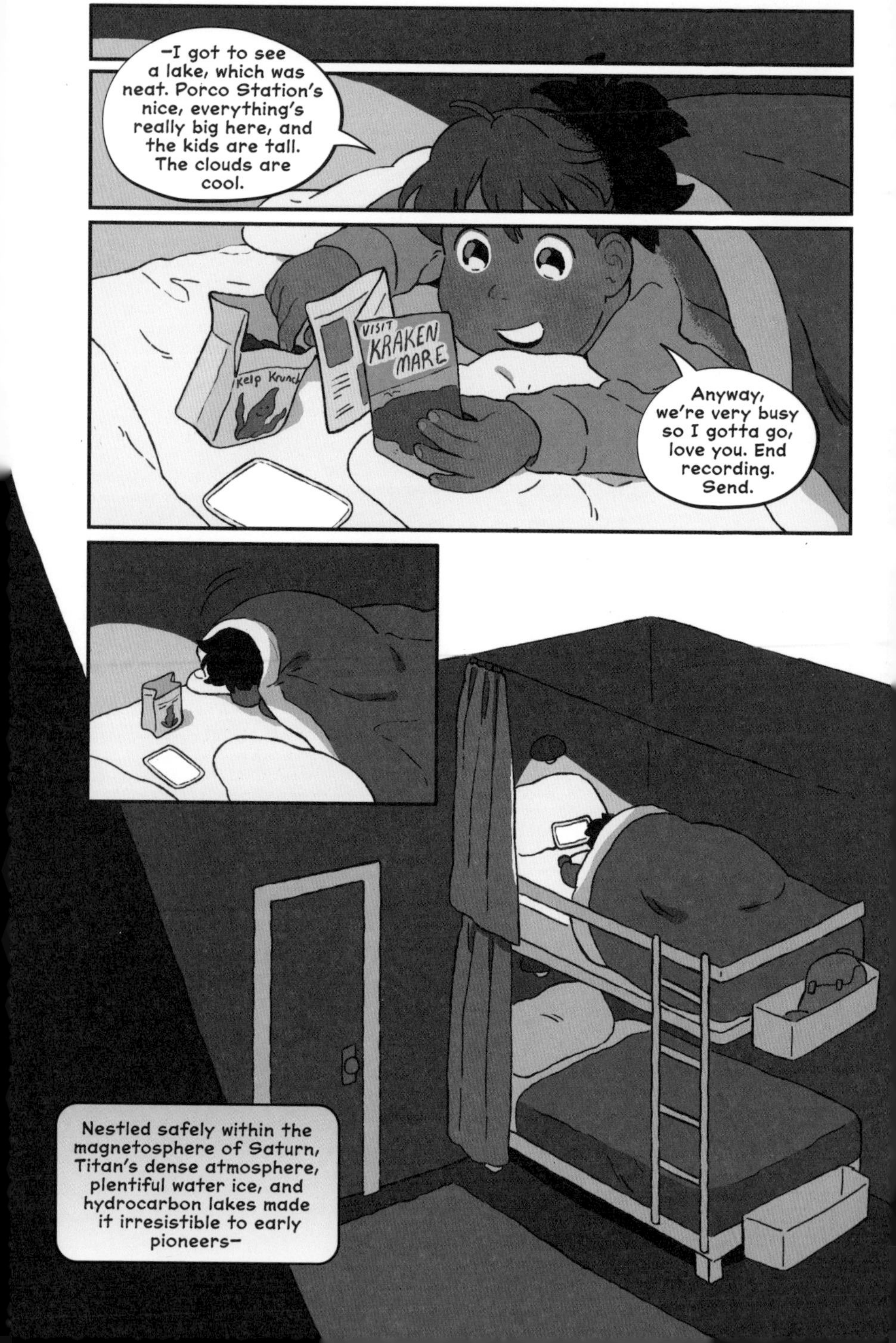
—I got to see a lake, which was neat. Porco Station's nice, everything's really big here, and the kids are tall. The clouds are cool.
VISIT KRAKEN MARE
Kelp Krunch
Anyway, we're very busy so I gotta go, love you. End recording. Send.
Nestled safely within the magnetosphere of Saturn, Titan's dense atmosphere, plentiful water ice, and hydrocarbon lakes made it irresistible to early pioneers—

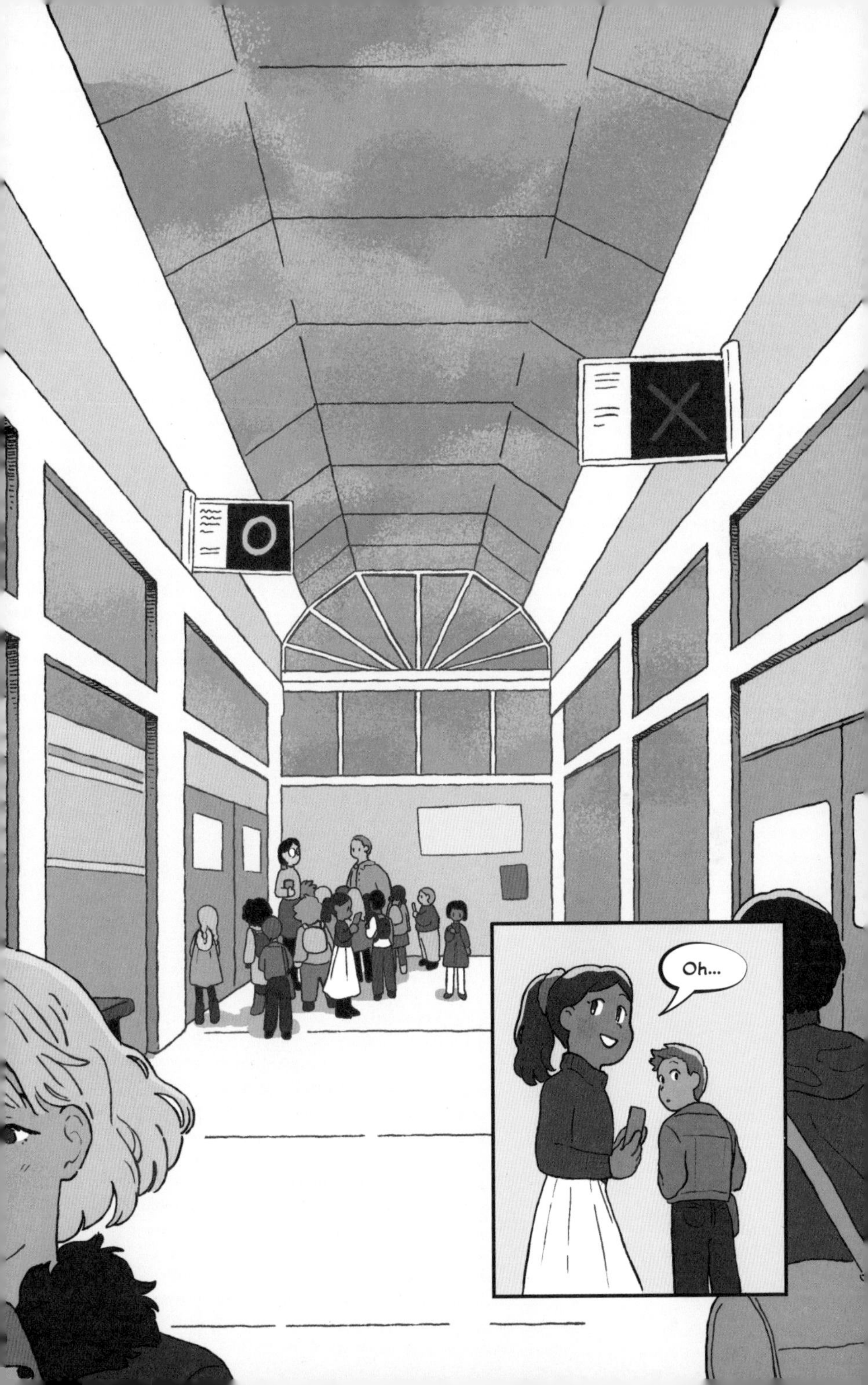
Oh...

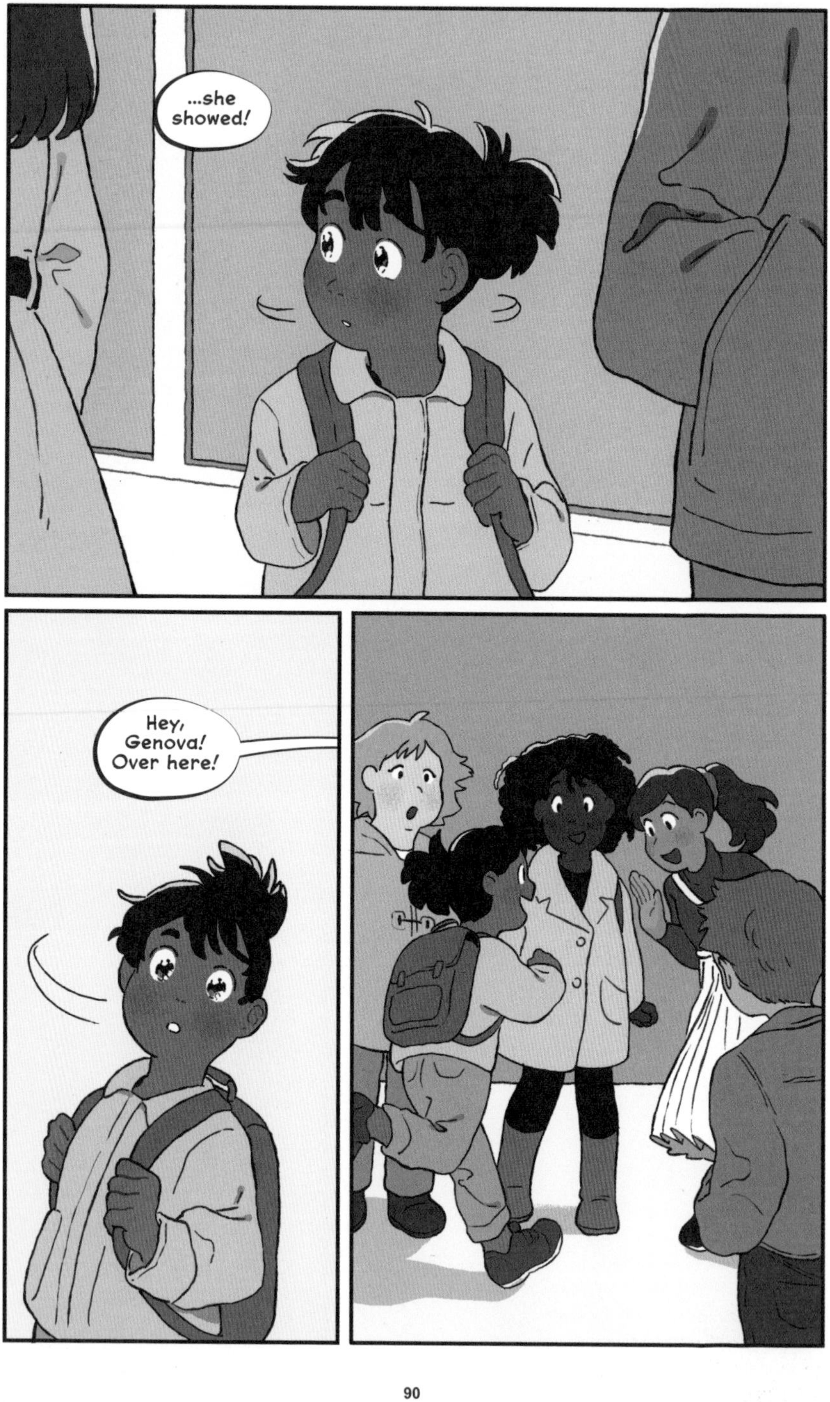
...she showed!
Hey, Genova! Over here!

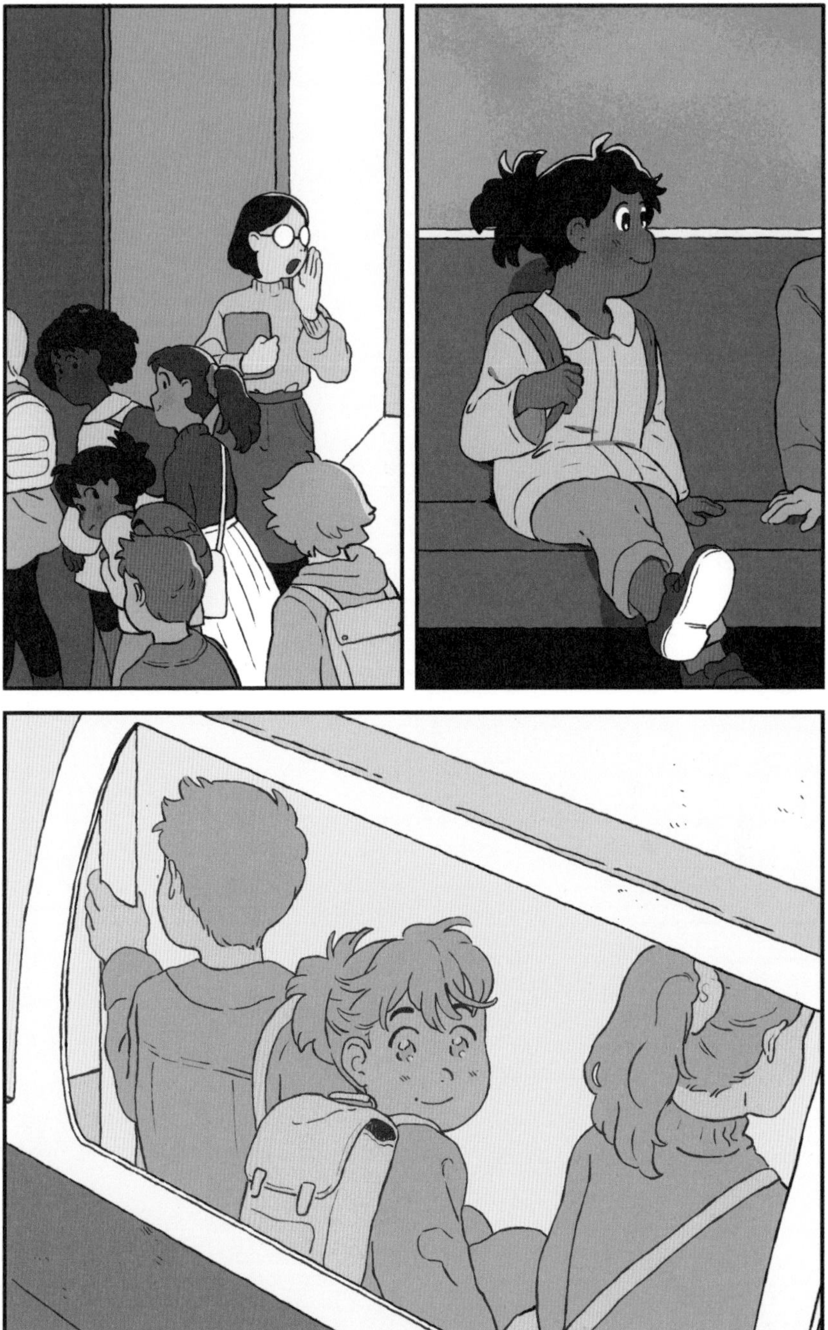

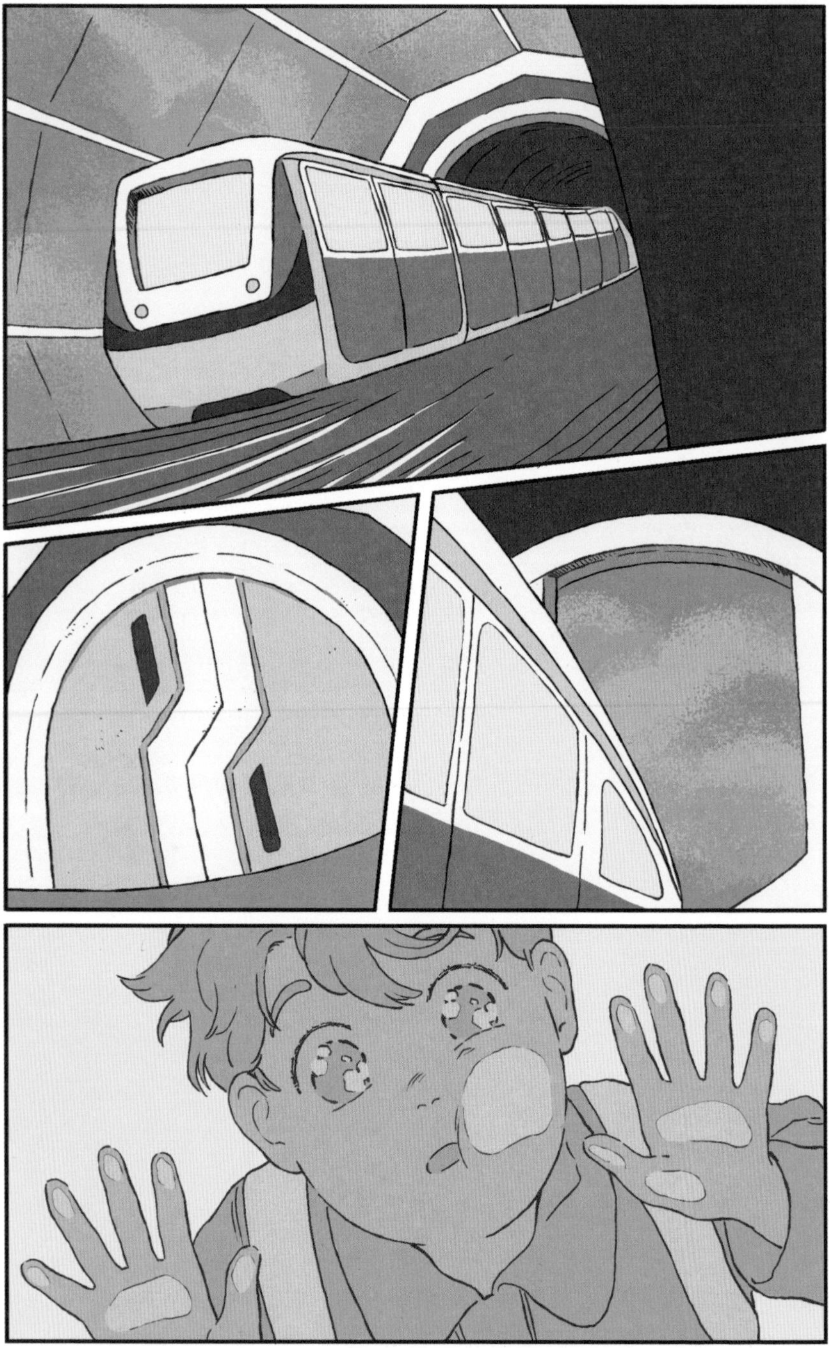

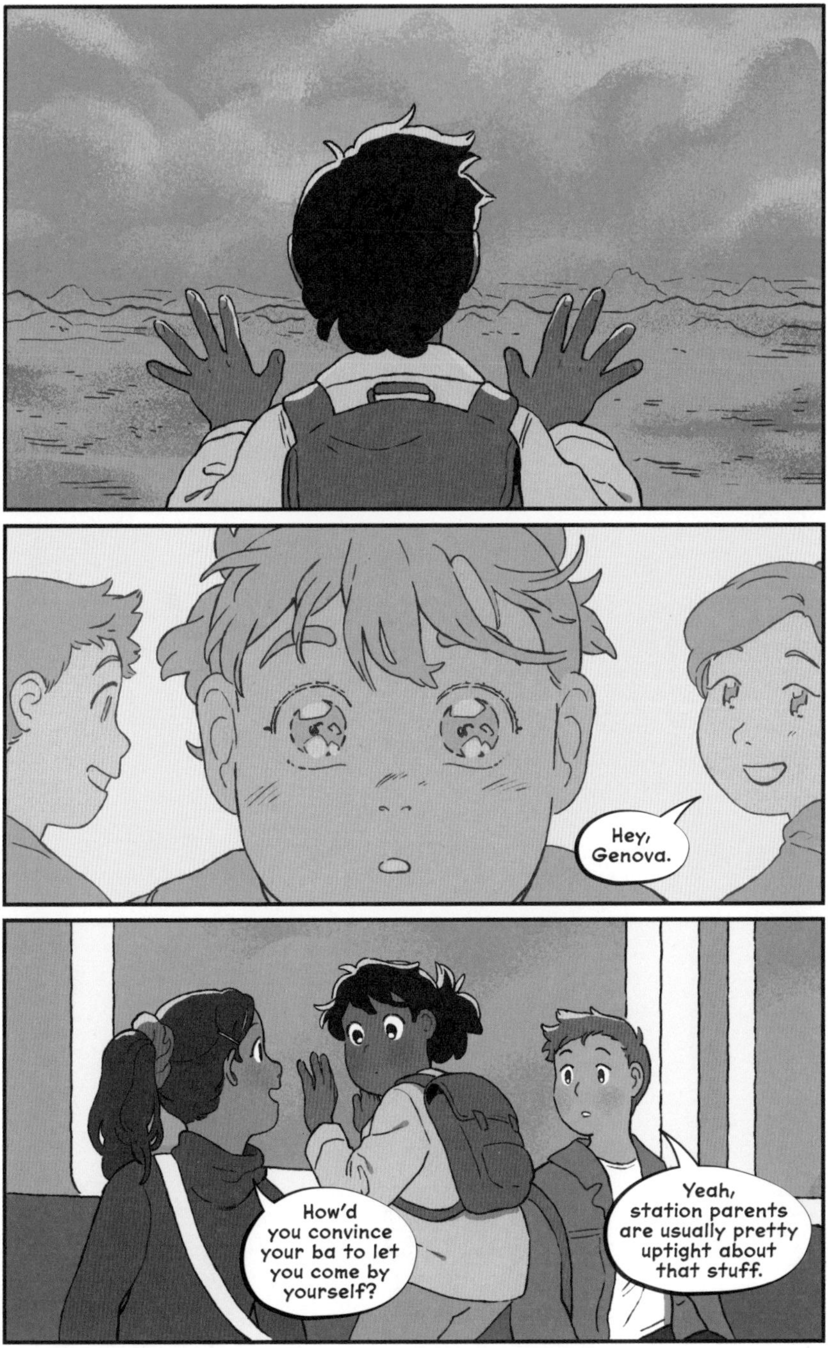
Hey, Genova.
How'd you convince your ba to let you come by yourself?
Yeah, station parents are usually pretty uptight about that stuff.

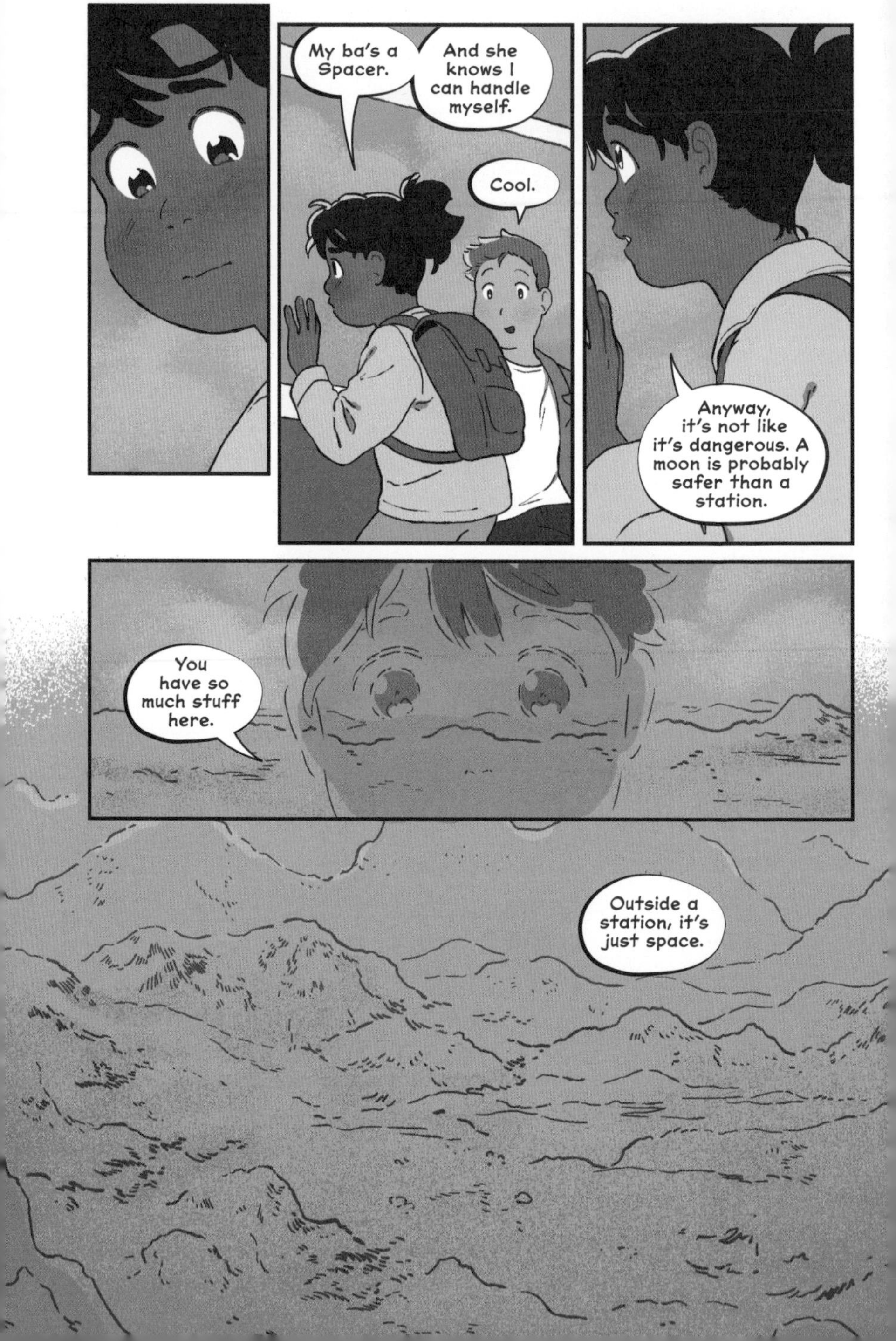
My ba's a Spacer.
And she knows I can handle myself.
Cool.
Anyway, it's not like it's dangerous. A moon is probably safer than a station.
You have so much stuff here.
Outside a station, it's just space.

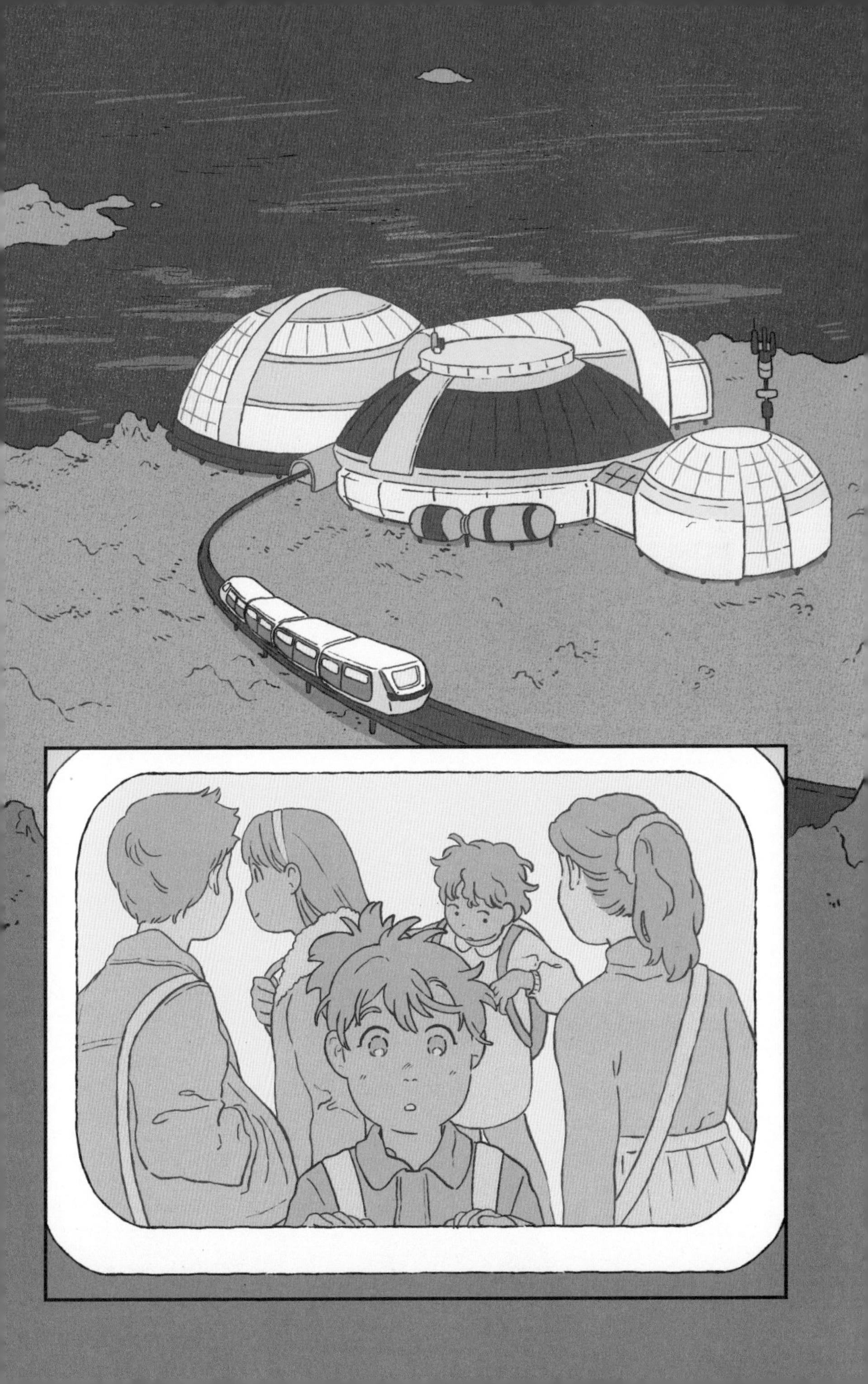

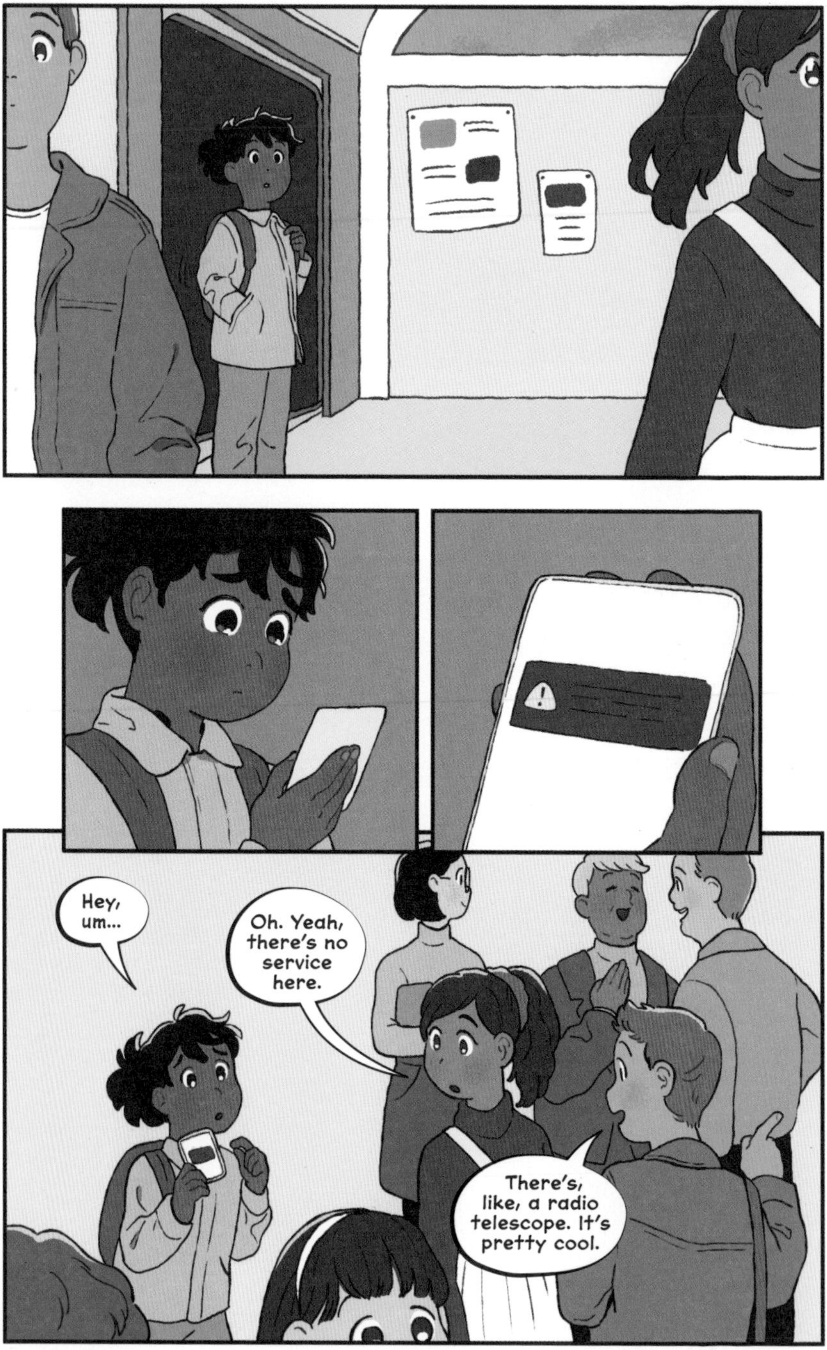
Hey, um...
Oh. Yeah, there's no service here.
There's, like, a radio telescope. It's pretty cool.

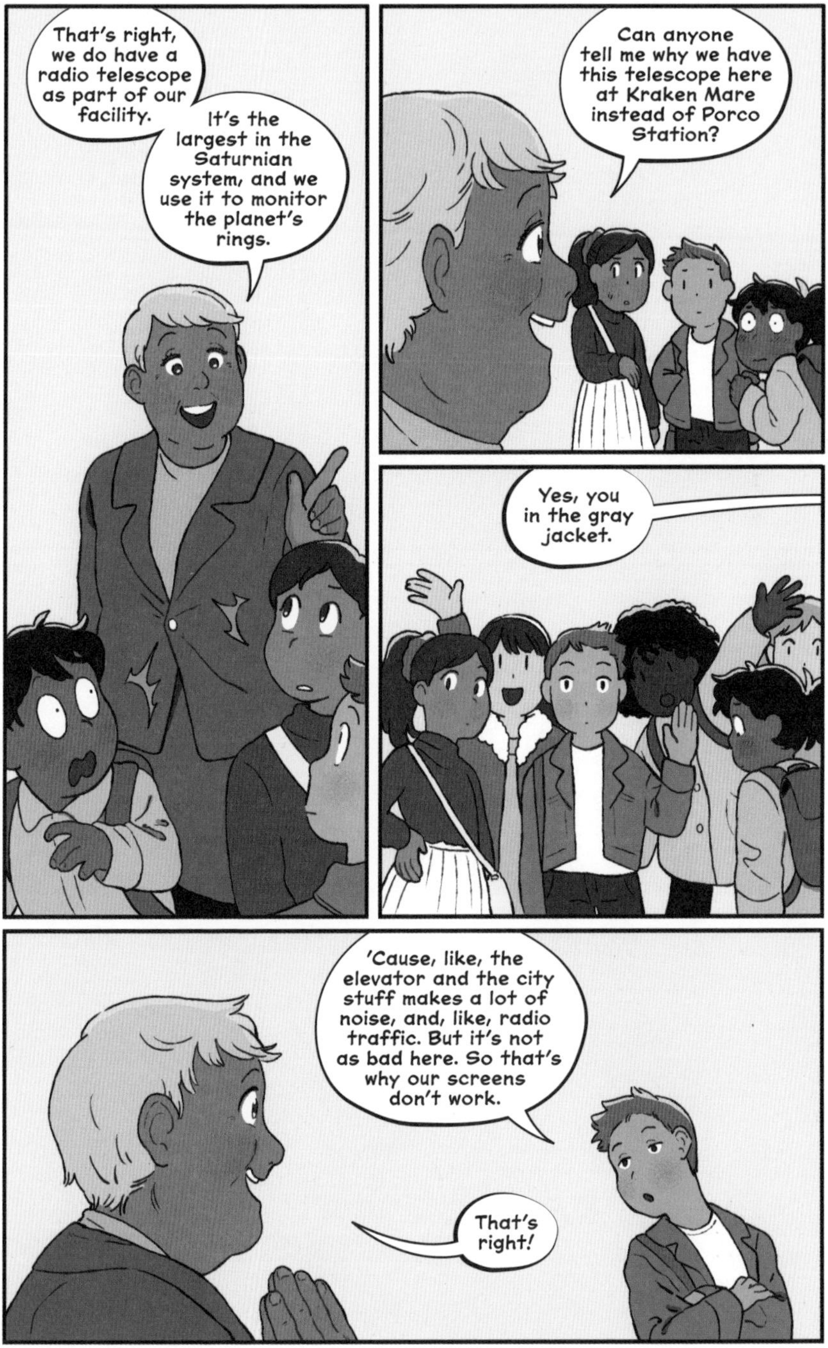
That's right, we do have a radio telescope as part of our facility.
It's the largest in the Saturnian system, and we use it to monitor the planet's rings.
Can anyone tell me why we have this telescope here at Kraken Mare instead of Porco Station?
Yes, you in the gray jacket.
'Cause, like, the elevator and the city stuff makes a lot of noise, and, like, radio traffic. But it's not as bad here. So that's why our screens don't work.
That's right!

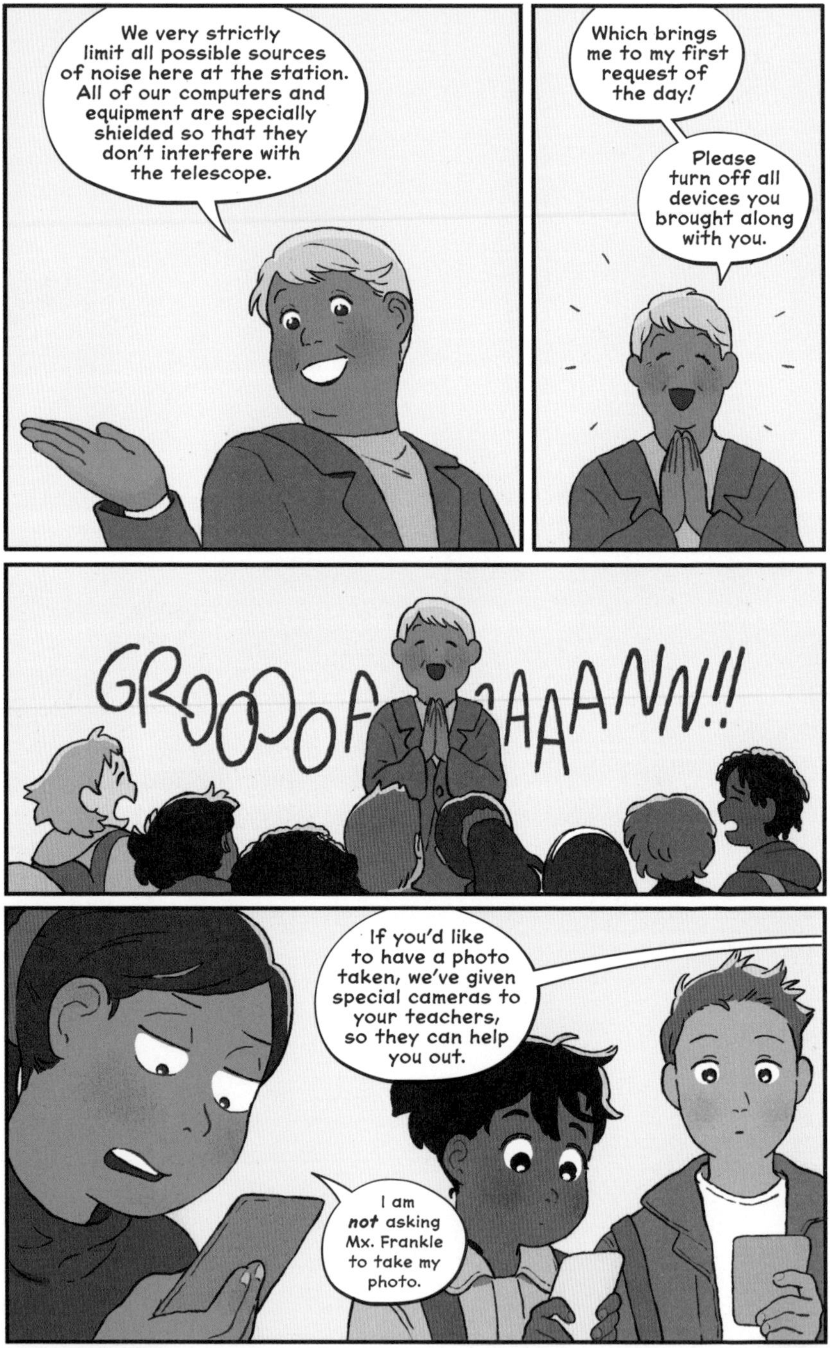
We very strictly limit all possible sources of noise here at the station. All of our computers and equipment are specially shielded so that they don't interfere with the telescope.
Which brings me to my first request of the day!
Please turn off all devices you brought along with you.
GROOOOAAAAANN!!
If you'd like to have a photo taken, we've given special cameras to your teachers, so they can help you out.
I am ***not*** asking Mx. Frankle to take my photo.

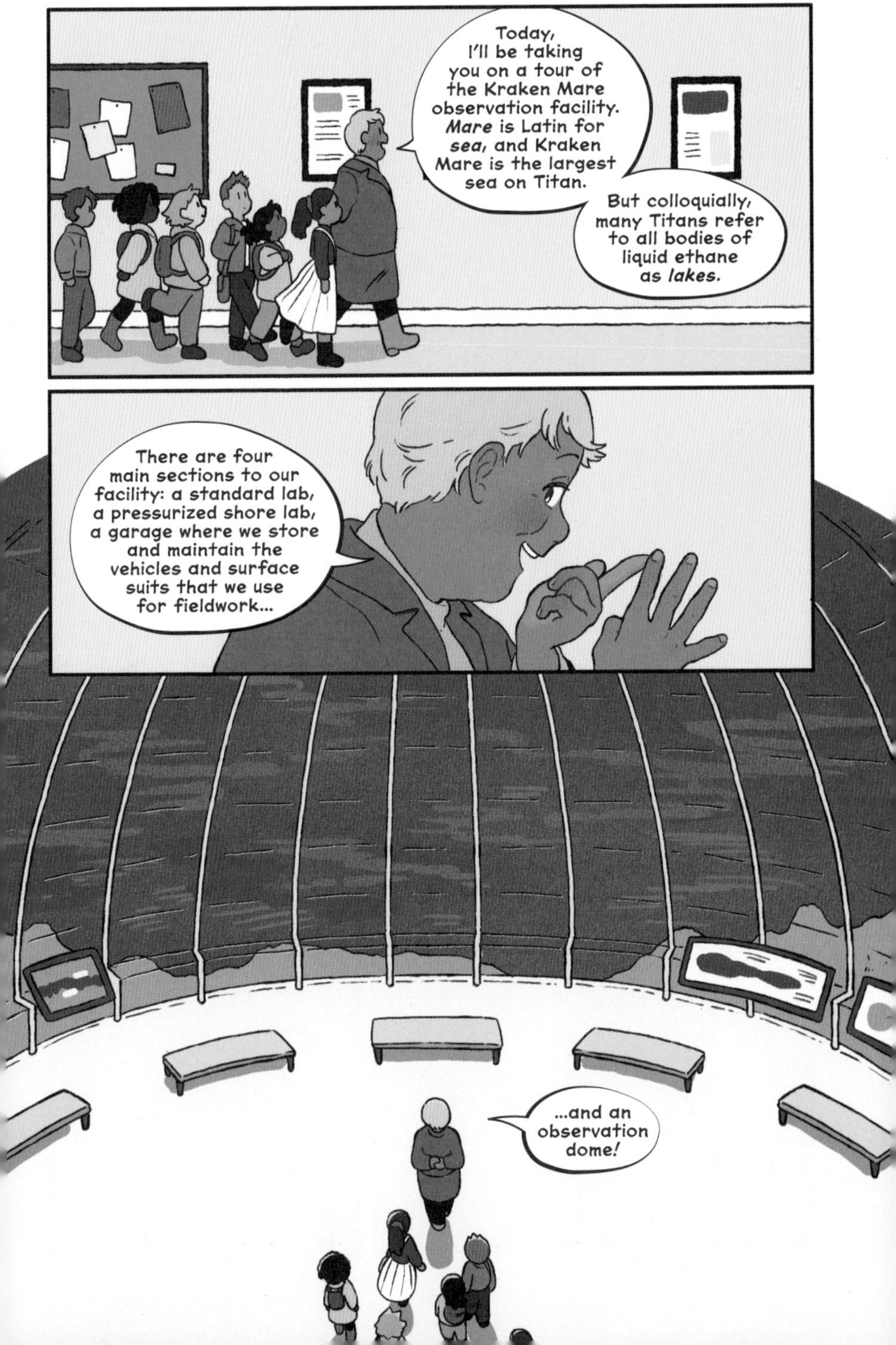
Today, I'll be taking you on a tour of the Kraken Mare observation facility. *Mare* is Latin for *sea*, and Kraken Mare is the largest sea on Titan.
But colloquially, many Titans refer to all bodies of liquid ethane as *lakes*.
There are four main sections to our facility: a standard lab, a pressurized shore lab, a garage where we store and maintain the vehicles and surface suits that we use for fieldwork...
...and an observation dome!

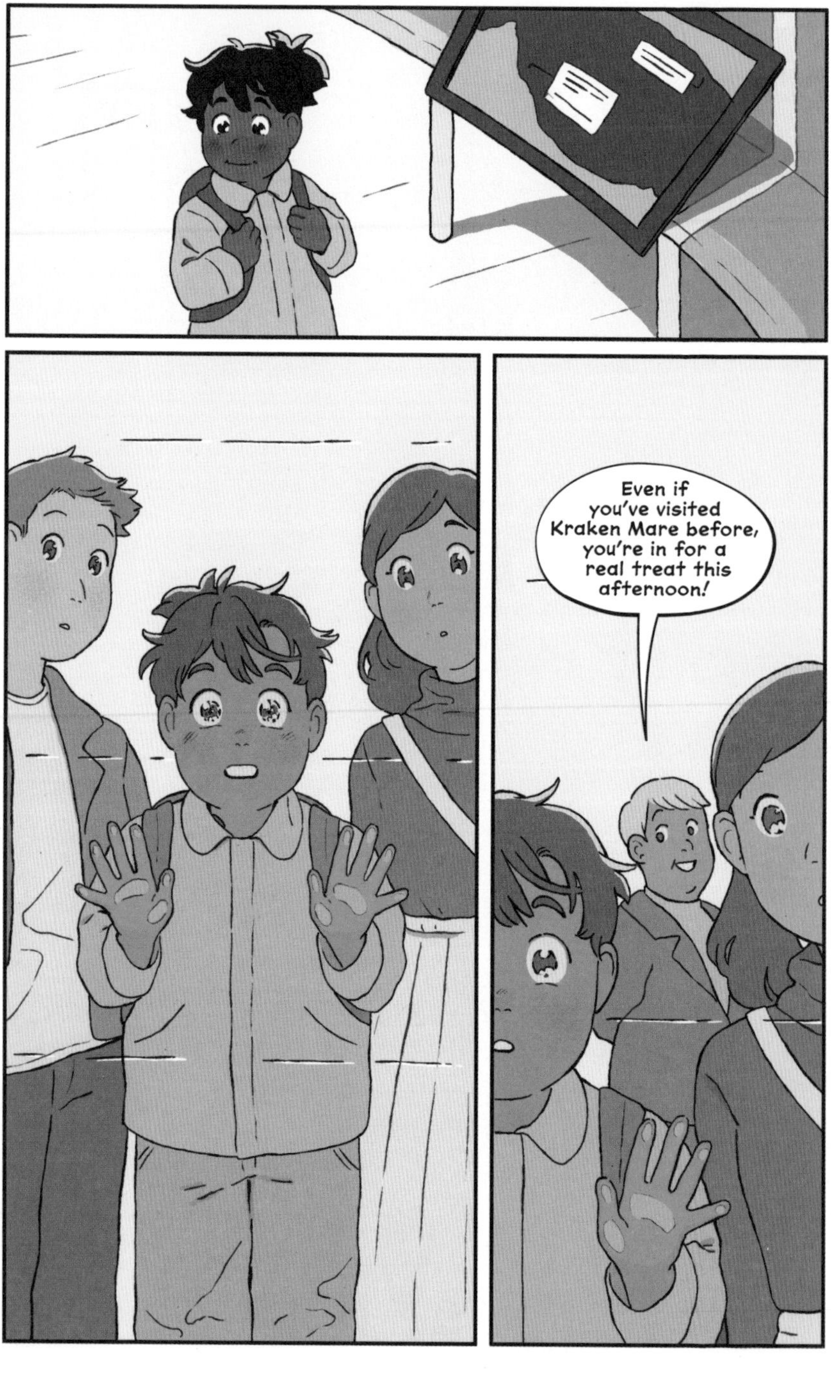
Even if you've visited Kraken Mare before, you're in for a real treat this afternoon!

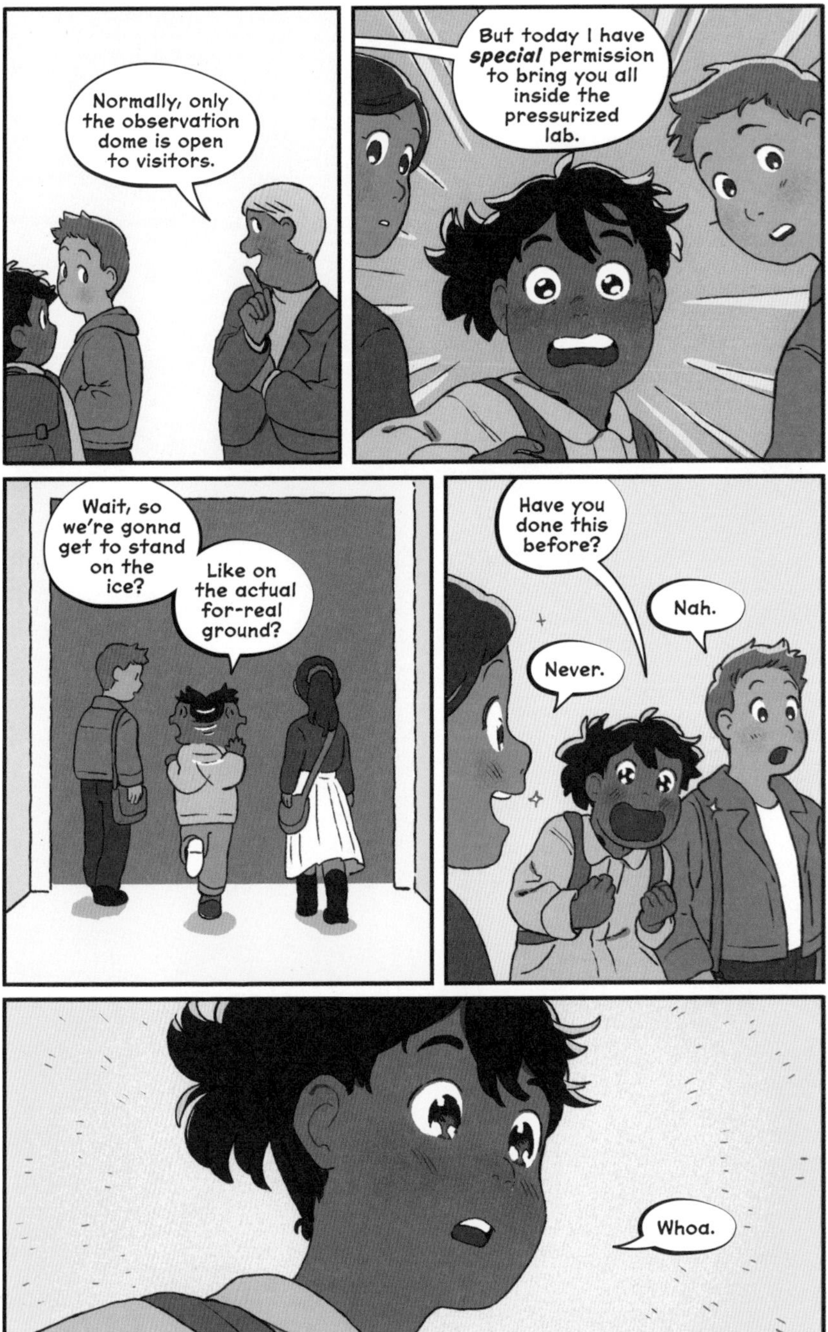
Normally, only the observation dome is open to visitors.
But today I have *special* permission to bring you all inside the pressurized lab.
Wait, so we're gonna get to stand on the ice?
Like on the actual for-real ground?
Have you done this before?
Nah.
Never.
Whoa.

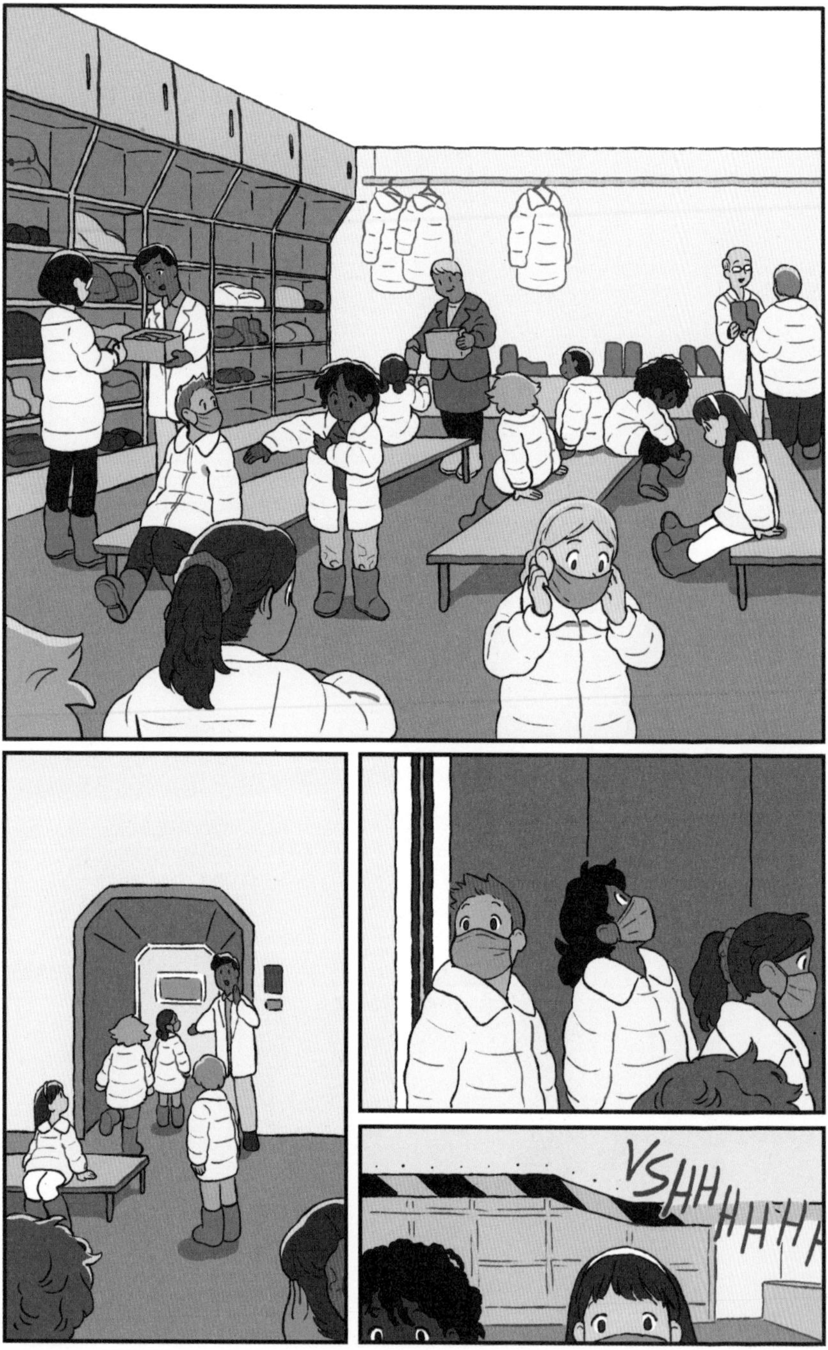
VSHHHHHHH

Watch your step! *The ice can be slippery!*

Make sure to keep your mask in place. Our breath can contaminate the surface and damage the researchers' work.

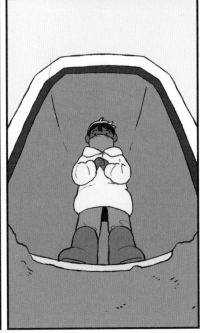

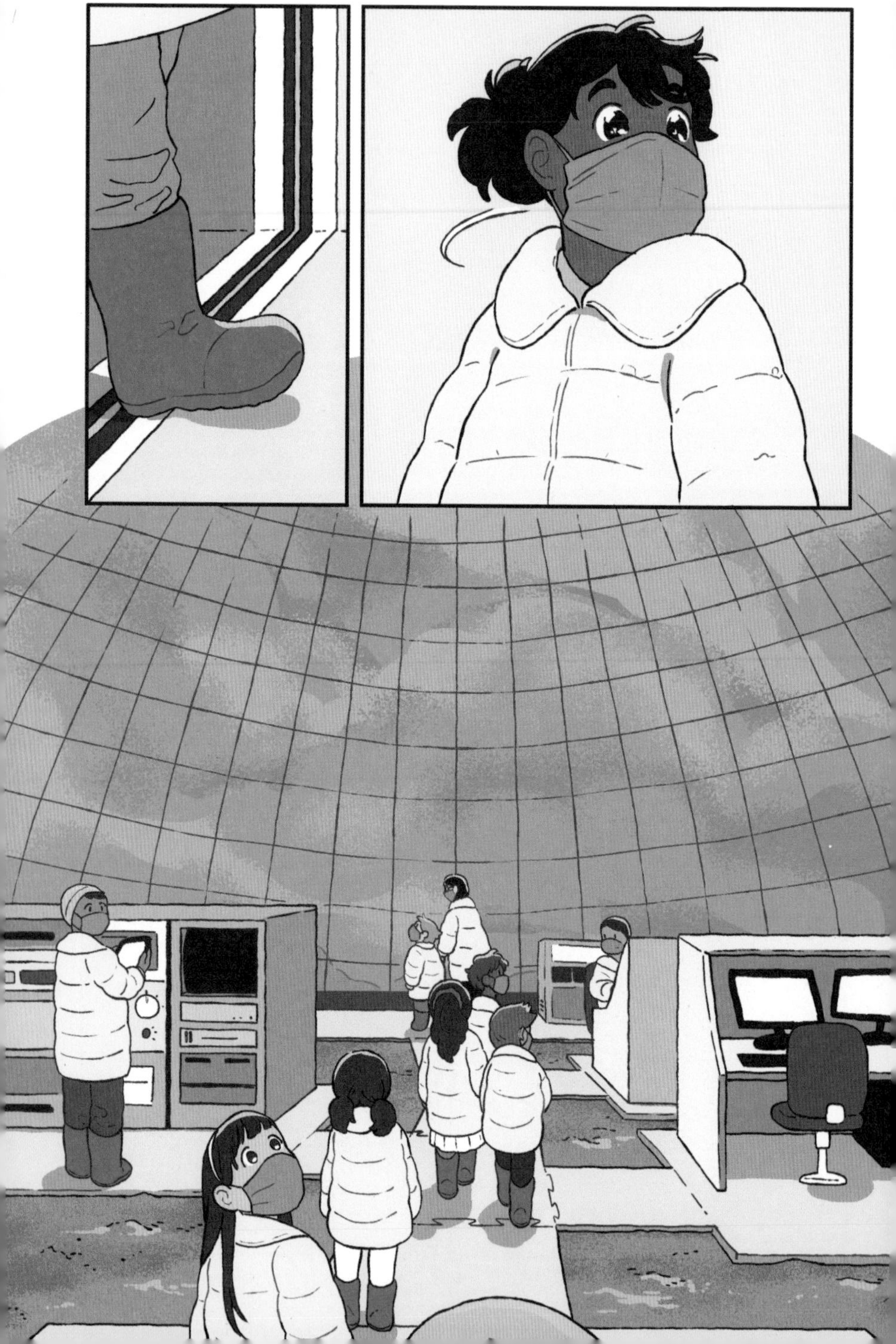

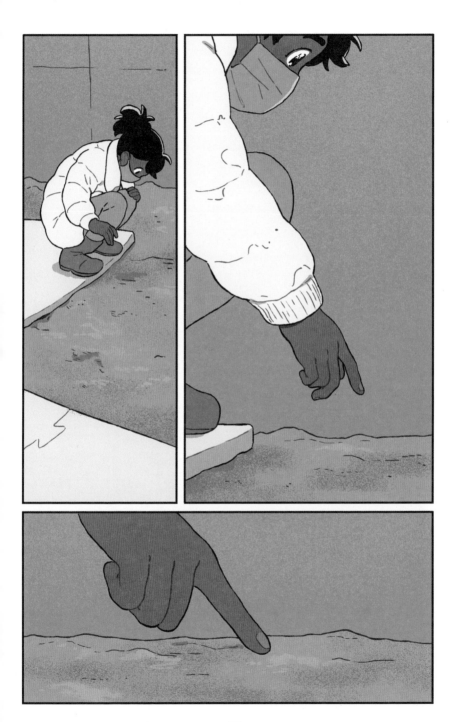

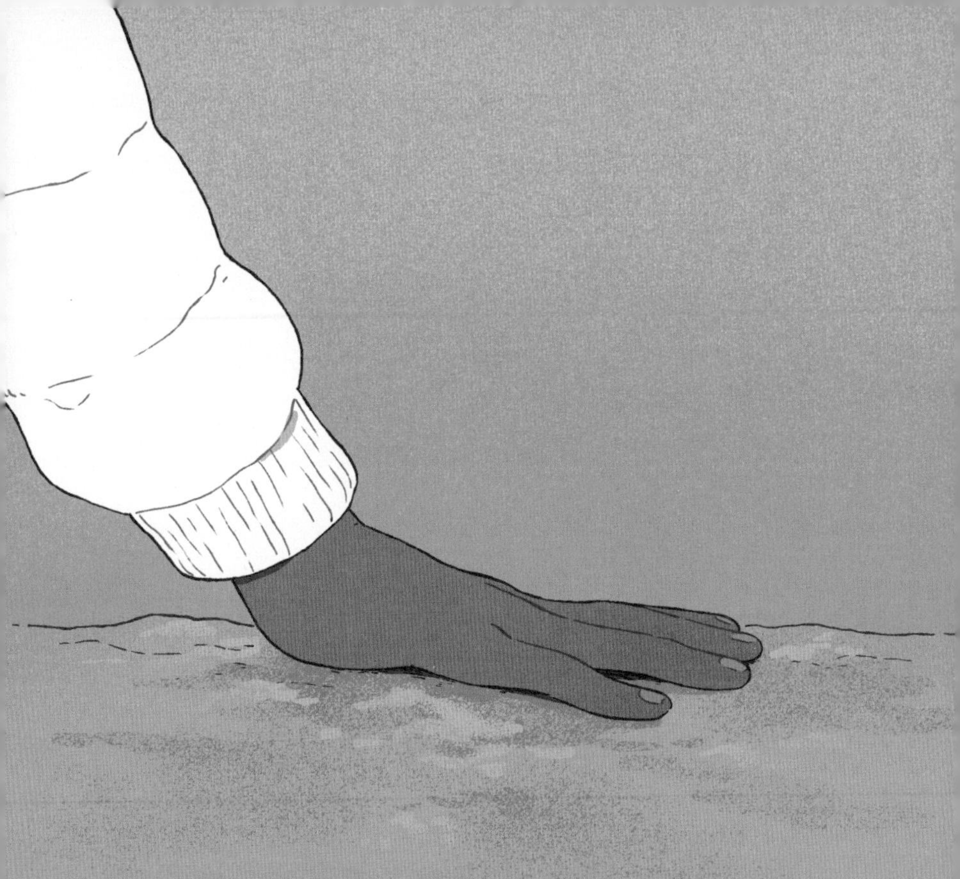
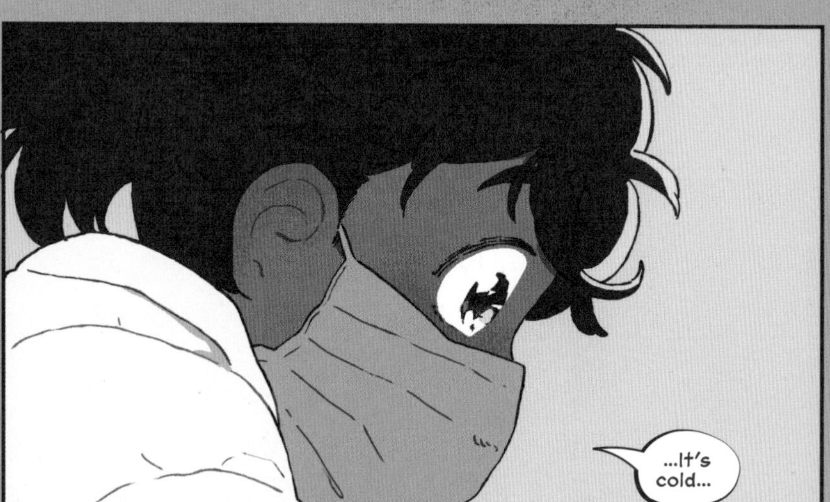
...It's cold...

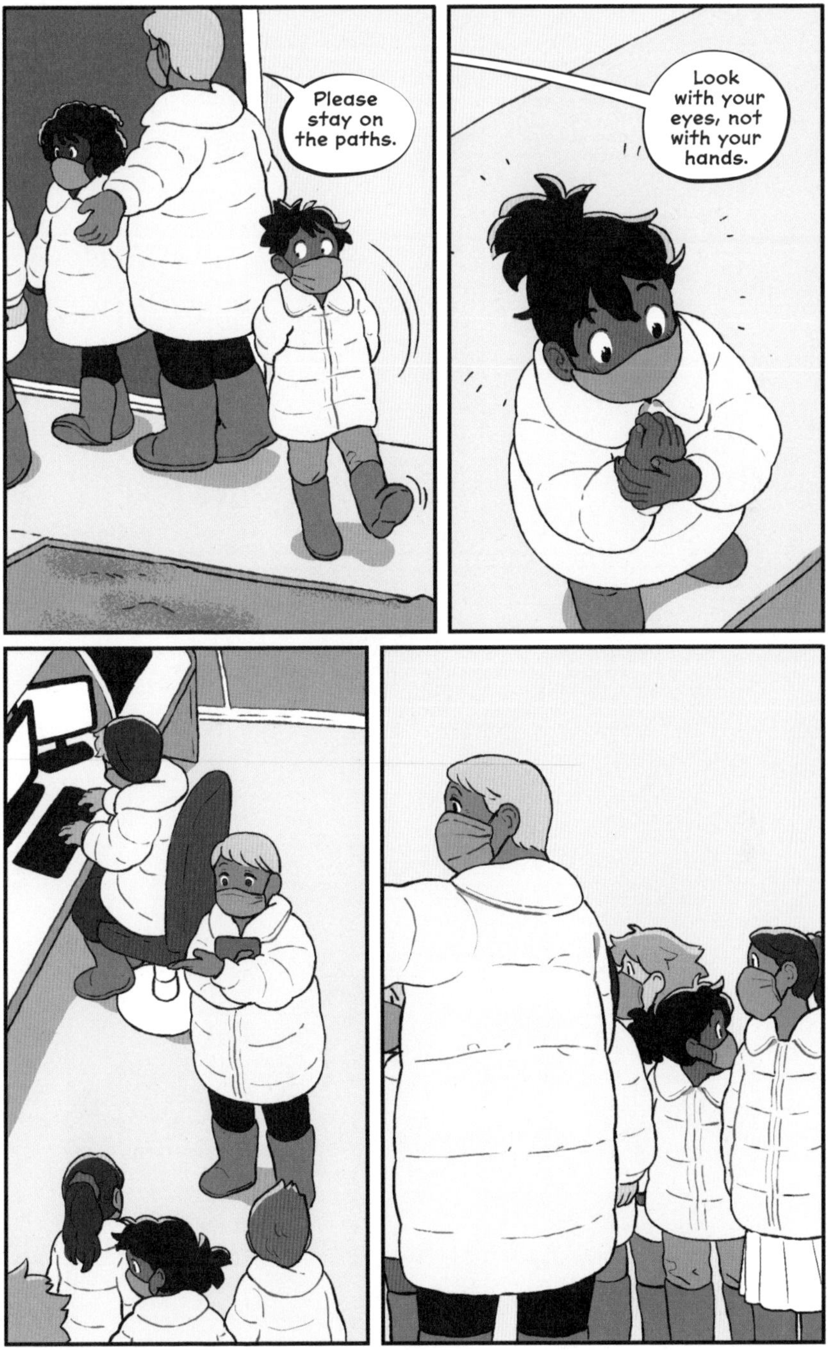
Please stay on the paths.
Look with your eyes, not with your hands.

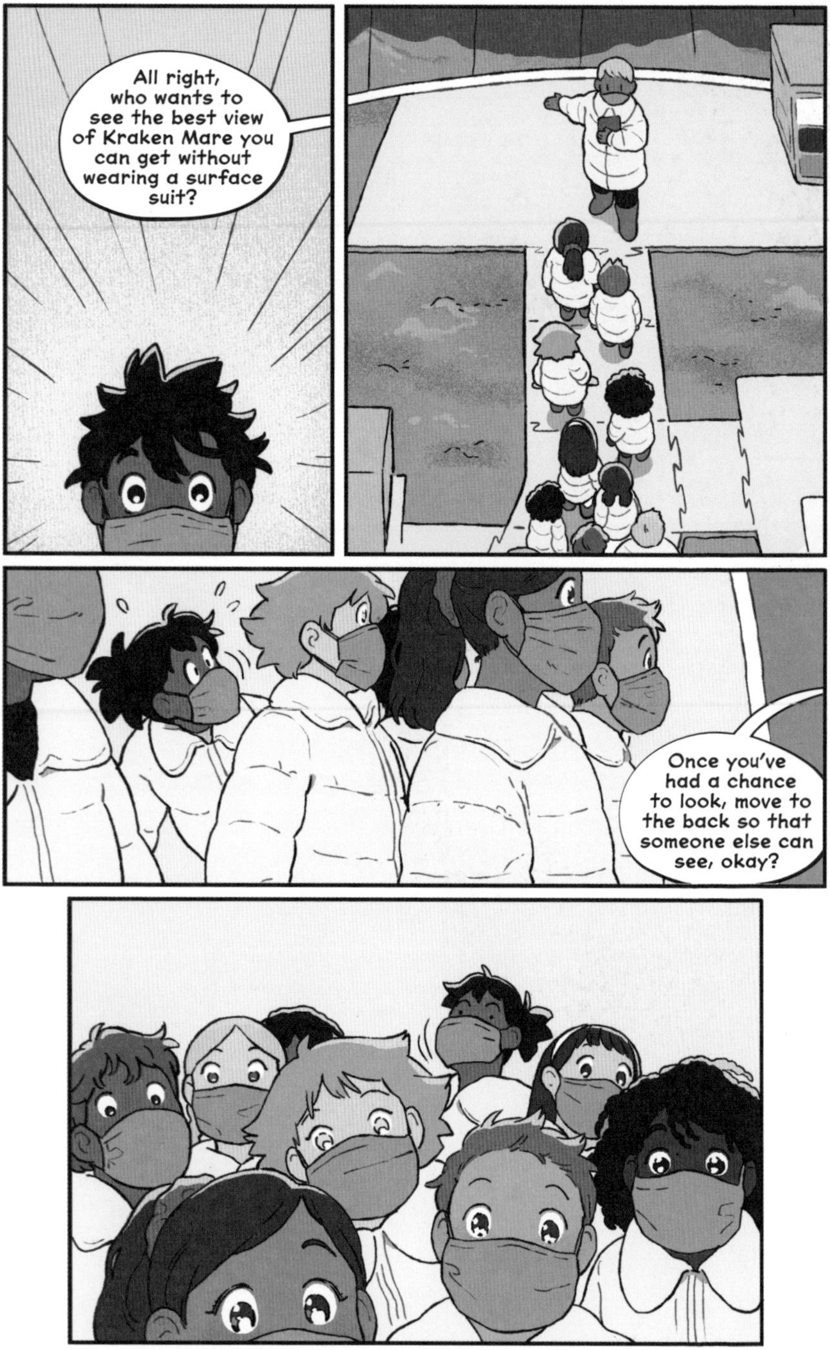
All right, who wants to see the best view of Kraken Mare you can get without wearing a surface suit?
Once you've had a chance to look, move to the back so that someone else can see, okay?

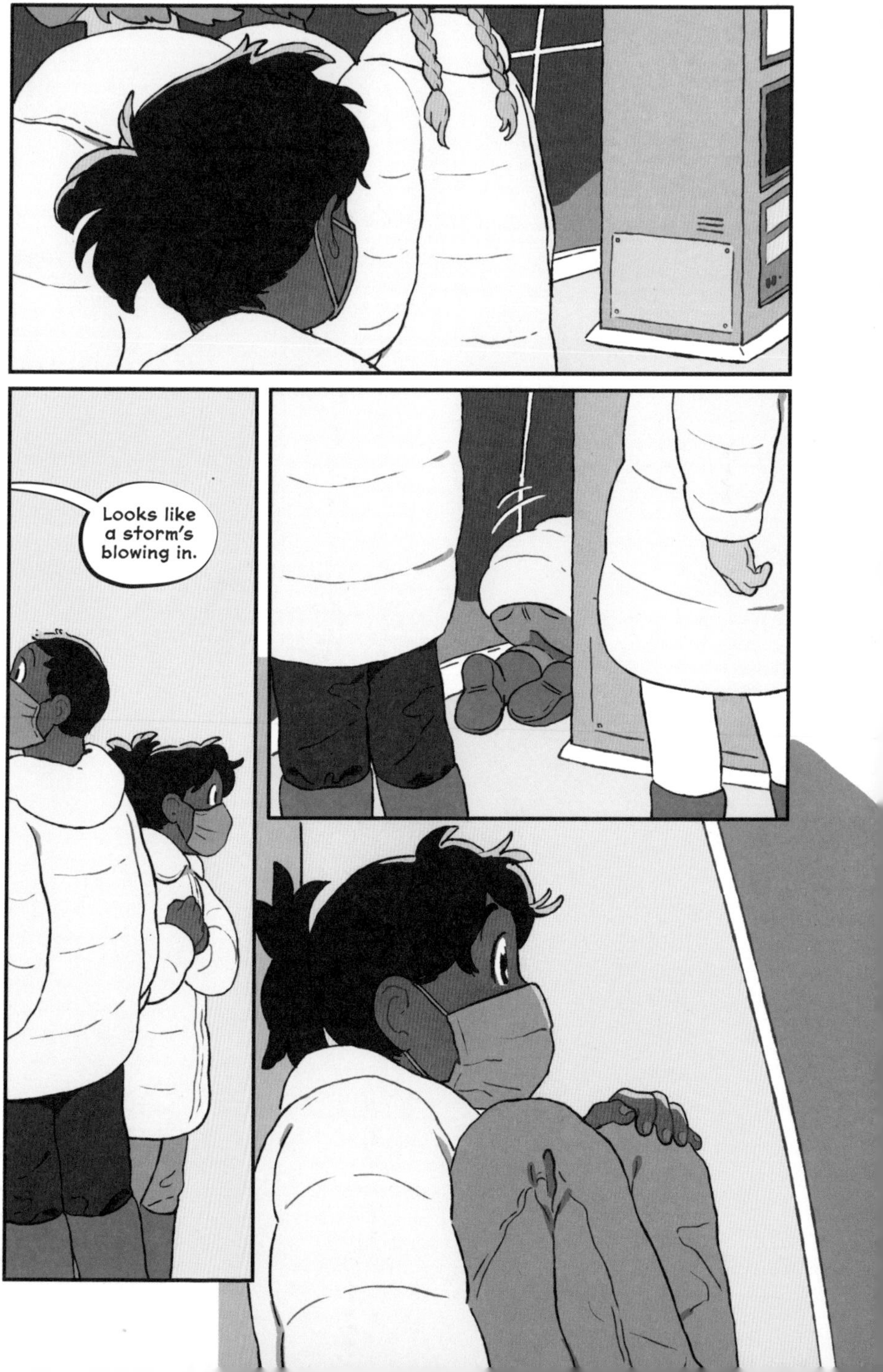
Looks like a storm's blowing in.

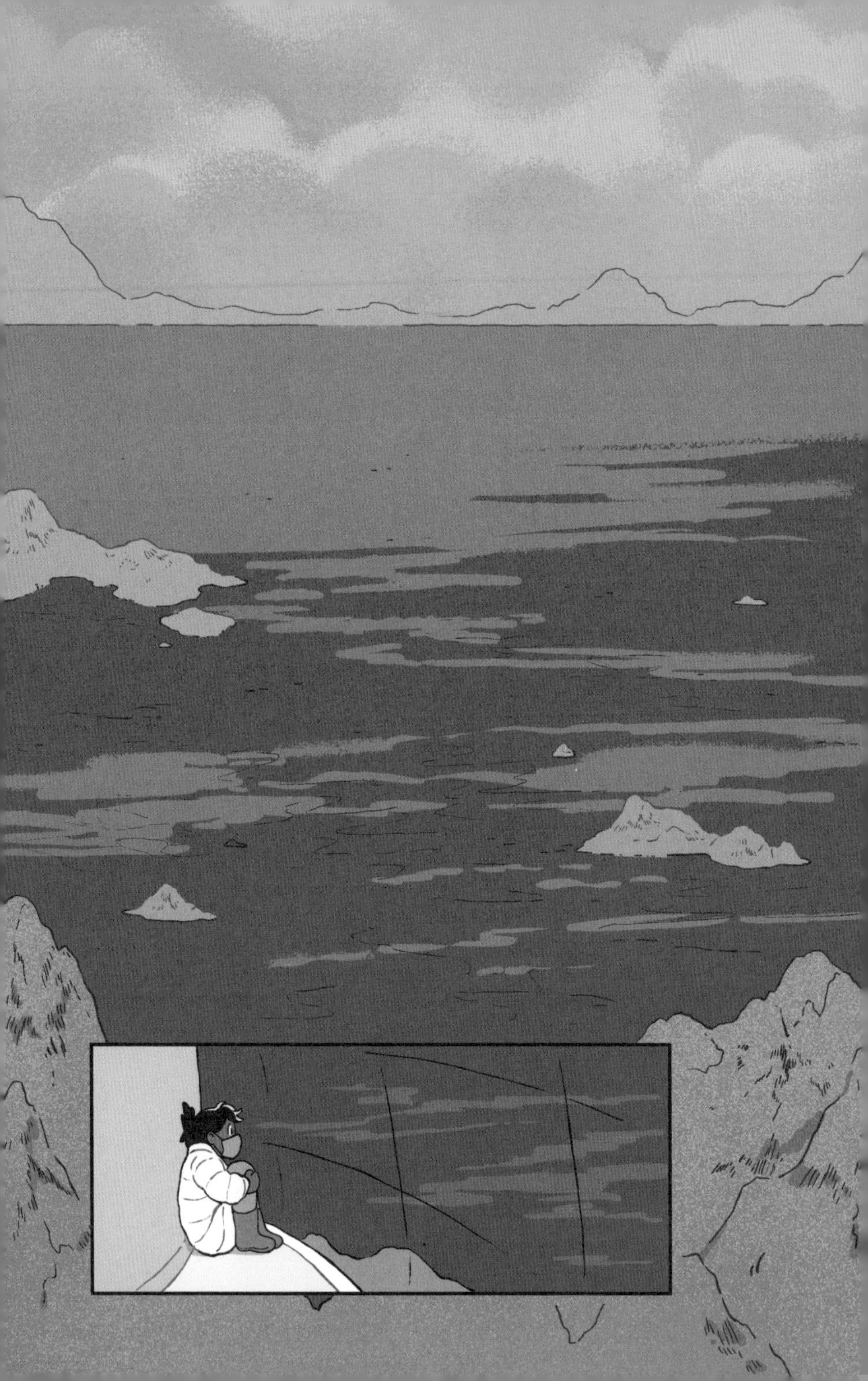

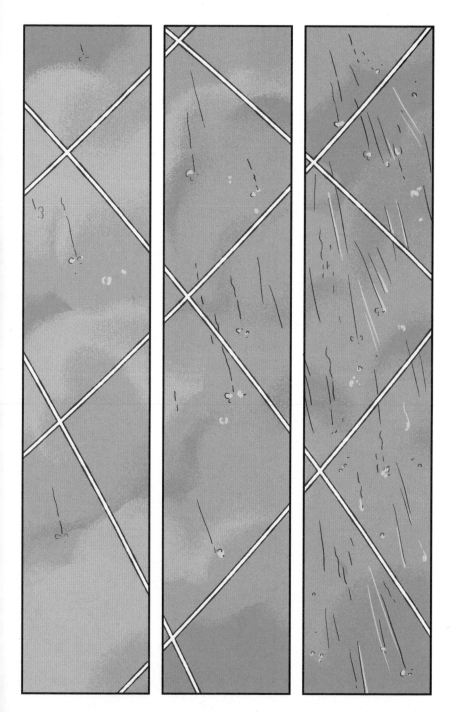

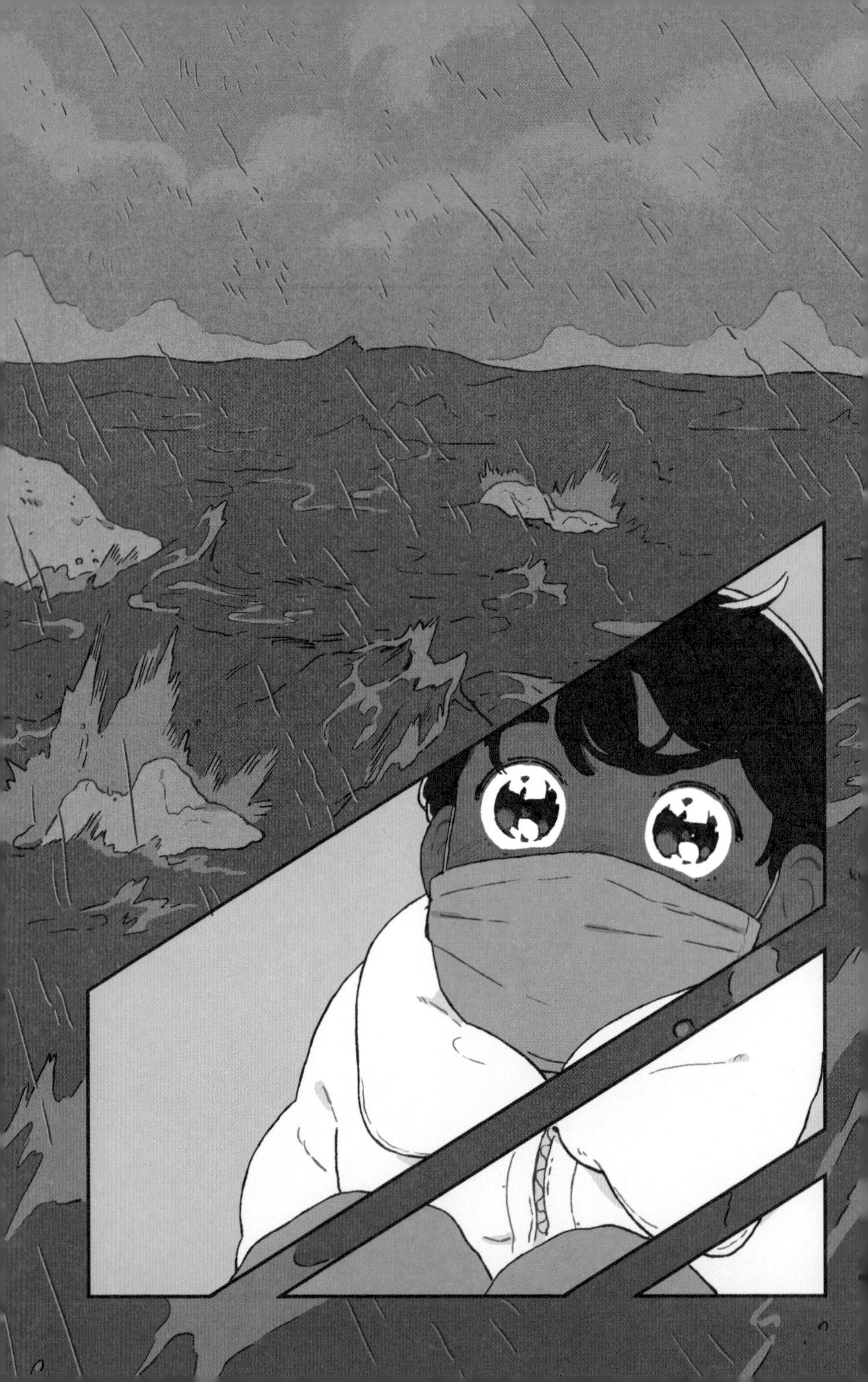

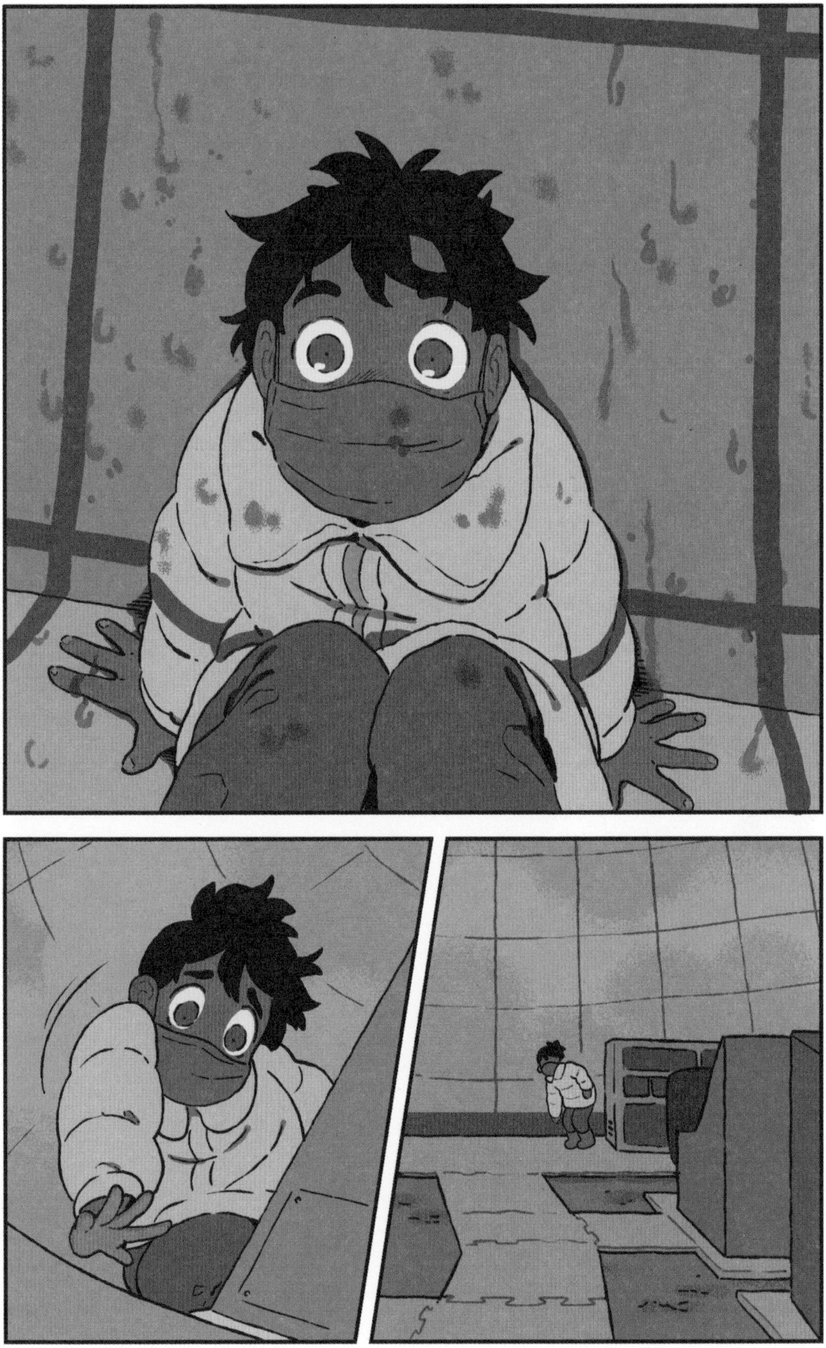

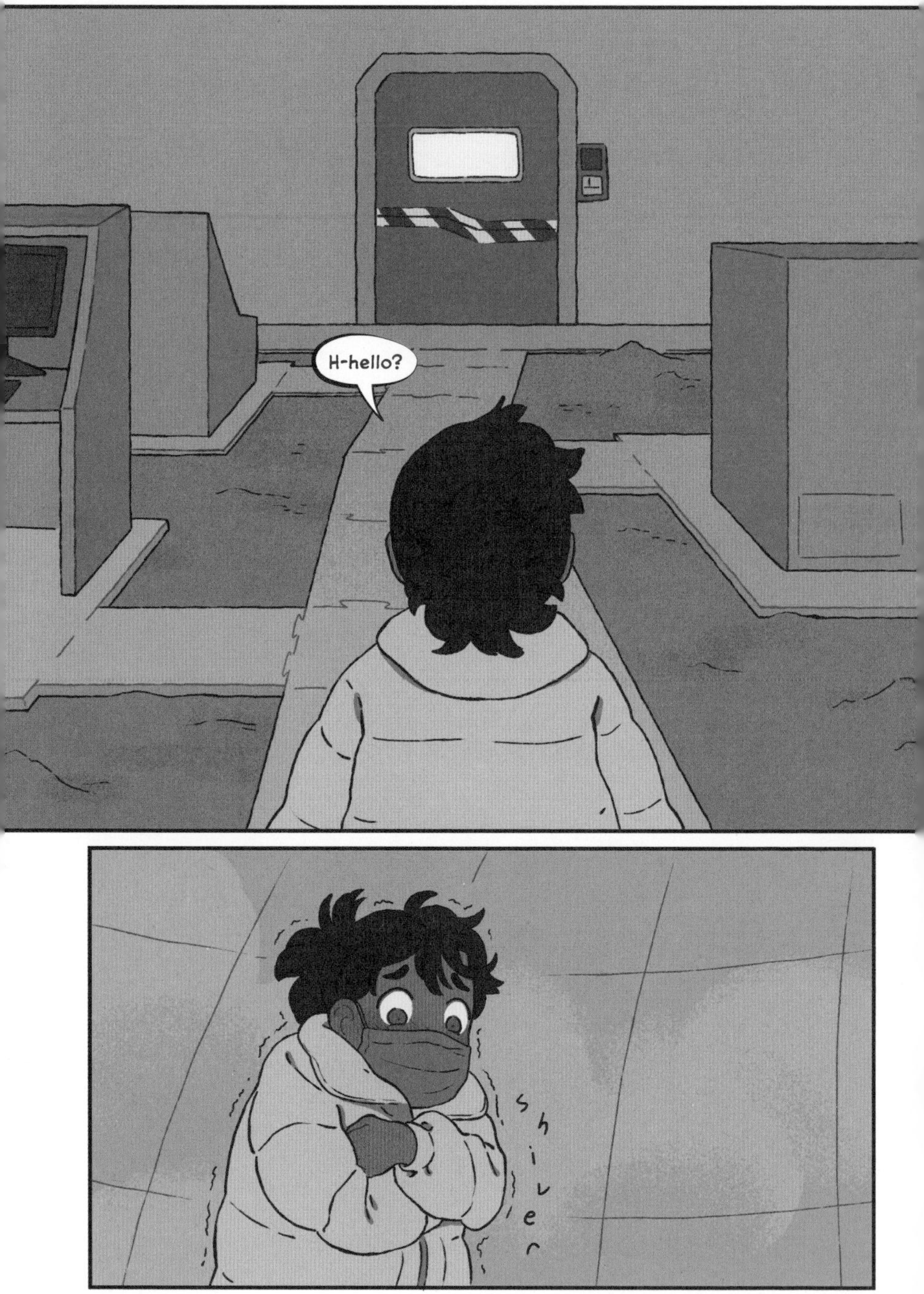
H-hello?
shiver

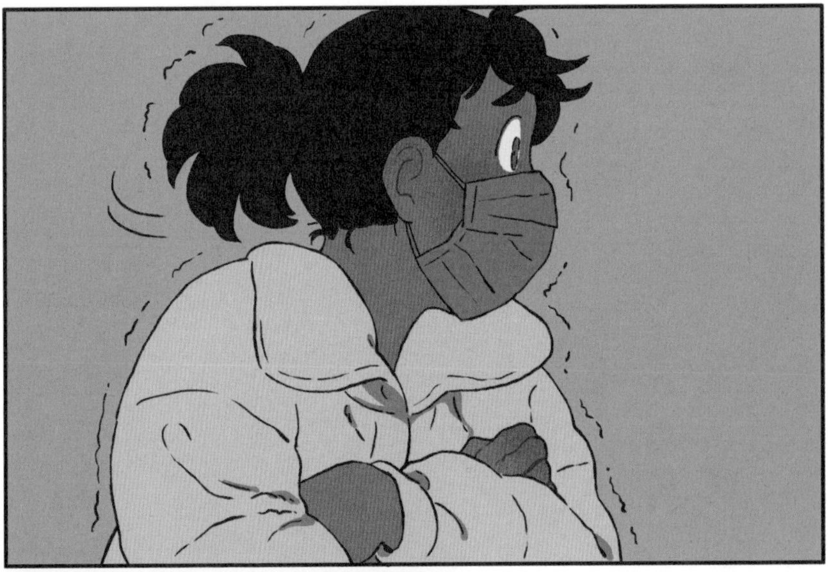

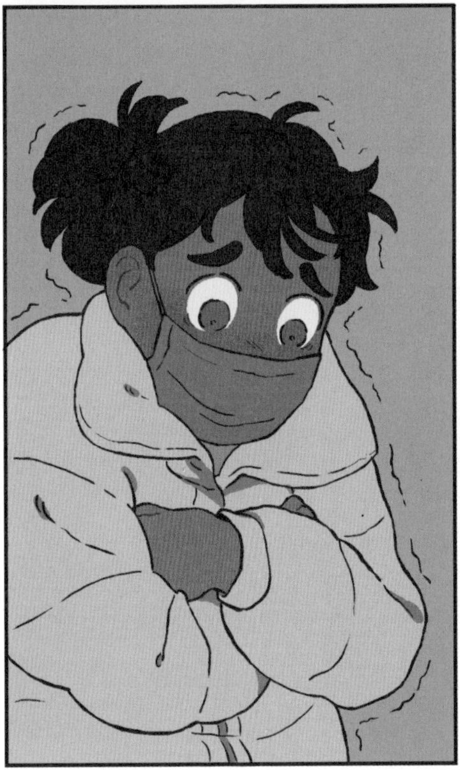

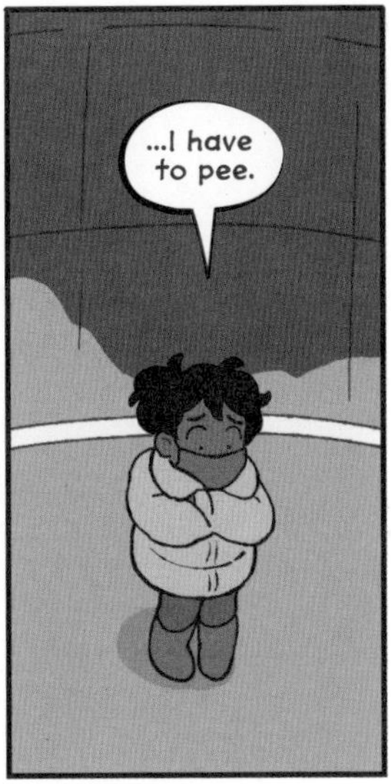
...I have to pee.

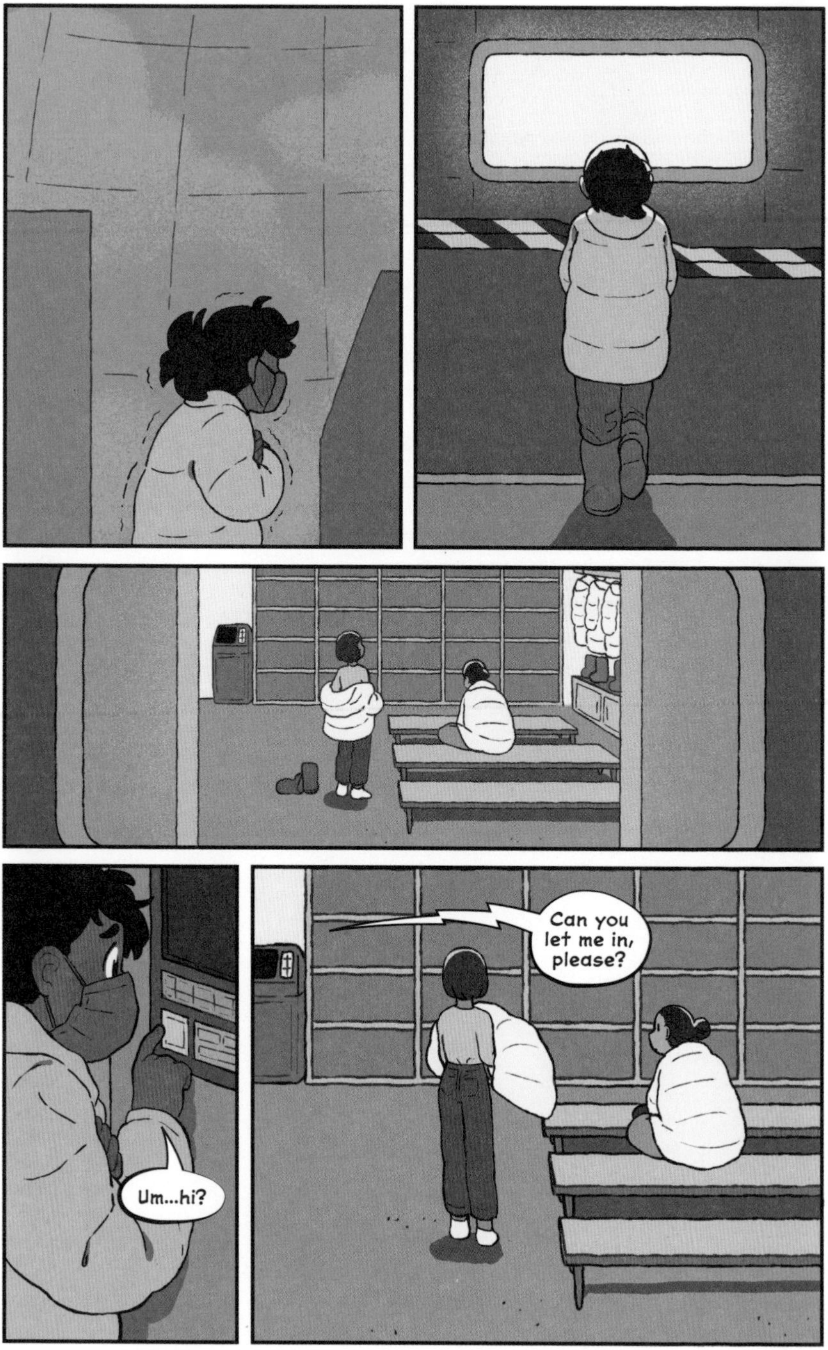
Um...hi?
Can you let me in, please?

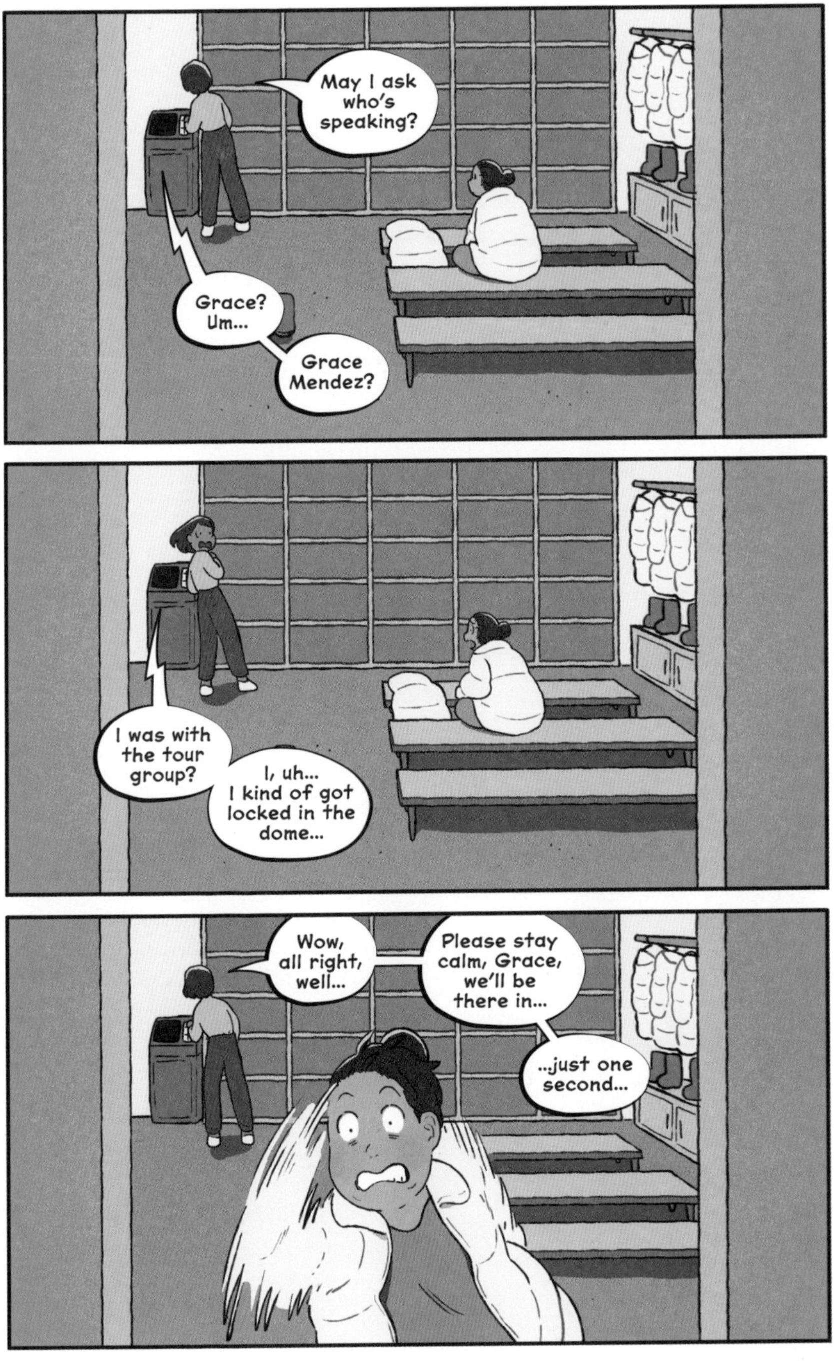
May I ask who's speaking?
Grace? Um...
Grace Mendez?
I was with the tour group?
I, uh... I kind of got locked in the dome...
Wow, all right, well...
Please stay calm, Grace, we'll be there in...
...just one second...

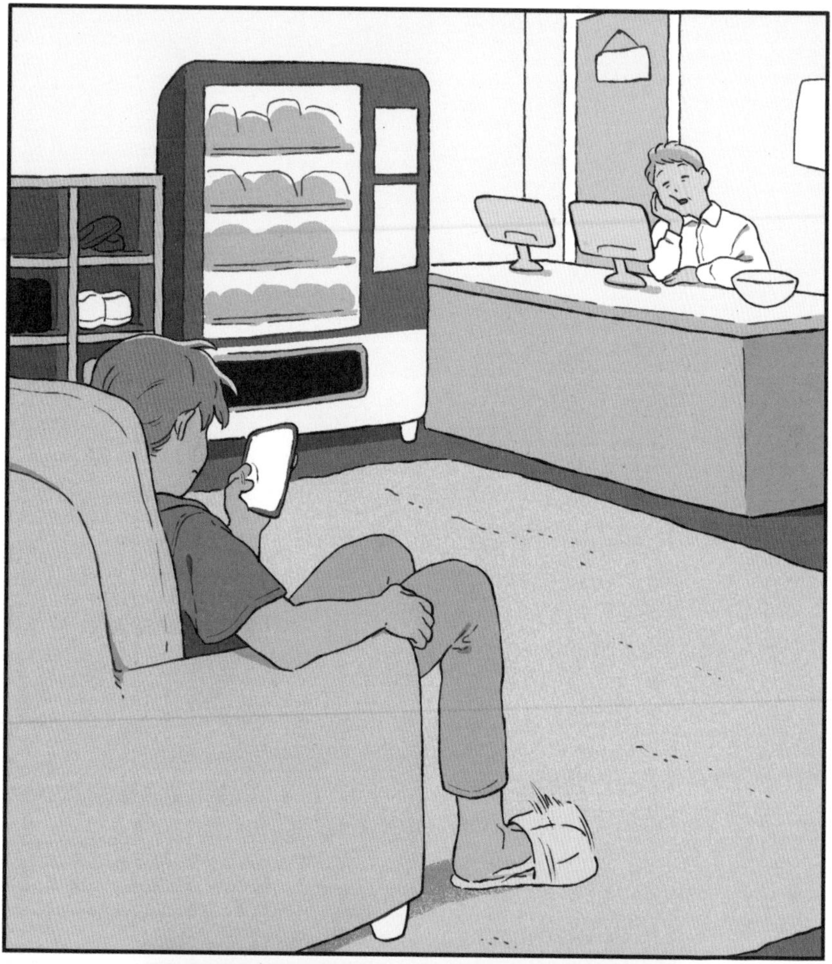

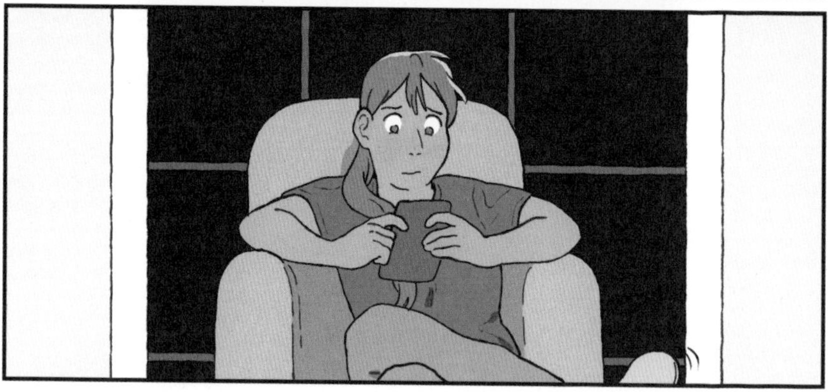

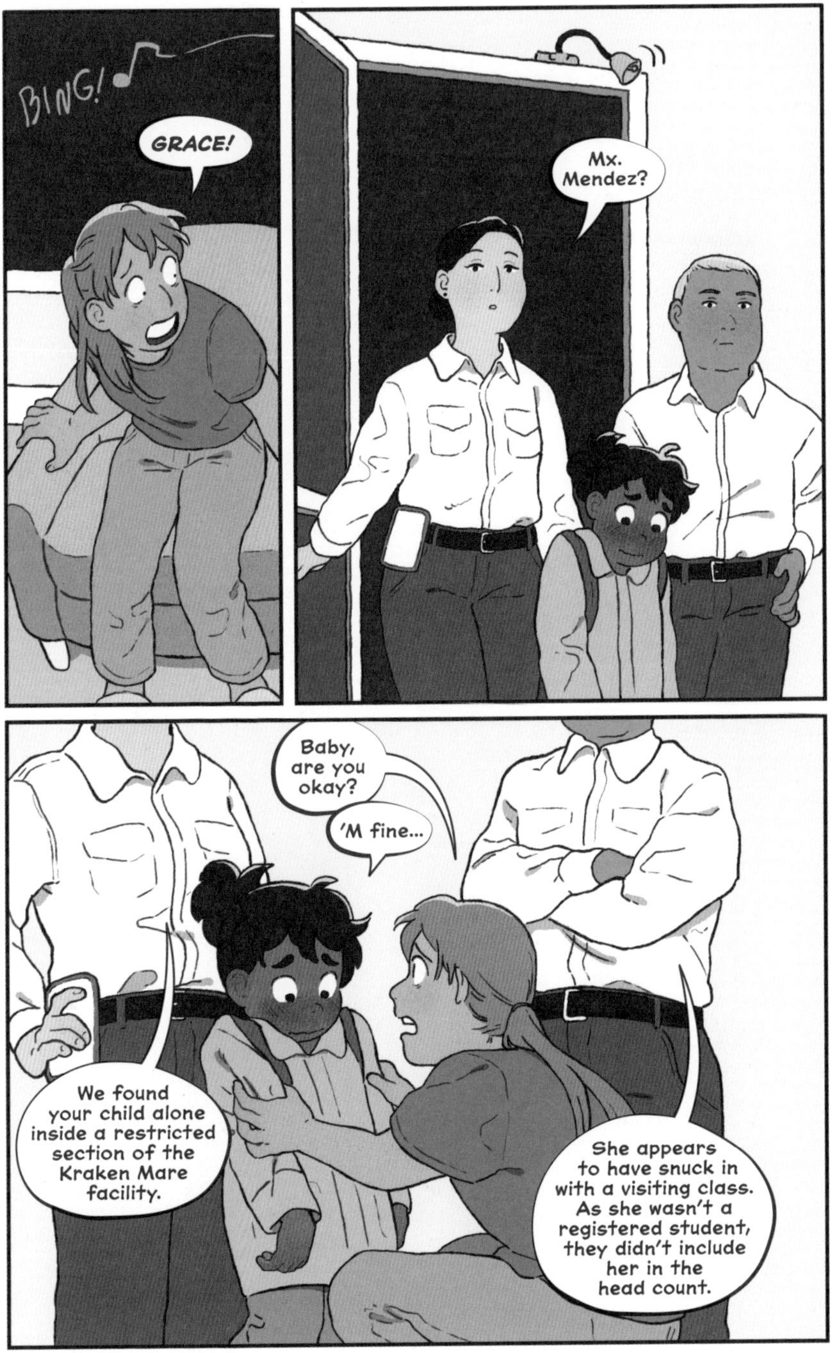
BING!
GRACE!
Mx. Mendez?
Baby, are you okay?
'M fine...
We found your child alone inside a restricted section of the Kraken Mare facility.
She appears to have snuck in with a visiting class. As she wasn't a registered student, they didn't include her in the head count.

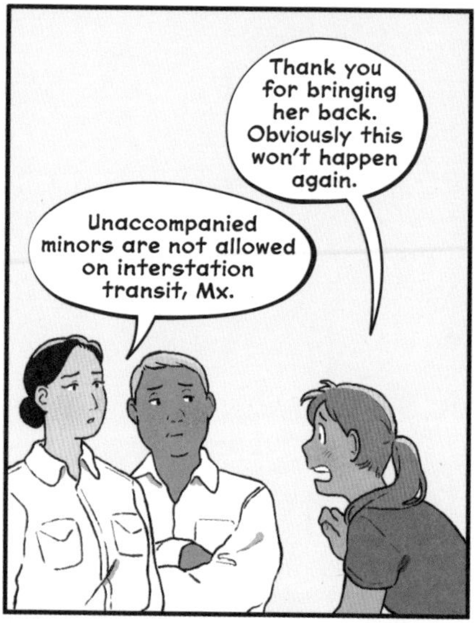
Unaccompanied minors are not allowed on interstation transit, Mx.
Thank you for bringing her back. Obviously this won't happen again.
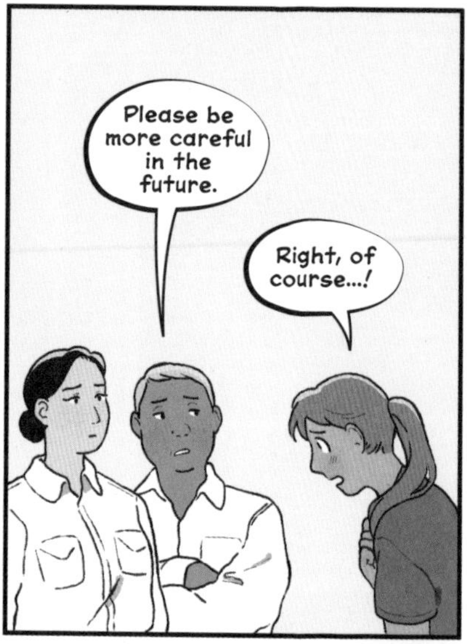
Please be more careful in the future.
Right, of course...!
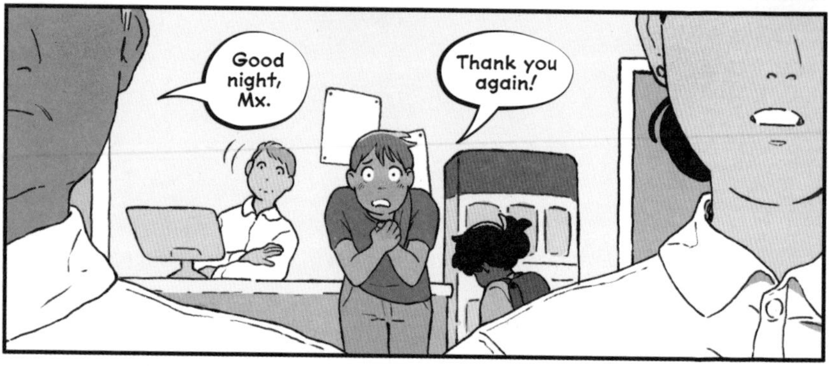
Good night, Mx.
Thank you again!
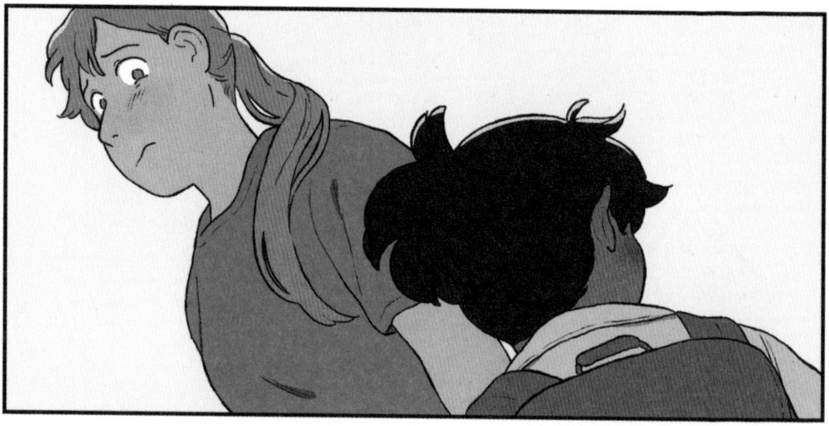

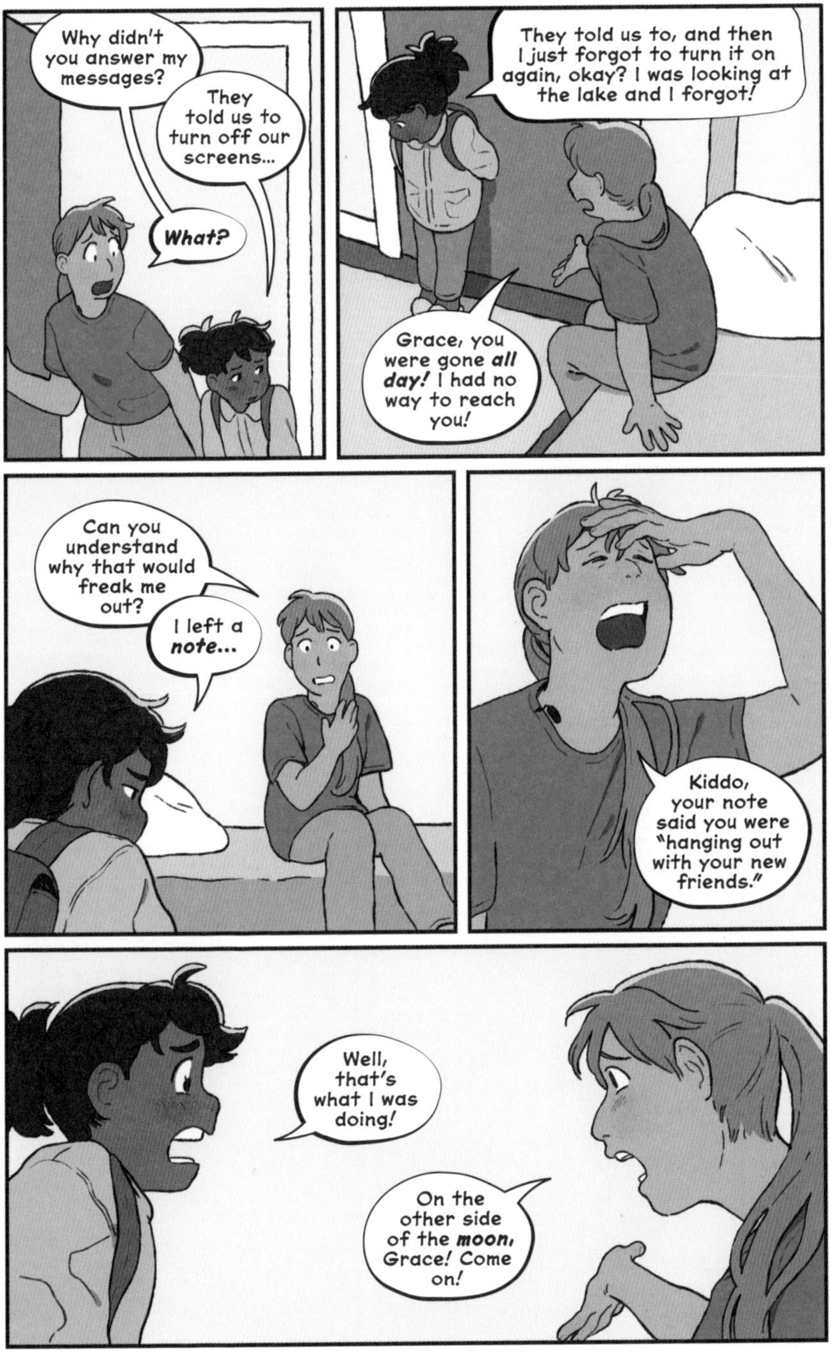
Why didn't you answer my messages?
They told us to turn off our screens...
What?
They told us to, and then I just forgot to turn it on again, okay? I was looking at the lake and I forgot!
Grace, you were gone all day! I had no way to reach you!
Can you understand why that would freak me out?
I left a note...
Kiddo, your note said you were "hanging out with your new friends."
Well, that's what I was doing!
On the other side of the moon, Grace! Come on!

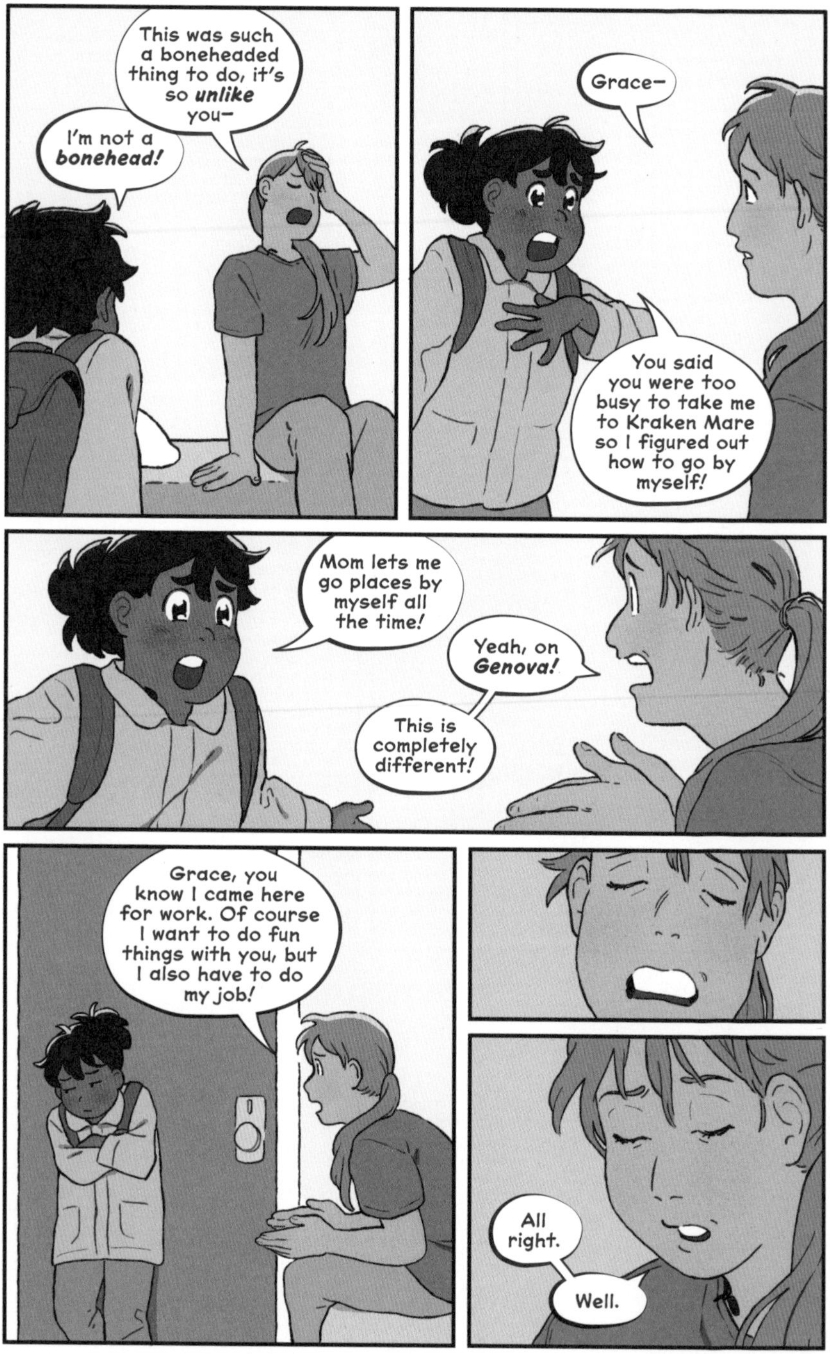
This was such a boneheaded thing to do, it's so *unlike* you–
I'm not a *bonehead!*
Grace–
You said you were too busy to take me to Kraken Mare so I figured out how to go by myself!
Mom lets me go places by myself all the time!
Yeah, on *Genova!*
This is completely different!
Grace, you know I came here for work. Of course I want to do fun things with you, but I also have to do my job!
All right.
Well.

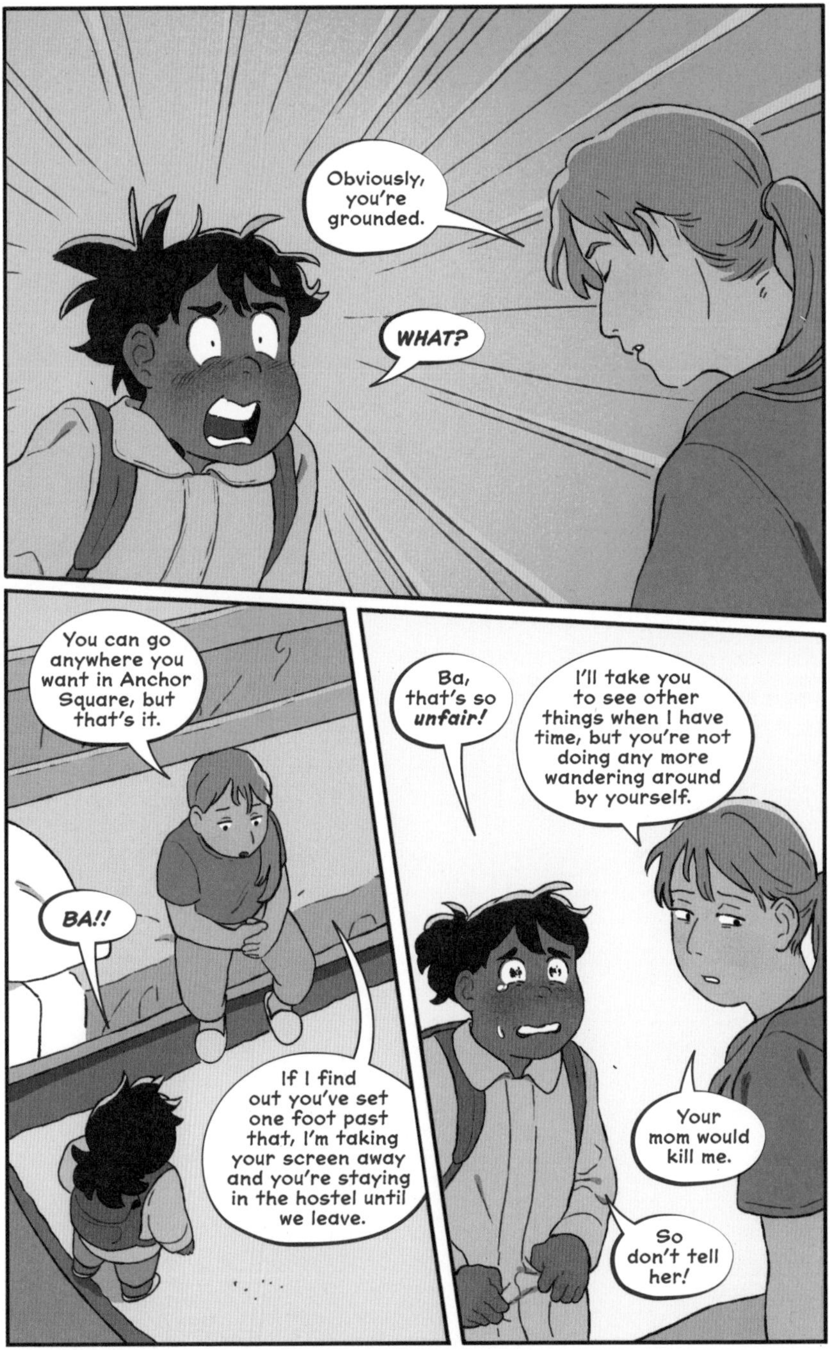
Obviously, you're grounded.
WHAT?
You can go anywhere you want in Anchor Square, but that's it.
BA!!
If I find out you've set one foot past that, I'm taking your screen away and you're staying in the hostel until we leave.
Ba, that's so *unfair!*
I'll take you to see other things when I have time, but you're not doing any more wandering around by yourself.
Your mom would kill me.
So don't tell her!

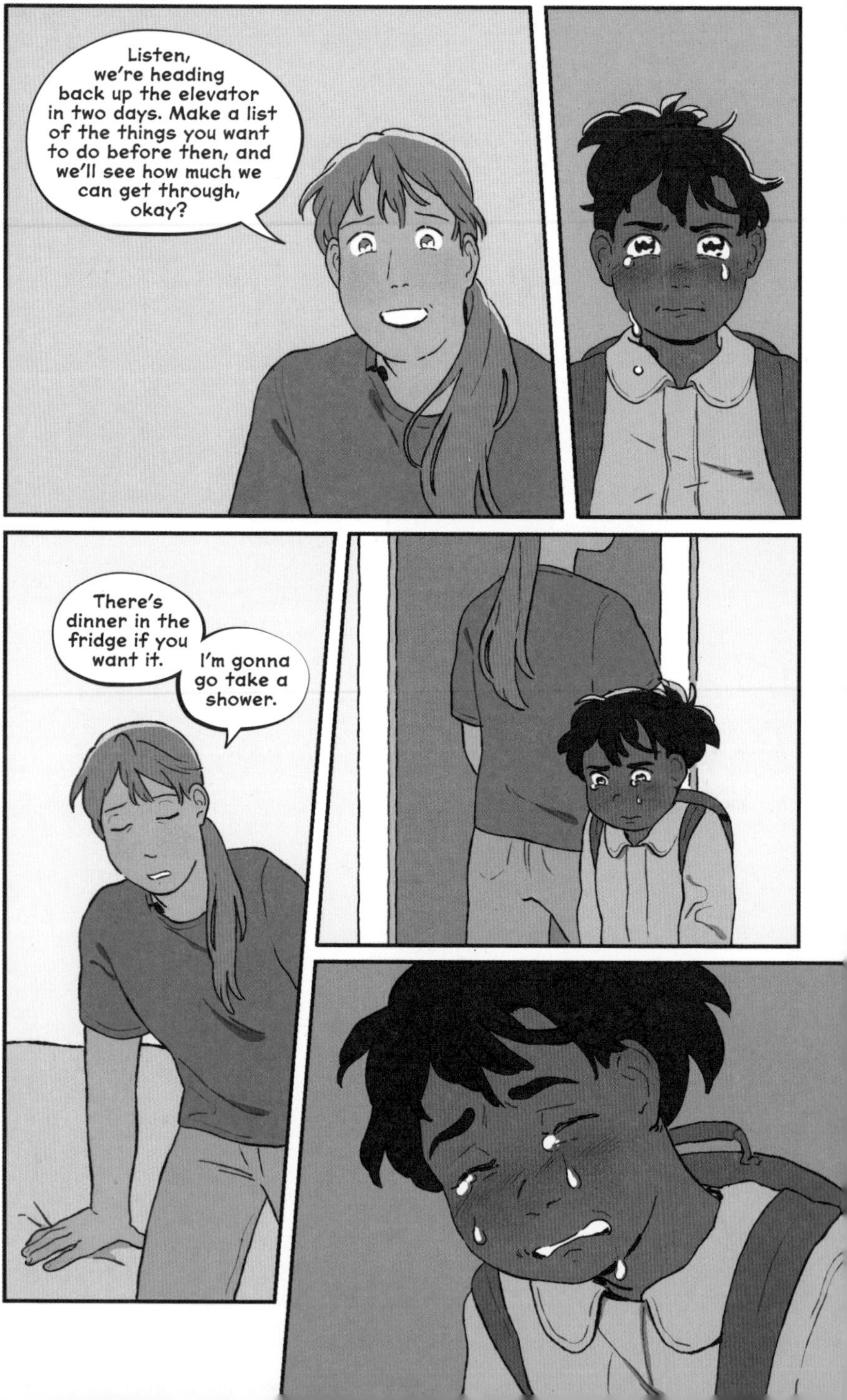

Listen, we're heading back up the elevator in two days. Make a list of the things you want to do before then, and we'll see how much we can get through, okay?
There's dinner in the fridge if you want it.
I'm gonna go take a shower.

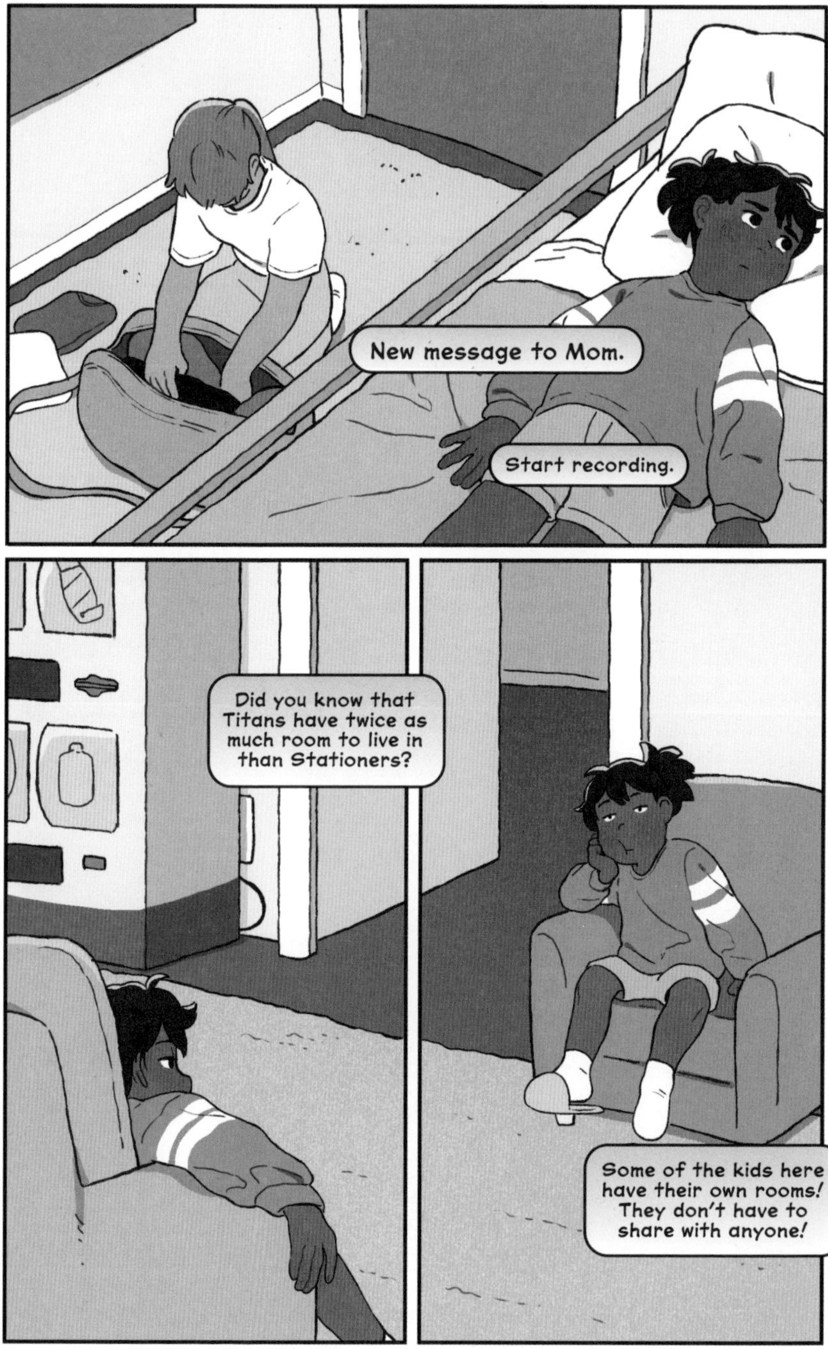
New message to Mom.
Start recording.
Did you know that Titans have twice as much room to live in than Stationers?
Some of the kids here have their own rooms! They don't have to share with anyone!

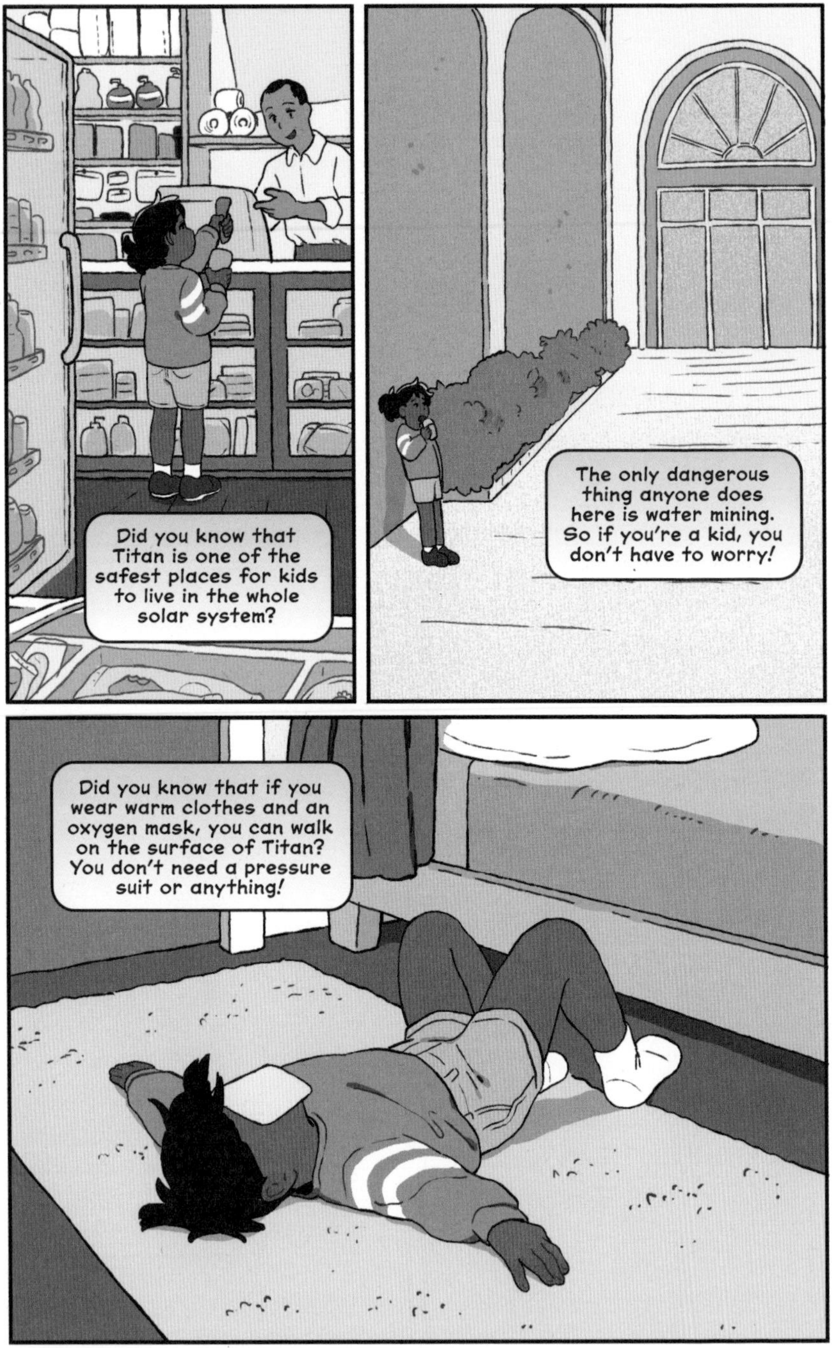
Did you know that Titan is one of the safest places for kids to live in the whole solar system?
The only dangerous thing anyone does here is water mining. So if you're a kid, you don't have to worry!
Did you know that if you wear warm clothes and an oxygen mask, you can walk on the surface of Titan? You don't need a pressure suit or anything!

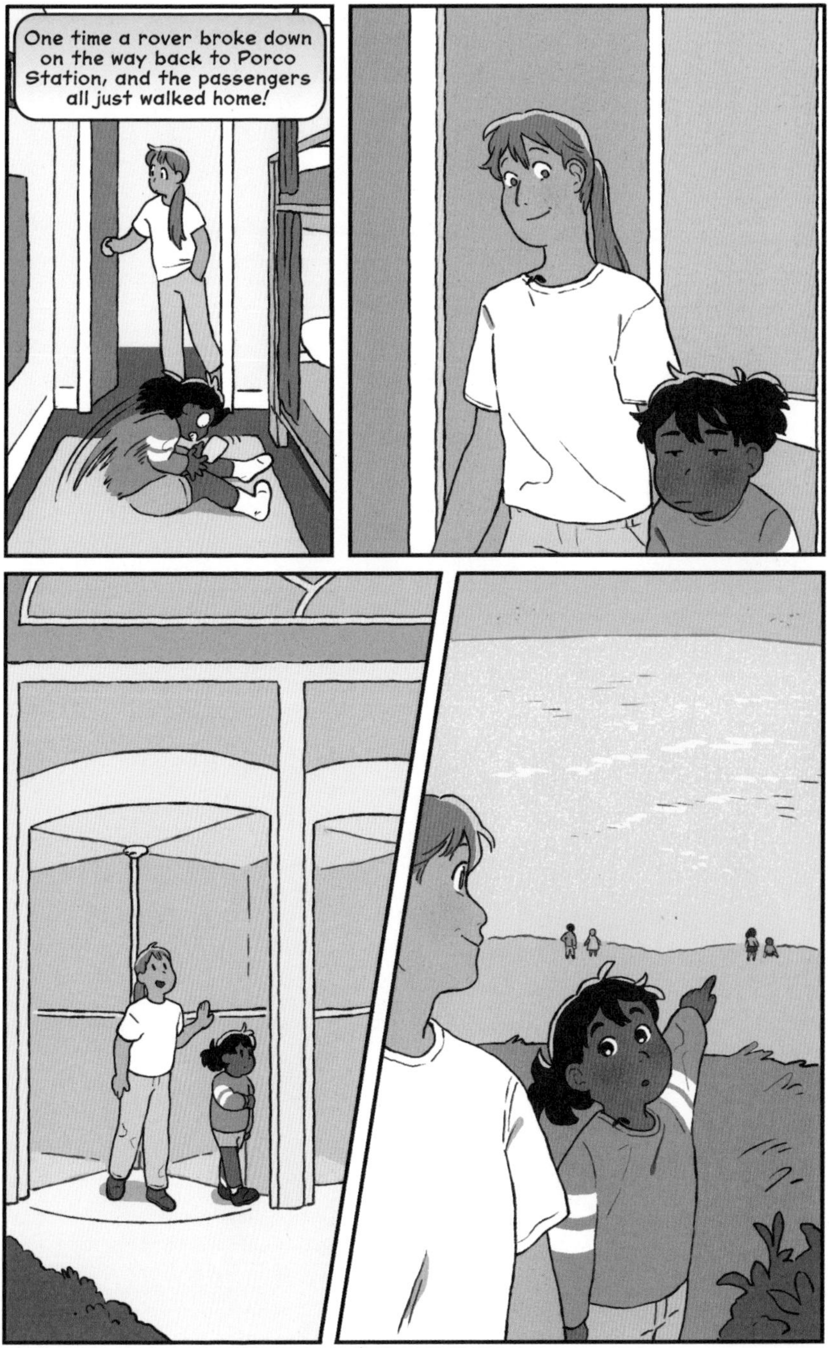
One time a rover broke down on the way back to Porco Station, and the passengers all just walked home!

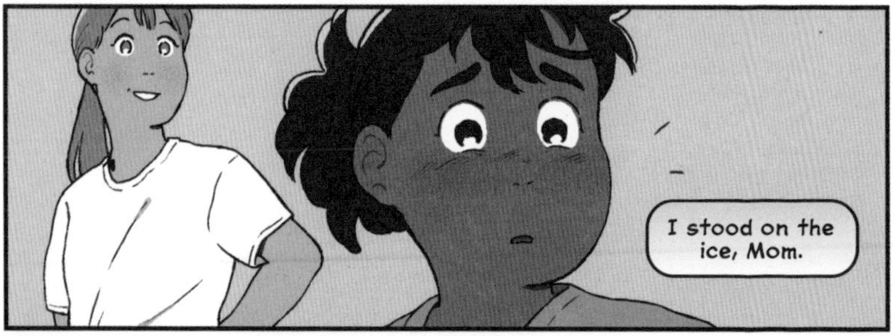
I stood on the ice, Mom.

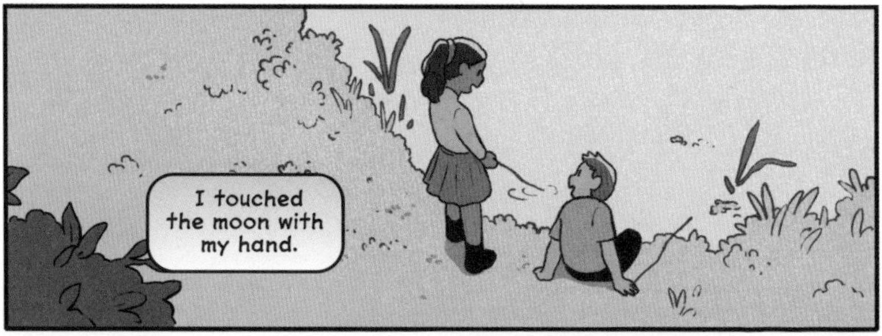
I touched the moon with my hand.

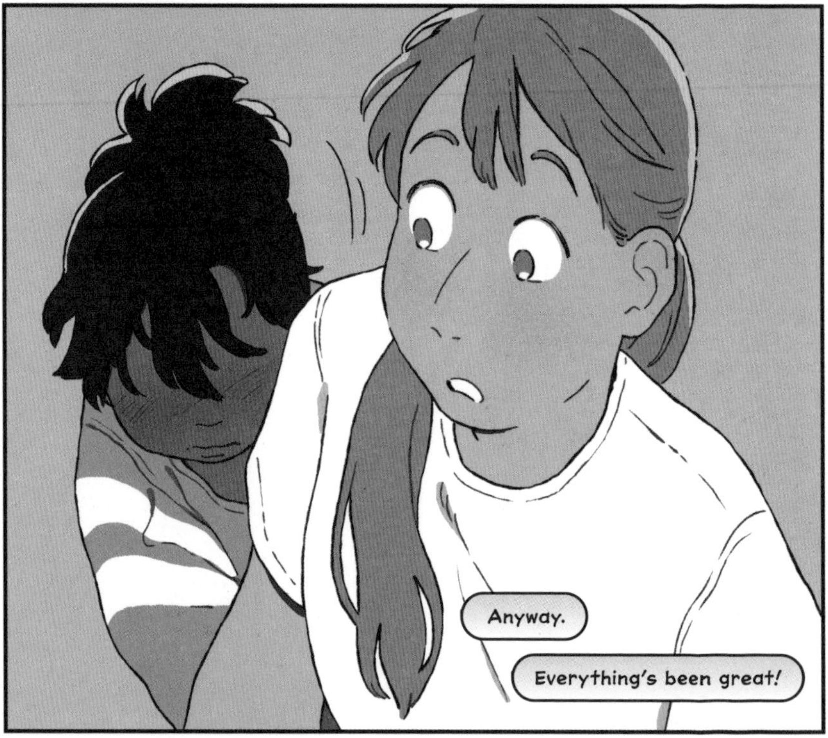
Anyway.
Everything's been great!

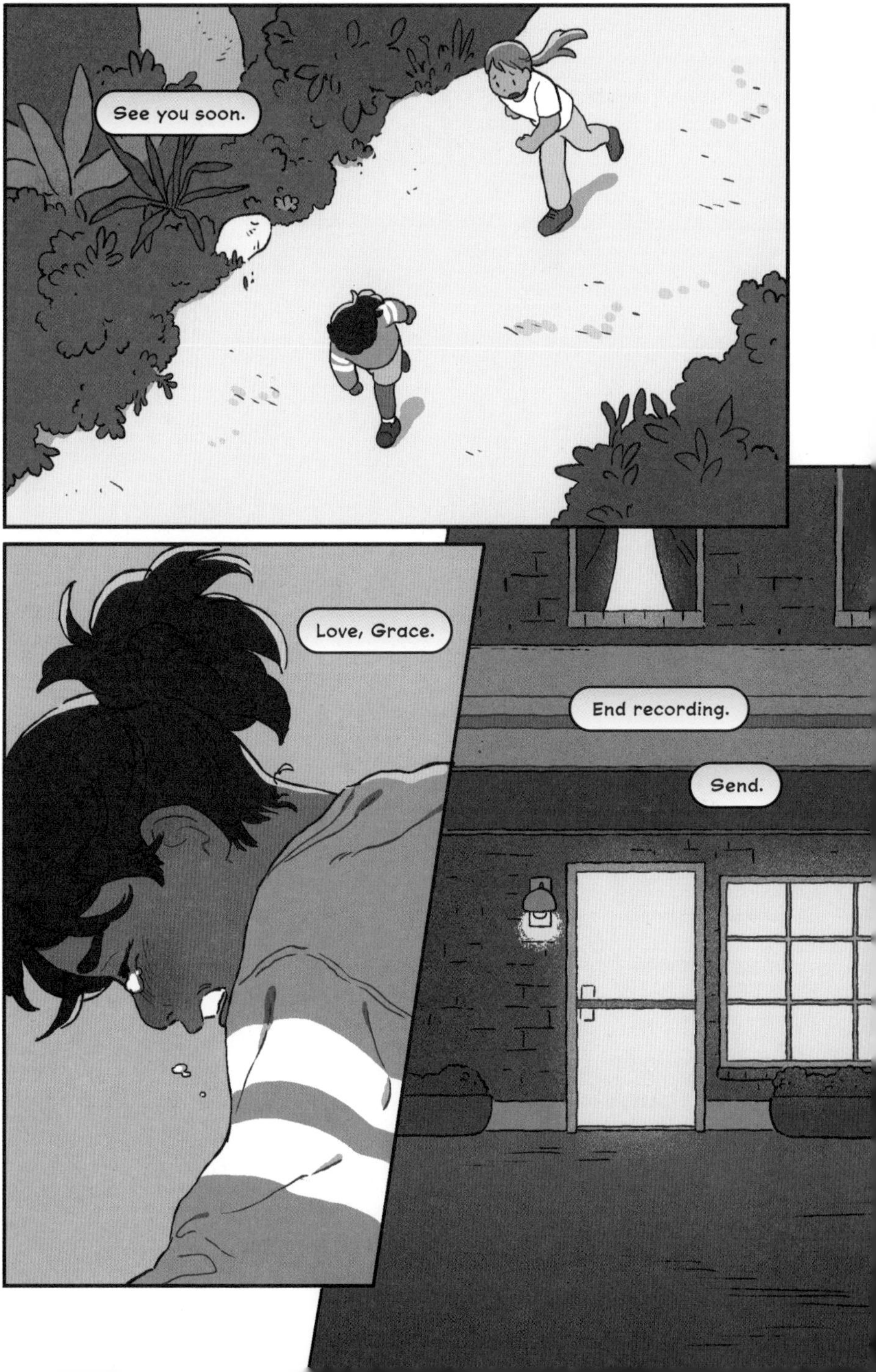
See you soon.
Love, Grace.
End recording.
Send.

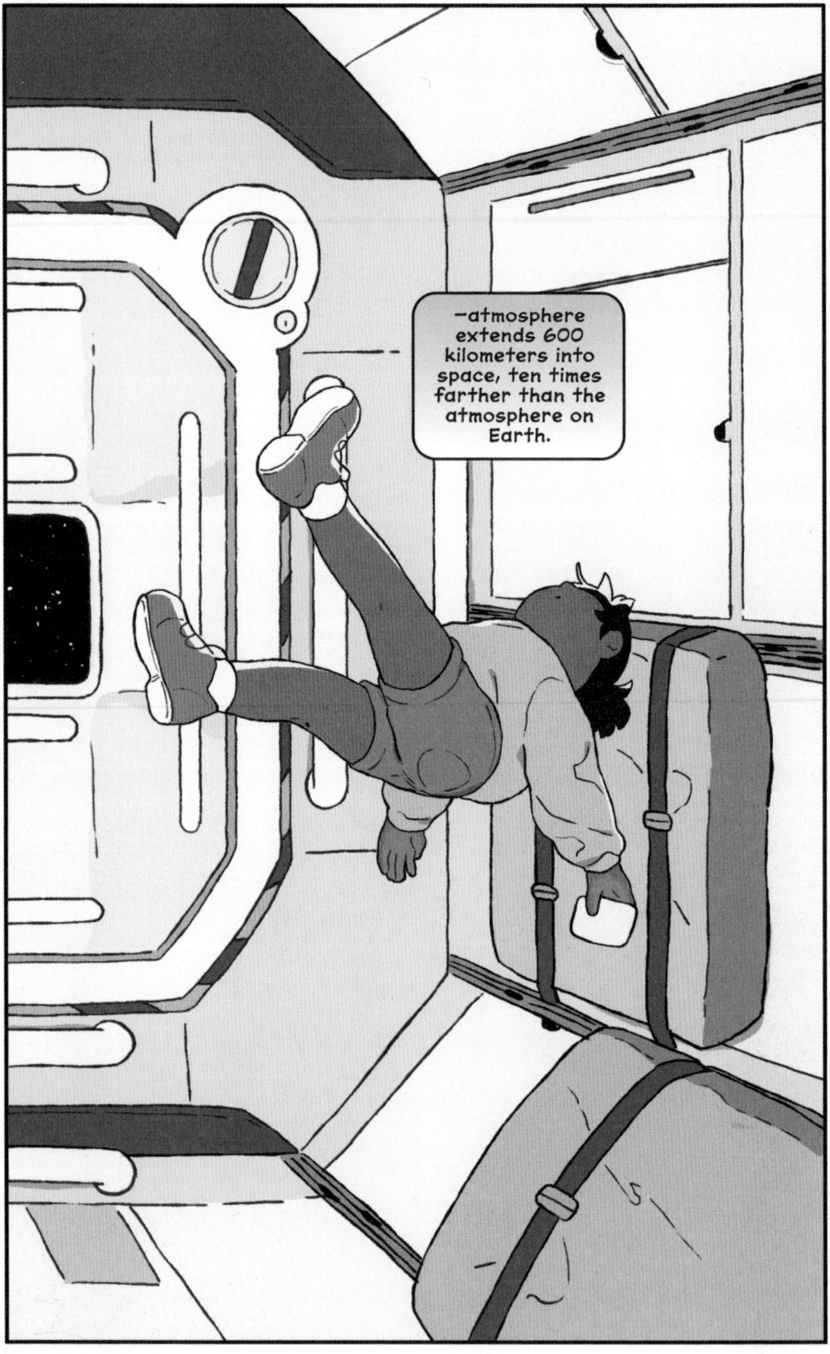
-atmosphere extends 600 kilometers into space, ten times farther than the atmosphere on Earth.

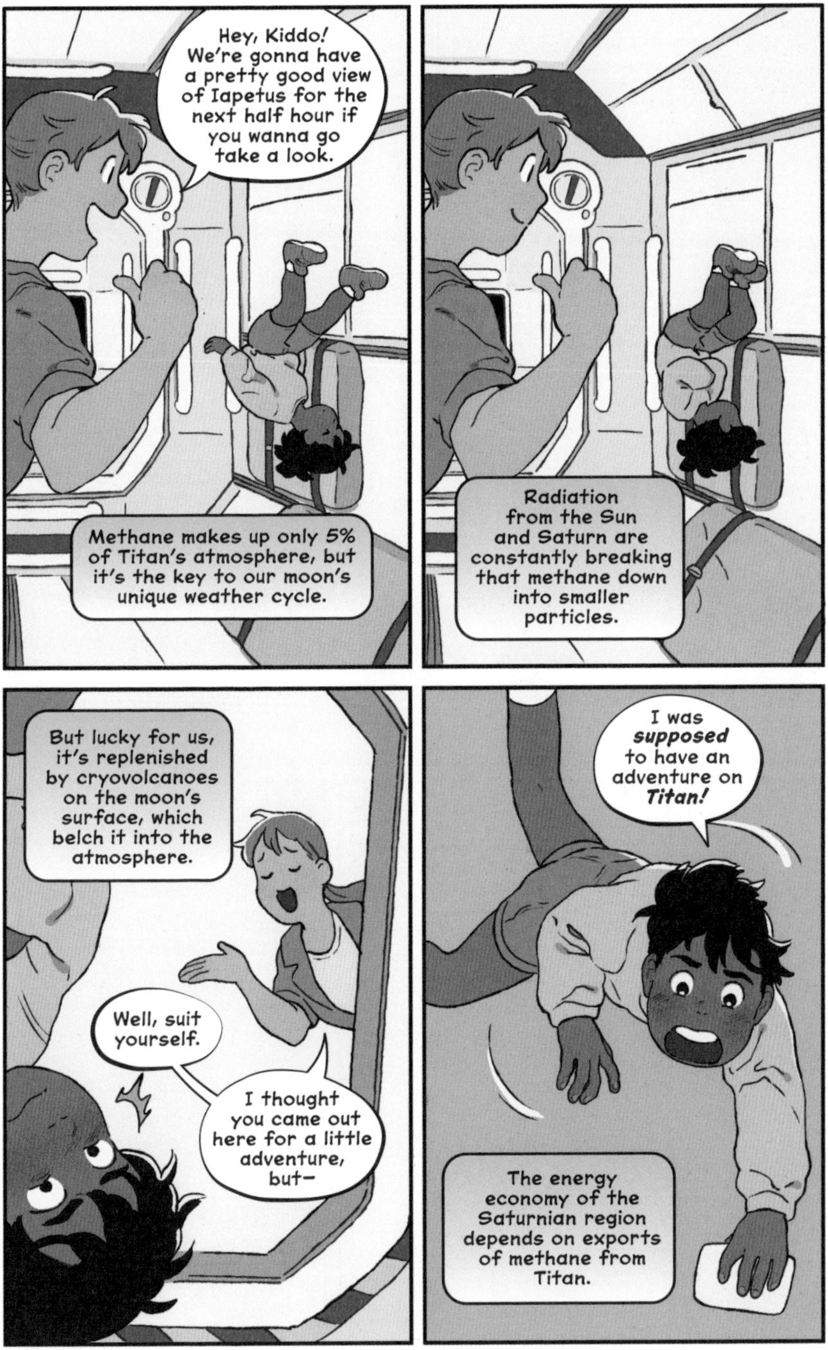
Hey, Kiddo! We're gonna have a pretty good view of Iapetus for the next half hour if you wanna go take a look.
Methane makes up only 5% of Titan's atmosphere, but it's the key to our moon's unique weather cycle.
Radiation from the Sun and Saturn are constantly breaking that methane down into smaller particles.
But lucky for us, it's replenished by cryovolcanoes on the moon's surface, which belch it into the atmosphere.
Well, suit yourself.
I thought you came out here for a little adventure, but–
I was *supposed* to have an adventure on *Titan!*
The energy economy of the Saturnian region depends on exports of methane from Titan.

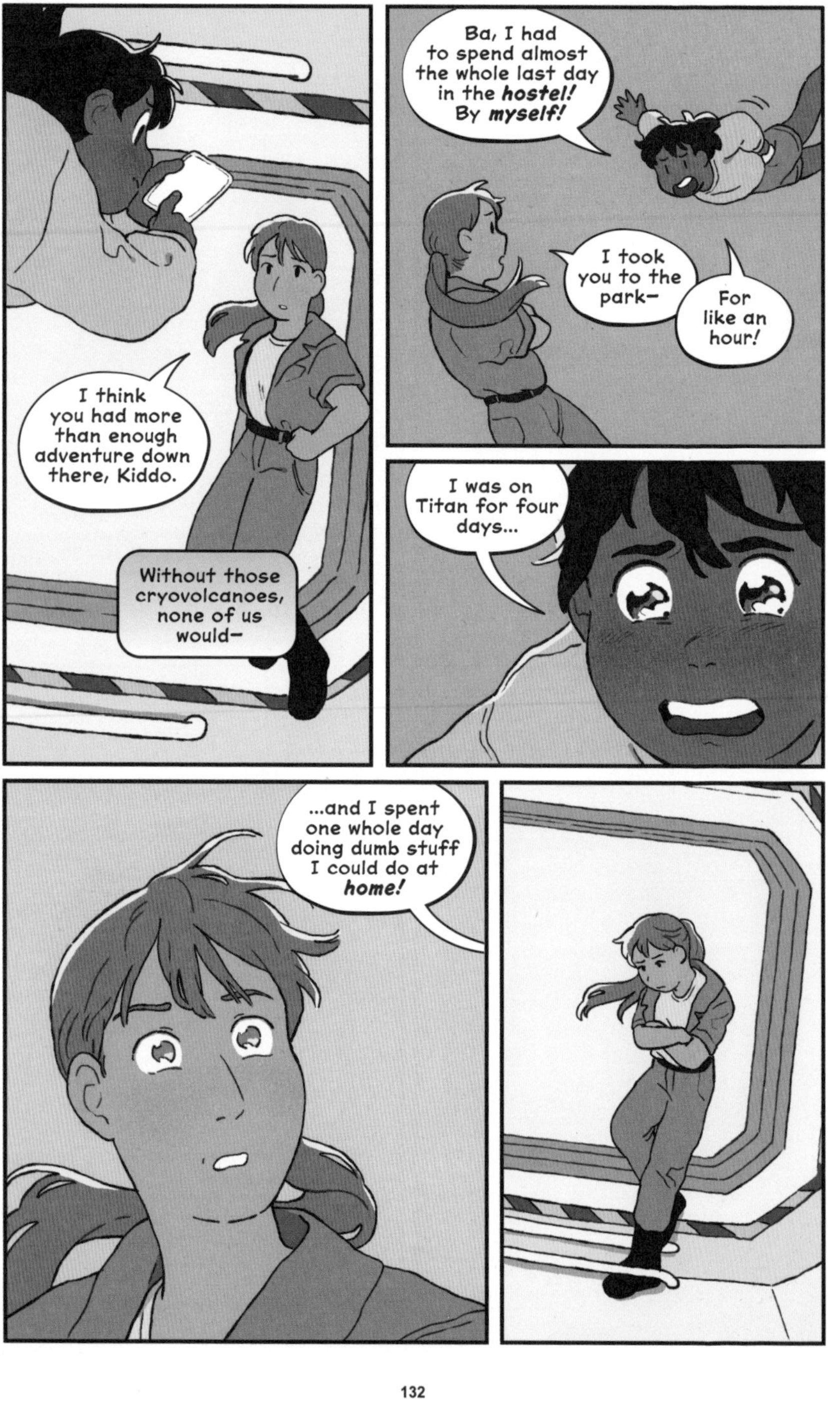
I think you had more than enough adventure down there, Kiddo.
Without those cryovolcanoes, none of us would–
Ba, I had to spend almost the whole last day in the **hostel!** By **myself!**
I took you to the park–
For like an hour!
I was on Titan for four days...
...and I spent one whole day doing dumb stuff I could do at **home!**

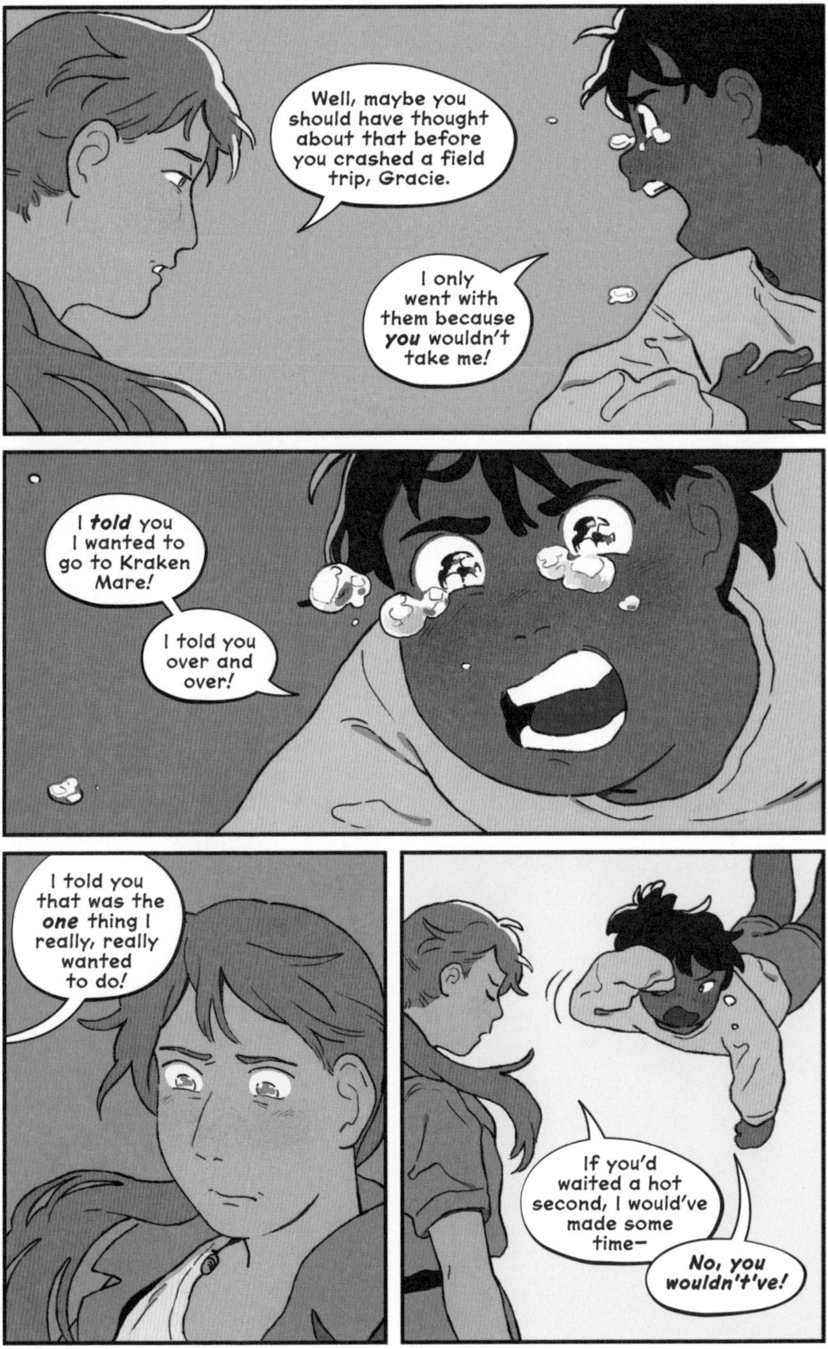
Well, maybe you should have thought about that before you crashed a field trip, Gracie.
I only went with them because *you* wouldn't take me!
I *told* you I wanted to go to Kraken Mare!
I told you over and over!
I told you that was the *one* thing I really, really wanted to do!
If you'd waited a hot second, I would've made some time—
No, you wouldn't've!

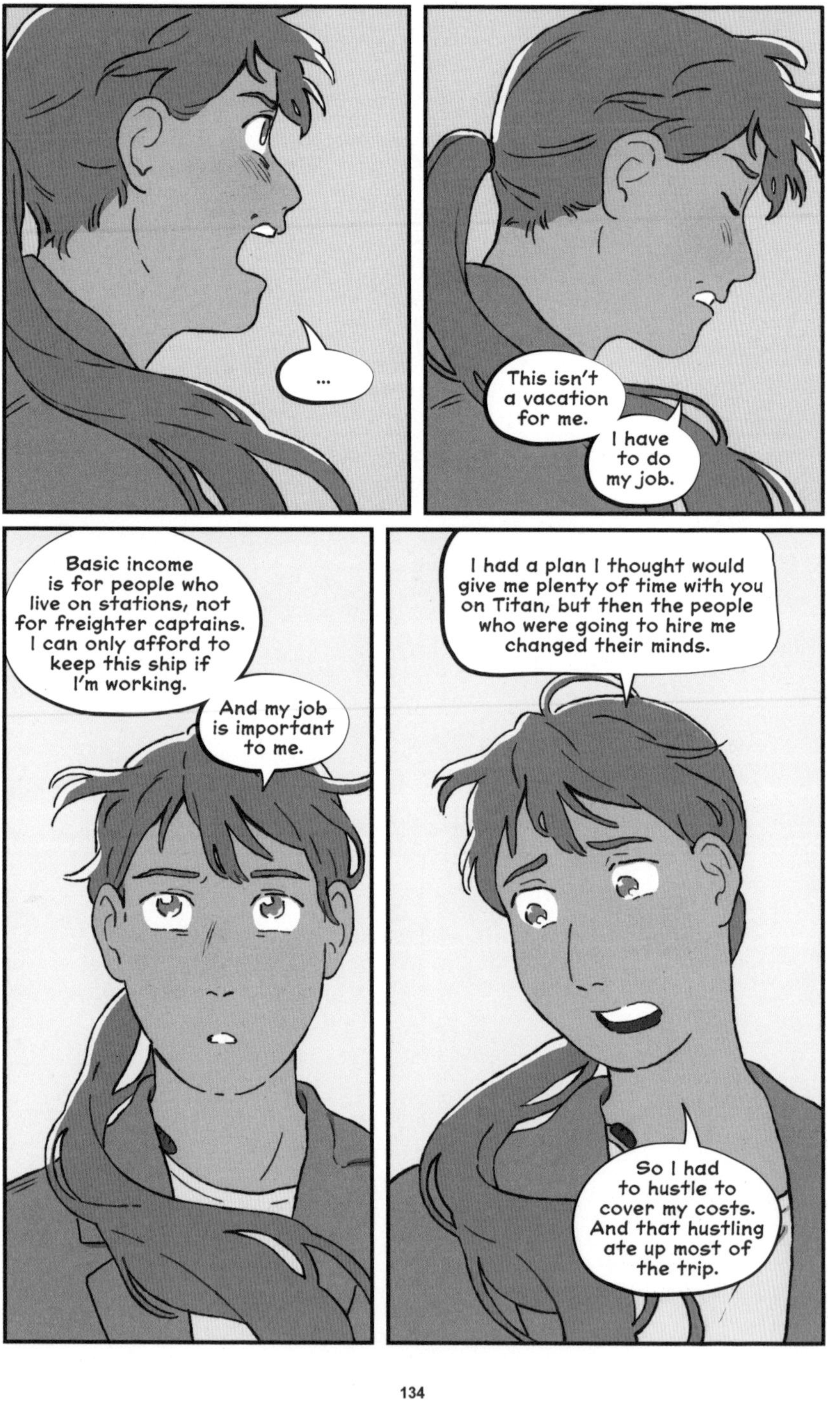
...
This isn't a vacation for me.
I have to do my job.
Basic income is for people who live on stations, not for freighter captains. I can only afford to keep this ship if I'm working.
And my job is important to me.
I had a plan I thought would give me plenty of time with you on Titan, but then the people who were going to hire me changed their minds.
So I had to hustle to cover my costs. And that hustling ate up most of the trip.

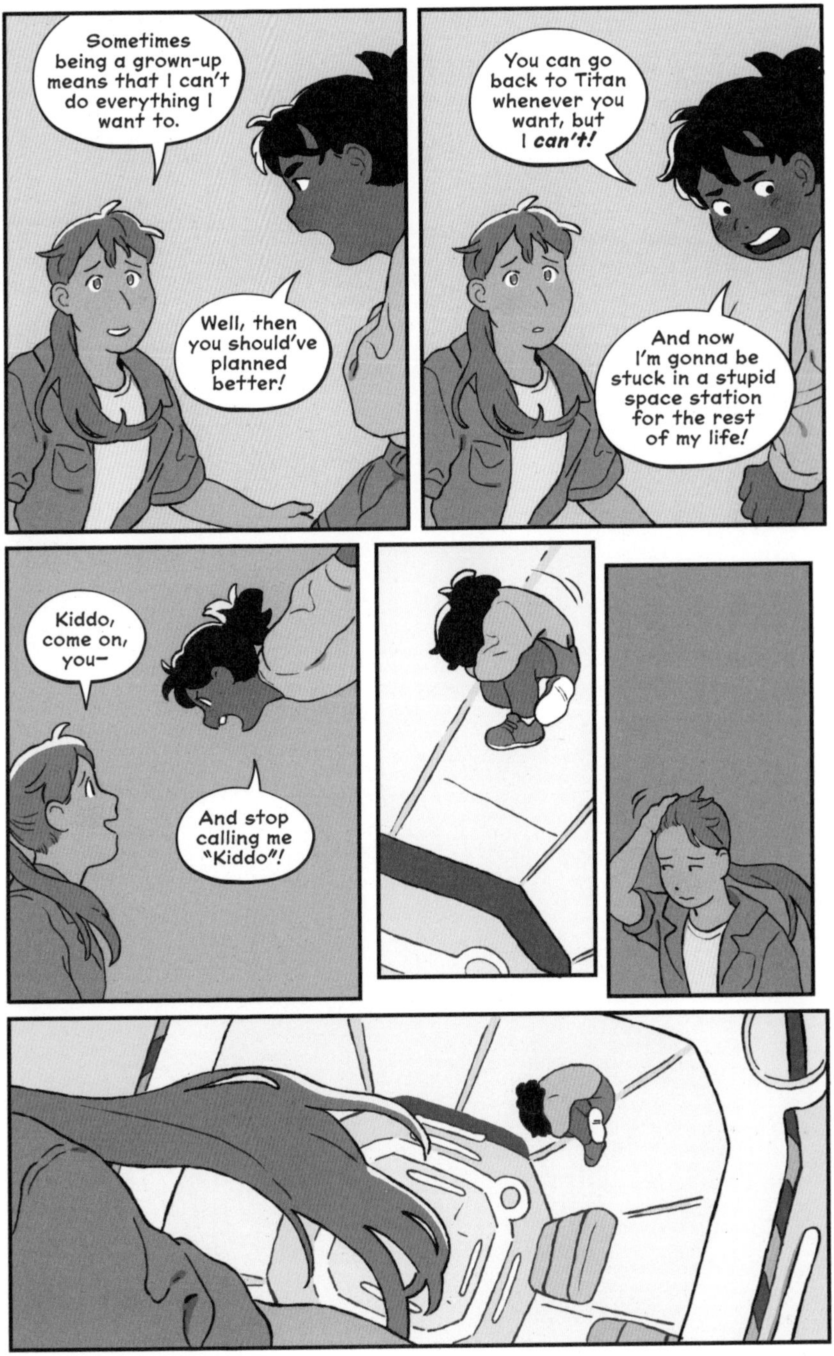
Sometimes being a grown-up means that I can't do everything I want to.
Well, then you should've planned better!
You can go back to Titan whenever you want, but I *can't!*
And now I'm gonna be stuck in a stupid space station for the rest of my life!
Kiddo, come on, you–
And stop calling me "Kiddo"!

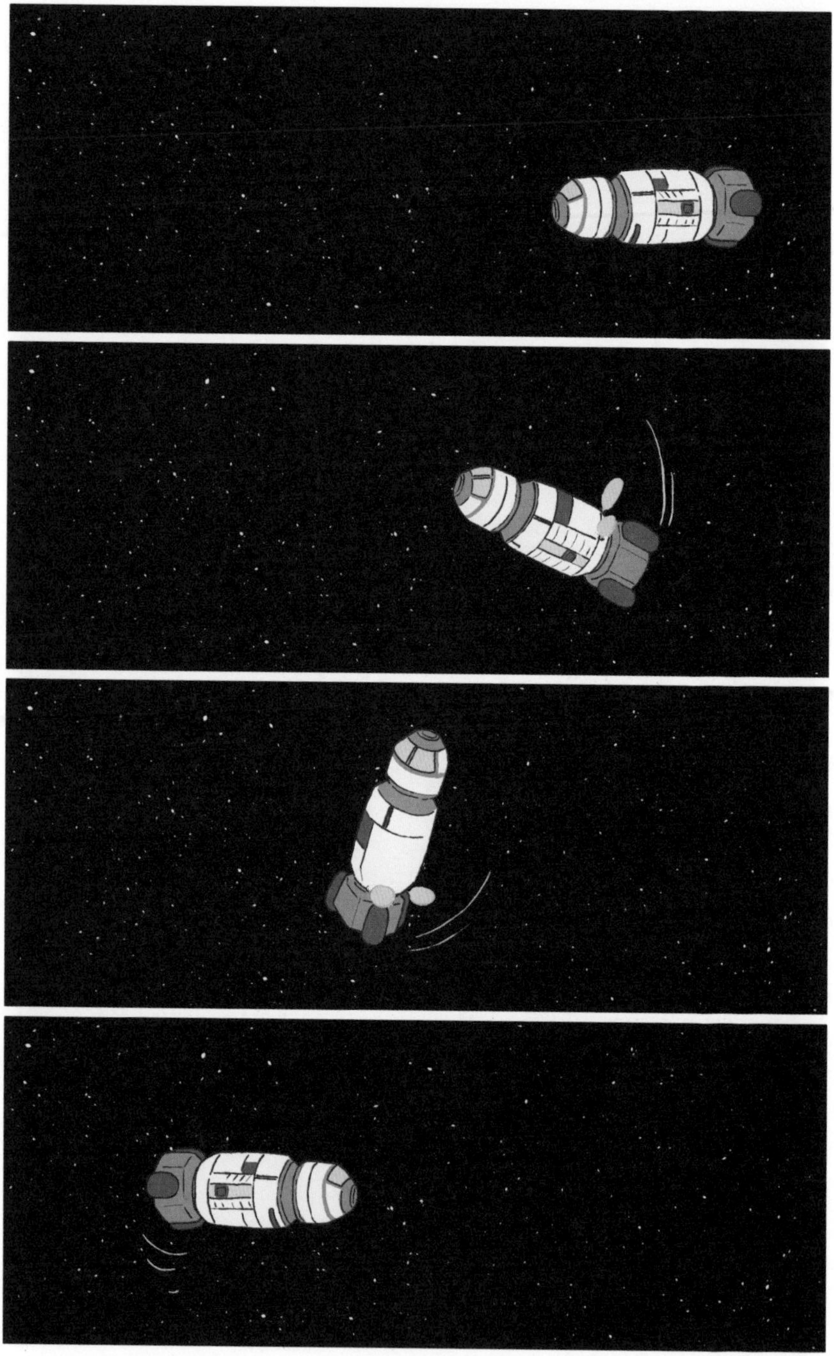

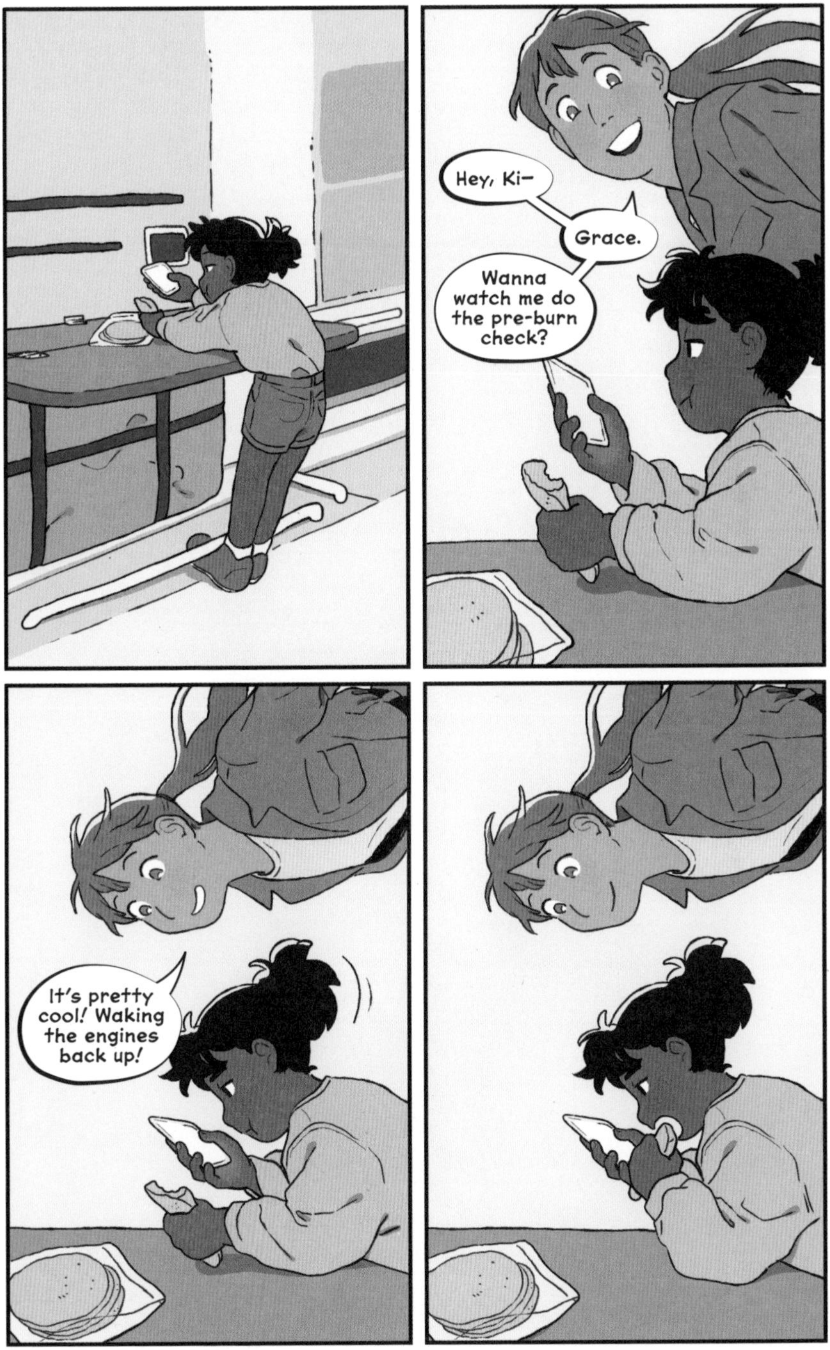
Hey, Ki–
Grace.
Wanna watch me do the pre-burn check?
It's pretty cool! Waking the engines back up!

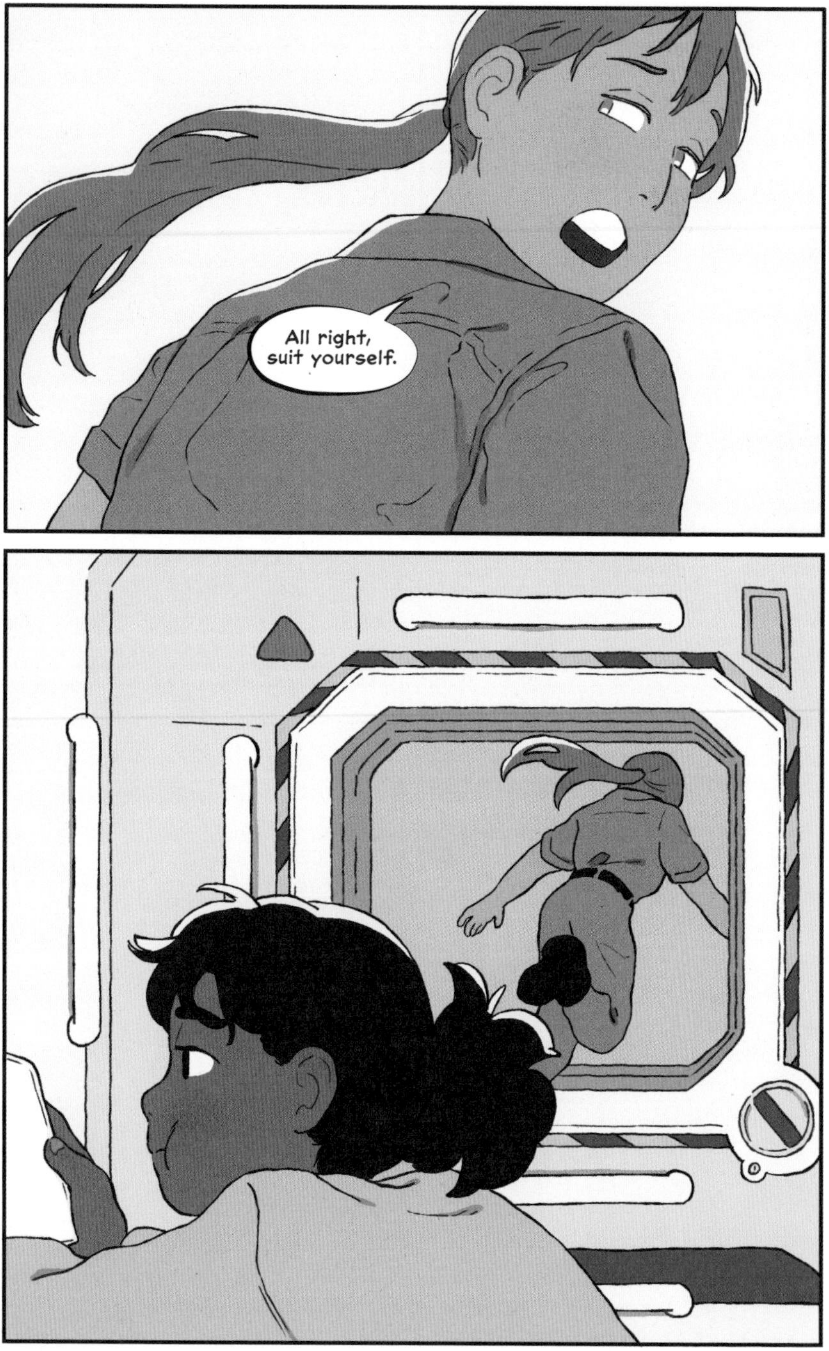
All right, suit yourself.

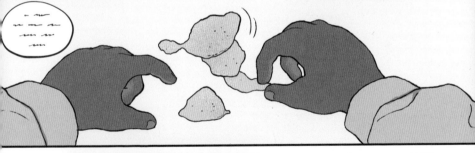
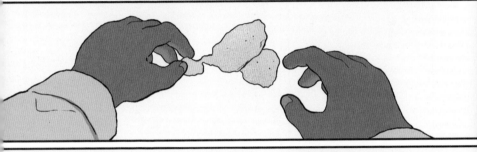

—gotta be kidding me with this...

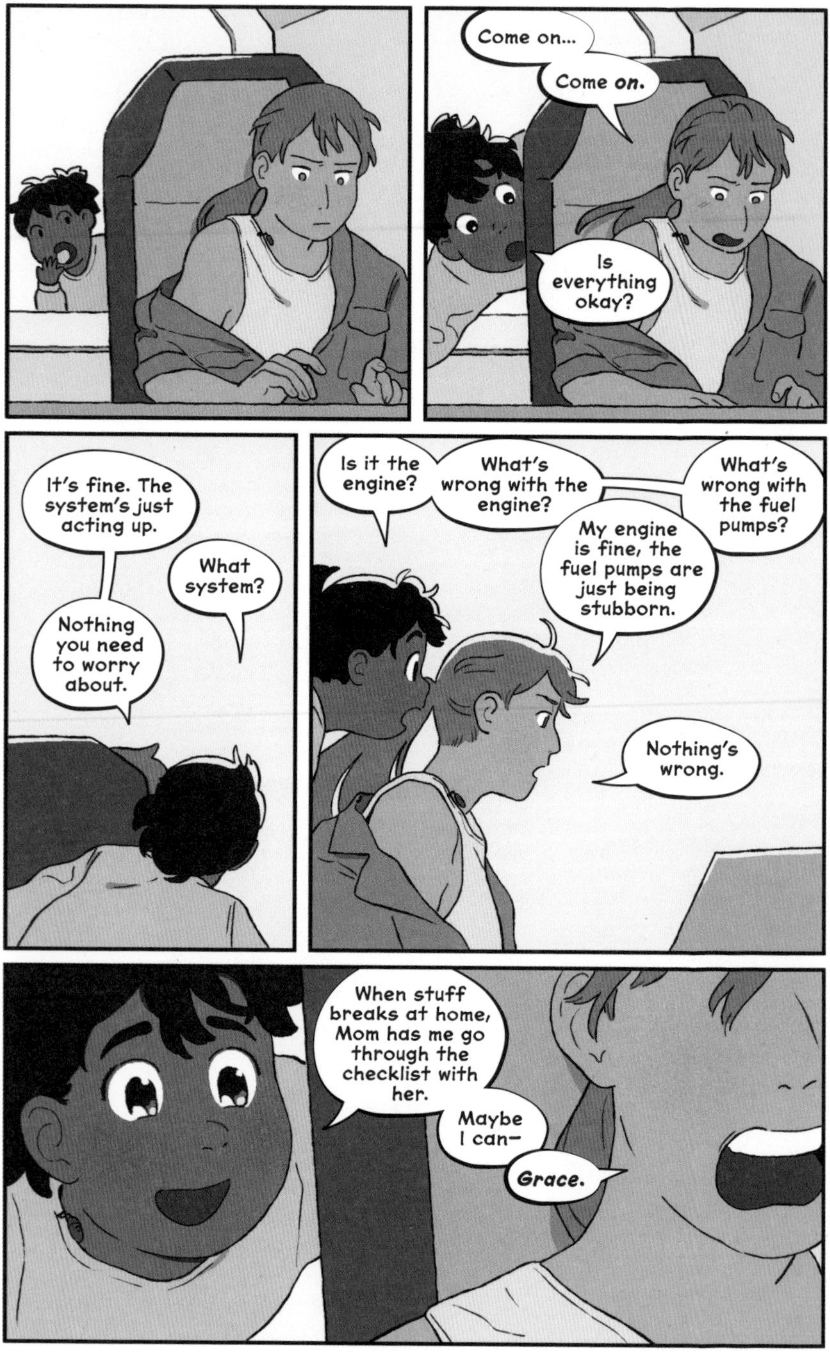

Come on...
Come on.
Is everything okay?
It's fine. The system's just acting up.
What system?
Nothing you need to worry about.
Is it the engine?
What's wrong with the engine?
What's wrong with the fuel pumps?
My engine is fine, the fuel pumps are just being stubborn.
Nothing's wrong.
When stuff breaks at home, Mom has me go through the checklist with her.
Maybe I can—
Grace.

How about you go wait in the main cabin while I'm figuring this out, okay?

You can get dinner started.

I just ate lunch.

Watch a video, then.

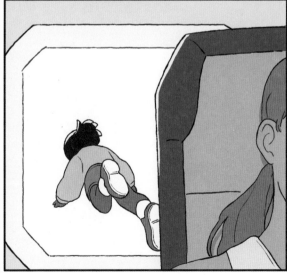

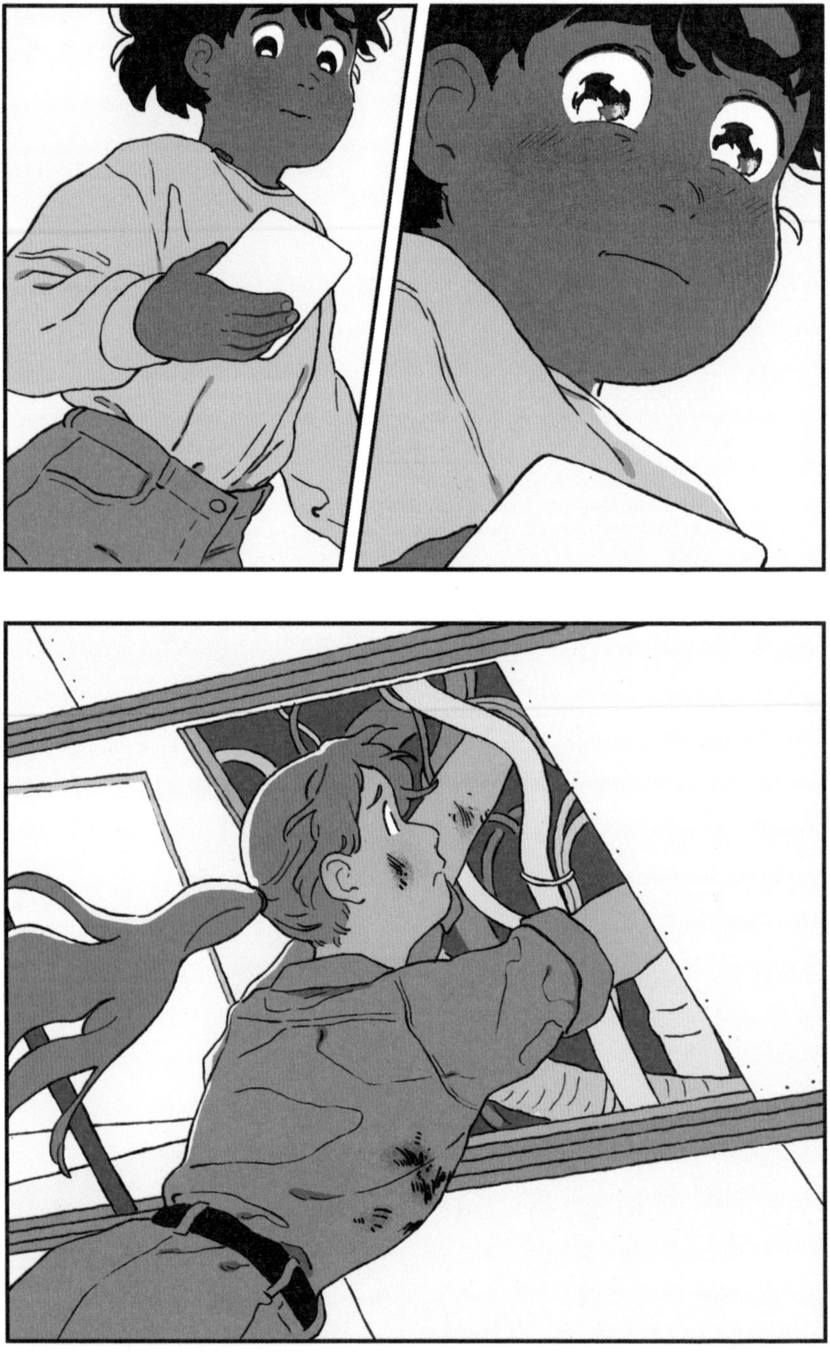

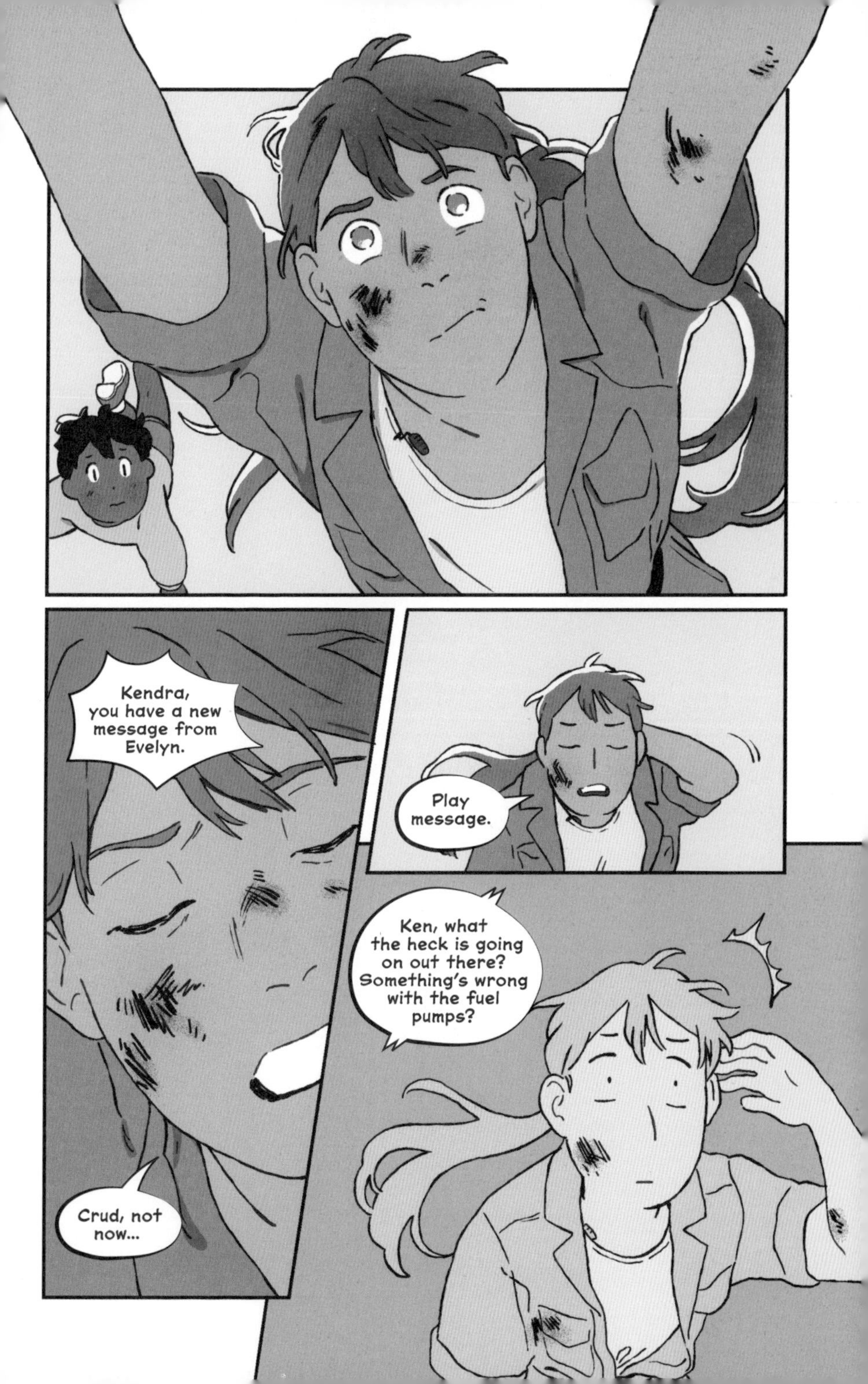

Kendra, you have a new message from Evelyn.
Play message.
Ken, what the heck is going on out there? Something's wrong with the fuel pumps?
Crud, not now...

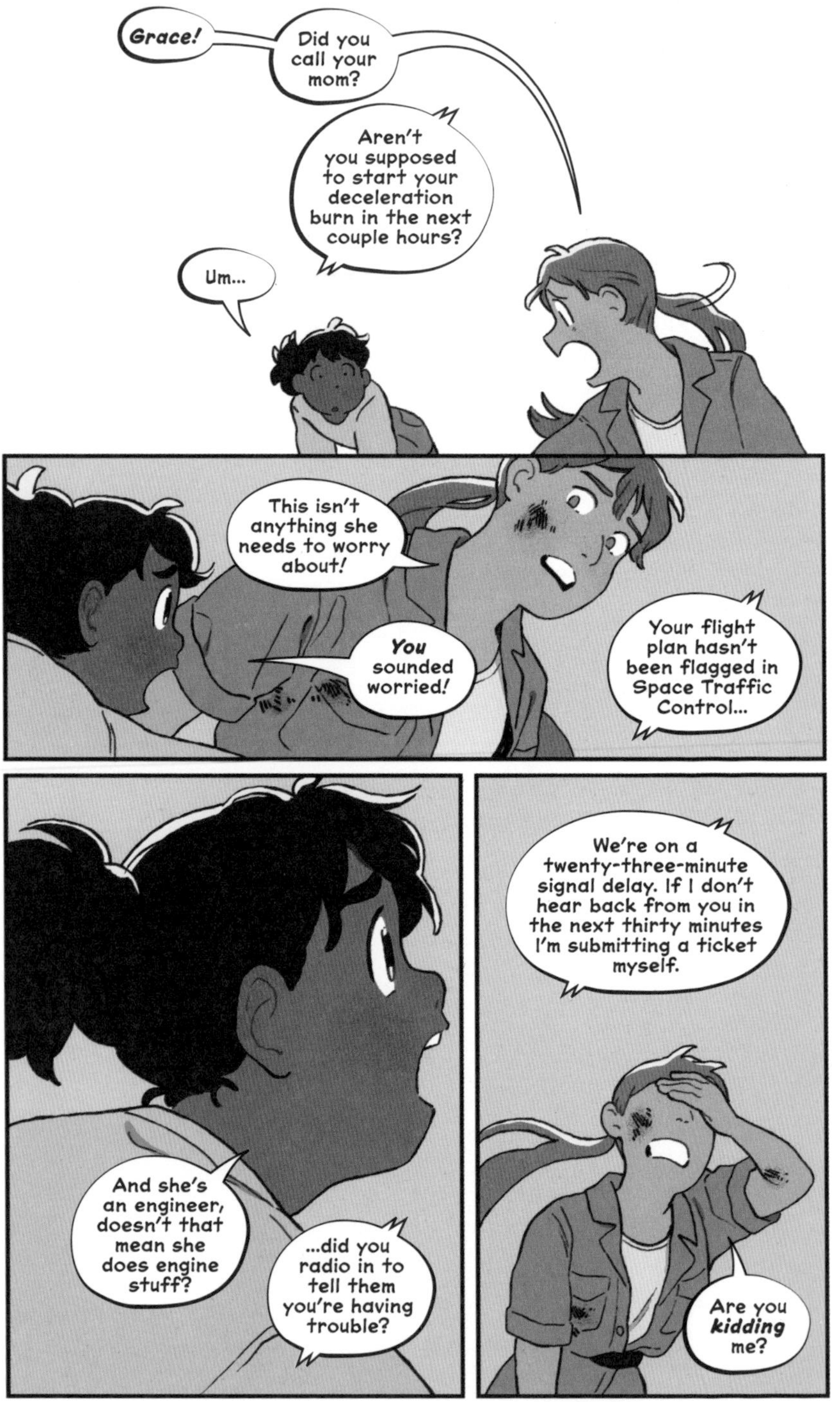
Grace!
Did you call your mom?
Aren't you supposed to start your deceleration burn in the next couple hours?
Um...
This isn't anything she needs to worry about!
You sounded worried!
Your flight plan hasn't been flagged in Space Traffic Control...
And she's an engineer, doesn't that mean she does engine stuff?
...did you radio in to tell them you're having trouble?
We're on a twenty-three-minute signal delay. If I don't hear back from you in the next thirty minutes I'm submitting a ticket myself.
Are you kidding me?

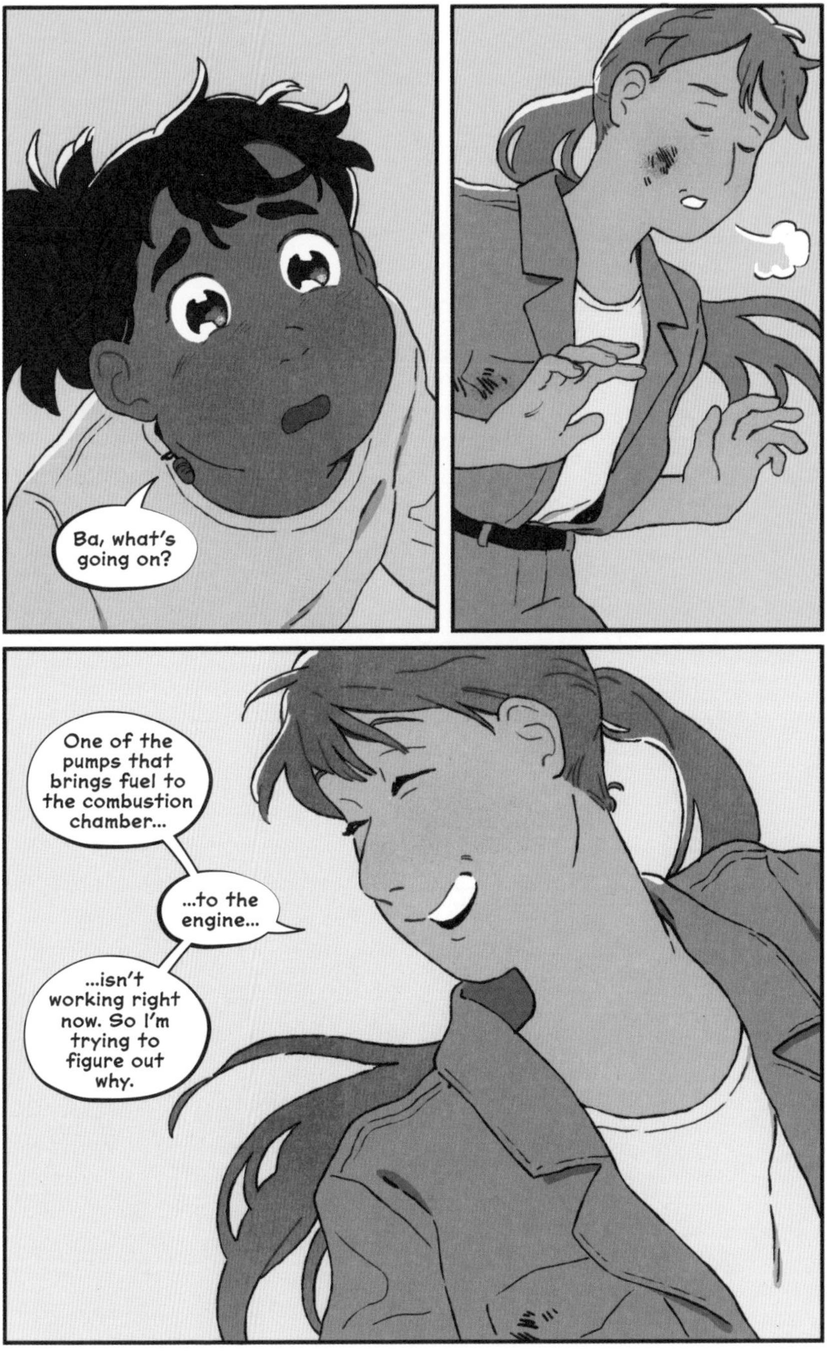
Ba, what's going on?
One of the pumps that brings fuel to the combustion chamber...
...to the engine...
...isn't working right now. So I'm trying to figure out why.

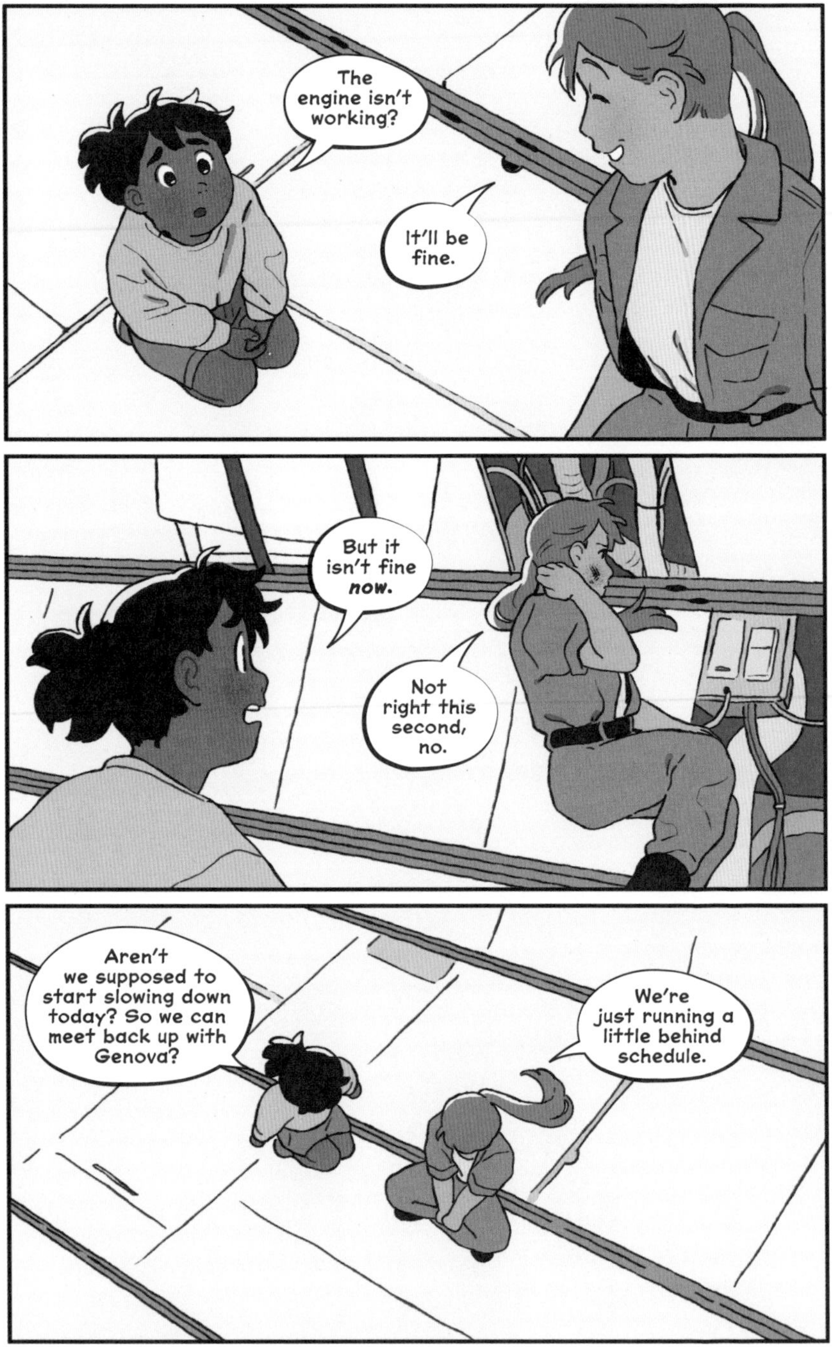
The engine isn't working?
It'll be fine.
But it isn't fine *now*.
Not right this second, no.
Aren't we supposed to start slowing down today? So we can meet back up with Genova?
We're just running a little behind schedule.

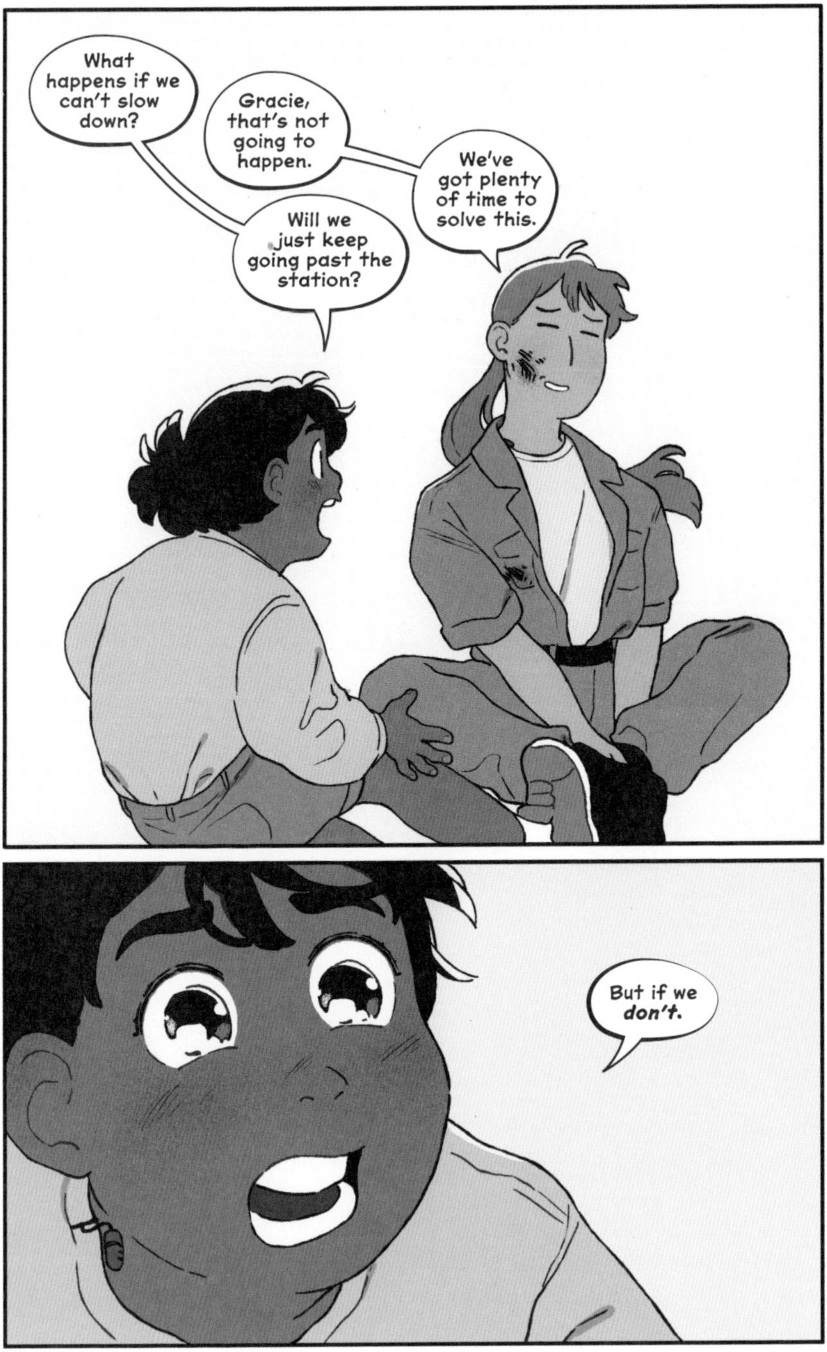
What happens if we can't slow down?
Gracie, that's not going to happen.
Will we just keep going past the station?
We've got plenty of time to solve this.
But if we *don't*.

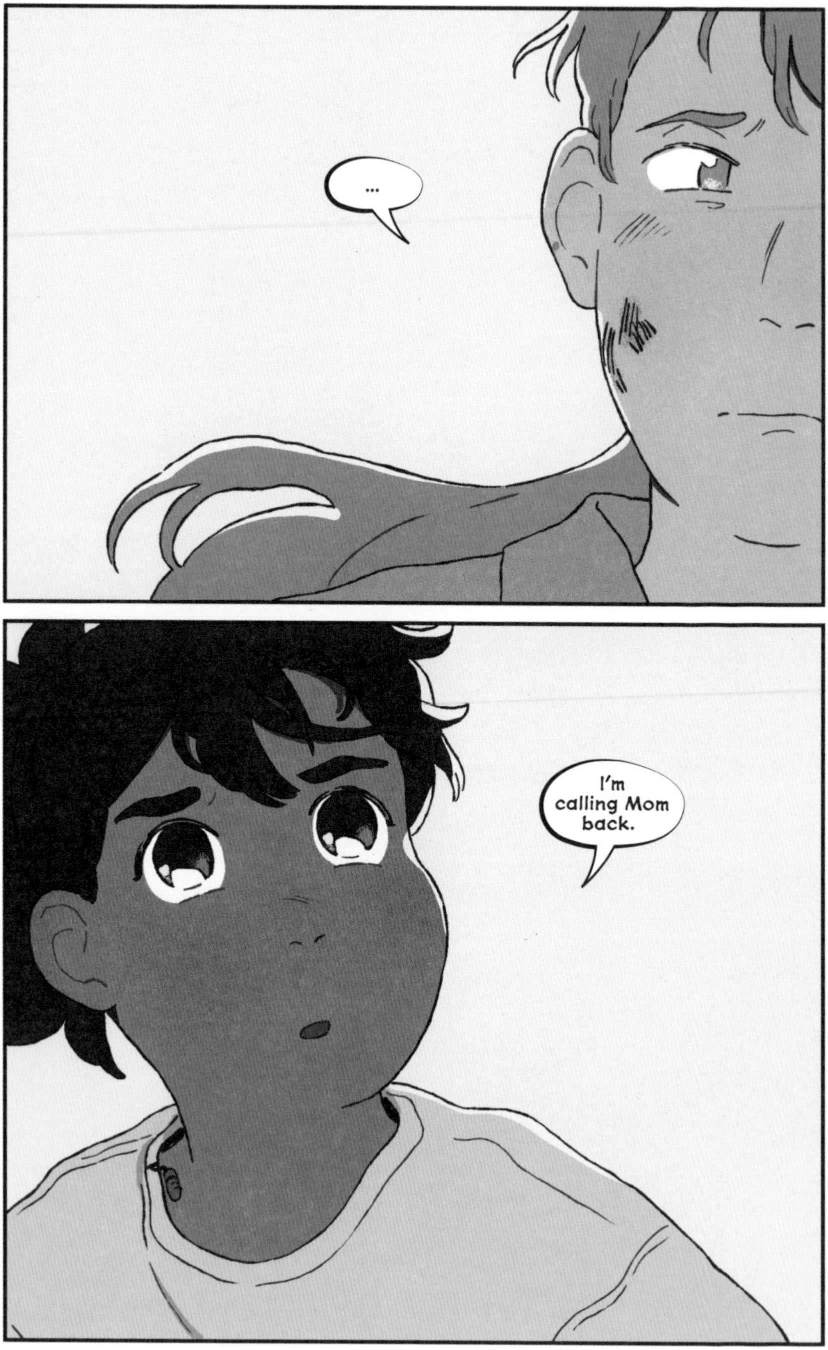
...
I'm calling Mom back.

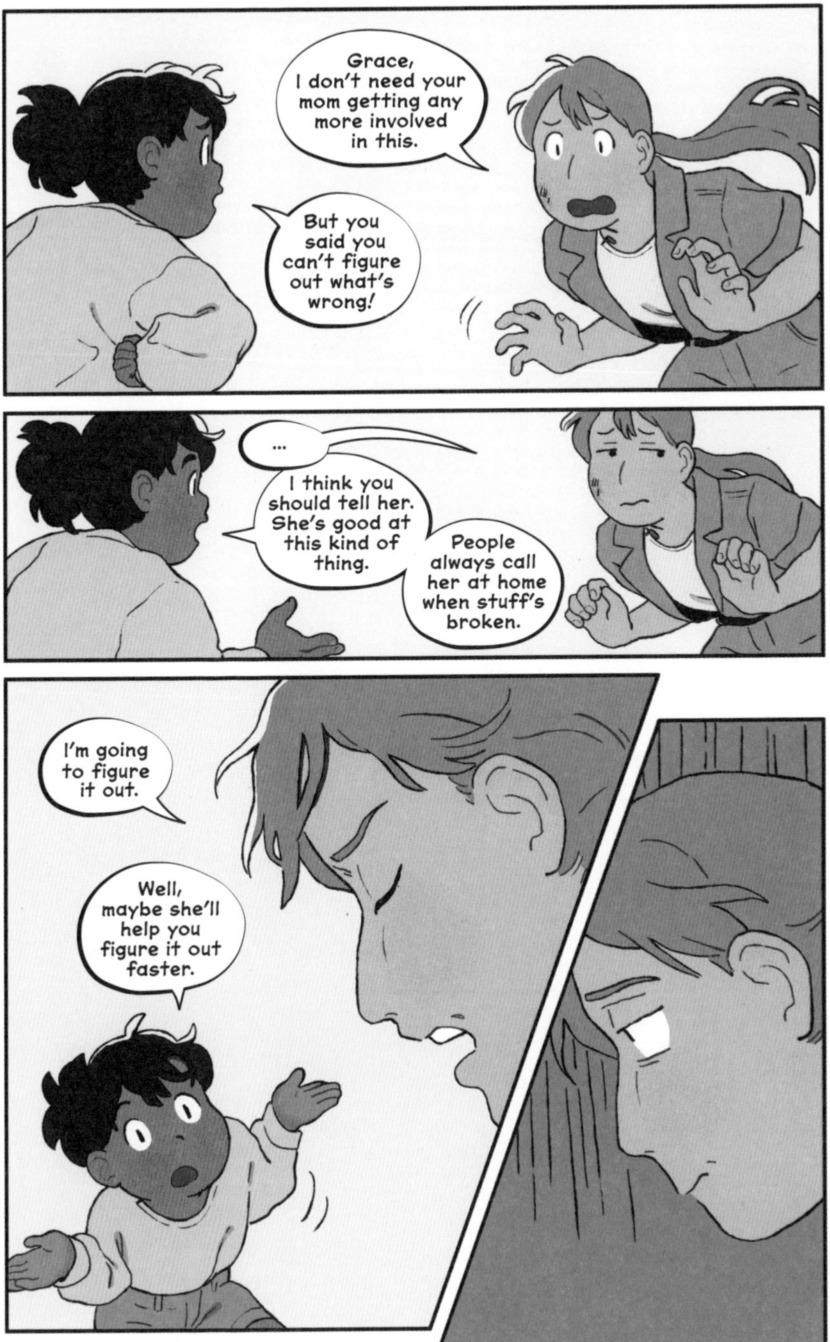
Grace, I don't need your mom getting any more involved in this.
But you said you can't figure out what's wrong!
...
I think you should tell her. She's good at this kind of thing.
People always call her at home when stuff's broken.
I'm going to figure it out.
Well, maybe she'll help you figure it out faster.

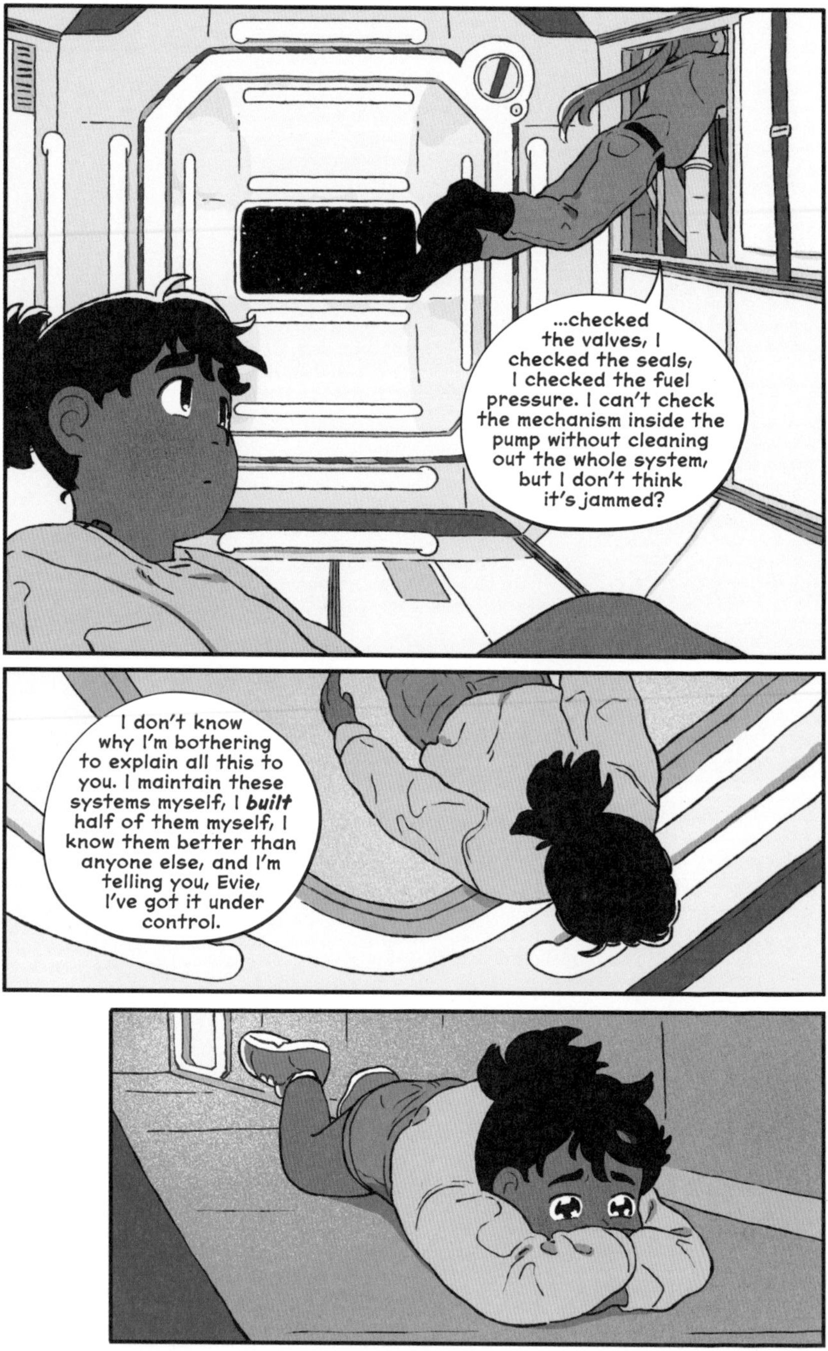
...checked the valves, I checked the seals, I checked the fuel pressure. I can't check the mechanism inside the pump without cleaning out the whole system, but I don't think it's jammed?
I don't know why I'm bothering to explain all this to you. I maintain these systems myself, I *built* half of them myself, I know them better than anyone else, and I'm telling you, Evie, I've got it under control.

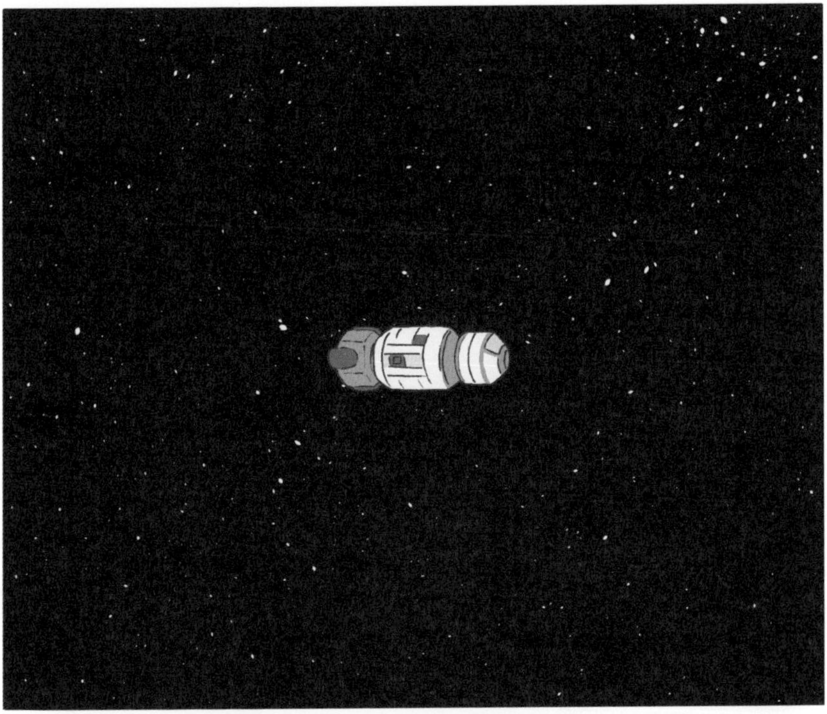

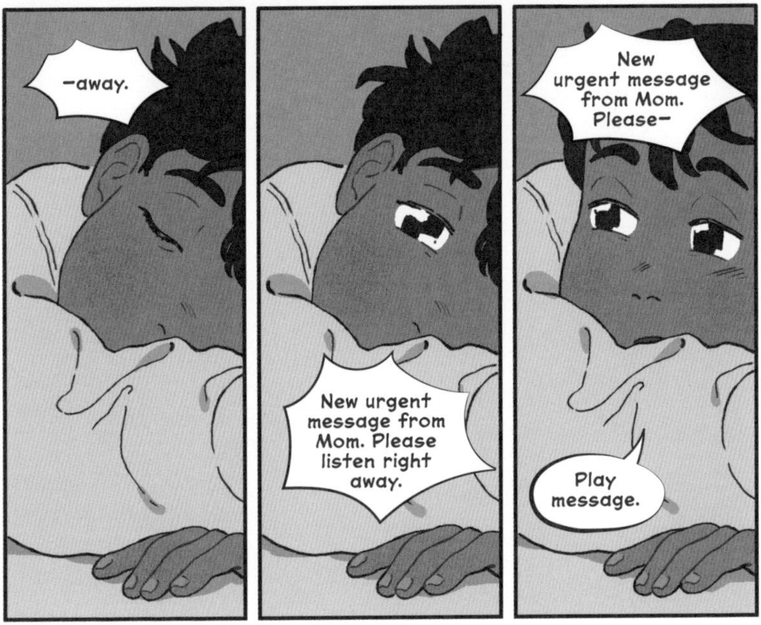
-away.
New urgent message from Mom. Please listen right away.
New urgent message from Mom. Please-
Play message.

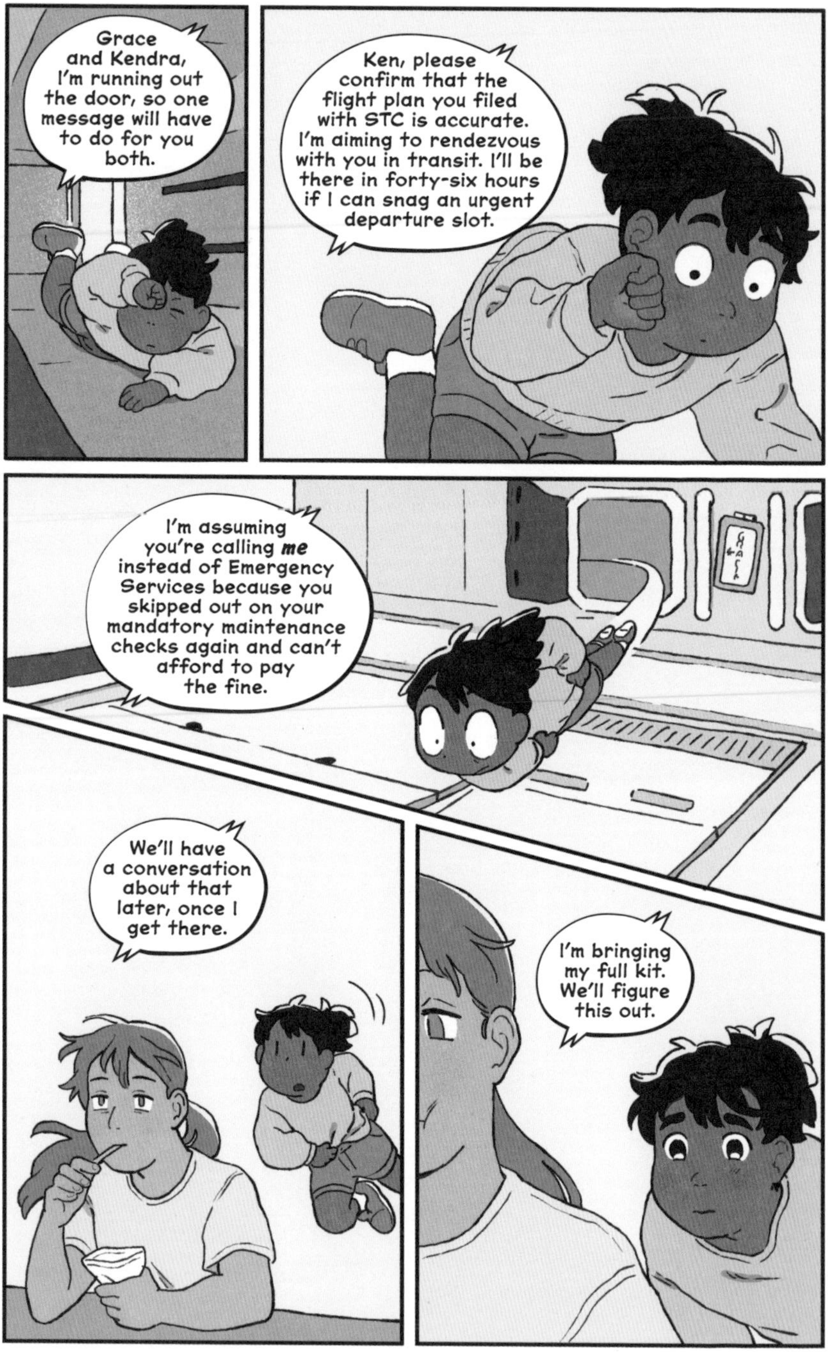
Grace and Kendra, I'm running out the door, so one message will have to do for you both.
Ken, please confirm that the flight plan you filed with STC is accurate. I'm aiming to rendezvous with you in transit. I'll be there in forty-six hours if I can snag an urgent departure slot.
I'm assuming you're calling *me* instead of Emergency Services because you skipped out on your mandatory maintenance checks again and can't afford to pay the fine.
We'll have a conversation about that later, once I get there.
I'm bringing my full kit. We'll figure this out.

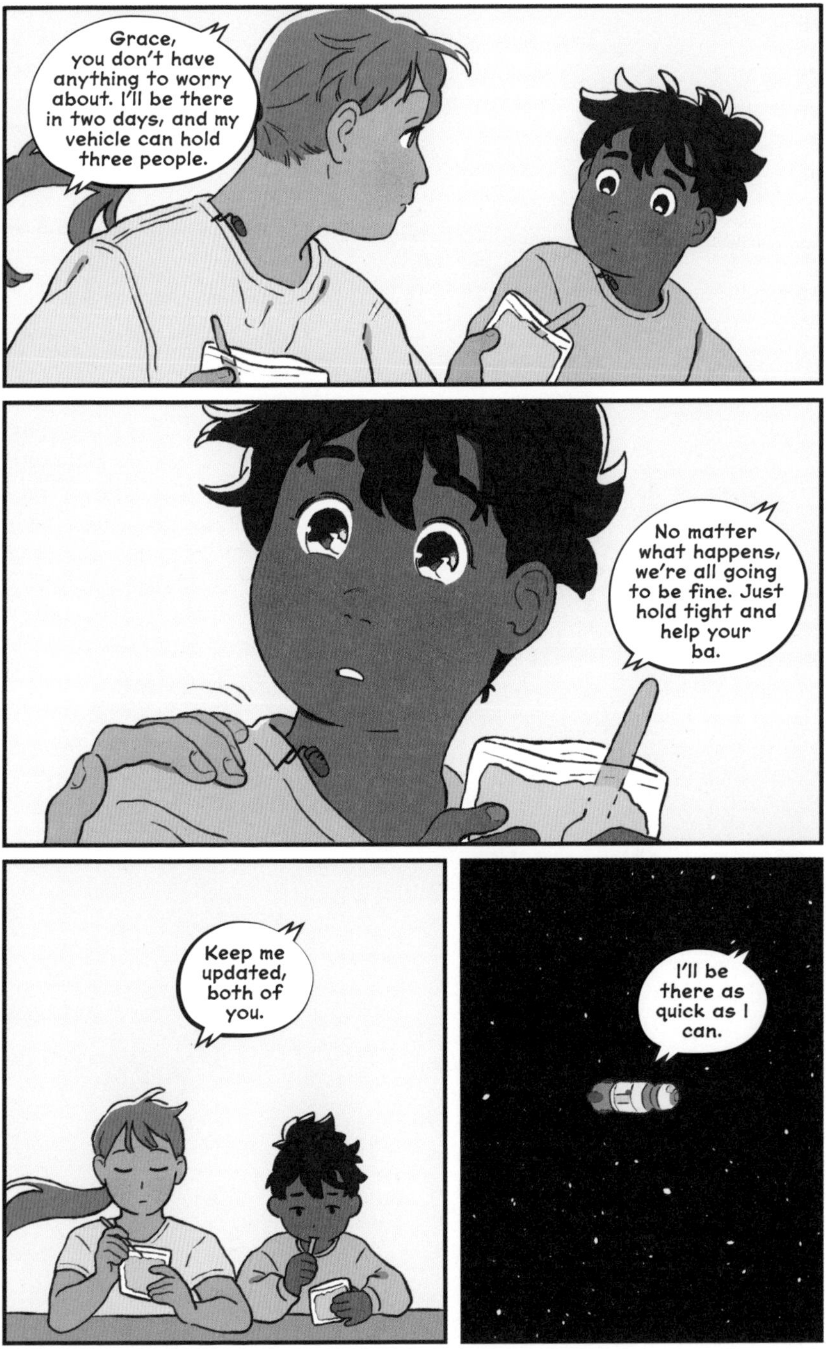
Grace, you don't have anything to worry about. I'll be there in two days, and my vehicle can hold three people.
No matter what happens, we're all going to be fine. Just hold tight and help your ba.
Keep me updated, both of you.
I'll be there as quick as I can.

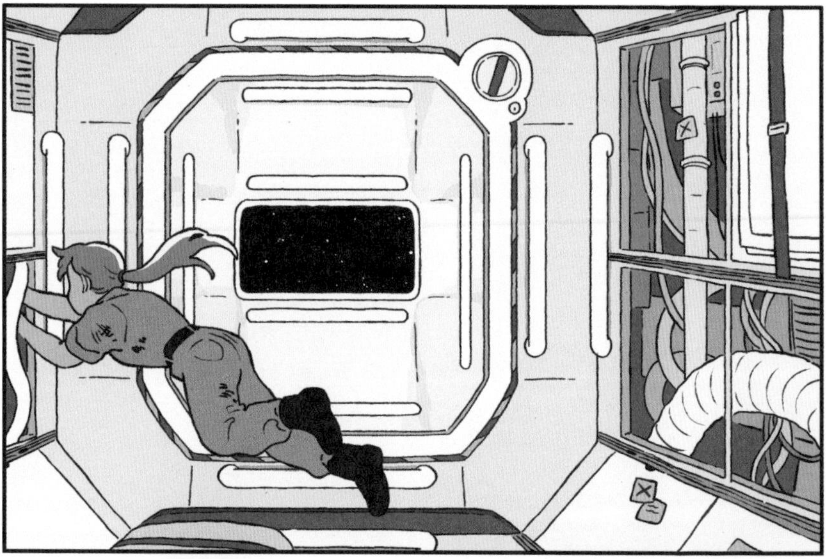

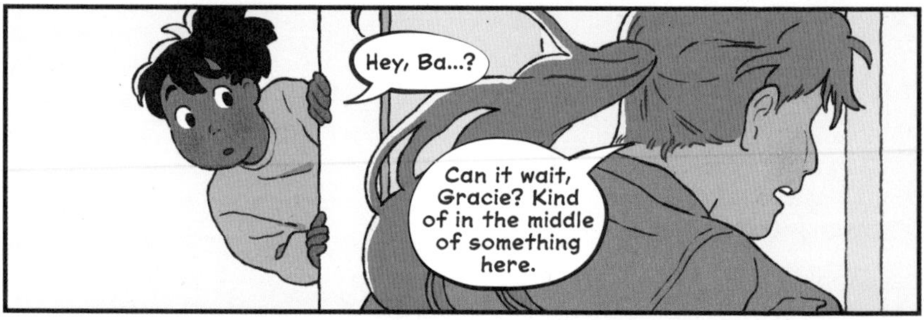
Hey, Ba...?
Can it wait, Gracie? Kind of in the middle of something here.

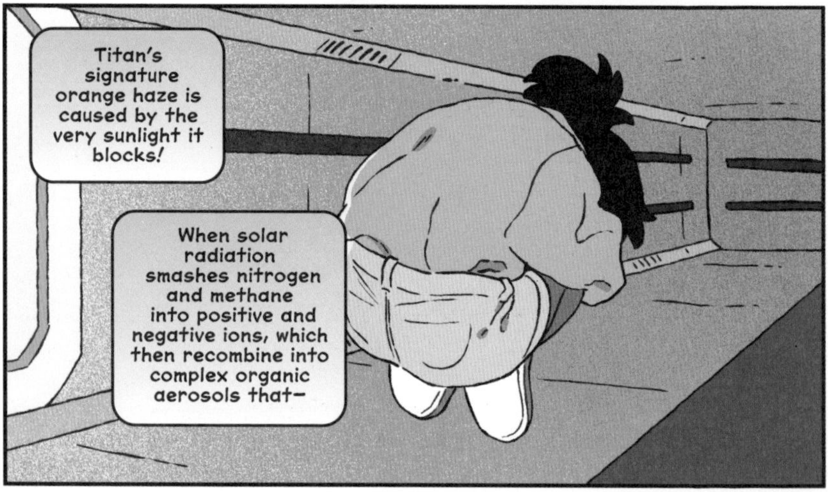
Titan's signature orange haze is caused by the very sunlight it blocks!
When solar radiation smashes nitrogen and methane into positive and negative ions, which then recombine into complex organic aerosols that–

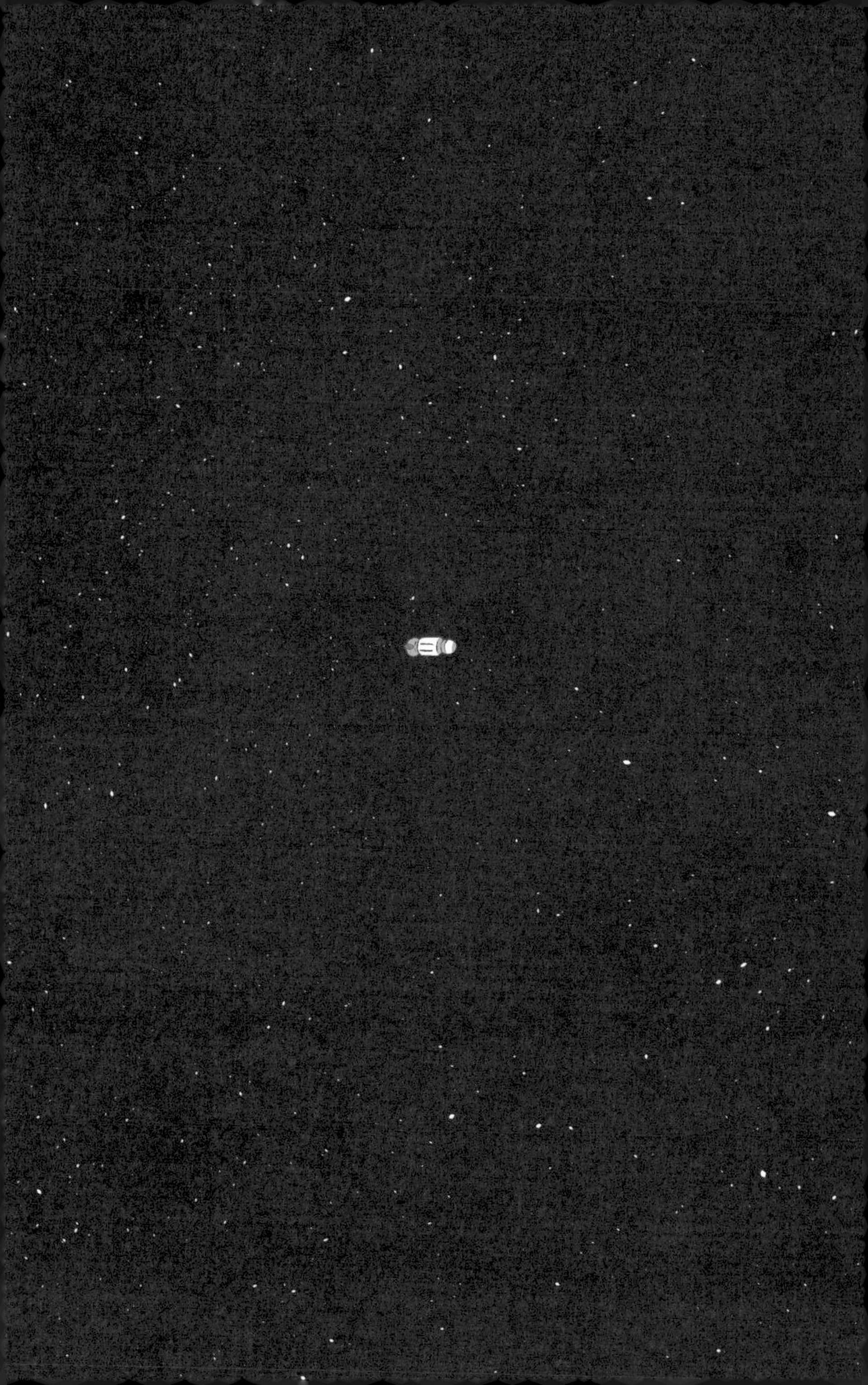

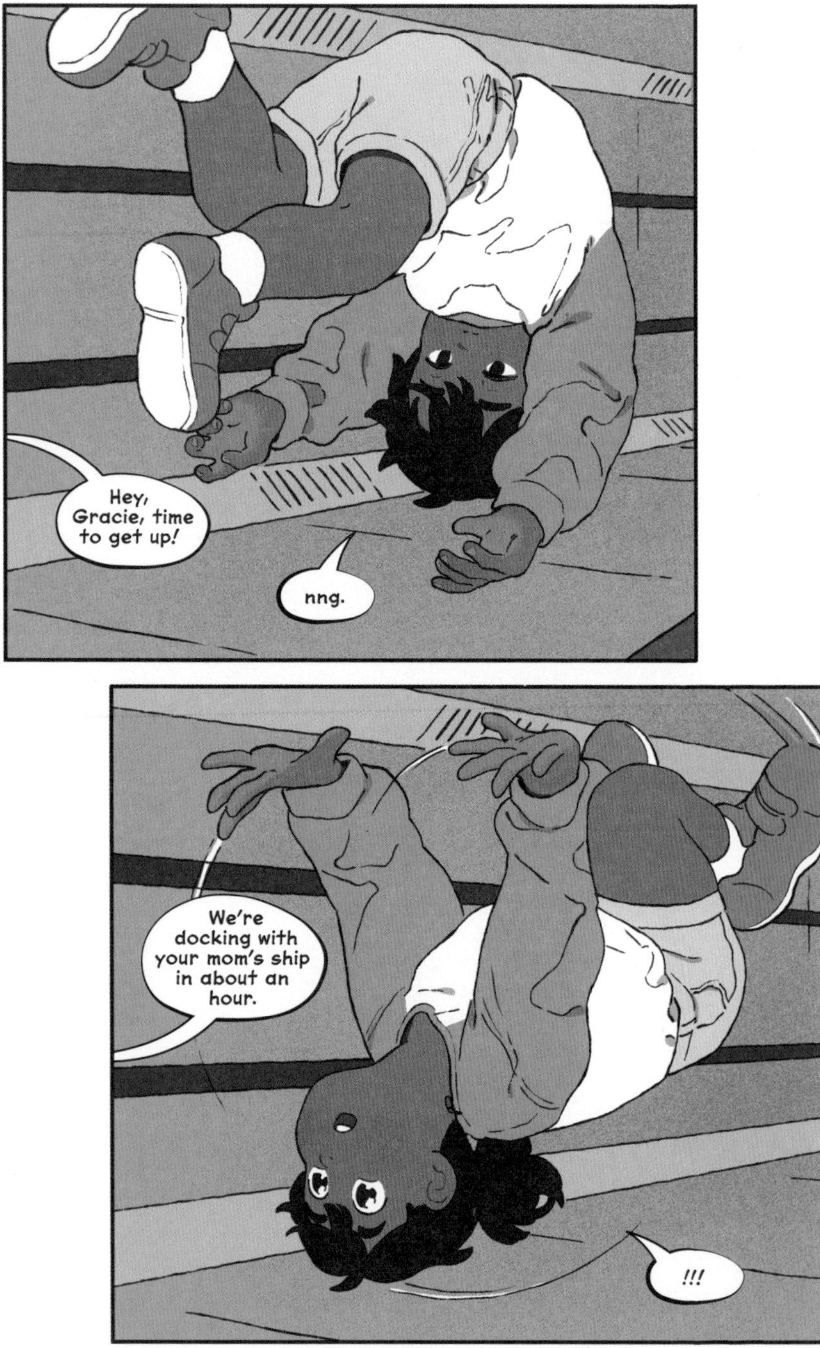
Hey, Gracie, time to get up!
nng.
We're docking with your mom's ship in about an hour.
!!!

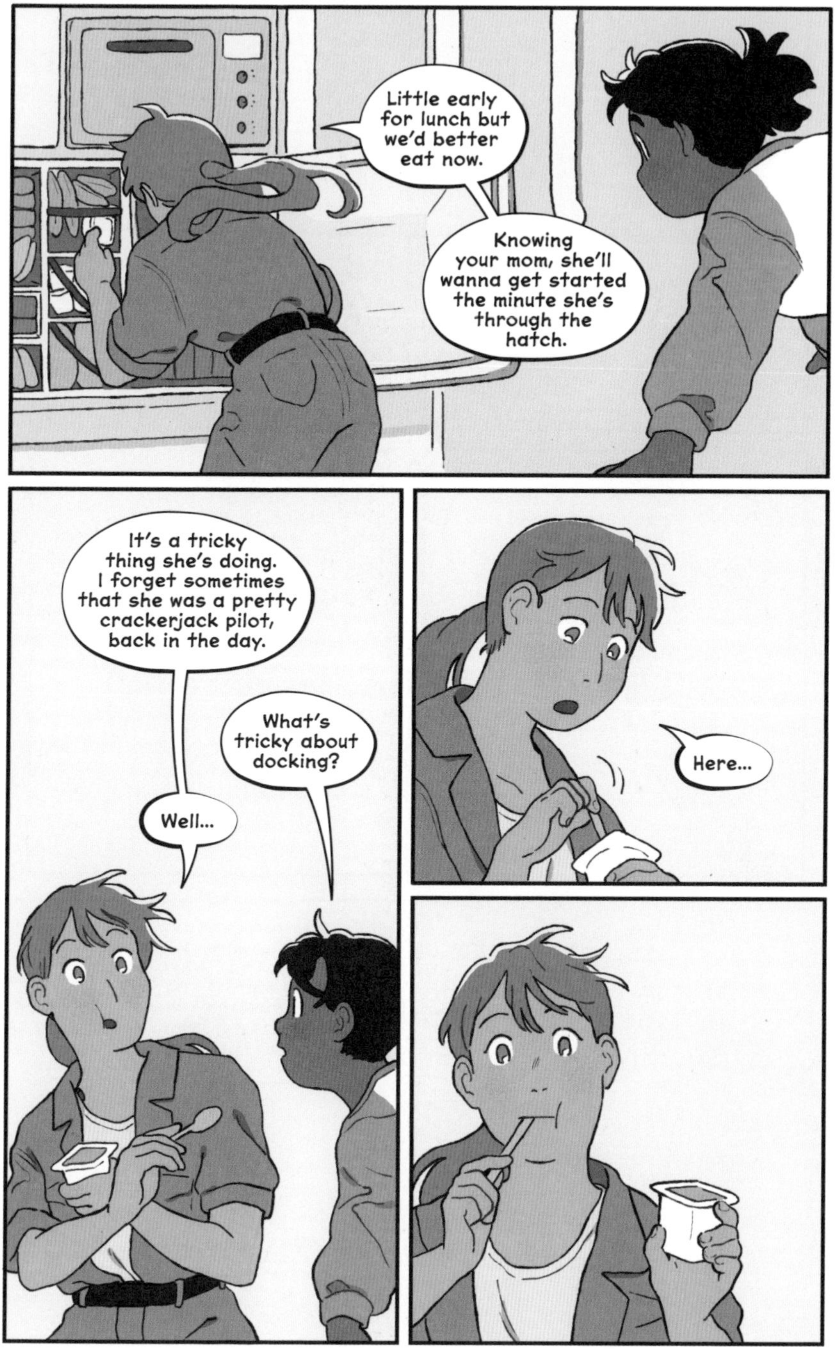
Little early for lunch but we'd better eat now.
Knowing your mom, she'll wanna get started the minute she's through the hatch.
It's a tricky thing she's doing. I forget sometimes that she was a pretty crackerjack pilot, back in the day.
What's tricky about docking?
Well...
Here...

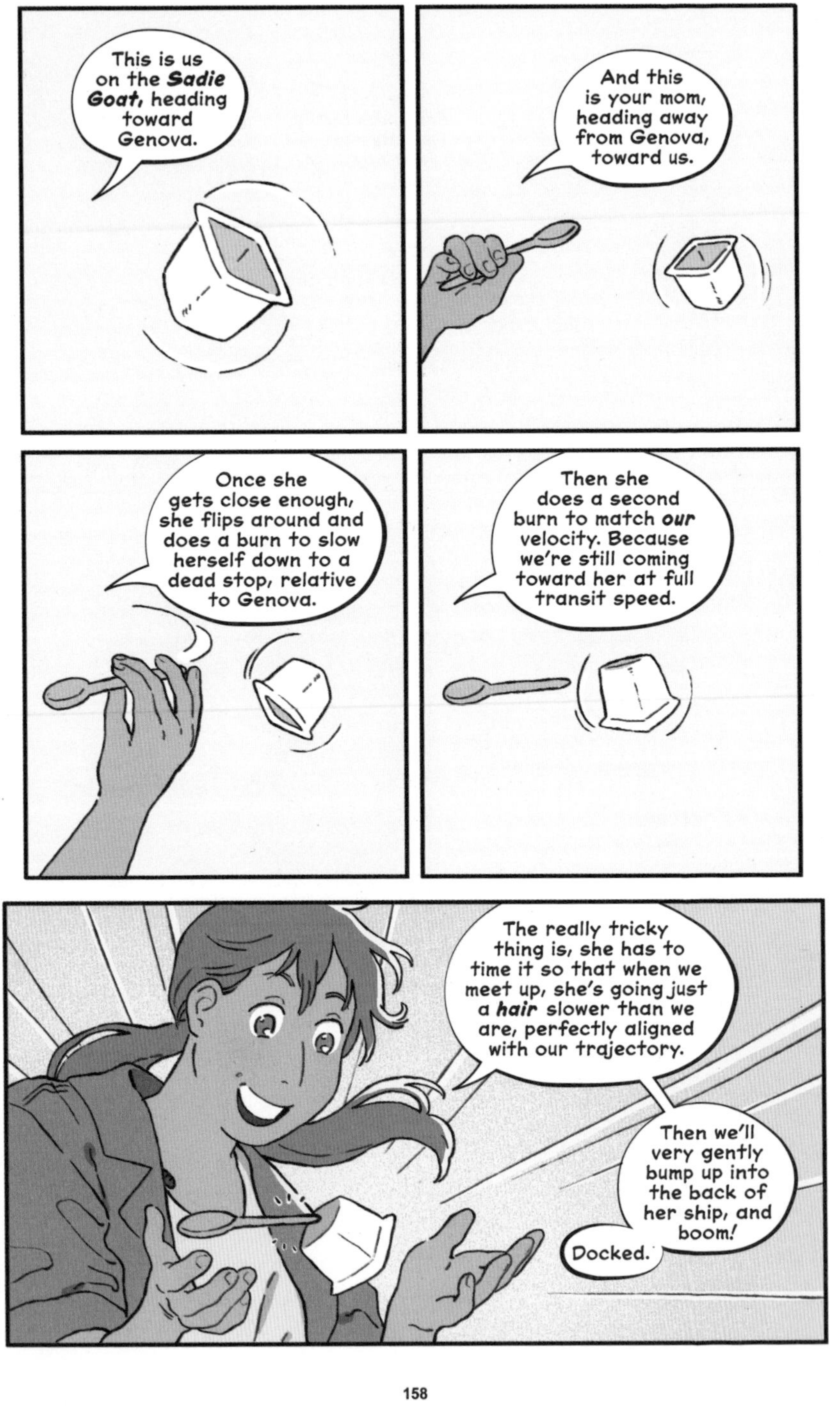
This is us on the ***Sadie Goat,*** heading toward Genova.
And this is your mom, heading away from Genova, toward us.
Once she gets close enough, she flips around and does a burn to slow herself down to a dead stop, relative to Genova.
Then she does a second burn to match ***our*** velocity. Because we're still coming toward her at full transit speed.
The really tricky thing is, she has to time it so that when we meet up, she's going just a ***hair*** slower than we are, perfectly aligned with our trajectory.
Then we'll very gently bump up into the back of her ship, and boom!
Docked.

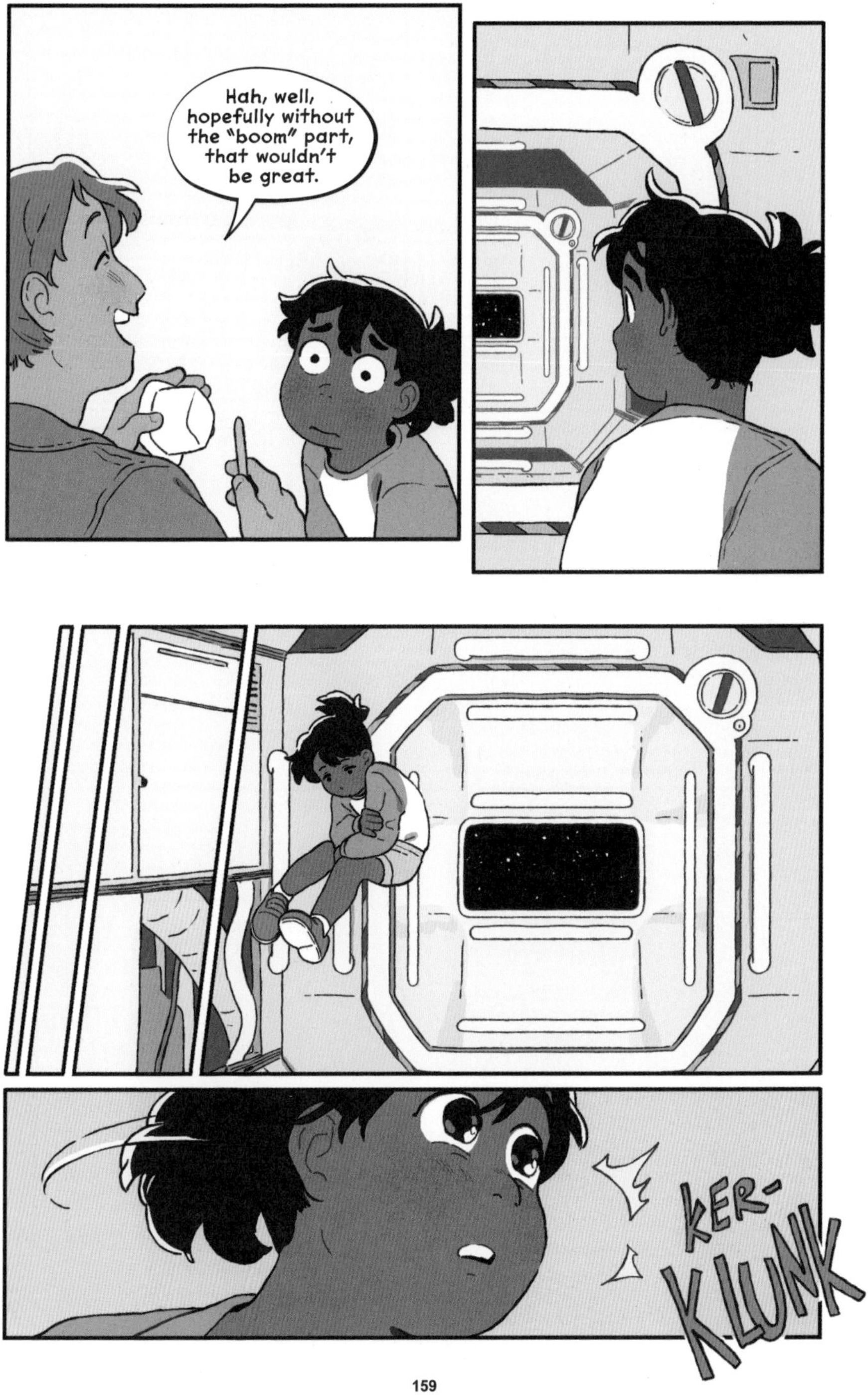
Hah, well, hopefully without the "boom" part, that wouldn't be great.
KER-KLUNK

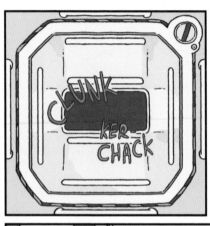

CLUNK

KER-
CHACK

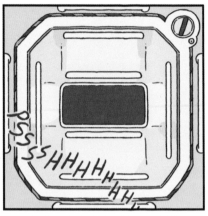

PSSSSHHHHHH,

BI-BING-BONG

Hold your horses, I'm coming...

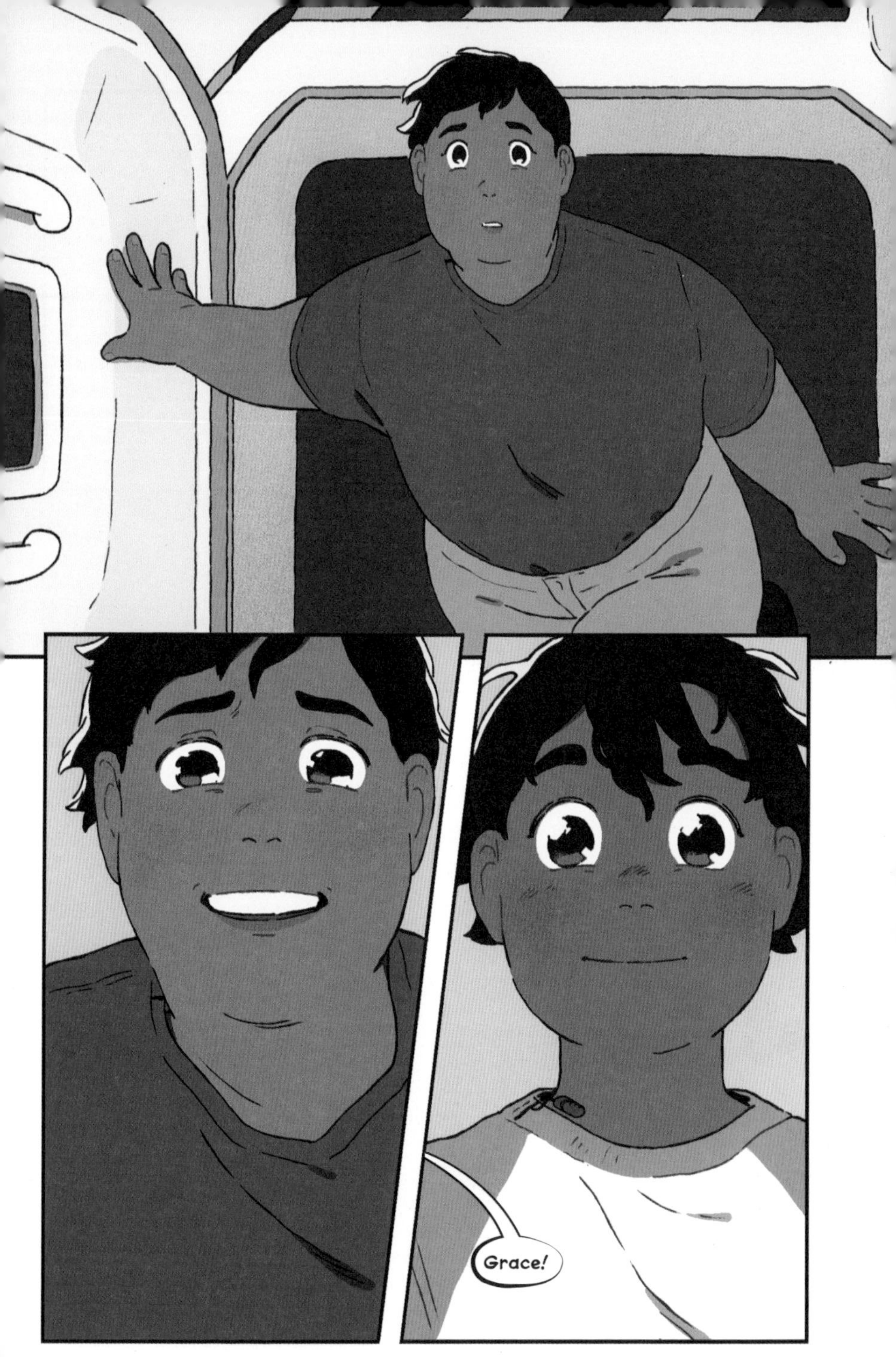
Grace!

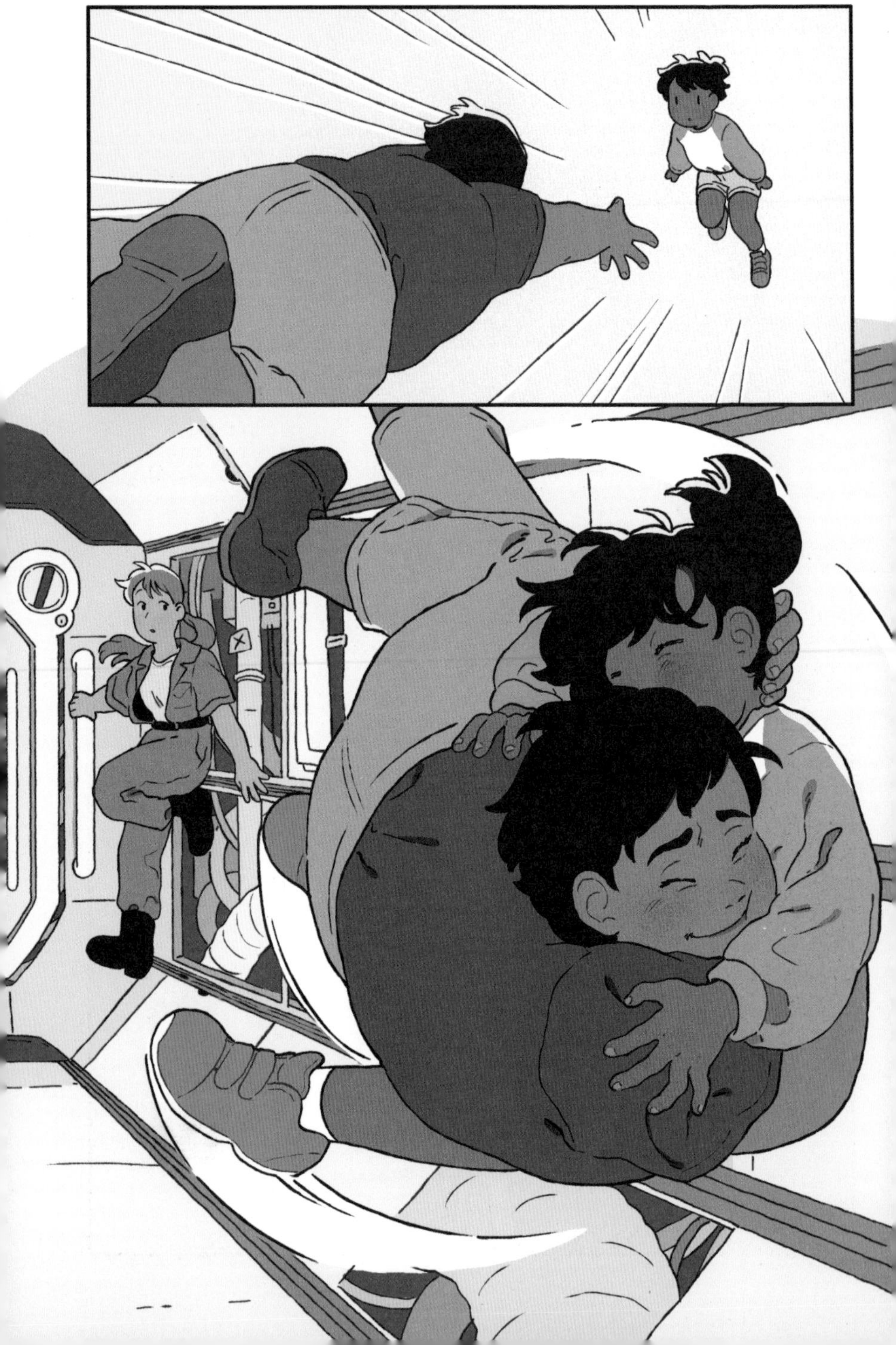

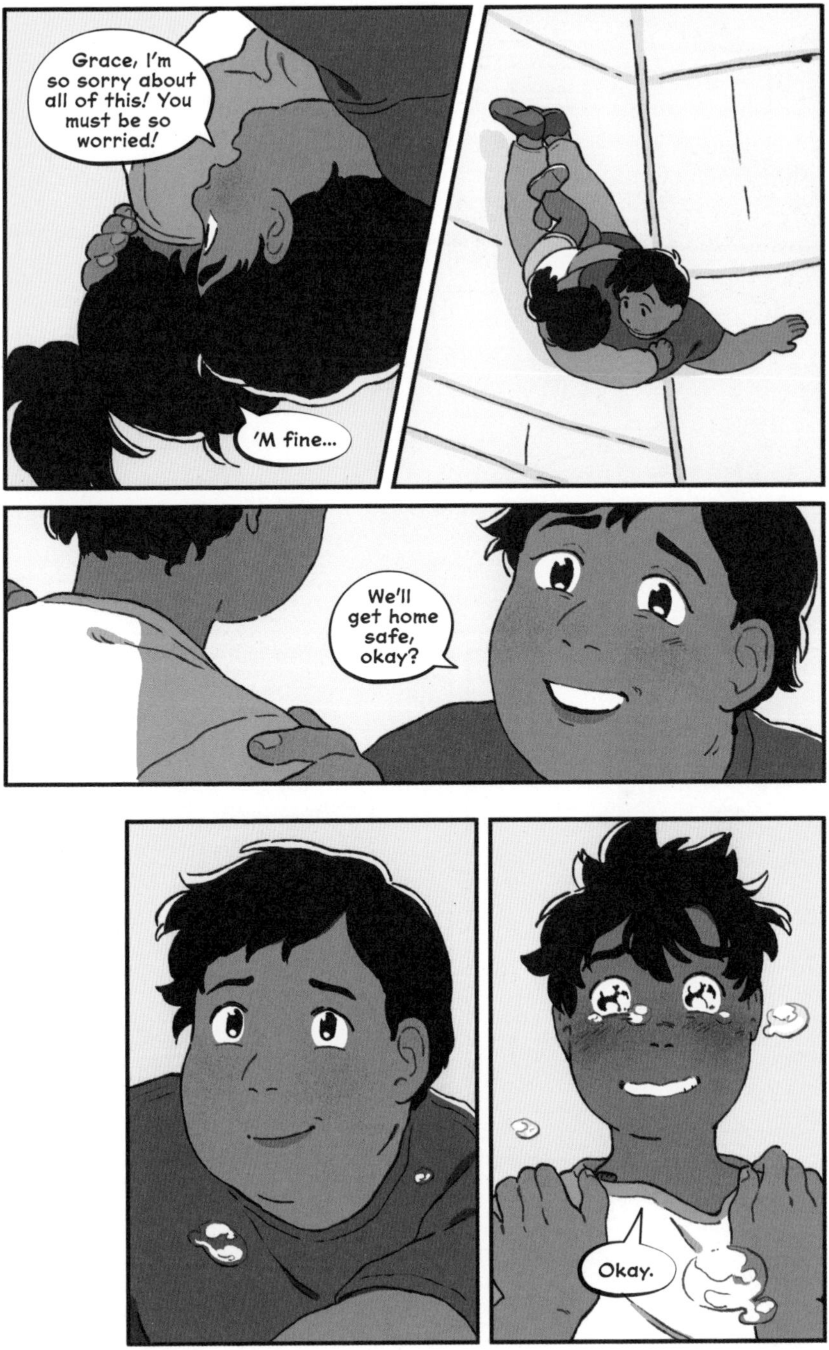
Grace, I'm so sorry about all of this! You must be so worried!
'M fine...
We'll get home safe, okay?
Okay.

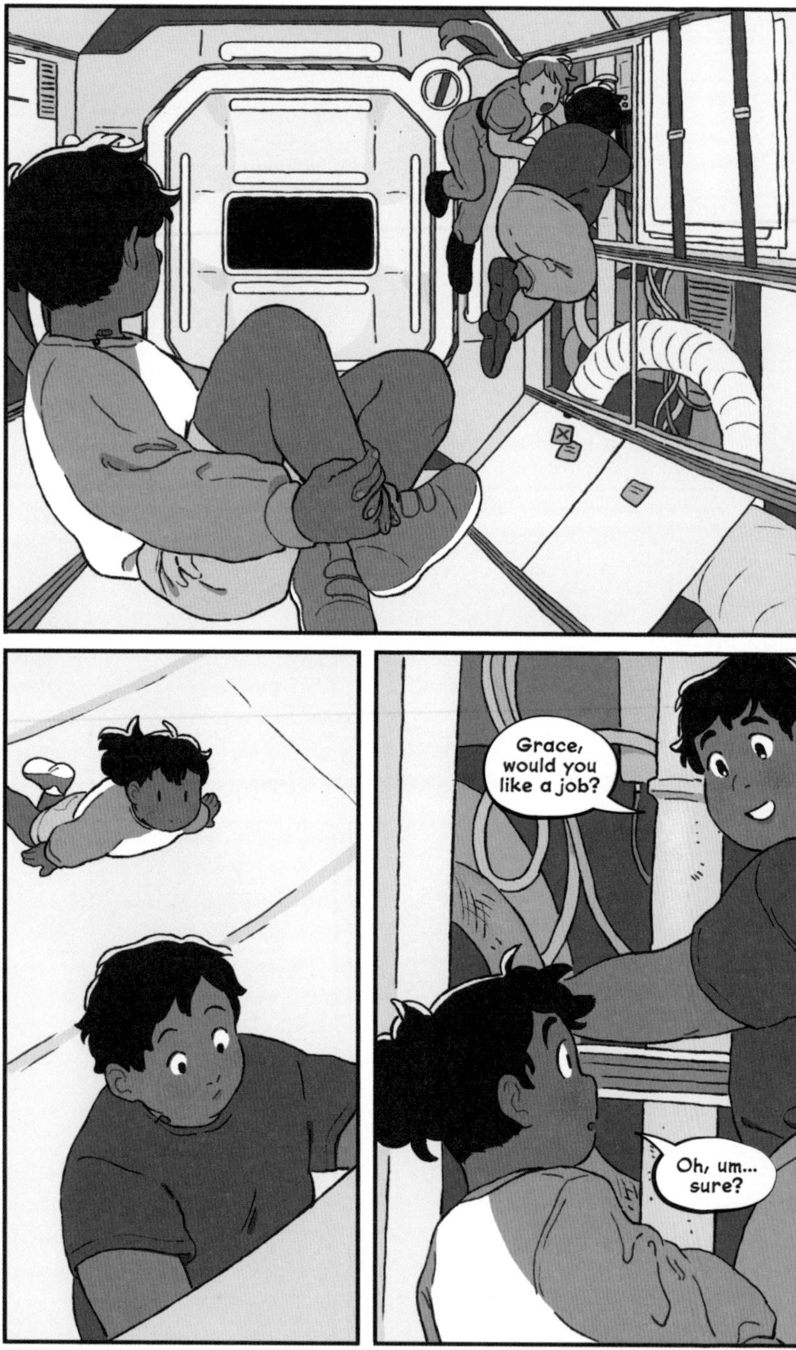
Grace, would you like a job?
Oh, um... sure?

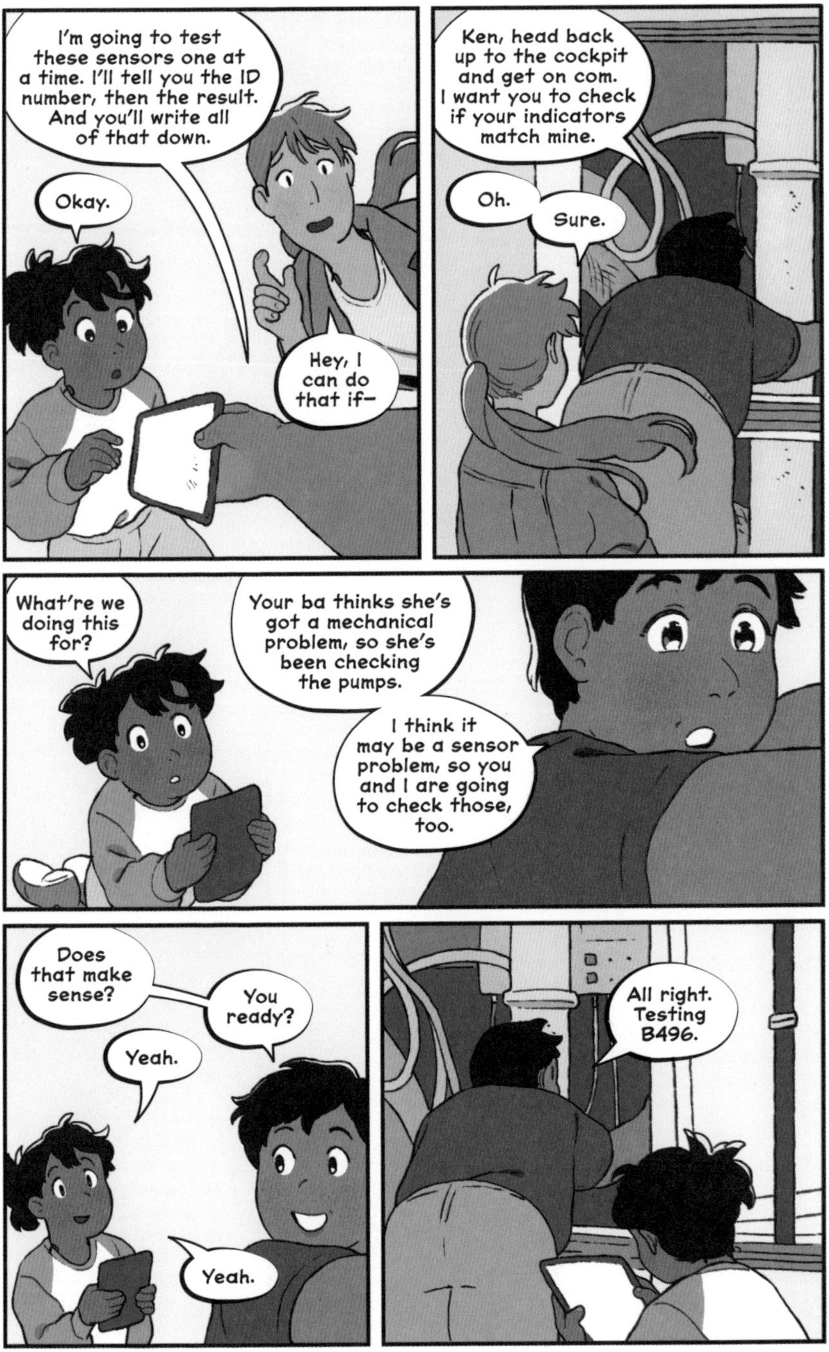
I'm going to test these sensors one at a time. I'll tell you the ID number, then the result. And you'll write all of that down.
Okay.
Hey, I can do that if—
Ken, head back up to the cockpit and get on com. I want you to check if your indicators match mine.
Oh.
Sure.
What're we doing this for?
Your ba thinks she's got a mechanical problem, so she's been checking the pumps.
I think it may be a sensor problem, so you and I are going to check those, too.
Does that make sense?
You ready?
Yeah.
Yeah.
All right. Testing B496.

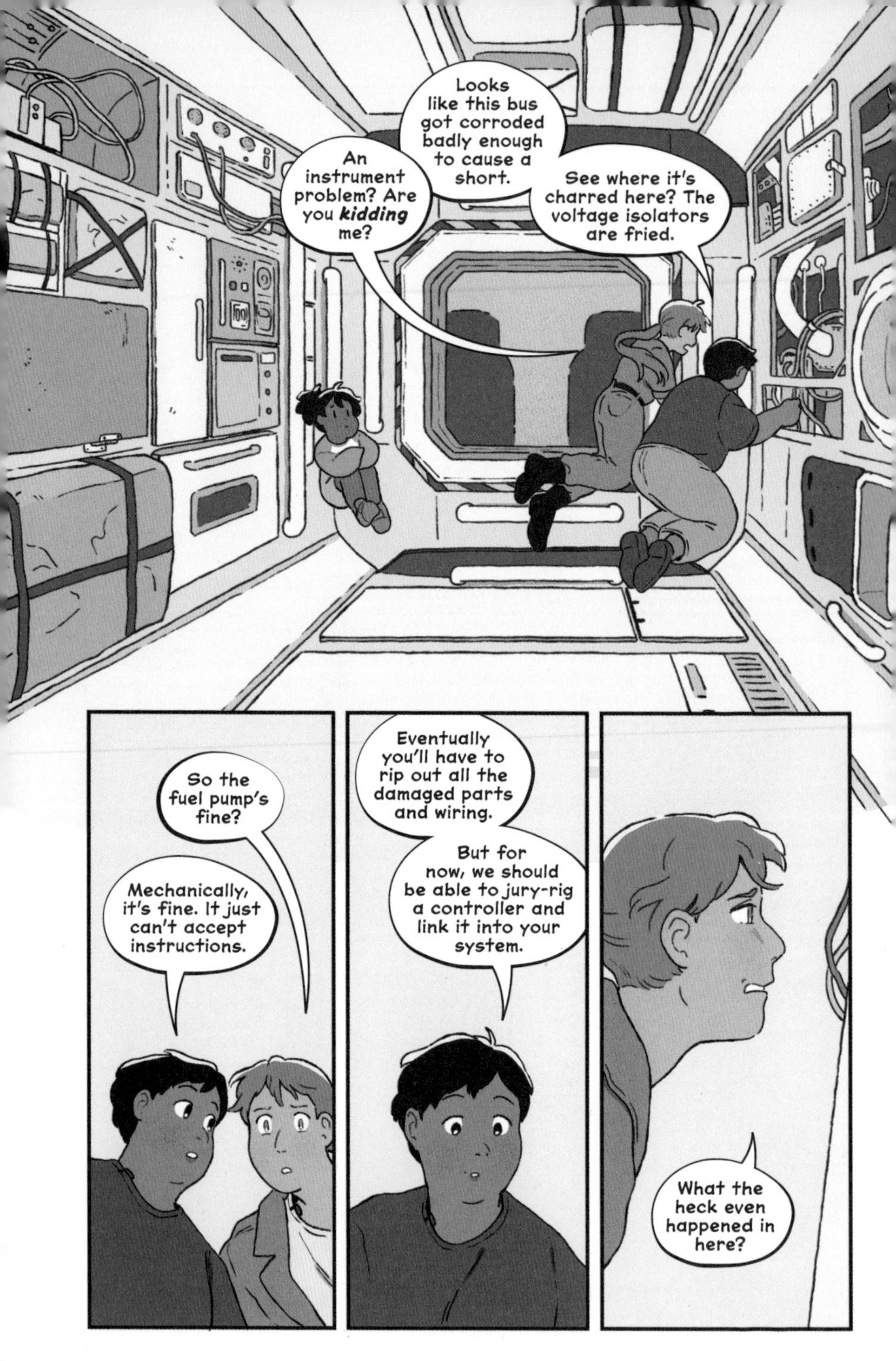
An instrument problem? Are you *kidding* me?
Looks like this bus got corroded badly enough to cause a short.
See where it's charred here? The voltage isolators are fried.
So the fuel pump's fine?
Mechanically, it's fine. It just can't accept instructions.
Eventually you'll have to rip out all the damaged parts and wiring.
But for now, we should be able to jury-rig a controller and link it into your system.
What the heck even happened in here?

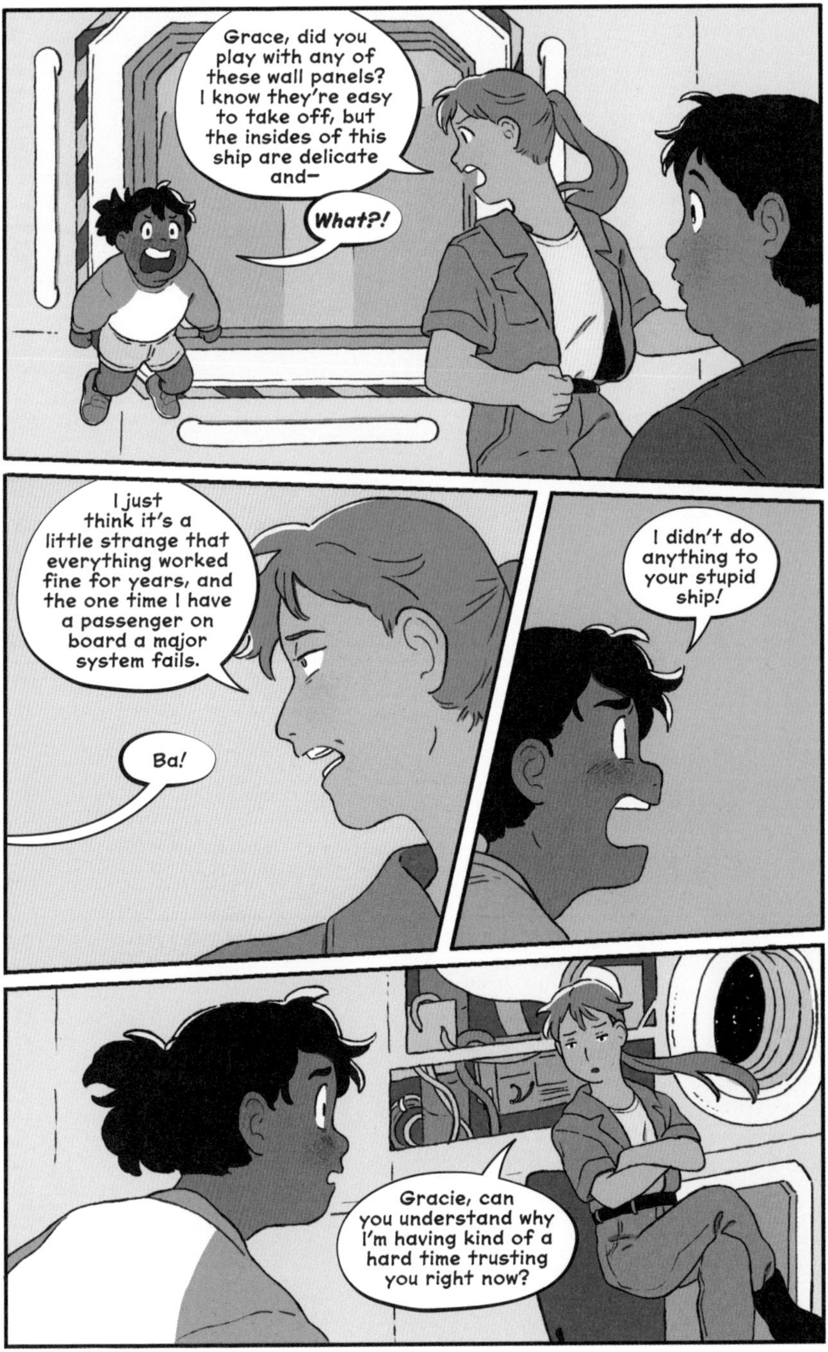
Grace, did you play with any of these wall panels? I know they're easy to take off, but the insides of this ship are delicate and—
What?!
I just think it's a little strange that everything worked fine for years, and the one time I have a passenger on board a major system fails.
I didn't do anything to your stupid ship!
Ba!
Gracie, can you understand why I'm having kind of a hard time trusting you right now?

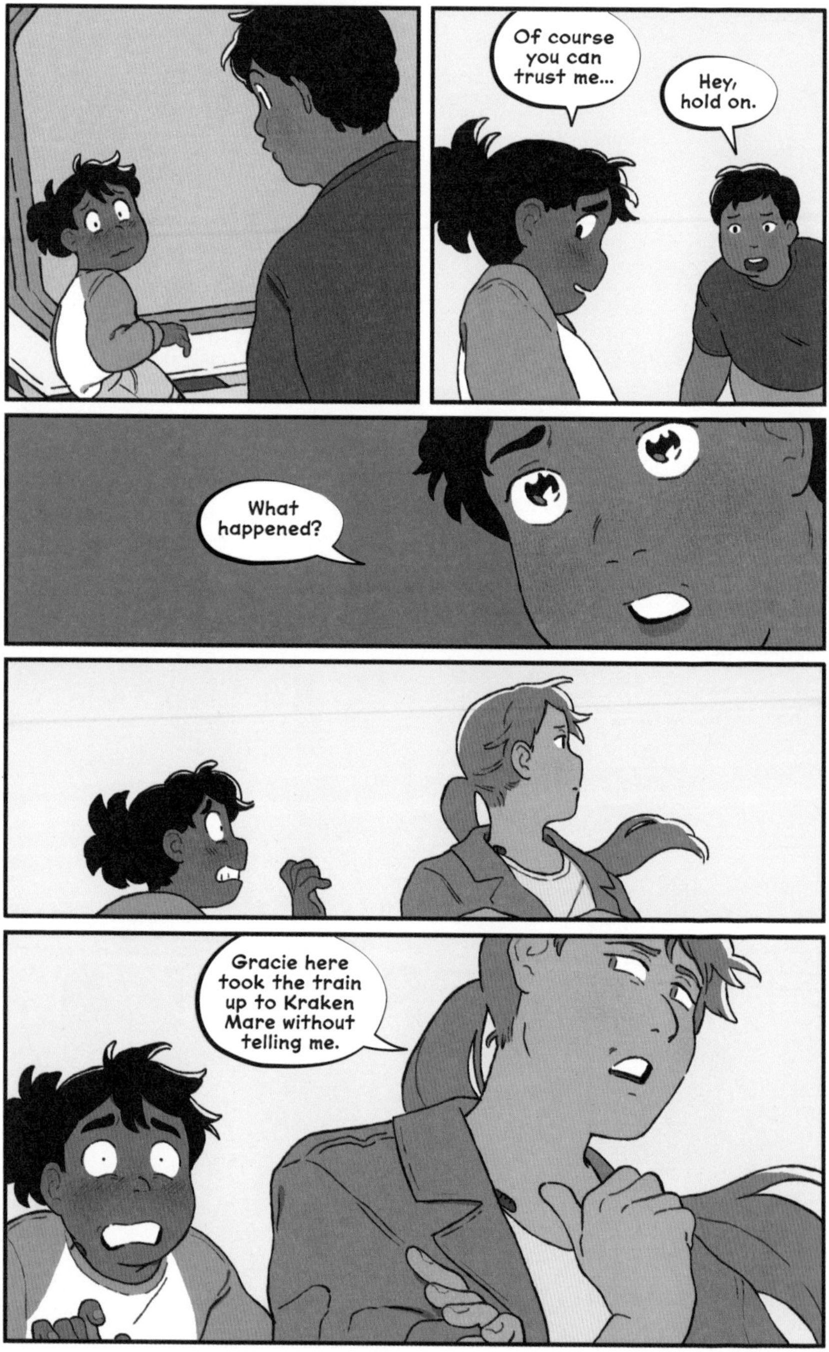
Of course you can trust me...
Hey, hold on.
What happened?
Gracie here took the train up to Kraken Mare without telling me.

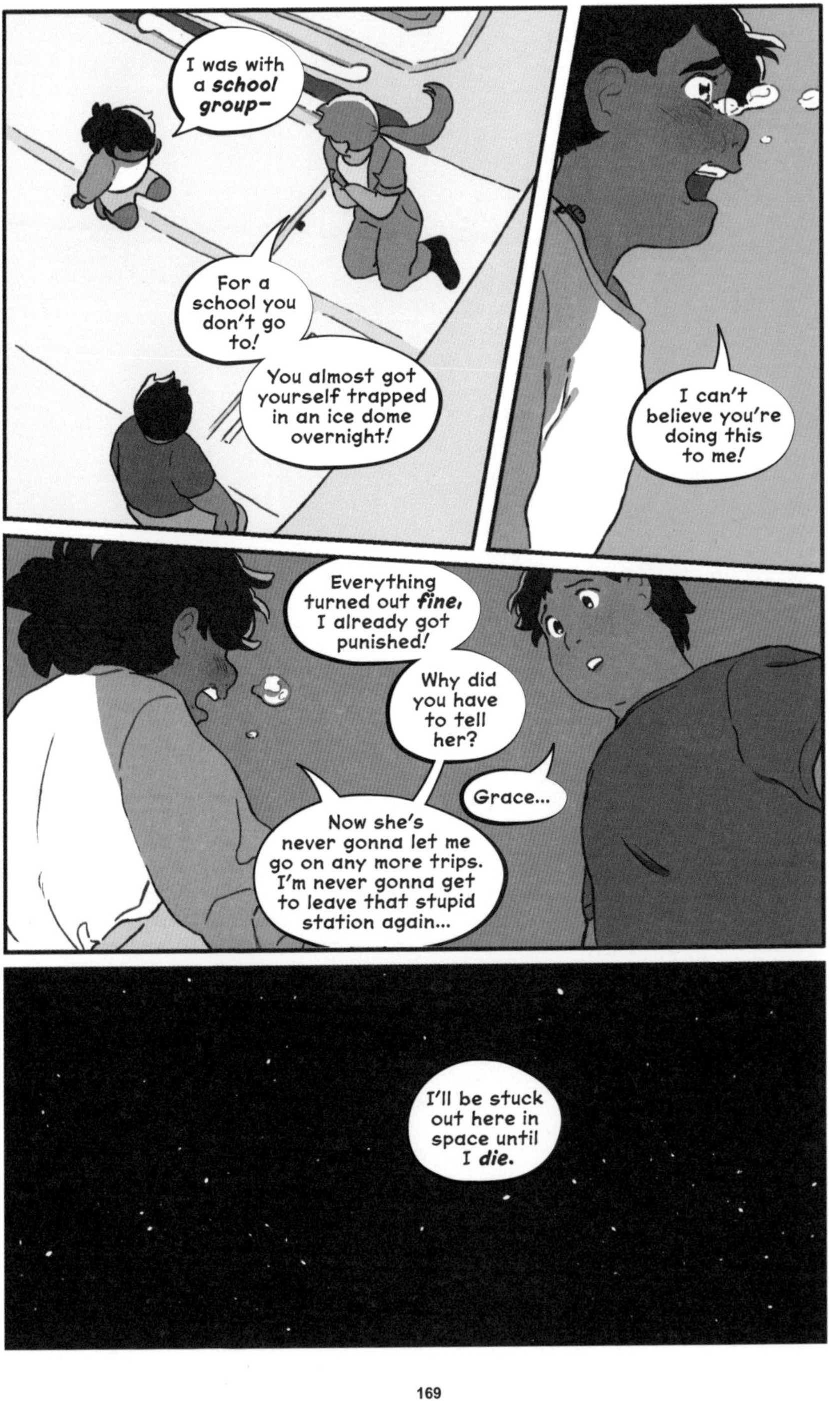
I was with a *school* *group*–
For a school you don't go to!
You almost got yourself trapped in an ice dome overnight!
I can't believe you're doing this to me!
Everything turned out *fine*, I already got punished!
Why did you have to tell her?
Grace...
Now she's never gonna let me go on any more trips. I'm never gonna get to leave that stupid station again...
I'll be stuck out here in space until I *die*.

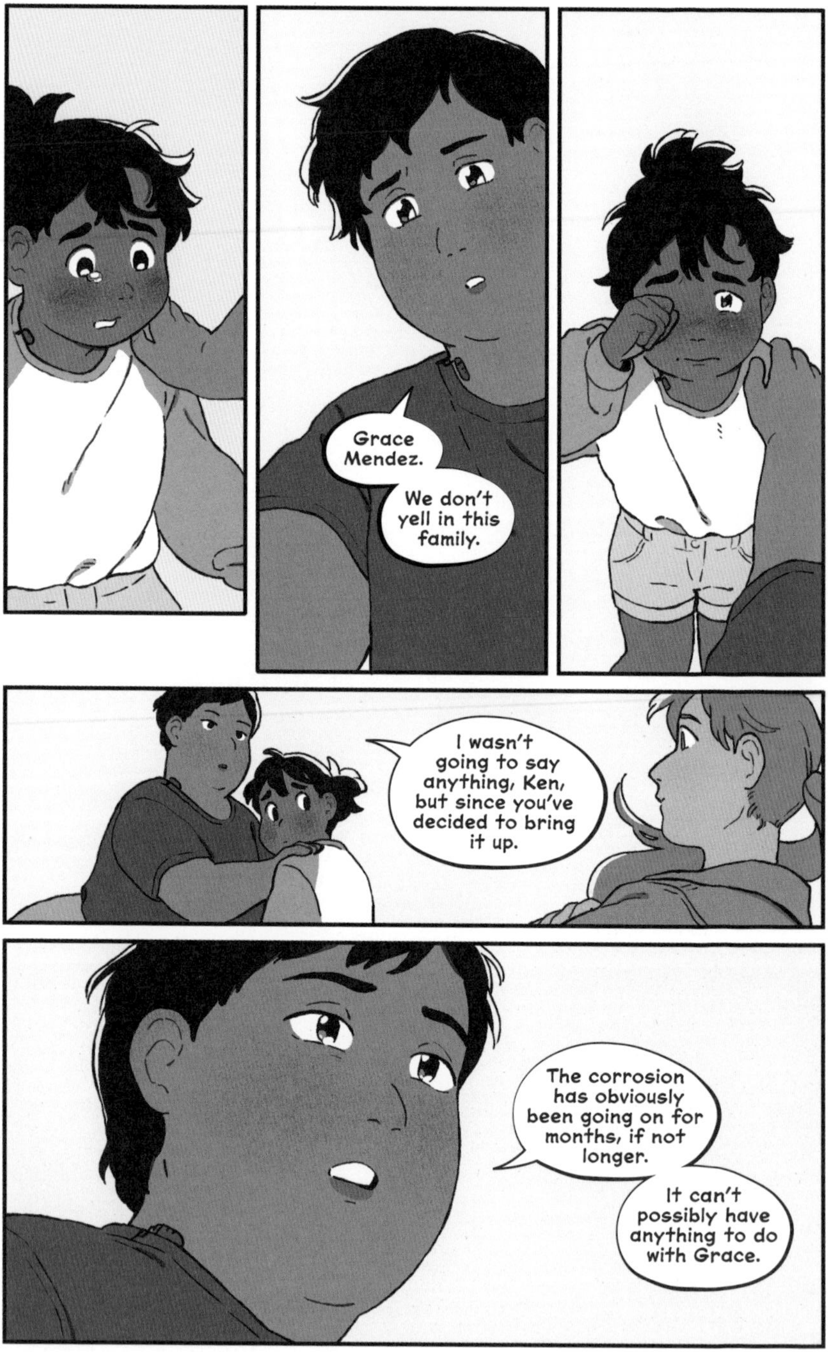
Grace Mendez.
We don't yell in this family.
I wasn't going to say anything, Ken, but since you've decided to bring it up.
The corrosion has obviously been going on for months, if not longer.
It can't possibly have anything to do with Grace.

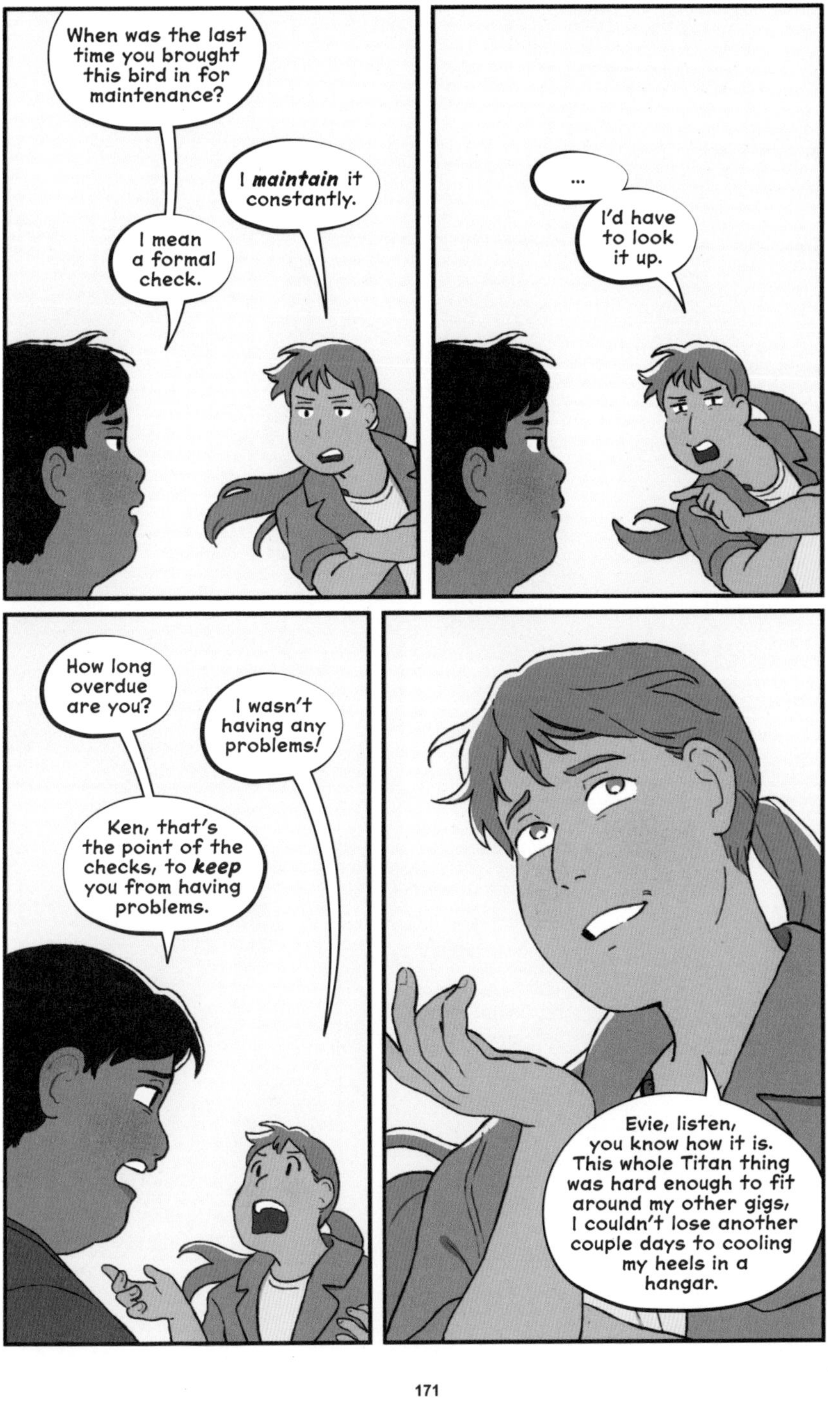
When was the last time you brought this bird in for maintenance?
I maintain it constantly.
I mean a formal check.
...
I'd have to look it up.
How long overdue are you?
I wasn't having any problems!
Ken, that's the point of the checks, to keep you from having problems.
Evie, listen, you know how it is. This whole Titan thing was hard enough to fit around my other gigs, I couldn't lose another couple days to cooling my heels in a hangar.

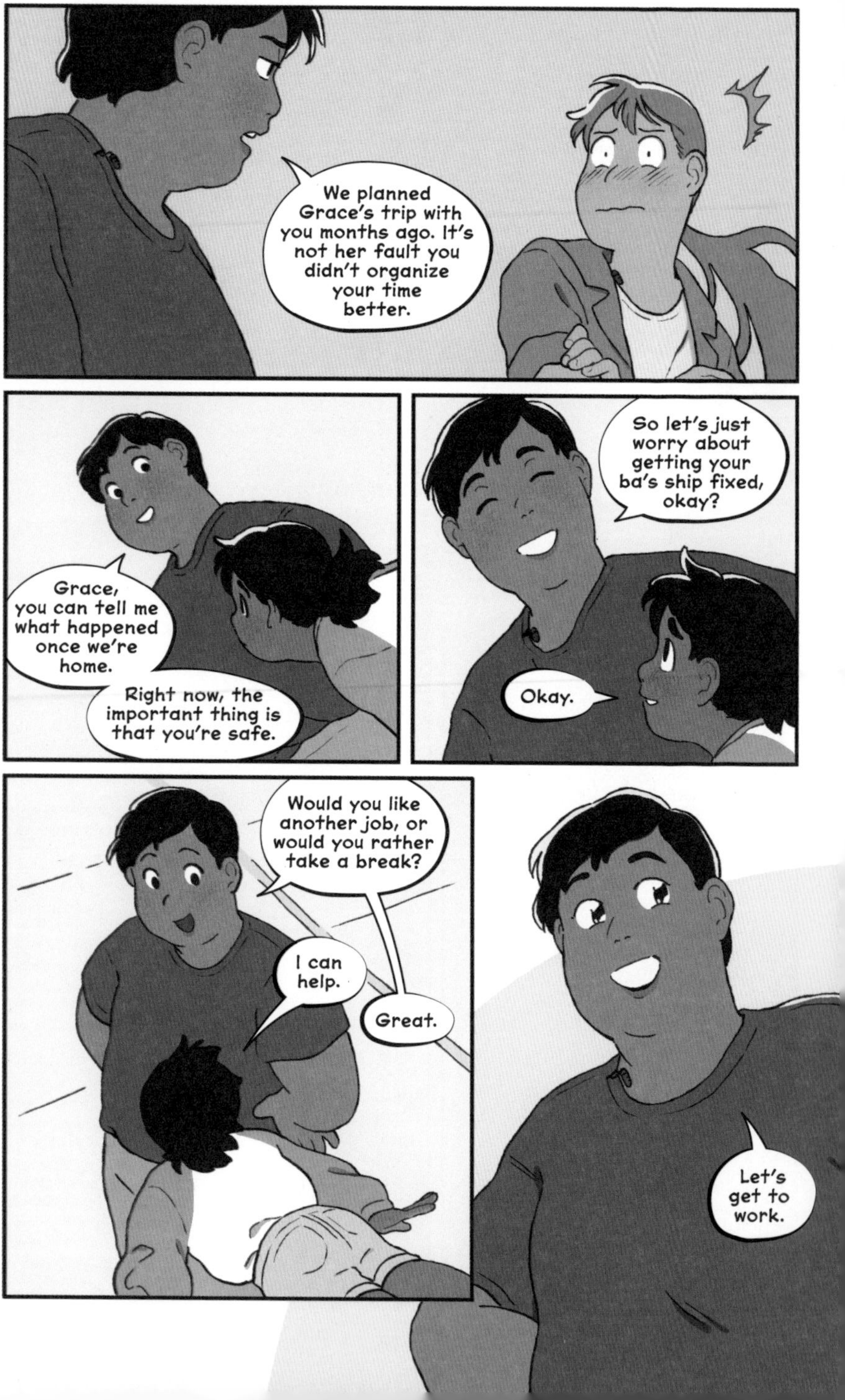
We planned Grace's trip with you months ago. It's not her fault you didn't organize your time better.
Grace, you can tell me what happened once we're home.
Right now, the important thing is that you're safe.
So let's just worry about getting your ba's ship fixed, okay?
Okay.
Would you like another job, or would you rather take a break?
I can help.
Great.
Let's get to work.

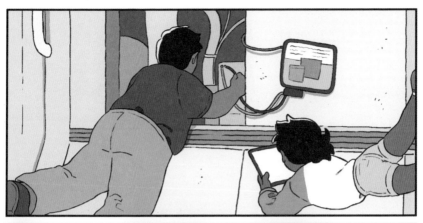

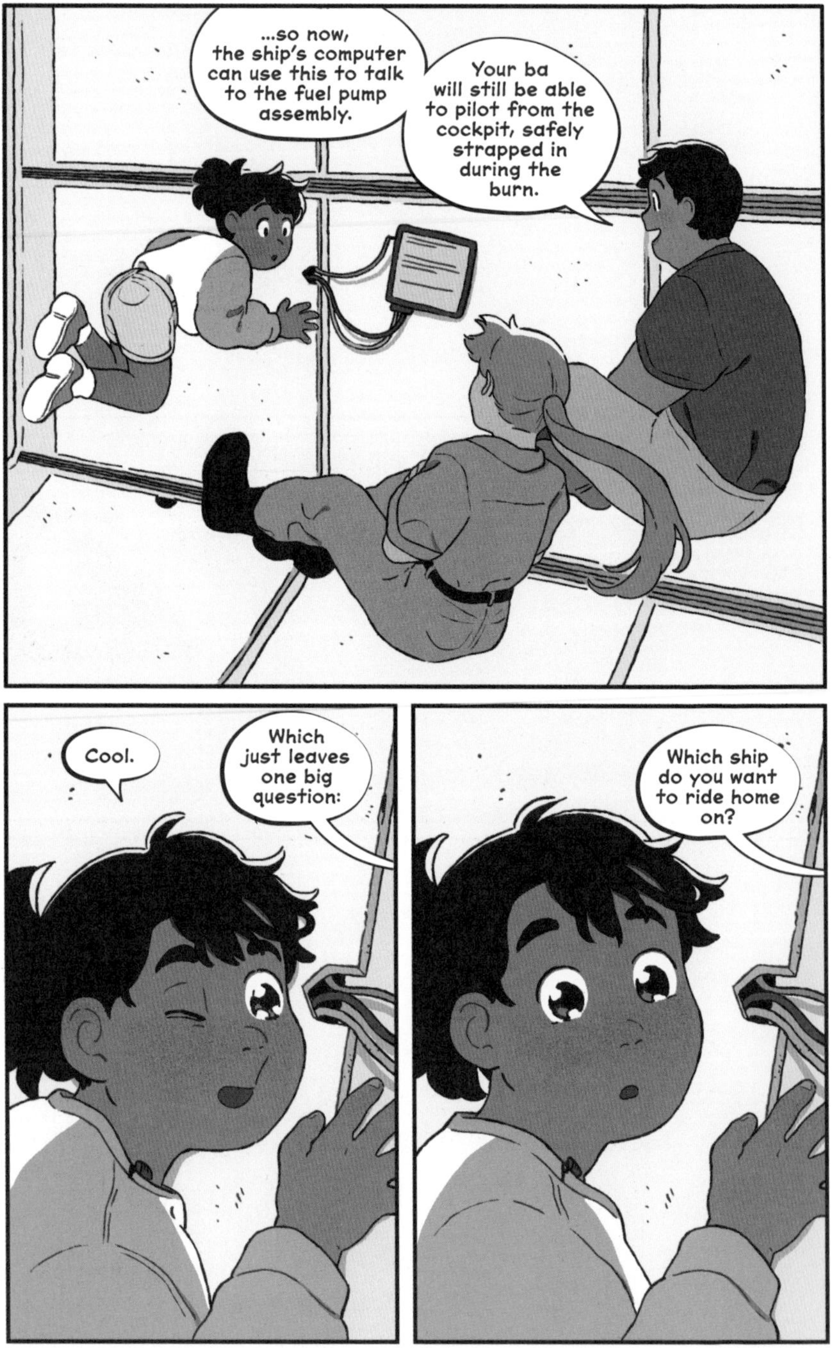
...so now, the ship's computer can use this to talk to the fuel pump assembly.
Your ba will still be able to pilot from the cockpit, safely strapped in during the burn.
Cool.
Which just leaves one big question:
Which ship do you want to ride home on?

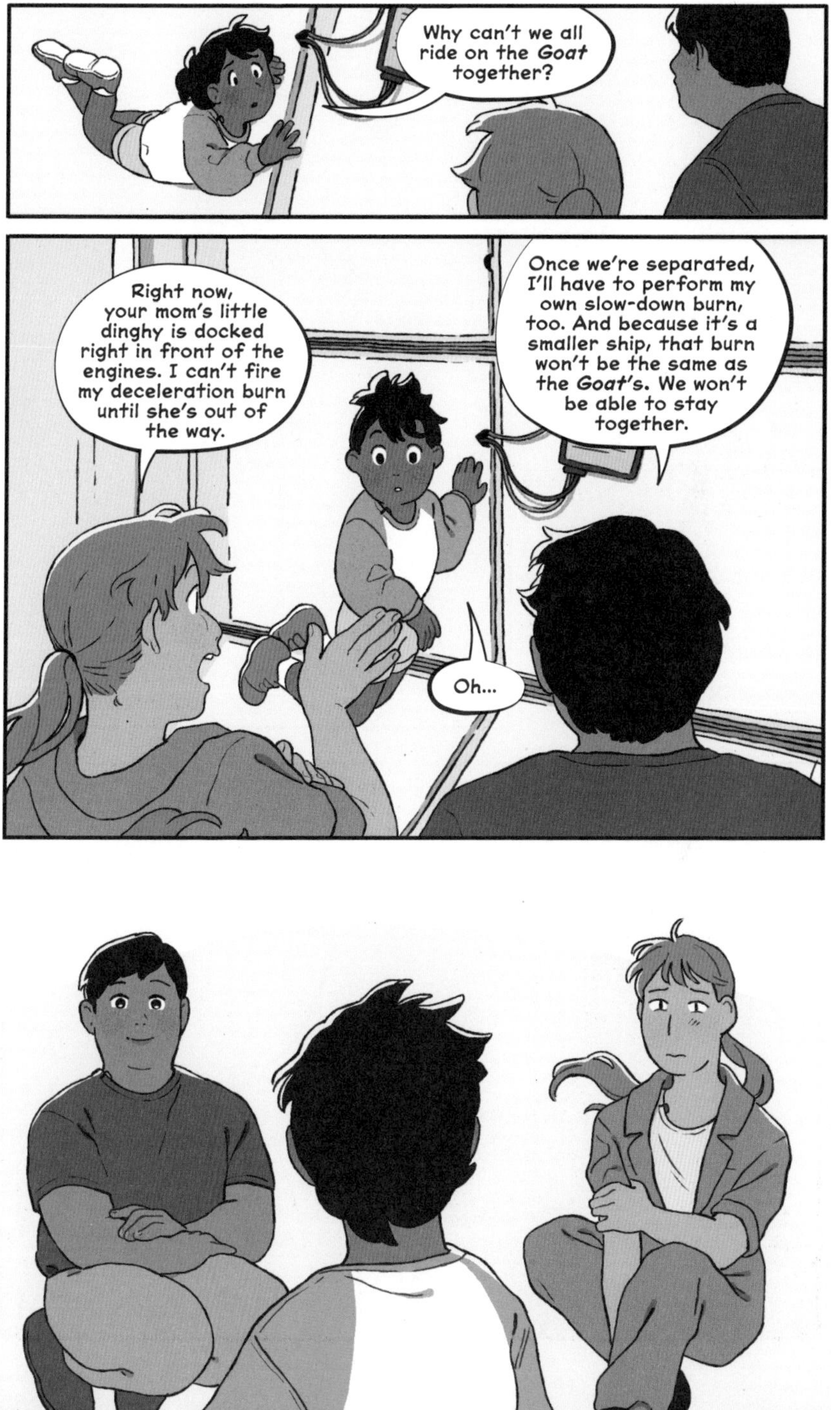
Why can't we all ride on the *Goat* together?
Right now, your mom's little dinghy is docked right in front of the engines. I can't fire my deceleration burn until she's out of the way.
Once we're separated, I'll have to perform my own slow-down burn, too. And because it's a smaller ship, that burn won't be the same as the *Goat's*. We won't be able to stay together.
Oh...

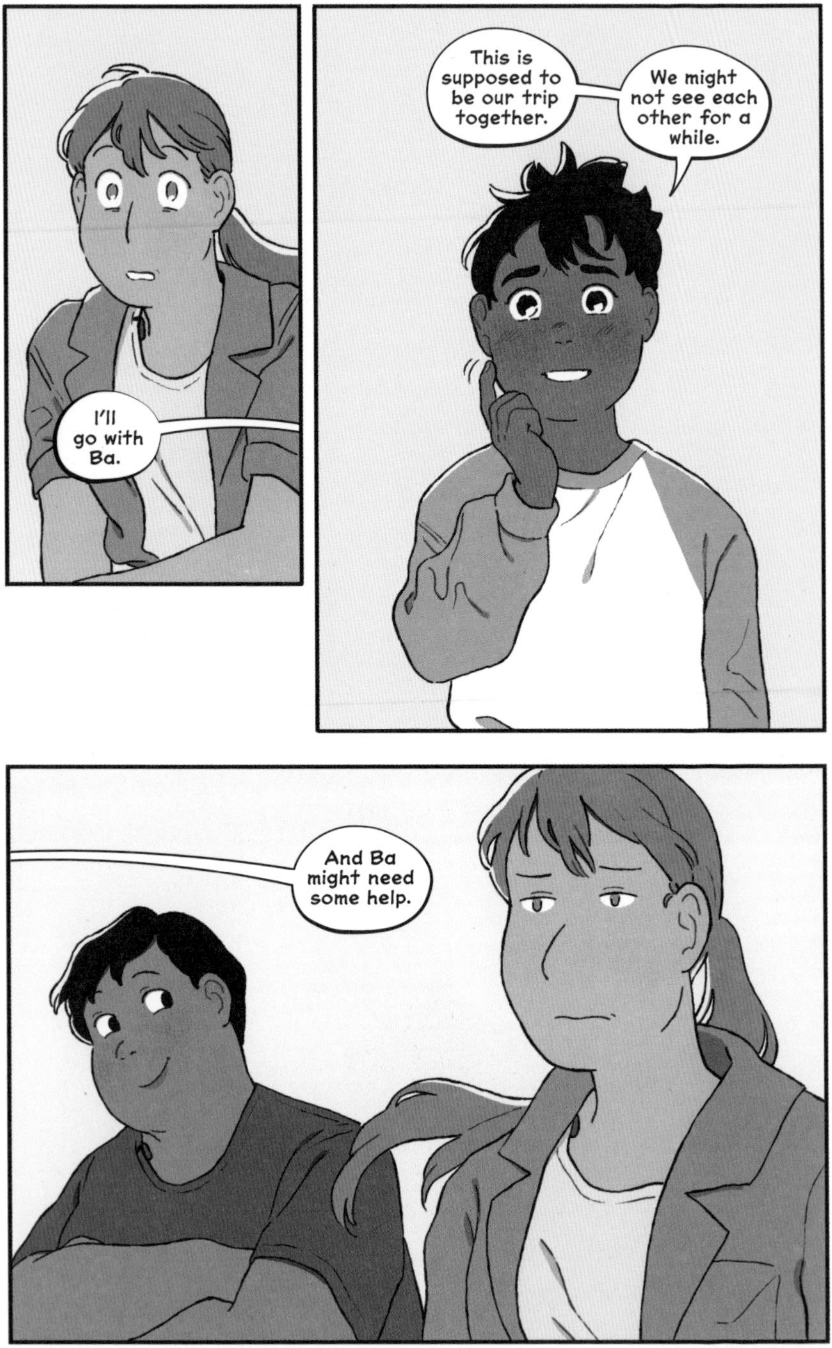
I'll go with Ba.
This is supposed to be our trip together.
We might not see each other for a while.
And Ba might need some help.

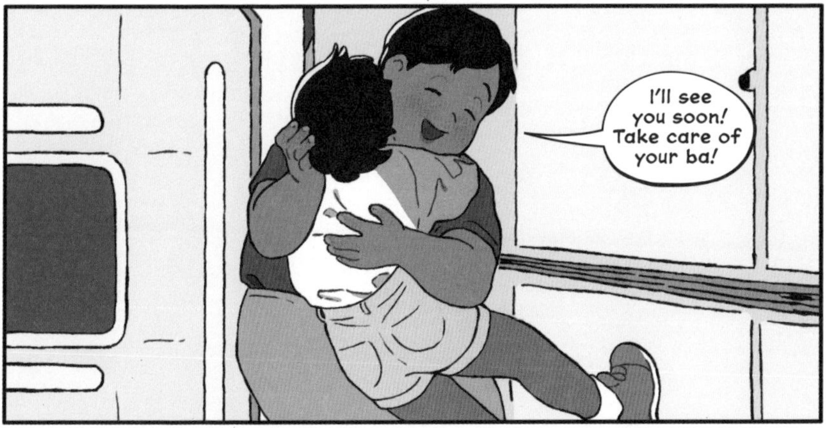
I'll see you soon! Take care of your ba!

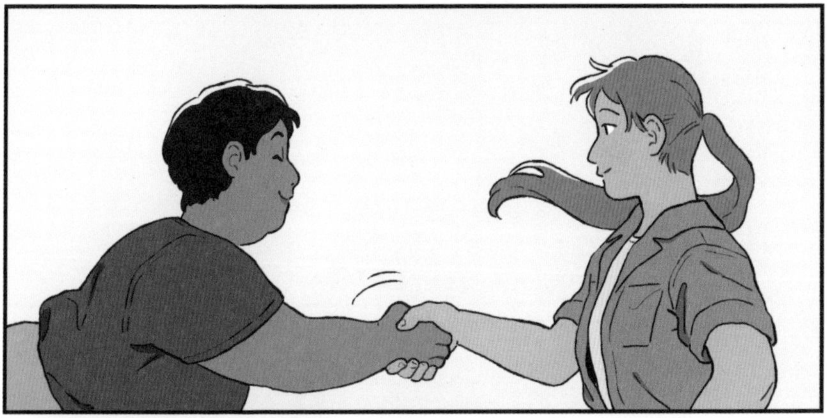

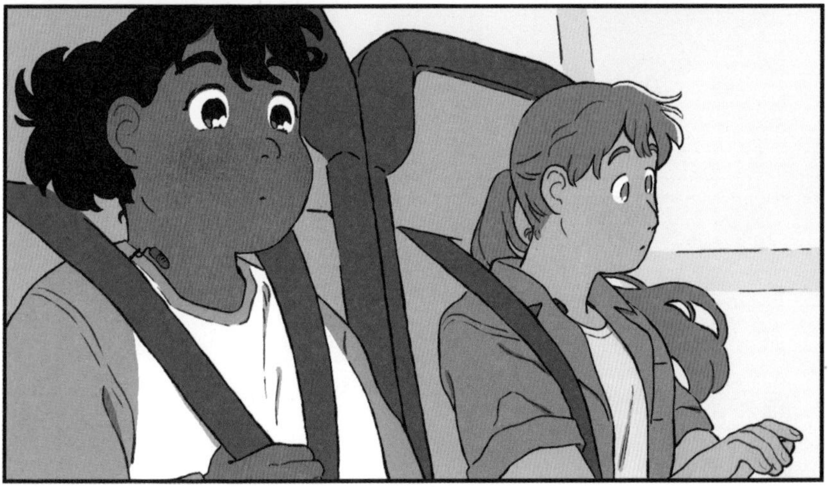

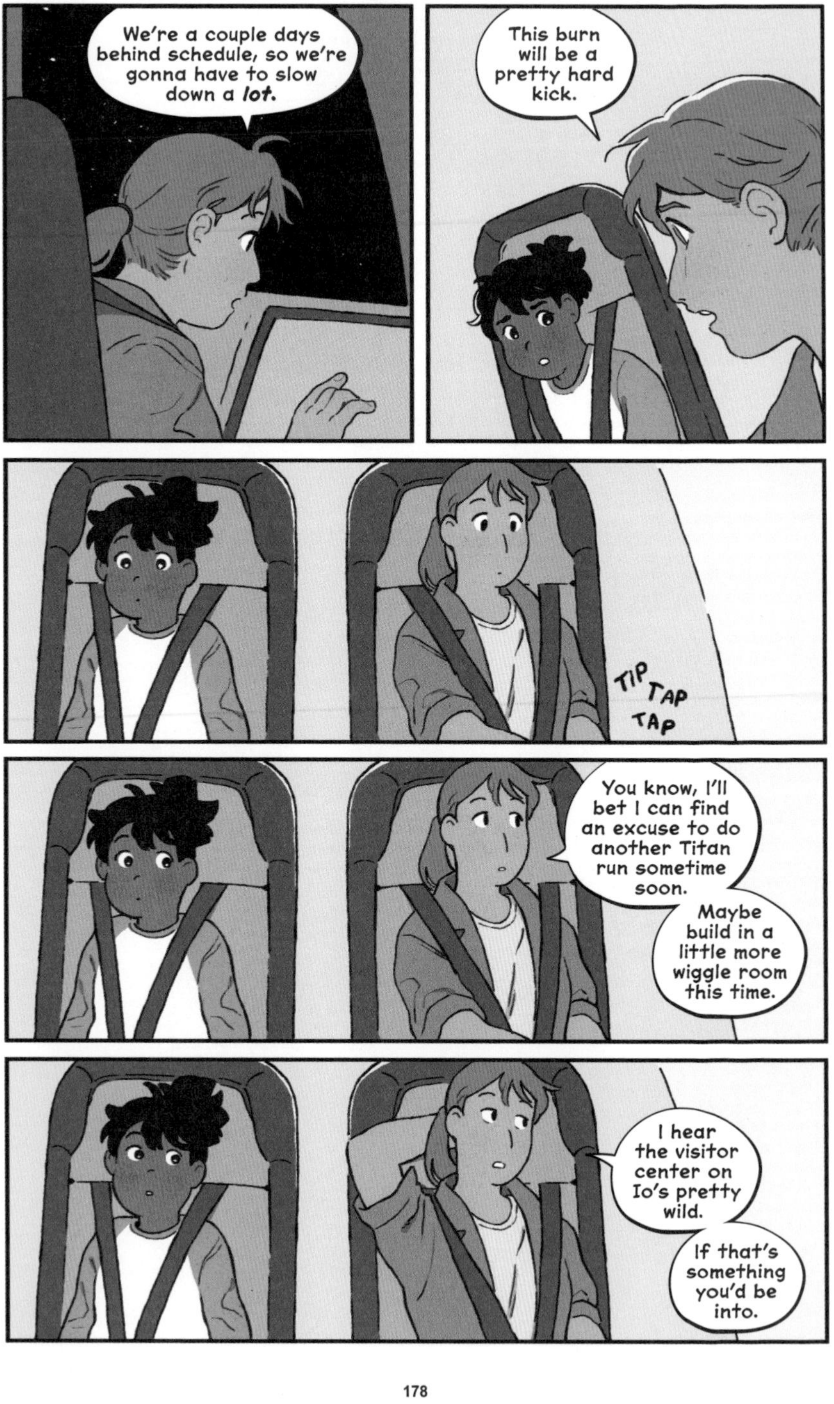
We're a couple days behind schedule, so we're gonna have to slow down a *lot.*
This burn will be a pretty hard kick.
TIP TAP TAP
You know, I'll bet I can find an excuse to do another Titan run sometime soon.
Maybe build in a little more wiggle room this time.
I hear the visitor center on Io's pretty wild.
If that's something you'd be into.

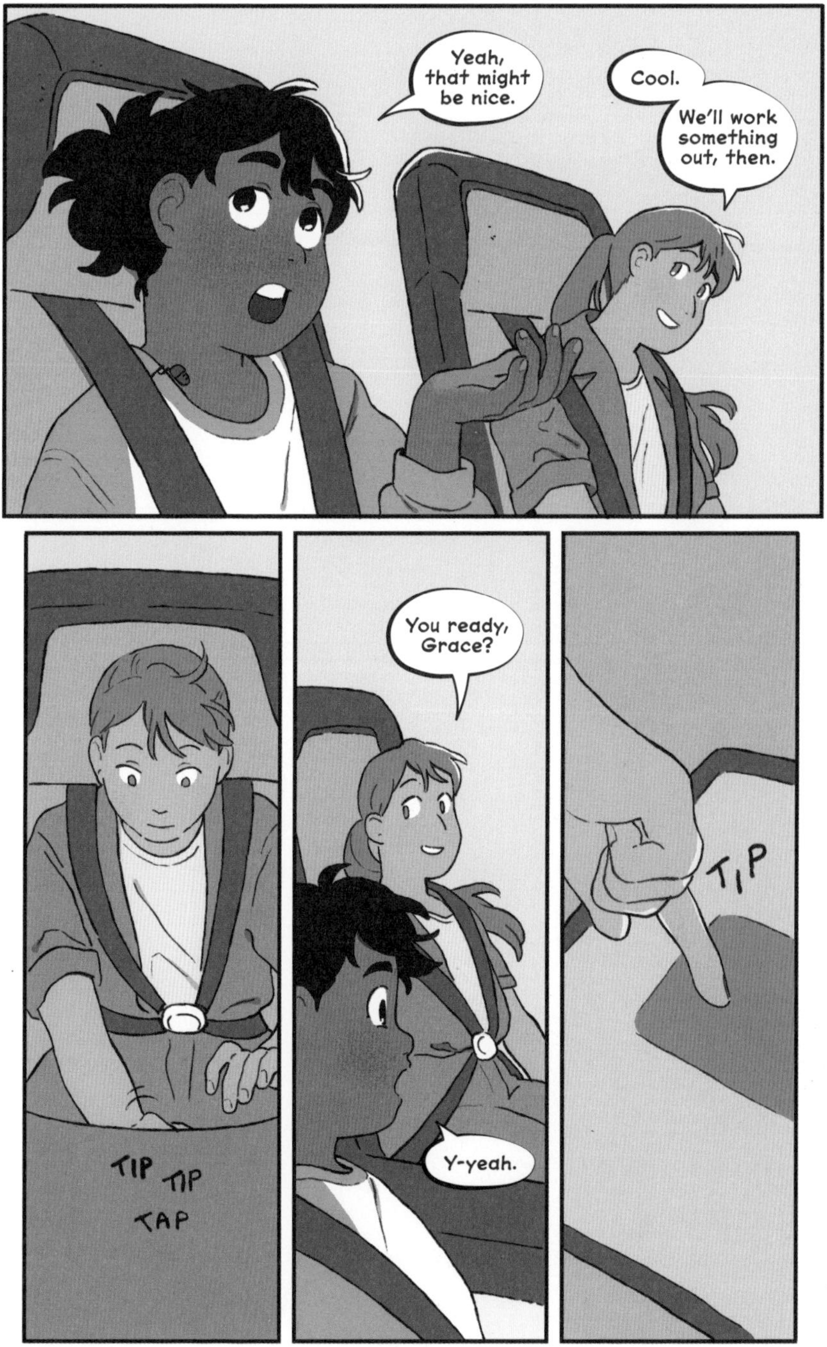
Yeah, that might be nice.
Cool.
We'll work something out, then.
TIP TIP TAP
You ready, Grace?
Y-yeah.
TIP

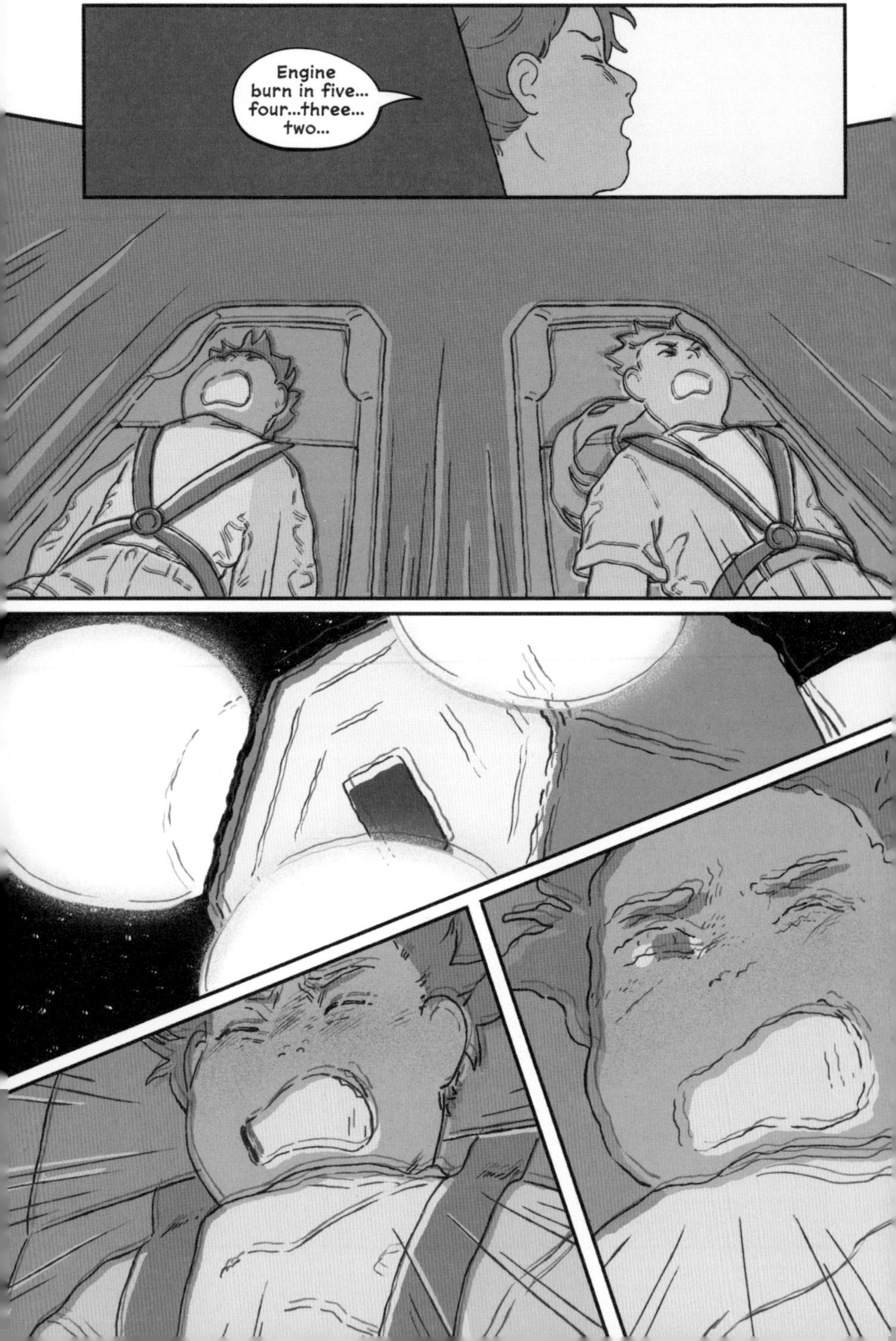
Engine burn in five... four...three... two...

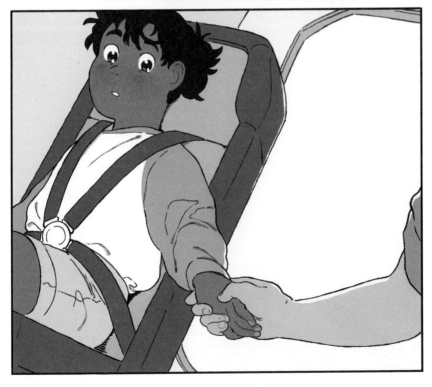

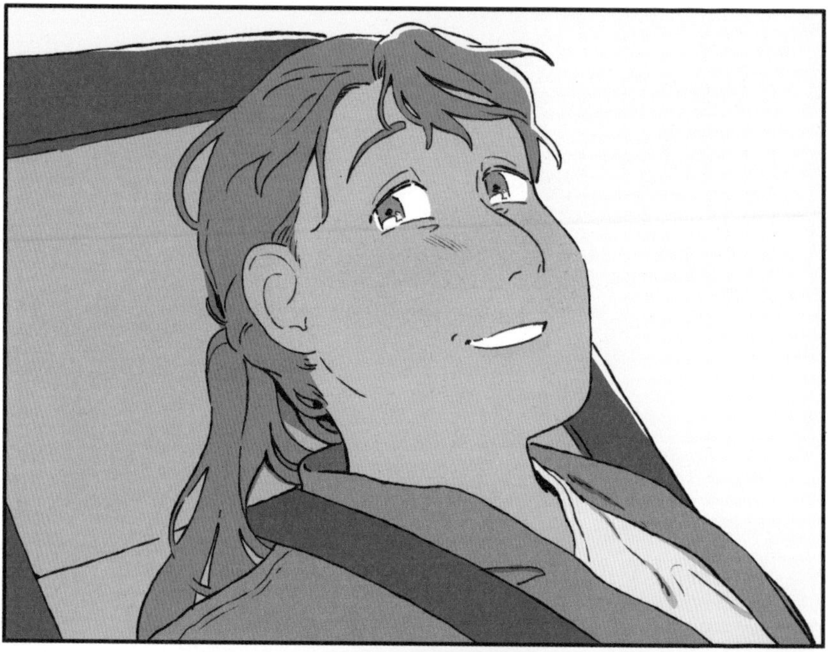

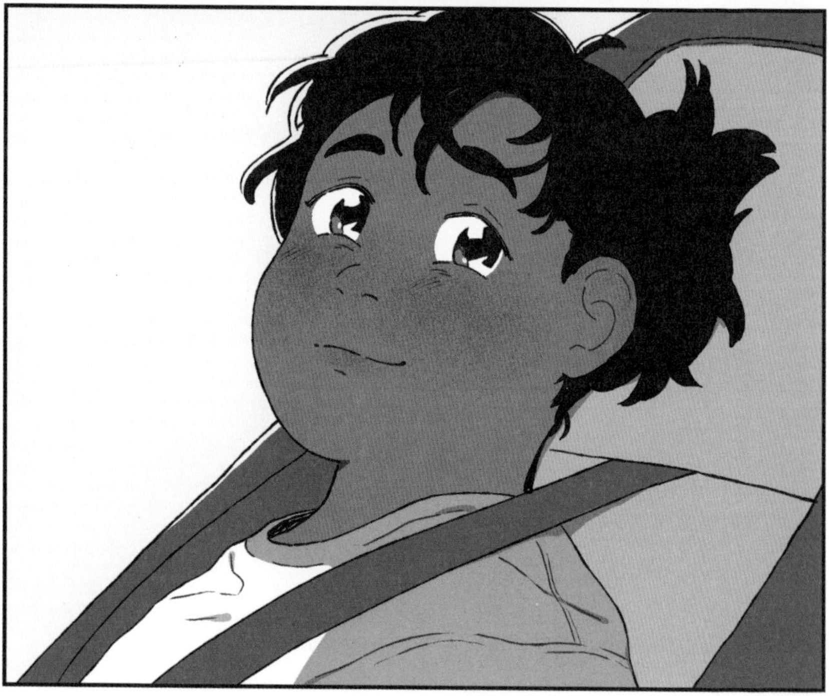

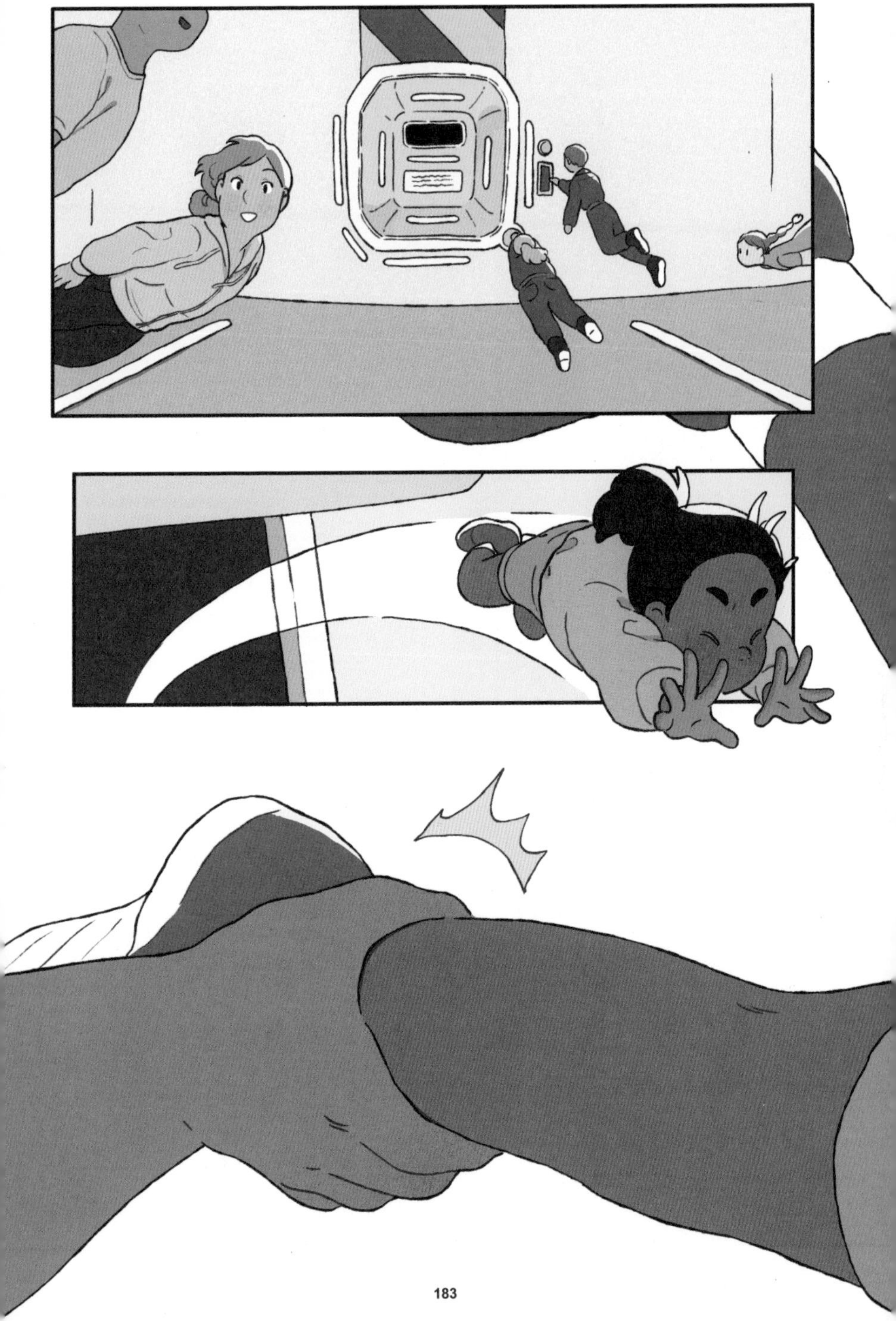

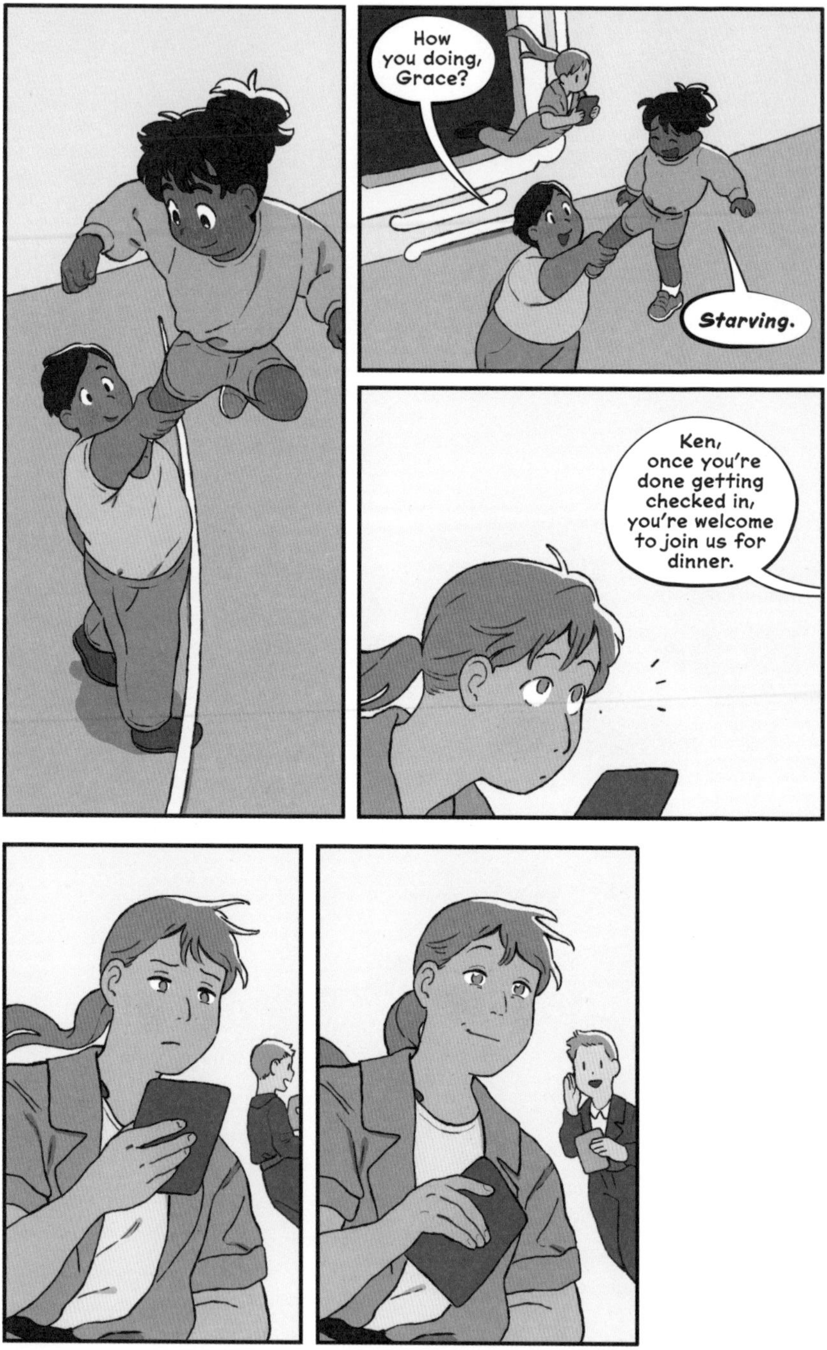
How you doing, Grace?
Starving.
Ken, once you're done getting checked in, you're welcome to join us for dinner.

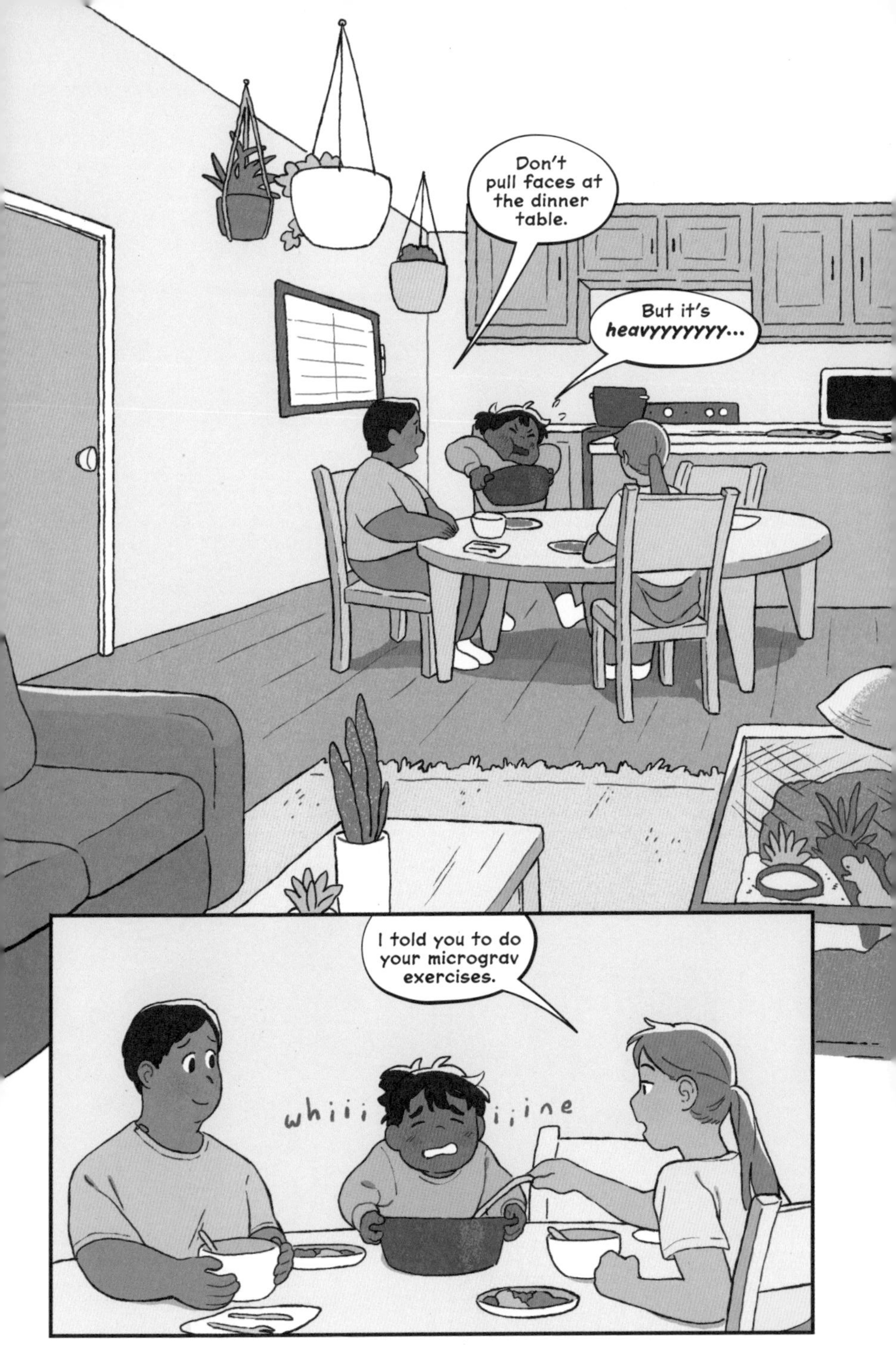
Don't pull faces at the dinner table.
But it's *heavyyyyyyy...*
I told you to do your micrograv exercises.
whiiiiiine

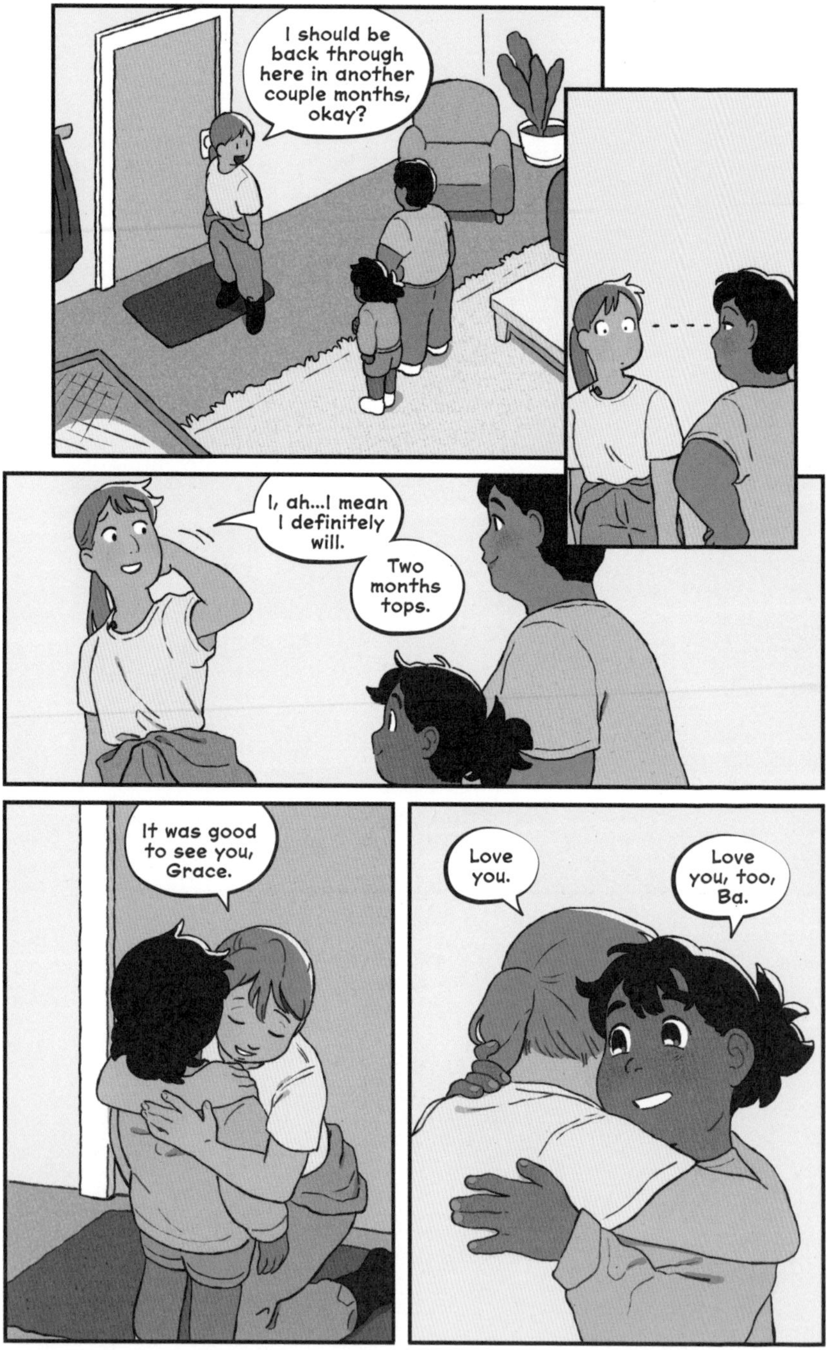
I should be back through here in another couple months, okay?
I, ah...I mean I definitely will.
Two months tops.
It was good to see you, Grace.
Love you.
Love you, too, Ba.

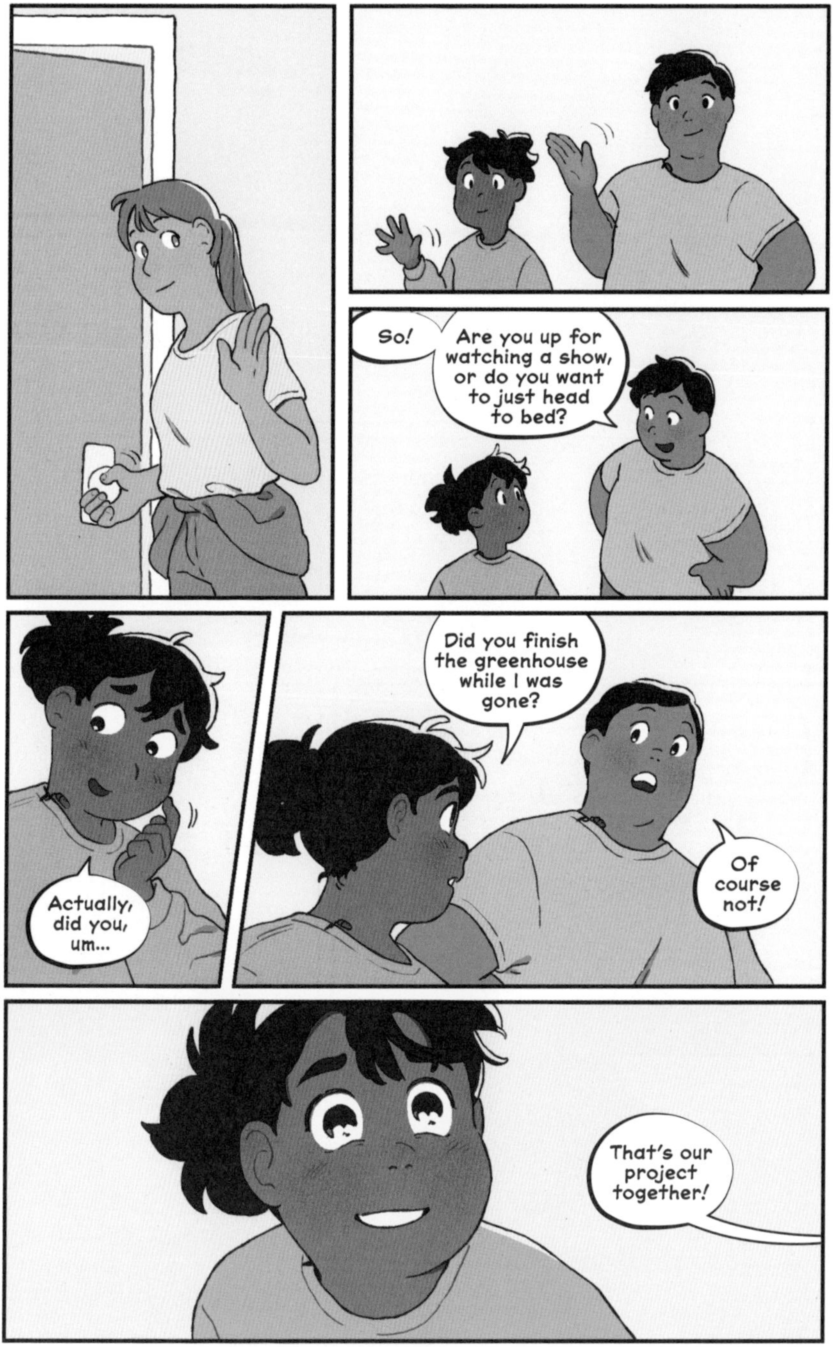
So!
Are you up for watching a show, or do you want to just head to bed?
Actually, did you, um...
Did you finish the greenhouse while I was gone?
Of course not!
That's our project together!

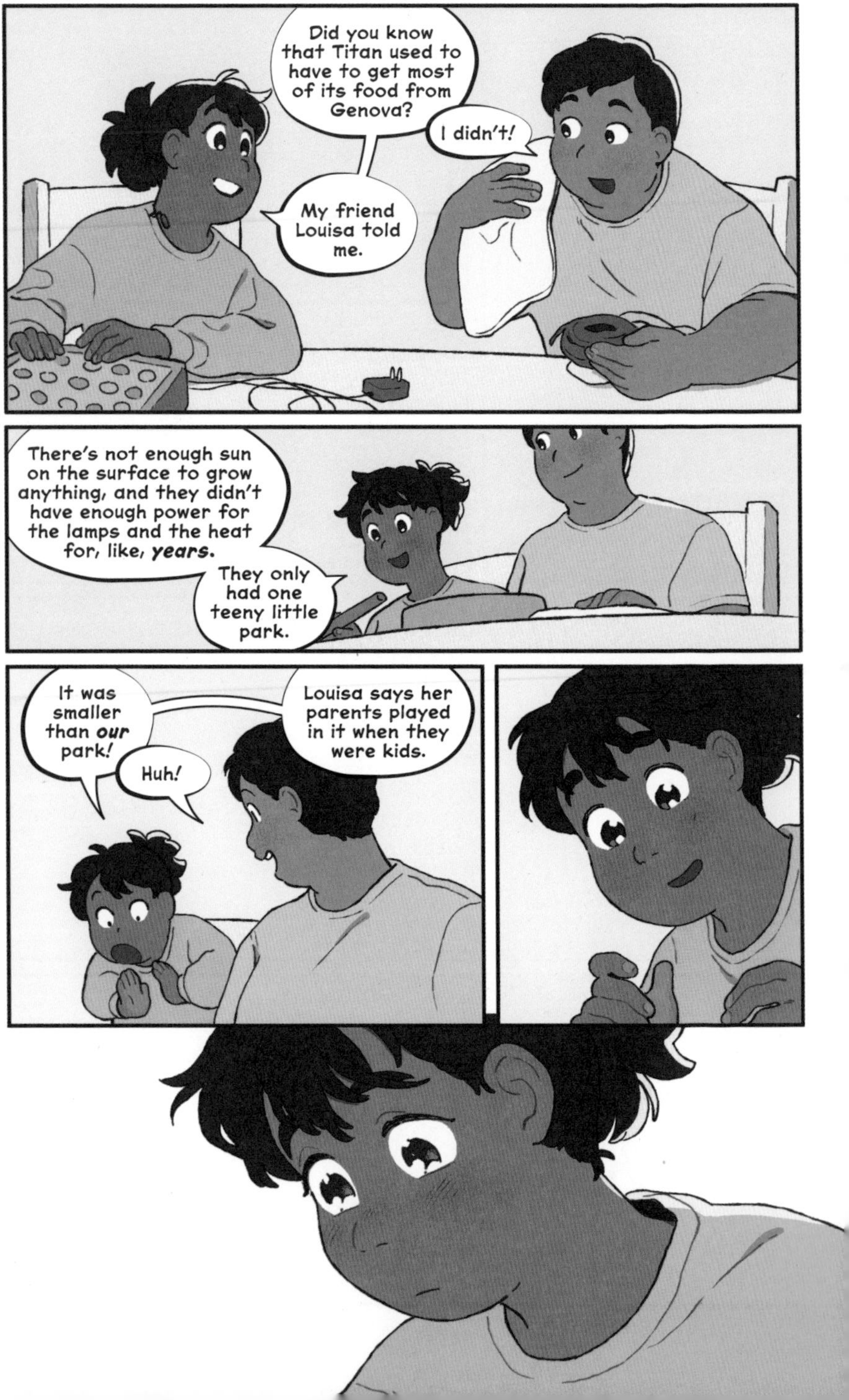
Did you know that Titan used to have to get most of its food from Genova?
I didn't!
My friend Louisa told me.
There's not enough sun on the surface to grow anything, and they didn't have enough power for the lamps and the heat for, like, *years.*
They only had one teeny little park.
It was smaller than *our* park!
Huh!
Louisa says her parents played in it when they were kids.

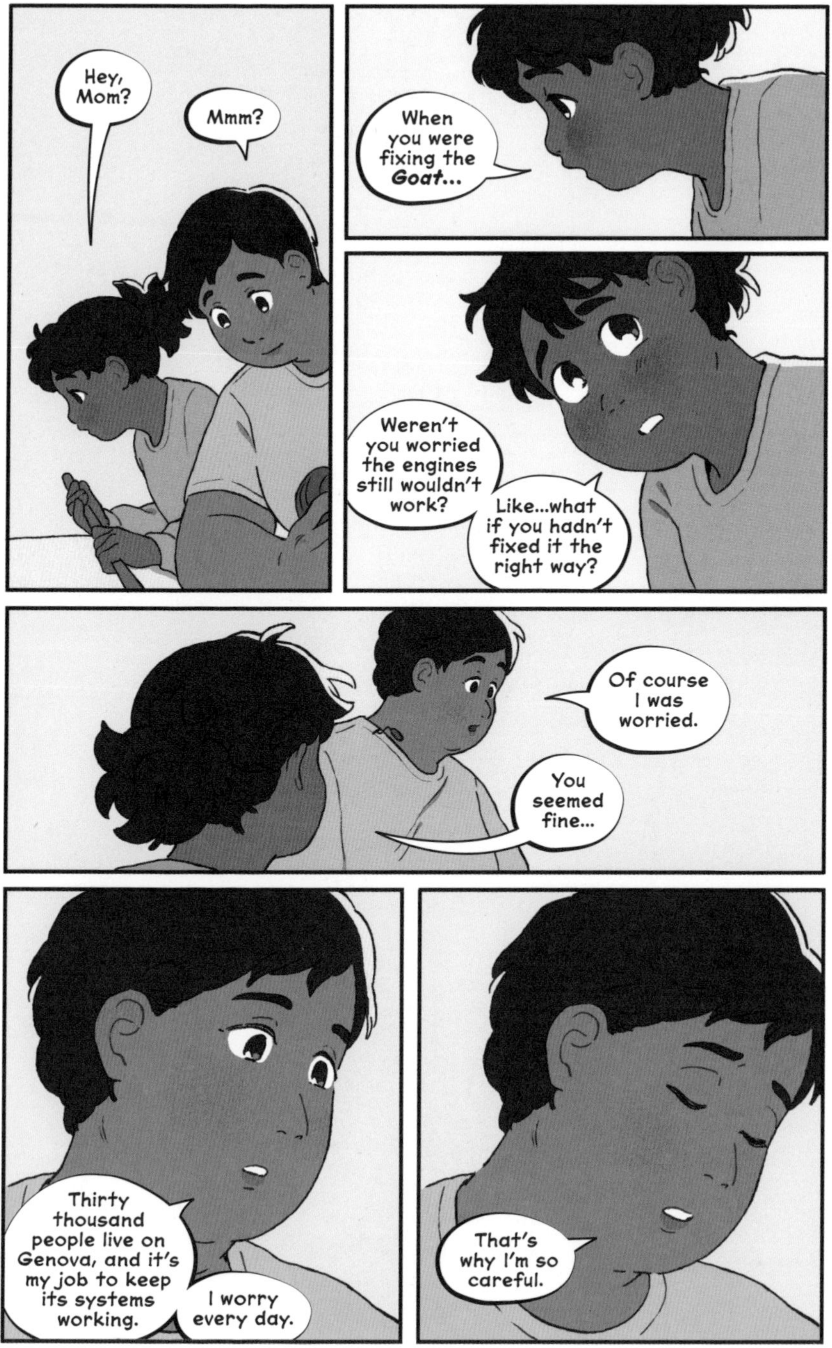
Hey, Mom?
Mmm?
When you were fixing the ***Goat...***
Weren't you worried the engines still wouldn't work?
Like...what if you hadn't fixed it the right way?
Of course I was worried.
You seemed fine...
Thirty thousand people live on Genova, and it's my job to keep its systems working.
I worry every day.
That's why I'm so careful.

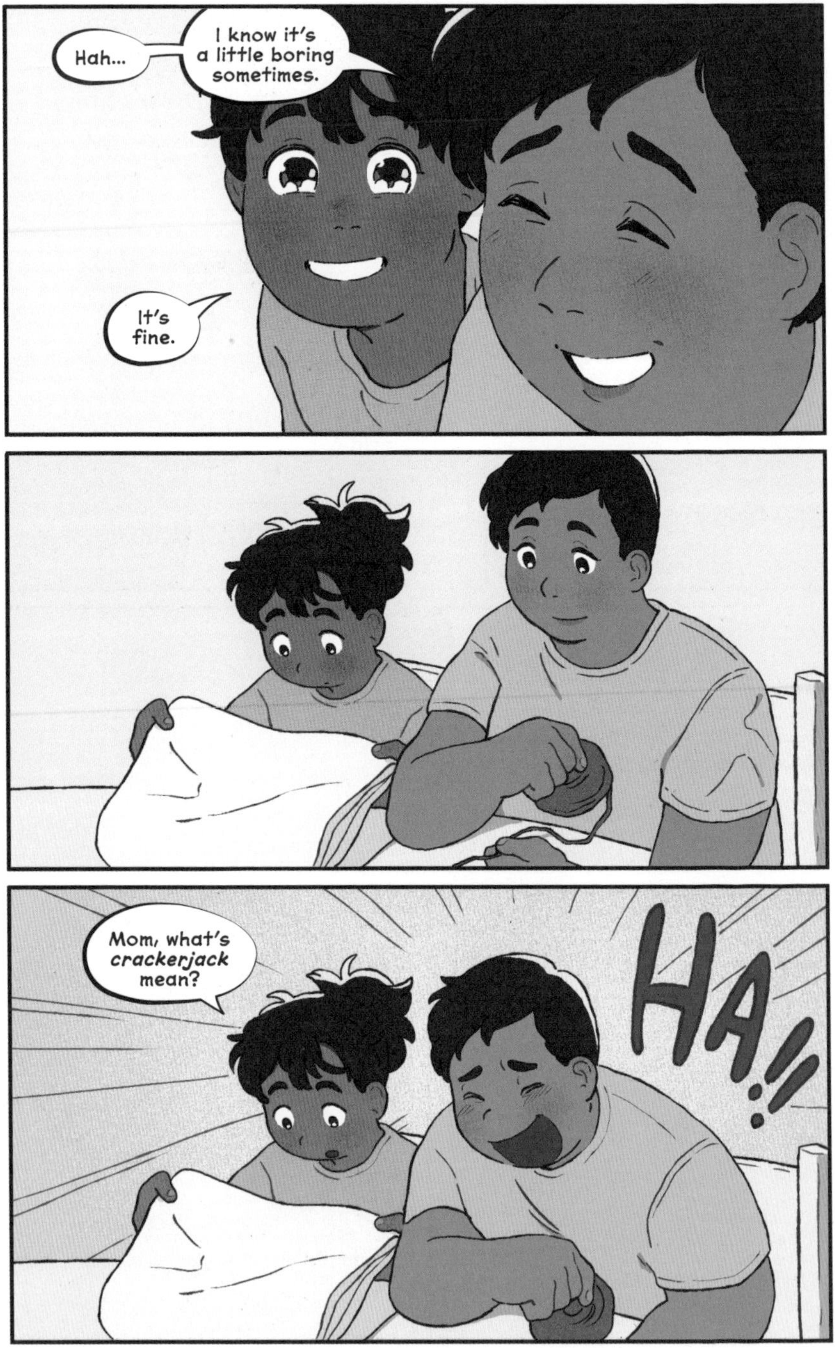
Hah...
I know it's a little boring sometimes.
It's fine.
Mom, what's *crackerjack* mean?
HA!!

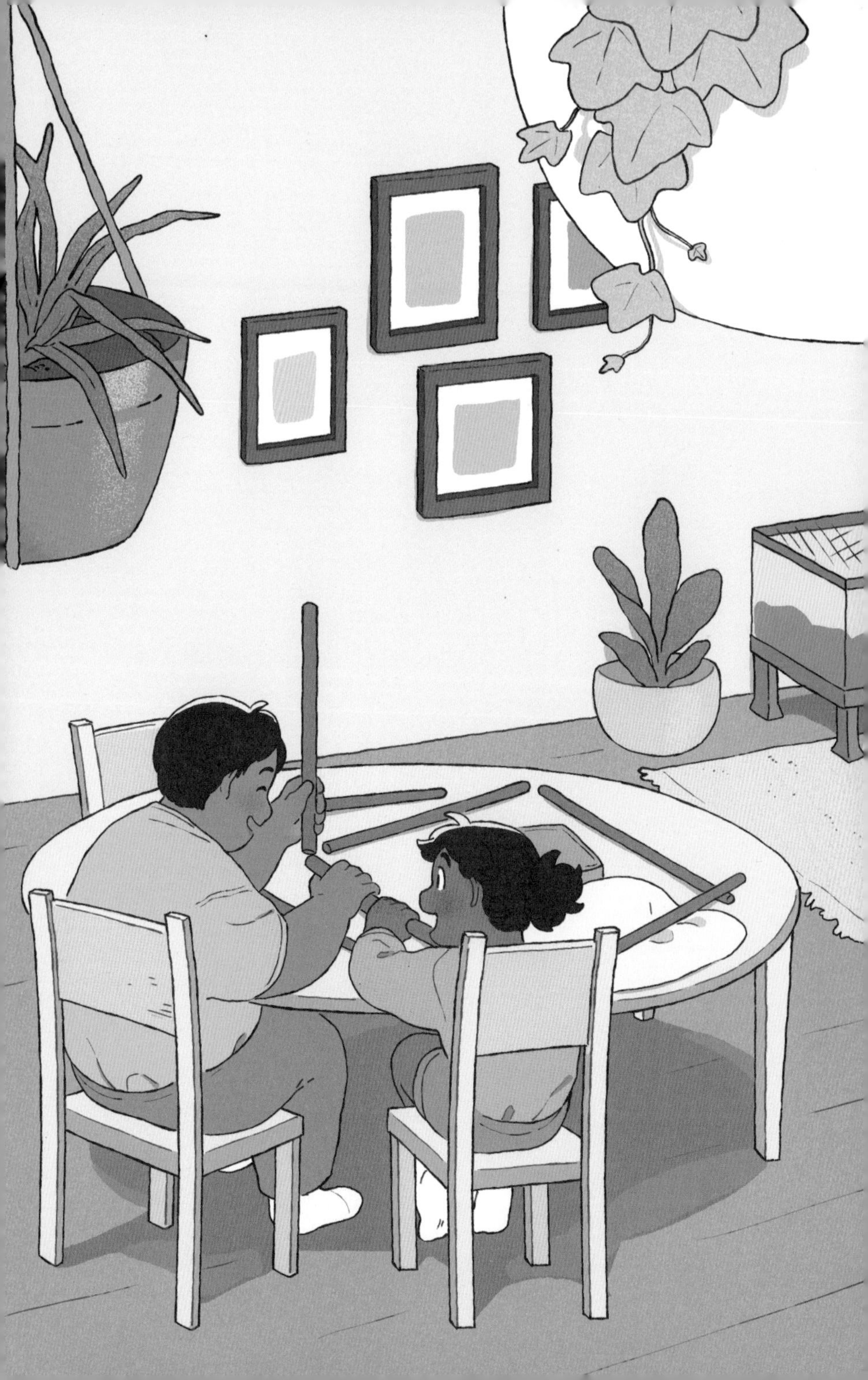

Acknowledgments

Thank you to my beloved agent, Eddie Schneider, and the rest of the team at JABberwocky Literary Agency for all their years of support and guidance. Thank you to our editor, Whitney Leopard, for shepherding *Grace Needs Space!* from a fragment of an idea to the book you're reading now, and to Patrick Crotty, our designer, for making it look fantastic. Thank you to Danny Diaz for all she does to keep things running smoothly. Thank you to our wonderful letterer, Mike Fiorentino. Thank you to the gang of pals who cheered me on and kept me sane in spring 2020, when I was banging my head against the script for "Space Moms" at the worst possible time.

And most of all, thank you to Rii for bringing Grace and her world to life. It wouldn't have been remotely the same with anyone else, and I'm so honored to have gotten to tell this story with you!

—B.A.W.

Thank you to Benjamin, Whitney, Gina, Patrick, Danny, and everyone else who had a hand in making this book a reality. It means so much that I was trusted with bringing Grace to life.

Thank you to Joe, my parents, my siblings, and my friends for your limitless support throughout the years. I wouldn't be doing any of this without your help. Thank you to everyone who has ever taken the time to pick up my work or cheer me on from the sidelines. And thank you to the incomparable Molly. I don't know what I would do without your constant guidance!

—R.A.

Name Notes

Some of the names of places and things in *Grace Needs Space!* have deeply nerdy origins. Here are a few!

Genova Station

Grace's home station is named for the Repubblica di Genova, the birthplace of astronomer Giovanni Cassini, who first observed Saturn's moons.

Porco Station

The station they visit on Titan is named after planetary scientist Carolyn Porco, who was the leader of the Imaging Team for the Cassini-Huygens mission that explored Saturn and its moons.

Sadie Goat

Kendra's freighter is named for Sadie Farrell, also known as Sadie the Goat, a possibly mythic nineteenth-century river pirate in New York City.

1997-061A

In addition to being the ID number for the *Sadie Goat*, this is the COSPAR (Committee on Space Research) number for the Cassini robotic spacecraft that orbited Saturn and its moons for thirteen years and gathered most of our current data on Titan.

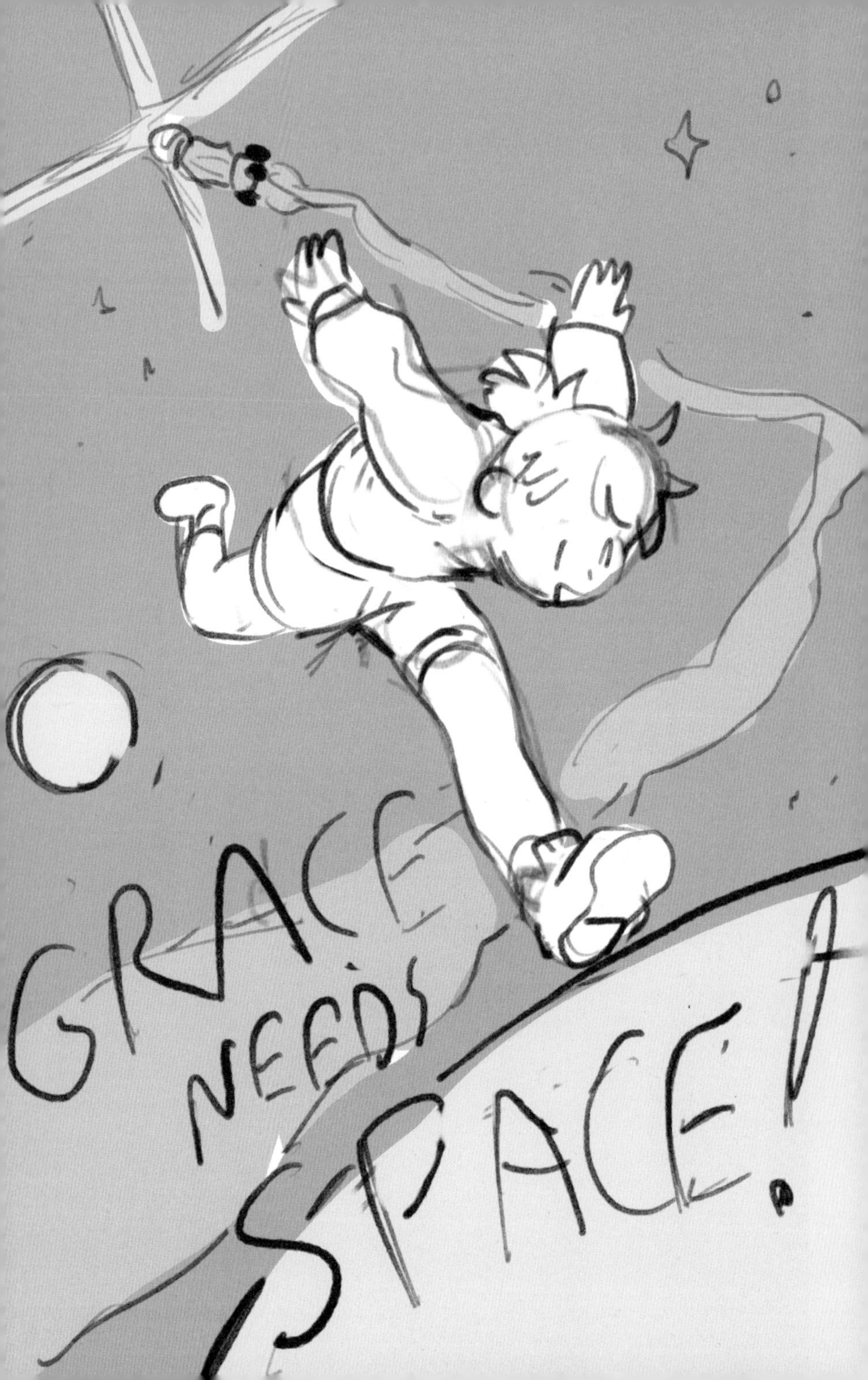
GRACE NEEDS SPACE!

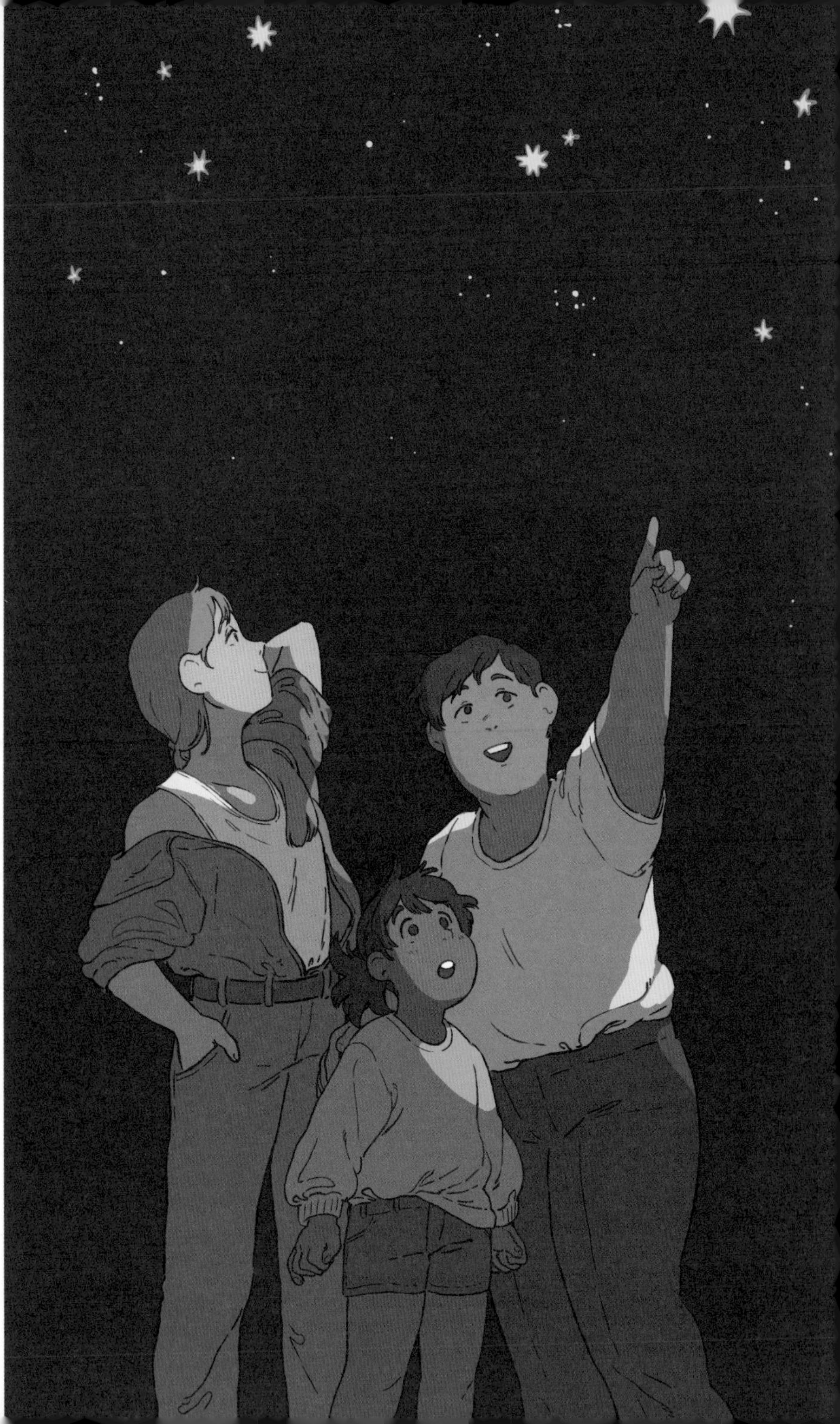

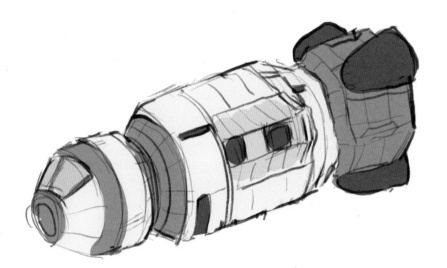

Cover Dev

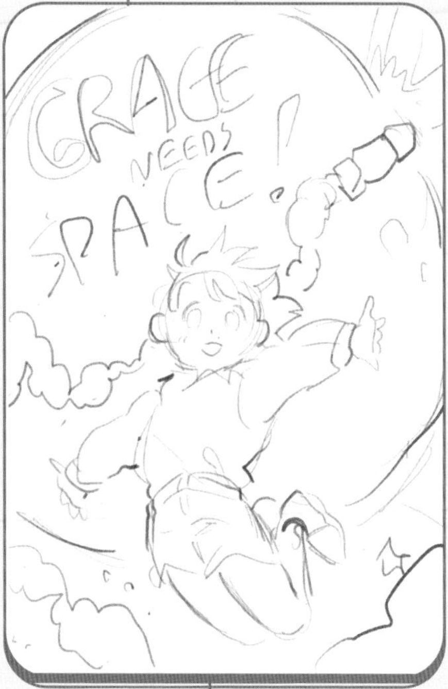
GRACE
NEEDS
SPACE!

This is the sketch that we decided to go with, but Rii drew a lot of others that we liked! Can you spot the big difference here? Grace's pose is really different! Plus, we put some rings around the planet.

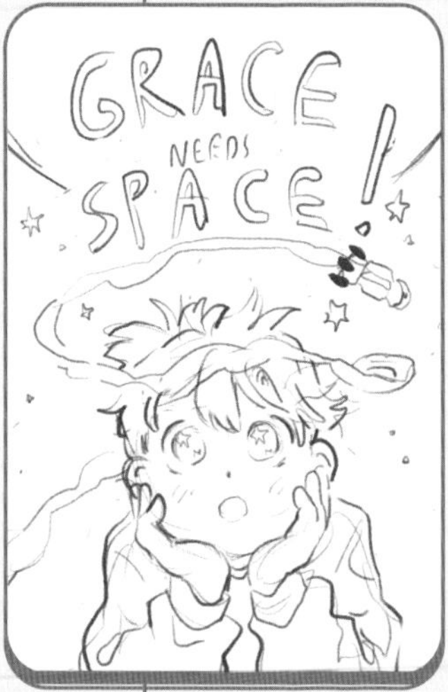
GRACE
NEEDS
SPACE!

We all really, REALLY liked this idea, but it made Grace look dizzy, which we didn't want on the front cover. That said, it inspired the design for the back of the book. Also, if you have the hardcover, take off the dust jacket for a surprise!

GRACE NEEDS SPACE!
GRACE NEEDS SPACE
GRACE NEEDS SPACE!

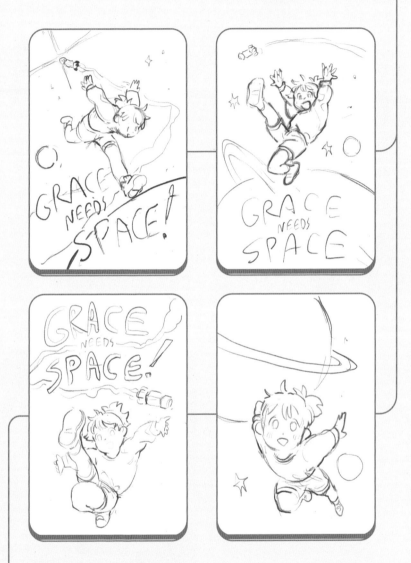

Here are more sketches that we love. The poses are very dynamic and fun, but we didn't use them for the cover.

Cover Dev

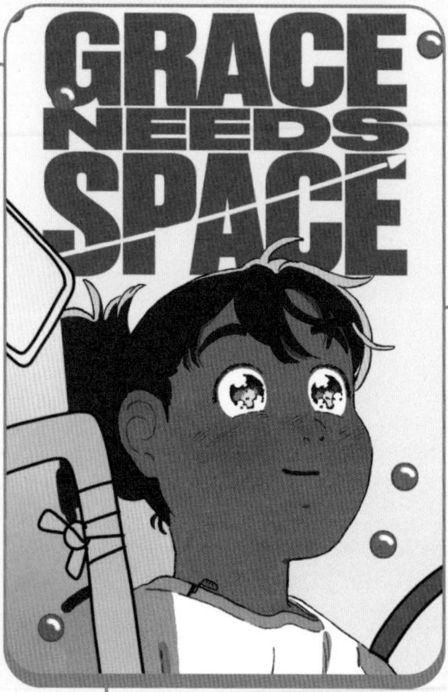
GRACE
NEEDS
SPACE

Some cover designs came directly from the designer. Here was one of his favorites, but it felt too much like a book about basketball.

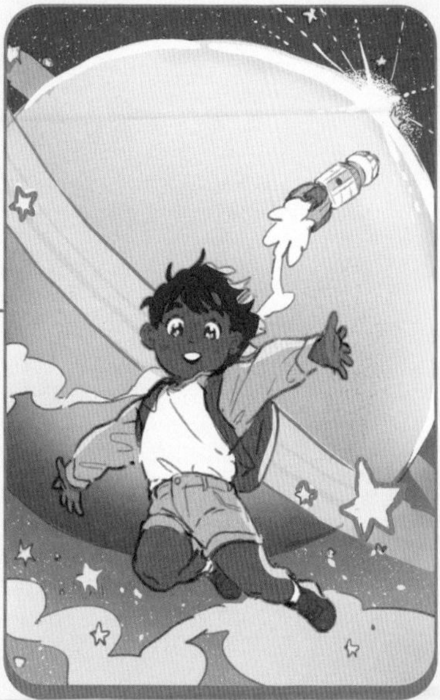

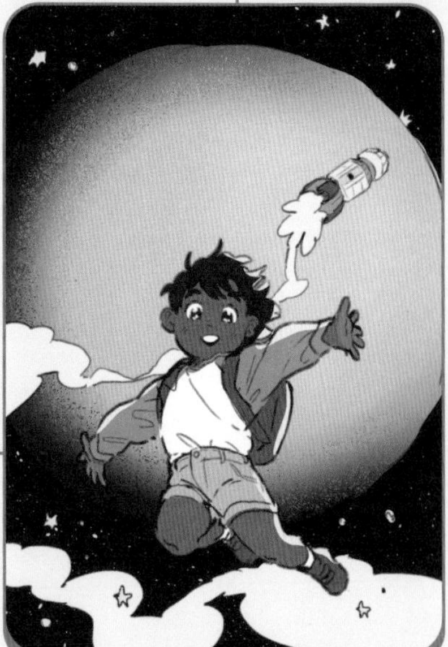

Color variations for the cover. Even after we find the perfect design, the colors can really change the mood of the cover, so Rii did a lot of testing to find colors that would fit the book.

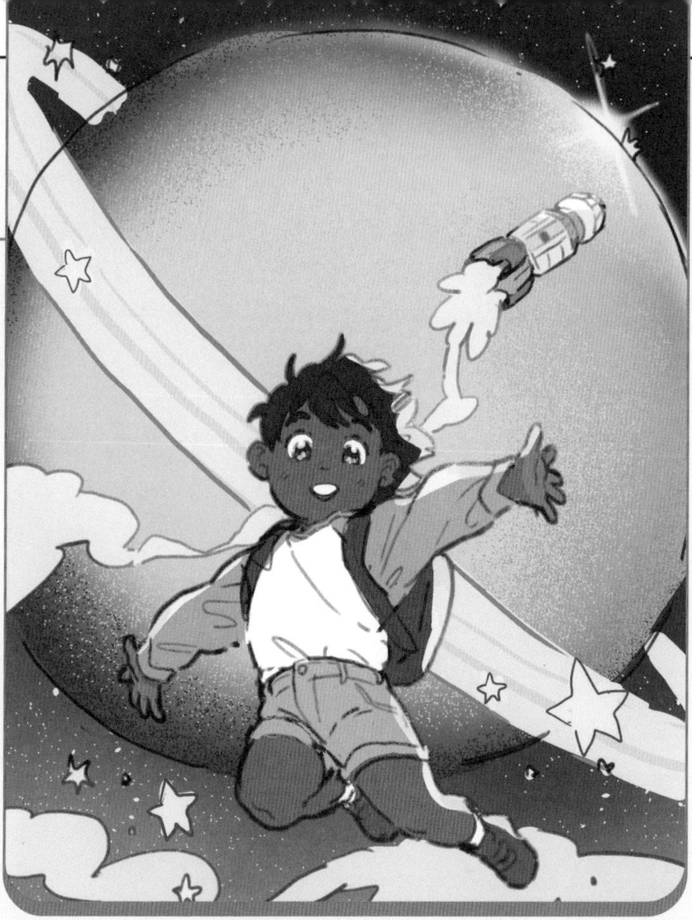

Another color variation we considered for the cover. This greenish yellow one was based on actual pictures of Titan!

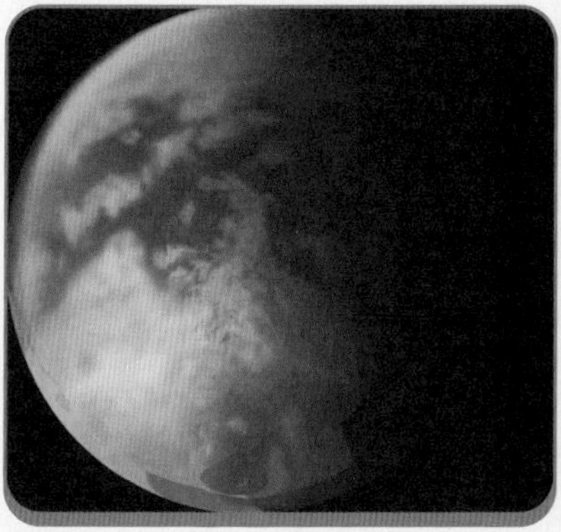

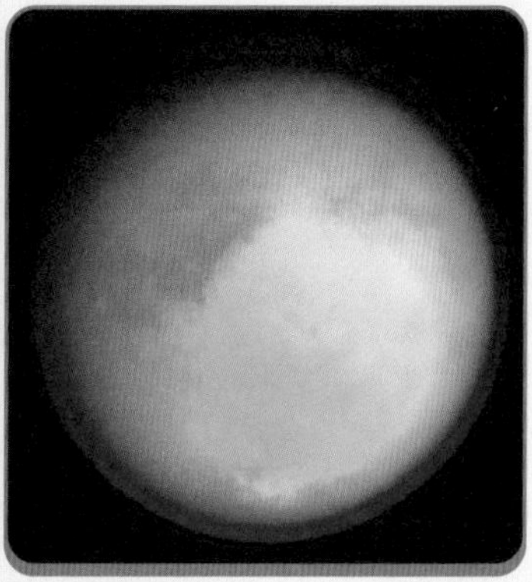

Benjamin A. Wilgus

is a Brooklyn-based Ignatz Award–winning comics writer and editor who tells emotionally intimate stories about small people in a big world. He studied film and television at NYU's Tisch School of the Arts, and while he got his start as a writer at Cartoon Network's *Codename: Kids Next Door,* he's made a home for himself in comics for almost twenty years. His previous work includes *The Mars Challenge* from First Second, a graphic nonfiction book about the history and hopeful future of human spaceflight, illustrated by Wyeth Yates; and *Chronin* from Tor, a solo graphic novel duology about time travel, queerness, and connection.

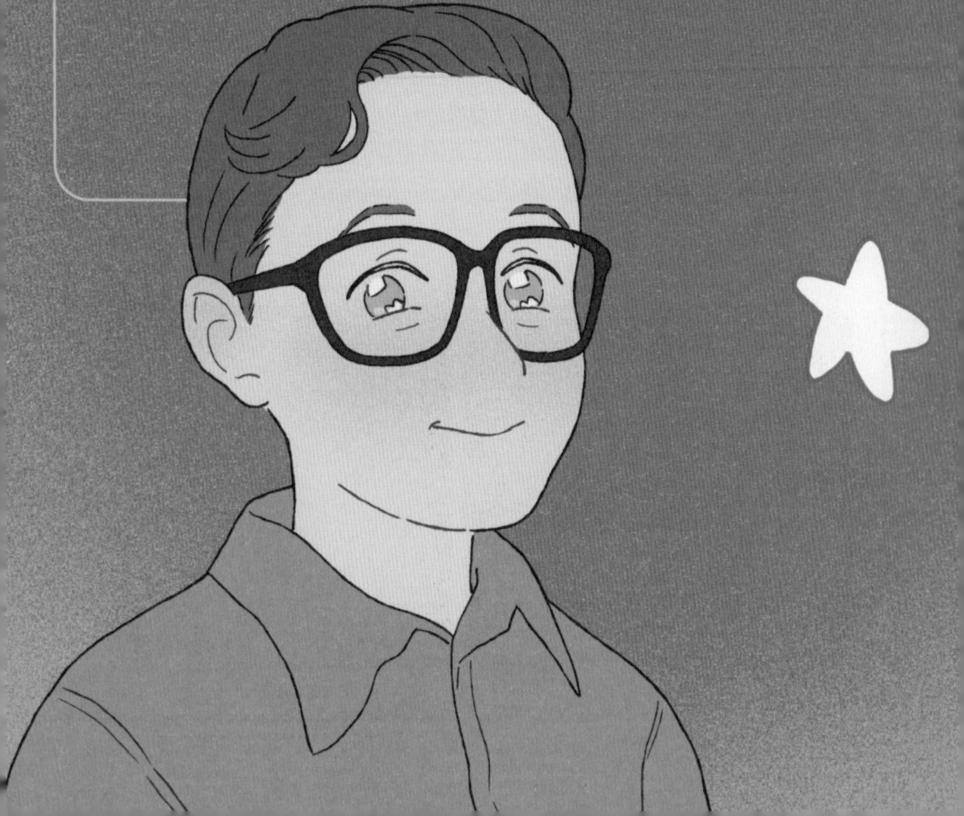

Rii Abrego is a Latina illustrator and cartoonist who resides in the very humid southern United States. She is the artist and coauthor of the graphic novel *The Sprite and the Gardener,* published by Oni Press, and has contributed art to a variety of comic titles, including *Steven Universe,* published by Boom! Studios. Rii graduated from the University of Montevallo, where she studied drawing and painting. In her spare time she enjoys creating work that celebrates the joy and magic of the every day, hiking, and fostering the stray cats that continue to relentlessly hurl themselves into her path.

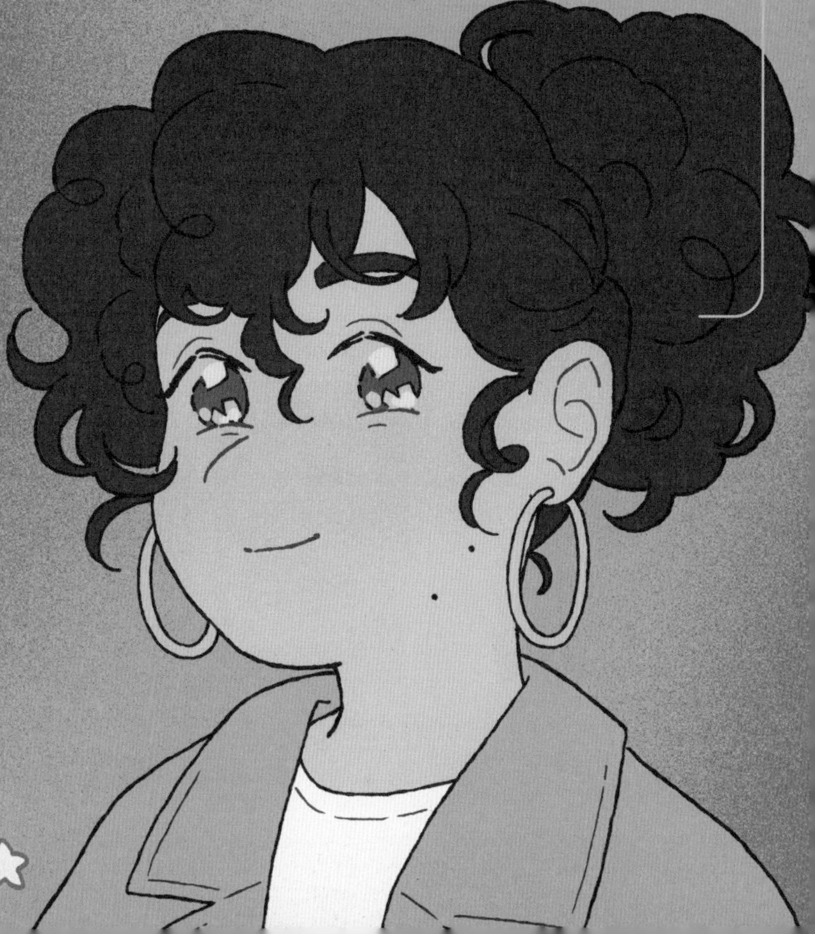

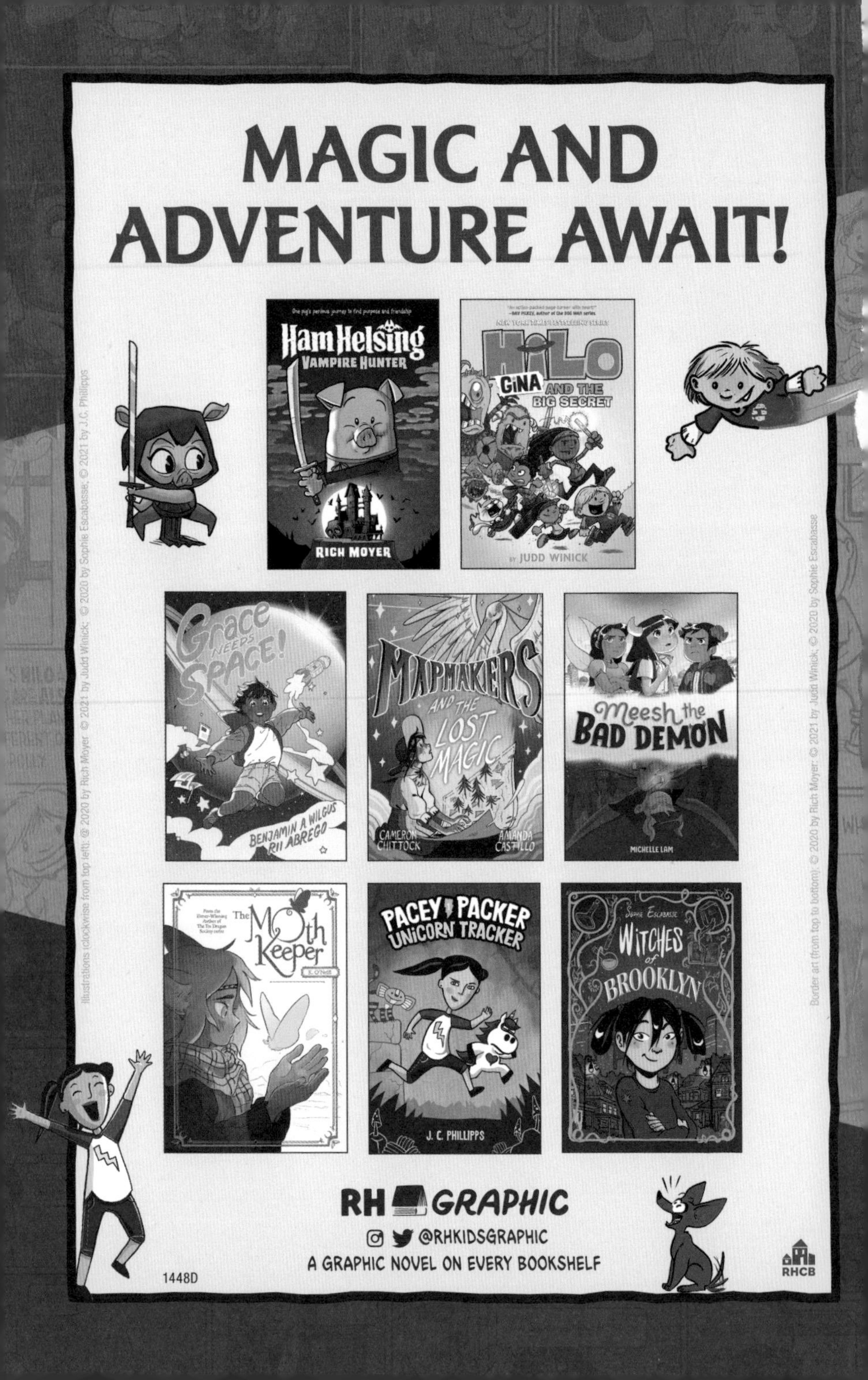
MAGIC AND ADVENTURE AWAIT!
One pig's perilous journey to find purpose and friendship
Ham Helsing
VAMPIRE HUNTER
RICH MOYER
NEW YORK TIMES BESTSELLING SERIES
HILO
GINA AND THE BIG SECRET
BY JUDD WINICK
Grace NEEDS SPACE!
BENJAMIN A WILGUS
RII ABREGO
MAPMAKERS AND THE LOST MAGIC
CAMERON CHITTOCK
AMANDA CASTILLO
Meesh the BAD DEMON
MICHELLE LAM
The MOth Keeper
PACEY PACKER UNICORN TRACKER
J. C. PHILLIPPS
Sophie Escabasse
WITCHES of BROOKLYN
Illustrations (clockwise from top left): © 2020 by Rich Moyer; © 2021 by Judd Winick; © 2020 by Sophie Escabasse; © 2021 by J.C. Phillipps
Border art (from top to bottom): © 2020 by Rich Moyer; © 2021 by Judd Winick; © 2020 by Sophie Escabasse
RH GRAPHIC
@RHKIDSGRAPHIC
A GRAPHIC NOVEL ON EVERY BOOKSHELF
1448D
RHCB